A DESPERATE YEARNING

"You've been put to a lot of trouble, Raider Prescott, with nothing to show for it," Blythe said softly. She looked down to hide her turmoil. Just once she wanted to know the deep tenderness and fierce, steamy passion of a man's love . . . of this pirate's love. It would probably be the only loving she would ever know. "Perhaps you should . . . take whatever booty you can."

Raider could scarcely believe his senses. When Blythe raised her head, her eyes were darkening, her lips were parted and reddened. Her breaths came shallow and quick. He felt her gaze turning him inside out.

"Love me, Raider Prescott . . . love me this once." Her voice was a seductive whisper, bouyed on a current of raw, unabashed hope. . . .

"Betina Krahn outdoes herself with this terrific, tender, touching and sensual romance . . . the most endearing pirate crew since Laura London's *Windflower.*"

— Kathe Robin
ROMANTIC TIMES

"Thoroughly uniqu........................al . . . a wonderful novel and..................put it together in such a d............

Leone
OEUR

PASSION'S RANSOM

BETINA M. KRAHN

ZEBRA BOOKS
KENSINGTON PUBLISHING CORP.

ZEBRA BOOKS

are published by

Kensington Publishing Corp.
475 Park Avenue South
New York, NY 10016

First printing: July, 1989

Printed in the United States of America

Prologue

March 1768

It was a bad night off the coast of Sussex in the English Channel. The frigid north wind whipped the gray night sky savagely, churning thick clouds into rounded masses that rolled across the face of the nearly full moon. Then the wind turned on the sea itself, bullying the waves higher, and the sea responded with an angry roar and spit at the faraway moon, thinking it to blame.

The tides of men's fortunes were as turbulent as the stormy elements of the earth and sky. In the midst of the clashing elements, one of the king's revenue cutters, *Harrier* by name, rolled in the white-capped waves and struggled to stay aright. Behind her, she towed the captured smuggler's sloop *Angel* and she barely succeeded in keeping the tow lines slack enough to prevent a disastrous collision in the heaving sea. The caprices of weather that had allowed her to find and capture the sloop had just as quickly turned to threaten her own survival.

Six unlucky smugglers were trussed and cuffed in iron hook chains, sprawled on the *Harrier*'s deck. They shuddered under successive drenchings with icy sea water, though some were almost grateful for the numbing effects of the cold on their injuries. The captured *Angel*'s crew were scarcely worse off than those of the *Harrier*'s men who had also sustained injuries in the brief fight and now still had to function as crewmen in the long, wind-

7

whipped night ahead.

An aristocratically chiseled face lifted from that miserable group of prisoners on the sea-washed deck and a deep voice rumbled forth to join the sea roar. "You miserable sod," Gideon Prescott growled at the sly-faced moon. "You were supposed to stay hidden tonight."

"What's that?!" a hoarse shout came from a coarse-featured man in a new officer's uniform stalking the deck nearby. "Keep yer yaps shut!" The toe of his boot caught the young captain of the *Angel* in the ribs. "That means you, too, yer *lordship!*" He stared down at the long sinewy frame, doubled up at his feet. "You'll have time enough to do your yammerin' before a magistrate. And I'll be there laughin' as they cart yer highborn arse off to rot in gaol. I waited months to get my hands on you!" The hard-eyed captain of the *Harrier* snarled an ugly laugh and lurched and groped his way along the rail toward the wheel, leaving the lanky young smuggler curled on the deck, his mind closed adamantly against the pain.

All around them, the cutter's crew were keeping a nervous eye on their short-hauled sails and the sloop they were attempting to tow to harbor. The rough weather and their absorbing concern over the lucrative contraband still tucked in the *Angel's* hold meant no one noticed the sail looming up behind them in the brightening moonlight. When she was finally spotted, the captain sent for his glass and scoured the ship as best he could for signs of identification. She appeared to be a solid brigantine, English built, a good fifty tons more than his own seventy-six-ton cutter. She darkly refused to answer their hailing and began to dog their wake.

The dark ship kept a wily distance on the wind-whipped sea that just eluded the range of the cutter's two carriage guns. In the full moonlight, the cutter's captain ordered more sail raised and made hard for Plymouth Harbor. The *Harrier* was now the harried.

Some three hours of hard running later, the challenging brigantine ran up a roger in the gray light of a calming dawn and put on a burst of speed to draw abreast of her quarry. A row of ports opened and a tier of guns were run out. The first bit of gunnery was mercifully lame at such close range, piercing the cutter's jib and foresail and splintering her long bowsprit. But was only a matter of minutes before the brig scraped alongside and grappling hooks appeared over the *Harrier*'s bulwarks, followed by a heaving wave of furious sea raiders. Sabers and knives clanged amid shouts and curses, howls and grunts. The fight was short and hard but surprisingly deathless. And soon the pirate crew was systematically pillaging both the cutter and her captive sloop.

"Well, what have we here?" A blocky, impressively muscular fellow wearing the *Harrier*'s captain's new coat finally came to stand over the cuffed and shackled smuggling crew. He wore an eye patch over his left eye and a wicked grin on his broad, square-featured face.

"Unlucky bastards, ain't ye? First ye lose yer cargo to His Highness's snoops, and then again to a band o' cutthroat pirates. Still," the burly pirate leader scratched his bristled chin, considering it, "ye got a right fine sloop, there. Which of ye lubbers is 'er captain?"

"I am," came that startling deep voice as the young captain of the *Angel* assessed his potential foe with calm eyes.

The pirate looked him over carefully. Tall, clean-limbed, and head-turning handsome, the burly sea dog mused. Still, he'd have to do. "If you've a wit in yer head, what in hell were ye doin' runnin' fer the Frenchie coast in full moonlight?"

"There wasn't a moon when we started; it was black as pitch" came the young captain's matter-of-fact response. "It was a perfect night . . . before we got caught in the changing winds. He was just lucky." He jerked his head toward the *Harrier*'s captain, who was being forced over the side and down to the deck of the *Angel*.

"Not anymore, he ain't," the burly pirate laughed. He was in a jovial mood. It wasn't often a crew could take two prizes for the price of one. "What be yer name, lad?" Something in his genial tone coaxed the truth from the *Angel*'s captain.

"Prescott . . . Gideon Prescott" came the even reply.

"Sounds sissy. Bet yer ma give it to ye," the pirate flashed a mischievous smile that was full of healthy white teeth. "I be Bastian Cane." He spoke it with a flourish and a wave of his muscular arm, as though he expected some reaction. He was piqued aplenty when none was forthcoming. "The Scourge of the Seven Seas . . ." he proclaimed insistently, ". . . Bastian Cane."

9

"Cap'n!" A ragged-looking seaman with a curved saracen cutlass stuck through his belt hurried up with a report. "Bales. Most of it's *bales!*"

In the pale morning light, the burly pirate's ruddy face grayed and his good humor of moments before deserted him. "Bales? Damn and blast!" He turned on Gideon Prescott with a furious glare of disgust. "*Owlers* . . . you be bloody owlers! Peddlin' soppy sheep's wool t'escape th' duties. Gawd! That's disgustin'! Probably in with the 'free trade-ers' and that *respectable* lot!"

"I am a proponent of free trade . . . and unafraid to get my hands dirty in it," the striking young captain declared with a spark in his light eyes.

"A pro-poe—what? Gawd. A fancy educated one at that." Bastian Cane turned and spat as if the very word "educated" fouled his mouth. He squinted as his eyes roamed the cuffed and chained group at his feet. Some looked promisingly seaworthy; at least they had callouses on their hands. He stalked away and stared out to sea, his hands on his hips. He stood there, thinking, while his own crew collected around the prisoners, awaiting word on what to do with their disappointing prizes.

A member of the ragged pirate crew came running up to speak to Cane in hushed tones, gesturing to Prescott with widened eyes. Cane turned on his jack-booted heel and stalked back to stare at the handsome, educated young blood. He was clearly pleased.

"So the night ain't such a loss after all . . . We got us a noble fish to ransom. The revenuer says yer pa be a baron. Likely he'll pay a pretty penny to have a fine whelp like you returned." His toothy grin was destined to fade again when a slow smirk spread over Prescott's cleanly sculptured features.

"Not hardly. The baron is notoriously tight with his coin . . . and never was exactly fond of me, wayward son that I am. And he'll be even less inclined to ransom back a captured smuggler with a price on his head." The young blood's posture remained a nerveless slouch and Cane's eyes narrowed in reassessment. He was a cool one, this young gent who didn't mind a bit of dirt on his hands. Cane found himself wondering just what it would take to get the young rake's dander up.

"Where were ye takin' her . . . yer cargo?" he demanded.

"None of your damned business," the gentleman smuggler

tossed back with a touch of well-born arrogance. Bastian Cane's broad, blunted features warmed with a cunning smile.

"Ye be wrong there, lad. But ye needn't tell me now. Ye'll have plenty of time on the trip across . . . It were France somewheres, I'll wager." He turned his sly, probing gaze on the rest of the *Angel's* crew. "Welcome aboard, men. Ye be part o' Bastian Cane's crew, now, *pirates* all!" There was a murmur through the clutch of men and in a blink Gideon Prescott had made it to his knees before the hard, punishing hands of Cane's crewmen on his shoulders forbade him to rise further.

"You can't mean you'll force us to join your crew?!"

"I mean just that, lad. I need men. Unless you'druther accompany the captain, there, back to gaol. Been in gaol myself . . . It ain't very pleasant. I bet you read charts, don't ye? Been needin' a navigator." Bastian Cane jerked up Prescott's iron-cuffed hands and scrutinized them. They were muscular, but uncalloused. "And we'll toughen the rest of ye soon enough."

"You can't force these men to join you —" Prescott jerked his hands away, rattling his bonds, and his square, patrician jaw set firmly. "Some of these men have families . . . wives and children."

"Families?! Which ones?" Cane's nose curled as though surprised and repulsed by the revelation. "Speak up!" he commanded the crew of the *Angel*. Three of the men spoke up warily, admitting to having responsibilities on land. Cane frowned, seeming oddly disappointed. "Well, they be better off with me than in gaol."

Prescott's crew beseeched their captain plaintively and his striking eyes narrowed, first on them, then on his mercurial new master. What he read of the self proclaimed "Scourge of the Seven Seas" interested him. The "free-trade-er" in him recognized and understood a strong profit motive in a man. "What would make it worth your while to set my familied lads ashore separately . . . say, near Hastings?"

Cane's broad face studied Prescott openly, then split with another of those enchantingly wicked grins. He rubbed his prominent chin and took note that the gent hadn't included himself in his question . . . only his familied crew. So the gent had a regrettable bit streak of nobility in him. He sighed thoughtfully and slid his eyes over his new navigator. But balancing it was a

11

promising bit of grit in the way the gent smuggler challenged and bargained, even though he held no cards.

"I didn't count on no damned wool . . . I ain't no pulin' shopkeeper. I want somethin' spendable; like brandy or gold."

"Brandy . . . was to be my return cargo." Prescott said it slowly and a roguish grin spread over his handsome face. "It still could be."

Bastian Cane's calculating expression muted to a knowing grin. With an exchange of eyes in the cold sunrise, a bargain was struck. "Then it *will* be. Ye've a pirate's heart, old son . . . and like it or no, the rest o' ye will soon match."

Chapter One

Philadelphia
August 1778

The fates play dice at night; it's a little-known fact, but true. Otherwise, why would deeds done in the dark of night often wreak such havoc on the affairs of mankind? It is further true that the last lot of the night is cast just as the sun's first rays creep over the horizon. And so the dice of influence must lay as they have fallen, quiet, exerting their capricious sway on events, until the last rays of light fade over the horizon again. For in the light, man's reason rules and free will is given free rein. Thus, dawn is often a time of tumult, of struggle between what can be and what must be . . . between the chancy determinations of fate and the reasoning choices of men. That is why armies usually attack, people frequently begin journeys, and lovers often part . . . at dawn.

When the fates tossed their celestial "bones" for the last time, that fine late August dawn, it was in Philadelphia area that the ivories came to rest. Many recent mornings had found them there, in that part of the American seaboard where the futures of continents and kings were slowly being unraveled. Often they rolled to a stop on or near centers of colonial power and rebel decision-making . . . and nudged a document toward signing, or shed a favorable light on a treaty or uncovered funds for a military need. But this morning, one rolled into the Society Hill district of the city, bumping into a stately, three-story Georgian home, and one rolled through the harbor district and down the Delaware channel toward the bay, managing to wedge itself securely between the hull of a ship and her anchor chain . . .

Blythe Woolrich was standing in her darkened bedchamber, dressing, as the first tumultuous rays of the new day crossed the boundary of the horizon. There was a violent ripping and pop and she found herself staring at a broken corset lace that dangled in her hand.

"Drat and blast!" She blinked at it, then winced at the sight of her reemerging curves, wondering why she was cursed with body parts that didn't match . . . a tiny waist, annoyingly full breasts, and shoulders that could only be called handsome . . . on a man. If she were only endowed more sensibly, she wouldn't have to wear one of these cursed contraptions in the first place!

Well, she wasn't one to just stand and moan about things she couldn't change. She hurried to the darkened outline of a mahogany highboy and opened drawer after drawer. She sifted and examined the contents of each with knowledgeable fingers; odd, short pieces of lace, hooks sensibly salvaged from old garments, frayed and often-pressed ribbands, and — *ouch!* — the odd silk pin that had never found its way back into her sewing basket. She thrust a bleeding fingertip into her mouth to soothe it and leaned her side against the tall chest. Her eyes closed and she released a hard sigh. No more laces.

"Be sensible, Blythe!" she muttered, forcing herself upright and squaring both her shoulders and her fine-boned jaw. "A broken lacing is nothing to come unstrung over. Just go without today and bring some strong twine from the shop when you come home this evening. Surely you can get through one day without a corset . . . you *hate* corsets!"

But as she pushed the failed garment down over her curvy hips and long, willowy legs, she had the strangest sliding sensation in the middle of her. She couldn't have known that on this particular morning she was shedding more than just a bony dictate of fashion; some of her legendary self-control was being shed, too. Blaming her odd shiver on the lack of fire in her mostly empty

14

bedchamber, she hurried to roll her stockings up and settle a petticoat about her waist.

The sturdy, moss-green woolen dress came next and soon she was tugging and tightening the dress's front lacings as much as she dared. She threw open the inside shutters, then hurried to the long cheval mirror to check the results. She squinted at her dim image in the glass. Without a candle, she couldn't be absolutely certain . . . But the respectable lines of her stark green woolen, with its scooped neck and severe, long-waisted bodice, seemed utterly ruined by the unladylike lumpiness caused by her full breasts. Groaning and tugging at the itchy woolen bodice, she tried to camouflage her blatant womanliness a bit better . . . and failed.

Making a disgusted face at her dim reflection, she turned on her heel and grabbed a brush to tame her unruly mass of hair. She'd been too fatigued last night to braid it properly for bed. There were tats and tangles aplenty from her restless night, and soon she was muttering and bemoaning the sheer quantity of her soft, voluminous brown mane. It was a bother, a pure irritation to have to mess with it each day. She had half a mind to take the shears to it and be done for good. There was no time for such idle pursuits . . . frittering away time on hair! But she clamped a hand on her rising frustration for a second time. A proper, respectable woman would never rid herself of her "womanly veil." And if Blythe Woolrich was anything, she was a proper and respectable young woman.

Soon she had her tresses in hand, constrained with simple tortoiseshell combs in efficient, if uninspired, sausagelike roles at the back of her head. She managed a last look in the mirror and a last irritable tug at her coarse, itchy bodice and headed for the door.

Lizzy, the frowzled little upstairs maid, was teetering toward Blythe's door at a half run, bent over by a huge copper kettle of hot water. Head down, she arrived just at the very moment Blythe jerked open the door and started through it. The collision splashed them both with hot water and brought squeals of distress and apology from the serving girl and a flurry of hands swiping at Blythe's wetted wool skirt.

"Sorry to be late agin, Miz Blythe," Lizzy groaned. "But Mrs.

Dornly sent me to Simmons the butcher, on account of she was too ashamed to face 'im again. I jus' got back. And now . . . yer old grandma be callin' for ye." Her wince betrayed her sympathy for her mistress and she turned on her heel for the stairs, muttering, "Ye pro'bly already heard her. All the neighbors did."

Blythe watched the tart-tongued little maid go, then stretched and smoothed the wetted spots on her skirt, praying they wouldn't draw and pucker when they dried. Her jaw was clenched and she swallowed back the irritation rising in her again. Hot water was the one luxury she still permitted herself . . . or tried to. What good was it when it came too late every morning and she ended up taking it to Nana anyway?

She squared her stiffening shoulders. Lizzy had her hands full in the kitchen helping Mrs. Dornly, their housekeeper, of a morning. The cook had left from lack of wages, and now the staunch housekeeper did their cooking herself, assisted only by young Lizzy. There was only one other servant left in the household that had once boasted a dozen: Old William, who was too old to worry about things like wages . . . and sometimes things like duties as well. She forced herself to repeat her frequent reasoning like an incantation against frustration: in these hard times, they all had too much to do; it just wasn't sensible to expect a luxury, even a little one, to continue. And if Blythe Woolrich was anything, she was a very sensible young woman.

She picked up the cumbersome kettle of water and trod the dark upstairs hallway from memory. There weren't any candles to light the way here either . . . though there were beautiful brass and crystal sconces on the walls. There were fine carpets, and elegant wainscoting, too, a fading splendor that was a remnant of a bygone era at Woolrich House. Three generations of Woolriches had lived proper, hard-working, and God-fearing lives in this splendid Georgian brick house that nestled in Philadelphia's "Society Hill" section. Each generation had added to its luxury and prestige as the Woolrich Mercantile and Freight Company grew and prospered. But for the last fifteen years, a slow decline had enveloped the house and its inhabitants and it now seemed the present generation would be the last to enjoy this heritage of industry and luxury. Both the Woolrich name and the Woolrich fortune were dying out . . . and it was all too clear that the fortune's demise would precede the end of the family line by a painful margin.

Nana Woolrich's piercing call smote the dignified silence of the fading hall and Blythe's eyes closed and her step faltered briefly. It never ceased to amaze her that such volume could be summoned from such a frail, infirm little body. Then, to make up for her unworthy thoughts, she quickened her pace and was soon suffering Nana's ear-splitting summons at very close range.

"Bly-y-ythe!"

"I'm here, Nana! No need to shout." Blythe stepped into her grandmother's spacious and well-furnished bedchamber and began throwing back the heavy brocade drapes at the windows and then at the bed.

"Nobody came this morning." Thin, small-framed Nana Woolrich huddled back into her pillows wearing a petulant frown under her white bedcap. "It's that girl of yours; she's determined to ignore me . . . whilst I lay here on my sickbed and . . . suffer."

"Nana, she's not ignoring you . . ." Blythe paused in the midst of tying back the bed drapes on the poster and bit back the part about how ships in the harbor would be hard pressed to ignore such caterwauling. "Lizzy had to go to Simmons the butcher this morning for Mrs. Dornly. She has a lot to do and she works very hard." Blythe saw the dramatic tightening of old Nana Woolrich's face as she struggled to rise to a sitting position and hurried to help her.

"Did you bring my water?" Nana craned her neck to search the floor for it as she eased back against the goosefeather bolsters Blythe plumped at her back.

"Yes, Nana." Blythe reached for the old lady's shawl, on a chair beside the bed, and settled it around her shoulders.

"And the soap I asked for?"

"Nana . . ." Blythe's squared shoulders braced for a stormy reaction, "I forgot your lavender soap. Maybe tomorrow—"

"Tomorrow—" Nana was abruptly seized by a fit of coughing, and it was a harrowing moment before she could continue. "It's always *tomorrow* . . ." she croaked, "and I don't have many tomorrows left. Here I am, trapped in this infernal bed, without the meagerest companionship . . . abandoned by friends and ignored by snippy, disrespectful servants . . . and now even you forget

17

about me!" Nana's voice clogged and she ground to a halt, sniffing and pressing her fingers into the corners of her aging eyes to prevent the tears. "I don't know how I can bear it another day . . ."

"Nana, please . . ." Blythe was beating back waves of guilt and came to put a consoling arm around her grandmother's slumped shoulders. "I don't forget about you; it's just that I have . . . a lot to do. I promise, I'll get your soap today." Though, in truth, Blythe had no earthly idea how or where she might acquire such a luxury. "Now come, let's get you washed and freshened and I'm sure after some barley coffee and a bit of food, you'll feel much better."

"I hate barley coffee. *Barely coffee*, they should call it." Nana burrowed deeper into her covers and had to be cajoled into her usual morning toilette. Blythe strained to keep a helpful mien as she helped her grandmother wash and don fresh line, bedrobe, and daycap. She dutifully refilled the stoppered earthern bottle at Nana's habitually icy feet with her hot water. Once the bedclothes were tucked securely, Nana caught Blythe's hand and raised a wan, suffering look to her.

"Be a good child and bring me my book." The old lady pointed a gnarled finger toward the small tilt-top table near the cold fireplace. "And my knitting . . . that pea-goose girl's put it on the windowseat again."

When Blythe nodded and went to fetch the book, Nana watched from the corner of her eye. "I simply must have some red wool yarn this afternoon for my needle piece." Nana saw the stiffening in Blythe's movement as she reached for the book. But no refusal was forthcoming and Nana's gray eyes crinkled with hidden satisfaction. "And you'll have to ferry a message to Reverend Warren, telling him he's forgot to visit me this week. I just don't know what the man can be thinking . . . to be so lacking in charity for the bedridden and the afflicted of his flock . . ." A Saint Joan-like tone had crept into her voice again.

"I'll . . . do what I can," Blythe strode back to the bed with her jaw clamped, and placed the book in her grandmother's hands. That same sliding sensation she'd felt earlier recurred in the middle of her and this time she dimly recognized its connection to the tenuous grip she held on her volatile feelings.

18

"And tell your father . . . he must come see me this morning!" Nana's voice rose in volume with every step Blythe took toward the door. "He simply must! It's sinful, the way he ignores—"

"I'll . . . tell him," Blythe declared tightly and escaped into the dim corridor. The door closed firmly behind her and she was halfway down the hall when her steps faltered and she found herself leaning against the wall. Her body was stiff and her fists were curled around balls of itchy green woolen.

It wasn't Nana's fault she was so difficult. Her unrelenting illness and the pain and isolation it caused would be enough to wear anyone down to raw nerves. And it must be especially difficult for a strong-willed woman used to ordering and commanding her world the way Nana Woolrich had in earlier days. As the working head of the family, Blythe had taken pains to see that poor Nana wasn't burdened with worries about their dismal financial condition, fearing that news of their miserable straits might weaken her precarious health. As finances worsened and Nana's health failed to improve, Blythe's protective pretense and daily duties with Nana had grown more and more difficult, but she never considered abandoning her ruse. For if Blythe Woolrich was anything, she was a dutiful young woman.

"*Bly-y-ythe!*" Nana's voice shook her out of her reverie and Blythe shot a guilty glance back over her shoulder and bolted for the stairs with burning ears. "Bly-y-ythe!"

Nana watched her door with narrowing gray eyes. It did not open. Her nose curled in irritation as her gaze shifted across the room to her knitting bag, still sitting on the window seat.

"Hell's fire!" she muttered, throwing back the thick covers and swinging her legs easily over the side of the bed to stand. She padded briskly across the cold floor and snatched up her knitting, then stomped back to her cozy sickbed.

The large center hall seemed especially barren this morning as Blythe came down the graceful stairs; no more Persian rugs, no marble-topped tables, no mirrors . . . She quickened to hurry through it, trying not to let the emptiness bother her. But once in the elegant Queen Anne dining room, she was confronted by blank walls and floorboards that bore discolored rectangles where

19

paintings and furnishings had once been and she could ignore it no longer. Her shoulders rounded and she halted, staring at the meager dishes set on one end of the long walnut table that seemed to be shrinking from embarrassment at its nakedness. No linen. No sense using it, when there wasn't anyone to wash it afterward. No silver candelabra, either. They'd been sold off more than a month ago, which was just as well, since there weren't any candles to put in them. Fully half of the luxurious furnishings that had once made Woolrich House a showplace of elegant living now graced other pantries and parlors.

Her stomach growled as the smell of hot biscuits reached her and drew her down the table. Well, at least she was able to keep food on the table . . . She was pulling out her chair when Mrs. Dornly came banging through the swinging kitchen door with a china pot in her hands and a forbidding scowl on her fleshy Scots-Irish face. Blythe could tell by the way she set her feet down especially hard and plopped the coffeepot down on the tabletop with meaningful force that they were about to have another of their "talks."

"Of course, it's none of my concern . . ." Mrs. Dornly always started off by disavowing all interest in the family's affairs. "It be no skin off my nose, if tongues be cluckin' all about the city. But, nits alwus come to lice and must be dealt with." She threaded her fleshy fingers together and brought them to rest at the front of her ample waist, her often-used gesture of martyred tolerance. Her plump face was puckered about the mouth and her eyes were hooded by scowling brows. She spoke her next words with the gravity of Moses speaking from the mountain, "We be cut off."

"Cut off?" Blythe felt that something in the middle of her sliding another notch.

"Cut off. No more meat from Simmons till the ledger's cleared. And he's not the only one. No more bread from Rausch, no produce nor sugar nor salt from Jacobson, and ye'll be sippin' the last milk in yer barley-coffee this morning. Dairyman Schultz's cut us off, too."

"But I thought the money from the last sale of silver should see us thro—" Blythe flushed under the housekeeper's expectant gaze and her hands withdrew from the tabletop into her lap, each to clasp the other.

"Something must be done, Miz Blythe." Mrs. Dornly raised both her chins to peer down her blocky nose.

"I'm doing all I can, Mrs. Dornly," Blythe managed through very tight jaws.

"I can see that, miz. But a slip of a girl like yerself ain't meant to run both a house and a business by herself." And having set up the argument with her own brand of logic, the housekeeper announced her own unshakable conclusion: "What you need is a man, Miz Blythe."

"I already have a man, thank you . . . my father!" Blythe bit her tongue to keep from saying more, knowing Mrs. Dornly meant another kind of man and had a candidate firmly in mind. And if she heard Neville Carson's name just now, she'd positively scream! She pushed up from her chair irritably, sending it clattering back across the bare wooden floor. "What I need is money — and a bit of cooperation!"

Blythe stared heatedly at the empty place at the end of the table, then fixed the stubborn housekeeper with a compelling glare. "Where is he?"

"He. . .?" That sent Mrs. Dornly back a step and she glanced at Lizzy, who was just entering the dining room with a tray destined for Nana. Lizzy slowed and shifted her grip on the tray uncomfortably as she, too, dodged her young mistress's demanding look.

"My *father*." Blythe watched between them and was suddenly incensed to realize that they were hiding something from her. "Where is he? The door of his room was ajar . . . and he's always first at breakfast . . ." Slow, creeping alarm made its way up her spine. Something was up . . . and from the looks on their faces, they knew about it.

"Never mind!" she declared, pivoting on her heel and striding for the door and the main stairs.

She already knew where to begin looking for him . . . the *attic!* It was the place he had stockpiled his "magnetite" when he went through his lodestone craziness . . . when he'd tried to enhance the flow of metal coinage into their coffers by making Woolrich House the "magnetic center" of the Colonies. It was the very same place he'd constructed "da Vinci" wings and insisted he'd discovered the secret of human flight. And it was also the place he'd

21

gotten his "North Star revelation," after which he'd walked, sat, slept, and lived in perfect polar alignment . . . facing the North Star exclusively. That had made for a few odd looks in the streets, walking backward and sideways . . .

Walter Woolrich was a genuine eccentric. He lived in harmony with a celestial tune heard by no one else on earth . . . or at least no one in Philadelphia. He'd inherited a large and lucrative commercial concern, but, unfortunately, none of the drive and financial acumen required to manage it. His talents seemed to lie in esoteric pursuits like philosophy, meditation, and the study of exotic natural phenomena. Since his beloved wife's untimely death, fifteen years before, he had immersed himself deeper and deeper in his odd blend of mystical and scientific dabblings. And as he increasingly abandoned control of the trading company, Blythe had been there to take it up. For if Blythe Woolrich was anything, she was a very responsible young woman.

She stomped up the main stairs trailed by a red-faced Mrs. Dornly and an owl-eyed Lizzy, who both vowed ignorance and noninvolvement in . . . well, whatever she might find. On the way through the upstairs hall, they collected white-haired Old William, who smelled a brouhaha in the works and fell in behind. The old fellow couldn't quite keep up with his mistress's pace up the second flight of stairs to the dusty third floor. But then, keeping a bit of distance might prove wise when the fireworks started.

Blythe didn't stop on the unused third floor, but went straight up the final narrow set of wooden stairs leading to the attic door. She paused with her hand on the doorhandle, drew a deep breath, and then charged into the room. An overwhelming blast of waxy fumes, heat, and light sent her reeling back and her hands came up to shield her eyes from the brilliant glare of more than two hundred candles. In the glare, she made out things darting—no, dangling—all about the bare attic. And then something brushed her shoulder, she squinted and recognized a handcut crystal prism, dangling from a string attached to the bare wooden rafters above. She looked again and made out . . . at least a hundred of them!

In the center of the attic, between two layered banks of wooden planking on which the candles were set, stood Blythe's father,

Walter Woolrich. He was dressed in his finest clothes: a scarlet brocade coat and waistcoat and white velvet knee breeches with scarlet knee bows. His once-handsome, fine-featured face was beaming, but the light that glittered in his gray-blue eyes had nothing to do with the brilliance of two hundred candles. At his feet was the shell of a once-magnificent crystal chandelier that had hung in the center hall for two and a half generations. Walter was busy tying more of its cannibalized crystal prisms onto strings to hang from the open rafters, and it was a moment before he realized he wasn't alone. He turned to behold Blythe standing just inside the doorway, her face blanched and her fists clenched at her sides. The crystal he was tying was thrust behind his back as he faced her with a guilty look.

"Blythe! How did you . . . find me?" But behind Blythe, Mrs. Dornly and Lizzy were edging into the attic, eyes wide and necks craning to take in the spectacle, and he knew. He gave them a look of grave disappointment. "You told."

"No, they didn't," Blythe declared as they shook their heads vigorously behind her. "I only wish to heaven they had!"

"Well, you're here now, that's all that matters. I was going to come for you anyway . . . afterwhile. Isn't it just magnificent?!" He turned around slowly and waved an enraptured arm about him at the dazzling display of light and shimmering miniature rainbows that were thrown by the crystals.

"What in God's name are you trying to do?!" she choked out when she could speak again. "Burn the house down around our heads?! Blow these candles out *immediately*!!" When he didn't move, she lurched forward and began furiously blowing them out herself. Smoke began to billow and choke the already meager air and her father grabbed her by the arms and grappled to pull her toward the middle of the floor between the blinding banks of candles.

"No, Blythe, you can't! I have to have the light! You must understand. I have to have the light . . . to end the war."

"To what?!" she stared at him in horror.

"You see, I've figured it all out. And I know the only way to reach the king's mind and free it from the darkness that enshrouds it." He pointed toward one of the small dormer windows and boyish excitement filled him. "You see that window? It faces east

23

by northeast . . . *England*, don't you see! And if I can just focus the light, enough light, and magnify it into a beacon . . . I can reach all the way to King George! All I have to do now is concentrate . . ."

In his tight grip, Blythe trembled between horror and anguish as her mind raced to take it in. She stared slowly about them at the fine beeswax candles . . . a small fortune, literally going up in smoke. For the past fortnight she'd not even had a tallow candle to see her to her bed at night. Her eyes landed briefly on Mrs. Dornly, who could not meet her pained, searching look. The money from the silver they'd sold . . . this was where it had gone . . . to pay for another of her father's moon-witted schemes . . . while the rest of the household slowly starved and withered into oblivion. Heaven help them — was she the only one in this wretched household with a bit of sense?!

"*No!*" She clamped her hands over her ears and wrenched from his grasp, refusing to listen to his latest craziness. "I'll not hear another word about it! Your *light* can't possibly make it to England. For heaven's sake . . . use your head, Papa. The strongest shipping beacons can't be seen past a few miles at sea!"

"But this is special light . . ."

"No—no, it's not!" Blythe turned and snatched up a candle and blew it out furiously. "It's just wax and fire . . . like any other candle. And we're just people, like any other people. We freeze when we have no fuel for the fireplaces, we starve when we have no food. And we have to work to earn the means to live! Your crazy scheme has taken the very food out of our mouths and the heat from our hearths! And I'll not have another instant of it!"

She wheeled and began blowing out the candles as fast and furiously as she could. The acrid smoke billowed to fill her lungs and eyes, burning them. She choked on the smoke and on the slow accumulation of the morning's frustrations . . . and stopped, blinded by tears. Her tender frame was rigid, damming up the turbulent waters of emotions she could not afford to feel or to show. Her fists were clenched like bronze casts.

She turned slowly to find her father staring at her through the fine haze of the smoke of spent dreams. His beautiful gray eyes were darkening; the animation was leaving his features. The mouth that used to smile and laugh to tease his little daughter drooped at the corners with uncertainty and disappointment. Hands that had tossed little Blythe high in the air and always caught her to safety now clasped in awkwardness and shame under her aching eyes.

Blythe could scarcely breathe. She shuffled her feet toward him and forced her bloodless hands open so that she could grasp his sleeve. "Papa . . . you can't go on like this. Don't you see . . . we're nearly ruined." The misery in his face was real, but Blythe feared it was not understanding of their plight that prompted it, nor regret for his role in bringing it about. "You have to stop doing things like this . . ." she grabbed and shook his arms with growing desperation, "or someday you'll destroy us all! And I can't let you do that . . . don't you see? Somebody has to be sensible. Somebody has to take charge . . ."

When his tortured gaze met hers, waves of despair crashed over her and she fought wildly to keep from smothering under them. She couldn't go under now . . . she had to be strong . . .

"Extinguish these candles at once!" she choked, whirling to include Mrs. Dornly and Lizzy in her command. "Dismantle this mess and . . . use whatever you can salvage to reduce our accounts at Jacobson's and Simmons's." The housekeeper lowered her eyes and Blythe swallowed back the tears that clogged her throat. "Then I want the chandelier crated up. As long as we were doing without it, we may as well do without it permanently. I'll find a buyer for it this afternoon!" She rushed to the door and Lizzy and Mrs. Dornly skittered aside to let her pass.

Blythe Woolrich had a life that would try a saint. And it was destined to get even worse.

Chapter Two

Blythe didn't even break stride when she reached for her worn velvet short-cloak on a peg in the center hall and marched out the front door into the cool September morning. Traffic was already bustling on the brick and cobbled street; tradesmen who supplied the gracious houses lining the street, folk on their way to offices and shops, servants scurrying in and out of houses and calling to one another in greeting. She threaded her way through the foot traffic and vendors' carts, acknowledging greetings turned her way with a preoccupied nod.

Anyone seeing Blythe Woolrich exit Woolrich House and walk her customary route toward the docks might have noted the absence of her somewhat dated bonnet, but none would have guessed that she was only a hairbreadth from an eruption. The peachy brightness of her smooth skin and the clipped edge to her graceful stride were the only outward effects of the turmoil flaming inside her.

To the world she appeared a respectable, if solemnly garbed, young woman of slightly more than middling height. Her dark brown hair glowed with reddish-golden highlights that could not be buried completely in the tight, sensible rolls at the back of her head. Her heart-shaped face was framed on prominent cheekbones that tapered downward over sweetly curved cheeks to a squared chin that bore a noticeable dent. Full, cupid's-bow lips were set firmly enough to force some of their corallike color into her dewy cheeks. Slender hands clutched the front of her modest cloak together over a silhouette that began with broad, smooth shoulders, tapered sharply to a narrow waist, then flared to a gently rounded bottom. Beneath those sensible woolen skirts, lithe, willowy legs exerted a no-nonsense stride that was the product of several carriageless years of transportation.

It was only the molten glow of her unusual eyes that hinted at the volatile emotions swelling and subsiding within her. Blythe Woolrich's eyes were the color coveted by misers and prized by adventurers; a color which could be as cold as coinage or as hot as the setting sun. They were *gold*. Set in a thick whorl of feathery sable lashes, those burnished disks were one feature of her appearance Blythe had never quite come to terms with. In her formative years, Nana Woolrich had often called little Blythe to her side to stare intently into her unusual eyes and declare critically, "Well . . . I think they're getting darker."

Nana had never exactly approved of her extravagant eye color, or of the shameless reddish glint to her lush mane of hair—a "hussy" shade, she'd called it, proclaiming it a legacy from Blythe's very blond, very "French" mother. Nana had never approved of Blythe's mother, either, and was only too glad to resume control of the dignified household when Blythe's beautiful mother had little enough sense to die, leaving a five-year-old daughter and a husband driven to distraction by grief.

In a household under "Nana" Hortense Woolrich, the sterner the virtue, the more it was prized. As Blythe grew up, sensibility, restraint, self-denial, and especially duty, were the order of the day . . . every day. She learned early to stand on her own two feet and it wasn't long before she was supporting others as well. She learned to sew because Nana hated mending; she learned to cipher quickly because numbers gave Walter a headache. She learned to do her own laundry and lay her own fires because the maids were always overworked, and she learned to stretch and substitute nearly every commodity required to run a household because coin was always in short supply. And in the process, she learned to make allowances for the limits of others, if not for her own. Responsibility seemed her destiny in life, for, as Nana had so often pointed out, she was certainly born with the shoulders for it.

Nana's opinions about what constituted "respectable" looks

found fertile ground in Blythe's impressionable mind. She learned to constrain and suppress the enchanting womanliness of her emerging form, and to lower her lashes to hide the natural boldness of her eyes. It was a discipline that had taken long to perfect, for a girl with a hidden "French" half. But once mastered, it had served her exceedingly well. In all Philadelphia there was no unmarried woman considered more "respectable."

Blythe was one of the few females who had weathered the nine-month British occupation of Philadelphia and emerged with her virtue and her reputation intact. When General Howe's redcoats marched into the city, many of the respectable folk—including most of the respectable female population—had marched out the other side, to take refuge in the countryside. Women who stayed were either loyalists . . . or women with something to gain from embracing, often literally, the British. Blythe became a notable exception. Nana was quite ill and Blythe's heavy responsibilities left her no patience with smug redcoat provisioning officers, with their roving eyes and crude, insulting hands and propositions. Her frosty ripostes and heated set-downs soon became barracks legends. And the British and their sympathizers had no need to trade with Woolrich Mercantile, with so many others willing to be more "accommodating." They simply took their business elsewhere.

Blythe's frustration had cooled by the time she arrived at the large brick building in the waterfront district that housed both the Woolrich Mercantile Shop and the warehouse of Woolrich Freight Company. That was fortunate indeed. For no sooner had she stepped through the door of their worn office than their clerk of many years, Douglas Carrick, hurried in to inform her that their last remaining freight wagon and team had disappeared on its journey to a trading post in the western hills. Reportedly, the driver had staggered into the outpost a week late and spun a tale of Indians . . . very pale Indians, who spoke "damned fine English."

This, on top of everything else this morning! The ramifications of the loss were just too devastating to contemplate, especially on an empty stomach. She had prayed that the British withdrawal from Philadelphia would bring an appreciable improvement in their fortunes. But instead, there was a sudden proliferation of shops and "merchants" in the city, owing to a boom in profiteering. Old suppliers and customers had adjusted too easily to new arrangements under British rule and their business went from bad to worse.

Blythe stiffened, blinked back the moisture that sprang to her eyes, and swallowed this new frustration, sending it to join that mass of disappointment and shunted anger that roiled and burned in the empty middle of her.

Her wretched luck just seemed unending. When their last wagon disappeared, their last shippable wares went with it. There wasn't enough left in the warehouse now to even draw mice. And there was precious little on the wooden stack shelves in the shop at the front of the warehouse, either. Over the last two years, their credit with the reputable lenders in the city had been exhausted and their living was reduced to mere subsistence. She'd done everything prudence and industry demanded, literally worked her fingers raw to care for her hapless family. But every venture she tried ended in some horrible calamity or other. It seemed as though some implacable "fate" was intent on grinding the Woolriches into oblivion.

The sleepy-eyed shopgirl, Mary, was just arriving, and Blythe dragged her into the shop to begin cleaning and rearranging the meager goods remaining on the shelves. She donned a worn apron herself, hoping activity would stave off the worry that gnawed at her and might help her think what to do next. But every swipe of the scrub brush, every billow of dust, reminded her of the cycle of grinding toil and deprivation that stretched dismally into her future. The minute they finished cleaning, the dust would begin to settle again . . .

Midway through the morning, Blythe paused to lean against the side of the stack shelves near the door into the passage leading back into the office and warehouse. Her eyes were closed and her energy was at low ebb. Hushed voices in the empty shop reached

29

her; ones she recognized all too well.

". . . not a new item in months," pinch-faced Eudora Frankel whispered loudly, heedless of being heard. "I don't know why I bother to come here anymore . . . except out of loyalty to poor Walter."

"Don't you mean 'poor Blythe?' " came stout Beulah Henderson's "whispered" response. Beulah Henderson and Eudora Frankel were two of the most famous gossips in Philadelphia. They made regular rounds in all the shops, gleaning their juicy tidbits from the buying habits of the leading citizenry and infuriating the merchants by never buying anything themselves.

" 'Poor Blythe' . . . humph." Eudora's voice lowered. "Her troubles are her own brewing. Everyone knows she's on the shelf now . . . twenty years soon and not a prayer of a marriage without a decent dowry. Too good for any of the local lads when Walter was better fixed and now that he's penniless . . . She might have landed a British officer, like my Sarah, if she hadn't been so disobliging and uncivil. Made a royal spectacle of herself . . ."

There the old cats stood, in the middle of her own shop, gossiping about her as though *she* were somehow to blame for the Woolriches' mounting misfortunes! It was too much to suffer in silence—

"She's forgotten how a true lady behaves, she has," Beulah agreed, adding, "One look at those hands of hers and a body can see that. And those clothes . . . goes about dressed like a charwoman. A body would think she didn't have any better."

Blythe's anger was momentarily cheated. She stared at her raw, work-reddened hands, then hid them in her apron, flushing hot with shame. Their words stung an unexpectedly tender part of her pride. She didn't wear better clothing because she had none; everything had been sold! She didn't have time for coiffure or fancy stitchery, wasn't invited to proper socials . . . not since well before the British came. She swallowed hard and felt shamed tears pricking the backs of her eyes. She didn't have time to be a lady anymore.

She didn't have the comfort of a lady's dreams. In the last year, she'd very sensibly laid to rest the last of her secret hopes of ever being a bride. She would never have the thrill of making plans for a wedding gown, a household, a life at the side of an upstanding

30

gentleman. There would be no socials, no christenings . . . no admiring looks or gentle touches . . . no sweet, gentlemanly murmurings in darkened gardens. She was fated for a very different kind of life . . . a solitary life of responsibility. People depended on her . . .

That awful sliding, sinking sensation occurred in the middle of her again. It was so intense this time that she felt for some physical evidence of it with her hands. But there was only her growling, empty stomach after all.

Flame ignited in her middle and shot a dangerous spurt of steam into her blood. "Do you ladies wish to *purchase* something?" She stepped out from behind the shelves with her hands on her hips and her angry golden eyes barely veiled. She watched Beulah shrink behind Eudora's pinch-faced condescension, then turned her gaze pointedly to the bolt of shopworn muslin Eudora was fingering. Eudora's hand slid from the fabric and hurried to clutch the handle of her empty market basket.

"No . . . I don't believe you've any yard goods suitable for a wedding gown," Eudora's tone was heavy with insinuation. "My Sarah's being married shortly, you know. *Lieutenant* Richard Grevell . . . of the British Grenadiers."

"Then she has my heartfelt condolences." Blythe scowled and this next just came tumbling out: "I'm sure you'll find the proper volume of yardage . . . somewhere."

Eudora reddened, for her daughter, Sarah Frankel, was a young woman known more for her width than her depth. There was an indignant flurry for the shop door and Blythe stood alone in the empty shop, hearing echoes of the old cat's cruel assessment of her. On the shelf now . . her own fault . . . forgotten how to behave . . .

What was happening to her? She felt herself teetering on the very brink of some unknown and frightening cataclysm in her life, in her very soul. She had to get hold of herself! She swallowed against that choking in her throat and clutched the wooden counter, trying to make herself think clearly. She always coped, always found a way to hold things together and she had to find one this time . . . somehow.

She shook herself straighter and stiffened her trembling chin. Her empty stomach growled again and she looked down.

"Hush."

At midday, Blythe dispatched their shopgirl, Mary, to Woolrich House to fetch them a bit of dinner. With Clerk Douglas Carrick dismissed to his own humble lodgings for the noon meal, Blythe sank into the worn leather chair behind the ink-marked desk in her father's sparsely furnished office. She rubbed her tired eyes, trying to banish the sight of stark red columns of numbers from the backs of her eyelids, then looked around the sunlit room. The once immaculate walls were lined with the furniture of commerce; a standing clerk's desk, two tall, wooden cabinets stuffed with paper and documents, and a covey of worn and empty pigeon holes above another small cabinet. The charter granted her great-grandfather to begin a trading company hung in a frame on the wall beside the door. In the middle of the room, opposite the large, leaded window sat the heavy walnut desk that was once the seat of power of a lucrative trading concern. Behind it, in the wide, stuffed chair, Blythe sighed tightly and rubbed her aching shoulders.

She had so many things to worry about . . . but right now, all she wanted was some hot food and a few moments of blessed silence. Those angry red numbers in her mind faded and permitted her quarreling stomach to be heard in earnest. Lord, what she wouldn't give for a hot beef pasty and a slice of tart, English "cheddared" cheese . . . not to mention a plum and sugar tart or a caramel custard showered with her favorite: sweetened coconut.

Her head drooped against the wing of the chair. Her mouth was watering. Her thoughts slowed and sorted and narrowed until a great juicy apple dumpling was all her mind could register. And then her mind went quiet altogether and she slept, sitting there, hungry and unhappy, in her father's, her grandfather's, and her great-grandfather's chair.

Something reached through that veil of sleep to call her forth a while later. And it was something not altogether agreeable. A sensation . . . a goad to memory . . . a smell. Something like . . . onions. And in her mind, there was only one connection to be made with that foul blend of soured ale and onion odors. She startled awake and her eyes popped open to stare straight into a

32

pair of narrow brown eyes embedded in puffy folds of flesh.

Neville Carson was leaning over her, his heavy arms braced on the arms of the chair. His hard velvet-clad legs pressed against and between her knees at the seat's edge and his fleshy face was crinkled with a hungry smile.

"Asleep at the tiller, my sweet Blythe? Can't expect to be doin' much trade that way. There's only one profession a woman can practice even while she's asleep." He laughed and another blast of beery onions issued forth as he purposefully let his gaze drift down the slim column of her throat to the limits of her strained bodice. "God, you look good enough to eat."

"You've already *had* dinner, Neville Carson," she gasped, trying to inhale as little as possible. "I can tell." Her straight, delicate nose curled in disgust as she waved a hand before her face to dispel the fumes of his breath.

"Actually, my delicious little dish, I was hoping to feast on your charms."

"Let me up," she demanded. His grin hardened, but did not fade altogether and she repeated it. "Let me up!"

He straightened and backed a step, just enough to allow her to stand. But when she gained her feet, his heavy arms clamped around her like a fleshy vise. His thick lips swooped down on hers with astonishing speed, and contact was made before she could prevent it. She pushed frantically against his wide, hard chest, twisting her head and squealing outrage.

"Neville Carson—" She managed to wrench her mouth free and gasped for air, "How dare you—" But Carson turned his feasting on the tender skin of her neck, just below her ear and she feared for a minute that he did mean to have her for dinner—literally! "Stop it!" She pushed against him valiantly and found herself moving backward, but only at the impetus of his wide frame. And soon she was pressed back against the wall between the clerk's desk and a cabinet. "Don't be ridiculous, Neville . . . stop it this instant!" she commanded, pushing at his velvet-clad shoulders and wriggling furiously in his grasp as he pinned her against the wall. His heavy, lecherous laugh was an indication of how ineffective her struggles were against his surprising strength.

Neville Carson was nearly as broad as he was tall, but his fleshy outer layers belied the hardness of the body beneath. Blythe knew well the strength he could employ in such a clinch, for he'd had her in similar predicaments before. And she hoped desperately this one would end as the others had . . . in his disappointment.

With a flash of inspiration, she went perfectly still, and his surprise was registered by an abrupt halt in his bodice-pillaging activity. She gambled that his vanity and pretensions were so imbedded that he'd not stoop to actually taking her here . . . on the floor of her own office. His head came up and his face darkened with desire as he stared into her glowing golden eyes. He'd seen those eyes each night in his tortured dreams and was determined to see them in the flesh in his bed before the first snow fell. He looked down at her perfectly bowed lips that were parted by panicky breaths, and he licked his own. He covered her mouth with his and sent his thick, oniony tongue to claim her surrender. And Blythe did the most natural thing in the world . . . she gagged.

Nothing is so likely to deflate a normal man's carnal desire as the feel of a woman retching under his kiss. And Neville Carson had a normal man's sensibilities, with regards to kissing. His dietary preferences were another matter altogether, and one of the chief reasons the refined female population of Philadelphia found him unacceptable . . . Blythe included. Though in truth, more than mere onions stood between him and the object of his desires.

Neville Carson was a self-made man who craved respectability almost as much as he craved riches and financial power. The cravings of the flesh usually finished a mere third in his estimate, but in Blythe's presence they were sometimes given precedence. He wanted to possess the venerable and respected Woolrich Mercantile and Freight Company and he wanted to possess Blythe Woolrich's delectable little body . . . in whichever order he could acquire them. He had a well-deserved reputation as a man who'd employ any means to an end and his patience with Blythe's obstinance was rubbing exceedingly thin.

"Dammit!" He jerked back as she clamped a hand over her mouth and retched for a second time. "*Damn!*" He stepped a full pace away, staring at her with horror in his dusky face. His blunted, bulbous features tightened and his fists clenched as humiliation burst and showered through the middle of him, followed by an explosion of raw fury.

Blythe's face drained as she watched him pound one fist into the other. She'd really done it this time! Her instinctive reaction had been as much a surprise to her as it had been to him. "I'm . . . not feeling well. I tried to warn you . . ." She stumbled to put the desk between them and skittered back when he lunged to plant his blocky fists in the middle of the desk and lean forward threateningly.

"You think you're so clever, Blythe Woolrich . . . so damned fine and untouchable. Well, I know better." His fists opened and turned on the desktop to engulf the littered sheets of paper that were covered with red ink. "These," he lifted the crumpled ledger sheets like prizes and shook them at her, "these say differently. These say you're a female . . . whose place is in a man's bed, not in a place of business. You're failing, woman, and you're too damned stubborn to admit it. You've lost your last wagon now and you've not got a shilling's worth of goods in the place."

So, he'd taken time to prowl through the shop and the documents on her desktop before awakening her to pursue his desires! Having him creeping and plundering around—it was like being violated in her sleep! Her face burned. "It's none of your concern how little I have on the shelves . . . or how my business is conducted!"

"I decide what's my concern and what's not. And I've decided Woolrich Mercantile *is* my concern," he snarled, tossing the papers aside. He began to stalk her around the desk and she moved to keep the furnishings between them. "I'm going to have Woolrich Mercantile and Freight. And like it or not, I'm going to have you, too. You're going to be Mrs. Neville Carson before spring. I'm going to dress you like a princess," his eyes gleamed, "and ride you like a mare . . ."

"Never." Blythe seethed it, feeling a dizzying rush of anger pouring into her veins. She'd never seen him in such a state! But not even the creeping fingers of dread up her spine could quell her open contempt for him. "Never!"

"On the contrary . . . as soon as possible. I've been too soft with you, Blythe, I see that now." His dark eyes burned like coals as he eased his bulk around the desk corner. He paused, and behind his deceptive flesh his ponderous muscles were coiling for the pounce. "If you come to your senses soon, you'll find I can be

35

a very generous . . . husband." His voice dropped menacingly. "I could be persuaded not to lock your lunatic father away."

"He's *not* a lunatic!" Blythe growled, searching wildly for an avenue of escape.

"And for certain *wifely considerations*," he watched her desperation with mounting excitement, "I could be persuaded not to kick that disgusting old crone you call your grandmother out on her arse in the streets. You see, your crazy father mortgaged your precious Woolrich House some time ago . . . and the gentleman who holds the note now finds himself in a bit of a bind. It's merely a matter of days before I relieve him of it."

He seized her brief moment of shock to spring at her, and this time the cold anger in his face said he'd not be denied his desires . . . whether on the floor of the office or not. Blythe grappled with him, fighting his punishing grip on her shoulders with everything in her, but losing ground steadily. "You foul, disgusting—I despise you!" His grasp only tightened and he wrestled her back against the desk and bent her back over it, forcing her down with his heavy body.

"You're mine, Blythe Woolrich," he panted, clasping a fleshy paw over one half-exposed breast as he groped for her mouth with his. When her head thrashed and he missed his target, his hand tightened on her soft flesh. "Count yourself lucky that I'm planning to marry you after—"

"I'd be luckier if I were to *die* first . . ." she gasped, struggling to raise her knee. It was suddenly raised for her . . . and pushed harshly aside. Carson ground himself against her pelvis crudely.

"Oh, I'll ride you, my proud little piece, make no mistake about it. Your only hope now is to dissuade me from wearing *spurs!*" And this time he managed to press her head down against the desktop and invaded her mouth fully.

Blythe's scream was muffled by his suffocating mouth, but she managed to break one hand free. She pushed and beat at his thick head and neck, managing to wrench her head to the side to gasp for air. His hands were busy trying to invade her dress, probing crassly. It was pure animal instinct that brought her short, hard nails up and drove them into his fleshy jowl. He shrank and howled with pain just as the office door flung back and Clerk Douglas Carrick blundered in, stopping, shocked, just inside the door.

"Miss Blythe?!" Carrick's doleful eyes were saucer wide as he took in the sight of his employer, stretched and pinned over her desk with a heaving-furious Neville Carson wedged between her thighs. "Merciful heaven! Miss Blythe—" He jolted forward to help, but was halted halfway by Carson's murderous glare.

Carson gauged the clerk's threat, then jerked upright and lurched back a step from Blythe's still tussling form. Holding his clawed face with one hand, he quaked with the need for violence. But some colder, saner urge reminded him that he wanted no breath of scandal over his marriage to Blythe Woolrich. There would be time afterward, in private, to avenge these insults.

Blythe sprang up on the desk, eyes blazing, dizzy with the unexpected release and yet steady enough to realize the threat was past, for now. "Get out, Neville! Get out and leave me alone. You'll never have Woolrich House . . . or Woolrich Mercantile. I'd rather see it burned to the ground!"

"You'll regret this, Blythe Woolrich." Carson turned a seething, slitted gaze on her that sent hot chills up her spine. "I'll have what I want . . . by God! And I'll see to it you rue the day you refused my . . . generous offer." He barreled for the door, nearly bowling poor Carrick over in the process.

The sounds of his furious passage through the shop and the door slamming behind him crashed over Blythe and she slid to the floor beside the desk. She was trembling all over, furious, steaming and chilling at the same time. The horror of what had occurred and what almost occurred settled firmly on her.

Sooner or later something like this was bound to happen. Neville Carson had pursued her since he came to Philadelphia almost two years ago. At first, his preoccupation with assembling his shady financial empire and his desire to be accepted socially had kept his attentions to her within bearable bounds. But lately, his advances had grown bolder and their confrontations had taken on an acrid, vengeful tone. Now she'd pushed him past his limits—retching at his kiss—Lord! She'd be fortunate if he didn't have her murdered in her sleep!

"Miss Blythe?" Carrick approached, and put a thin hand on her arm. "Are you all right?"

She forced her trembling hands to smooth and right her rumpled clothing and her quaking voice to respond. "I'll be . . . I'm fine, Carrick," she fairly choked on the lie. "Thank God you came when you did! You're not to let that disgusting lout set foot on the premises again, Carrick, do you hear? Never . . . not so much as a foot!"

"Oh, no . . . not a foot, miss." Thin, storklike Carrick shook his head gravely, then adjusted his fragile spectacles on his nose, wondering just what he could possibly do to prevent it.

Drawing on the waning reserves of her beleaguered strength, Blythe forced her shoulders back and her head high. She couldn't allow herself to be intimidated by the scurrilous likes of Neville Carson, no matter how wealthy and powerful and ruthless and vengeful . . . She gasped, scarcely able to breathe for the weight of something heavy and smothering settling on her chest. Dearest Lord . . . her entire life was crashing down about her head and she had nowhere to turn. What was she going to do?

Overwhelmed and robbed of all but despair by the day's mounting calamities, she shuffled toward the door and reached for the apron that hung on a nail there. Her tone was utterly lifeless as she whispered, "Is Mary back yet?"

"Not yet, miss." Carrick watched her rigid back, the bleak, frozen look on her face and the jerky, inept movements of her hands and he scowled. "Are ye sure you're all right, Miss Blythe?"

It was some time before she realized he had spoken, and she turned, her hands clamped on her apron strings. "What? Oh . . . I . . . I'll be . . . all right." He shook his head, unconvinced, and turned to his desk to begin sorting through his stubby, much-used quills. "Carrick?" Her voice was very small.

"Yes, miss?" He tilted his head back to peer at her through his scratched spectacles.

"We wouldn't have any food about the place . . . ?"

Carrick winced and shook his head apologetically.

She sagged. "I thought not."

The Gaff and Garter wasn't a very fancy accommodation for one of the largest trading concerns in Philadelphia, Carson Mercantile and Freight. Nevertheless, every day at noon, its business was moved from its respectable offices near Market Street and conducted there, amidst the pockmarked tables, loud, well-soaked patrons, and the ale-stained bar. The traffic was brisk, the food was hearty, and the rum uncut. That made the Garter just the place for the kind of business Neville Carson liked: business that sometimes needed a bit of a diversion in front of it.

He'd settled irritably at his usual corner table, accompanied by his chief minion, Dickey, and called for his usual dinner, when two men entered the Garter, asking for him by name. The plump tavern wench looked them over carefully and, under the taller one's intimate, caressing gaze, decided to be rather helpful. They wound their way through the noisy patrons and soon stood over Carson's table, staring down at the dwindling heaps of boiled beef and onions he was consuming. He was still stinging from his humiliating confrontation with Blythe Woolrich and was in no mood to have his table manners scrutinized by strangers. But a hot second look at the well-heeled gents and he forced his indignation to wait. Neville Carson never let emotions interfere with potential profit.

"Mr. Carson, I believe . . ." The taller of the two strangers spoke with a voice so deep and resonant that it vibrated the fork in Neville Carson's hand.

Carson lowered his intended mouthful and squinted, studying the man who'd spoken. "Yes. I'm Carson." The cut of the gentleman's clothing was exceedingly fine, excelled only by the cut of the man beneath them. He was broad-shouldered and clean-limbed, with classically wrought features and an easy, confident carriage that said *he'd* have no difficulties with stubborn, penniless heiresses . . . or any other women for that matter. One glimpse of the hard-eyed tavern wench's frankly admiring gaze on the man confirmed it. And Neville Carson took an instant dislike to him. "And just who are you, sir?"

"My name is . . . Gideon, and this is the captain."

Carson looked them over carefully and set down his crude cutlery. One was garbed as a gentleman and the other as ship's officer, eye patch and all. They had conspicuously short names. "What can I do for you, gentlemen?"

Carson's chief underling, the wiry and palorous Dickey, watched his employer's polite manner and came to attention. He knew from long experience that surly Neville Carson was never

39

more dangerous than when he was being polite.

"Perhaps it be what we can do for you, sir." The shorter, muscular-looking captain in his immaculate officer's uniform and leather eye patch spoke with a decidedly stuffed and nasal quality to his voice. A quick glance from the taller man caused him to defer to his companion.

"We've been told that Carson Mercantile is the largest freight hauler in Philadelphia . . . and the shrewdest" came Gideon's arresting voice again, its tone and timbre such as to ensure the listener would crave more. "We've a proposition that might interest a man such as yourself."

"A proposition?" Carson's dark eyes narrowed in their fleshy folds as he mulled it over. He waved a hand that sent Dickey up to roust two other patrons from their chairs and to commandeer them for the gentlemen. When they were seated opposite him, Carson raised his tankard and spoke over the rim of it before he drank. "What kind of proposition?"

"A very lucrative one." The gent calling himself Gideon smiled a cool, beguiling smile that nettled Carson further. Carson could just imagine its salubrious effects on the females of his acquaintance. "A shipload of goods, very fine goods. Silks and china, pepper and indigo dye. Worked iron implements, bolts of cotton —"

"And how did you come by these . . . very fine goods?" Carson drank very deliberately from the tankard and noted the slight pause before the answer was given.

"They were liberated from British ships."

"Under letters of marque?" Carson sat forward, hiding his piqued interest in his food as he resumed eating. He forked, then stuffed his mouth and a greasy onion dangled down his chin briefly before he slurped it through his thick lips.

"Naturally" came the handsome gent's casual response.

Naturally, Carson sneered silently. And as he mulled it over, searching for some way to turn this irksome encounter into some advantage, it came to him. A greasy smile spread over his bulbous features and he wiped his chin on the back of his hand. "Well, I'd be gratified to be doing business with the likes of such fine gentlemen, but I find myself embarrassingly short of warehouse space just now . . . havin' just taken on several loads of similarly 'liberated' goods. I'm afraid I couldn't offer very attractive terms. But . . ." He paused and laid a thick finger beside his nose as if he required its aid in remembering. "I might be able to put you in the way of a friend . . . with a fat purse and a keen desire for just such goods."

The one called Gideon and the "captain" exchanged glances that hinted at disappointment. Carson's greasy smile grew. "I happen to know that Woolrich Mercantile and Freight is in the market for goods; I just spoke with Woolrich myself . . . this very morning."

"They haul freight . . . have wagons and routes?" Gideon inquired evenly.

"They do." Carson saw Dickey's frown of consternation and slipped his hand beneath the table to dig harsh fingers into his companion's scrawny arm to keep him from speaking. "But I'll warn you. Woolrich hasn't made a massive fortune by spendin' coin freely, if you take my meaning. Damnable old-fashioned and don't like spendin' a penny of his 'got', even to 'get' more. You'll have to bargain hard. If there's aught left . . . come see me; I might be able to take a small bit off yer hands."

An odd flicker went through the handsome gent's eyes and he rose, extending his hand to Carson in thanks. Carson accepted it without bothering to rise and turned immediately back to his gaseous meal. Gideon and the captain strode out of the tavern and Carson noted the effects of the tall gent's lazy smile as he murmured thanks to the flint-edged serving wench. She followed them to the door and hungrily watched the tall gent's stride as he left. Carson's face darkened furiously as he watched her.

"But, Mr. Carson . . ." Dickey rubbed his arm and spoke up with the wariness born of experience, "ye be needin' goods and we got plenty o' place in th' warehouse. What'd ye send 'em over to Woolriches fer?"

Carson turned a slitted glare on his hireling and heaved a breath that cast noxious fumes. "They'll be back," he declared, "and they'll be willin' to accept my prices, after tanglin' wi' Blythe Woolrich and comin' away empty-handed." His forbidding scowl faded, and an ugly smile creased his fleshy face as he savored his little joke. And Blythe Woolrich would have the stock she needed so badly dangled before her big golden eyes . . . only to have him snatch it from her yet again.

"I wondered . . ." Dickey caught on and began to grin at his employer's impressive guile. "The Woolriches ain't got a single wagon left; we seen to that. And they ain't got no stock nor a penny to their name . . ."

"True enough." Carson laughed harshly, setting the voluminous flesh on his body aquiver. "The only wealth the Woolriches have left is what's between Blythe Woolrich's legs!"

Chapter Three

"A right good bloke, 'at Carson fella." The captain tossed a glance back over his shoulder at the fading signboards above the door of the Gaff and Garter.

"For a *respectable* sort, you mean? You wouldn't have thought so if you'd smelled him," Raider Prescott paused in the busy street and set his hands at his waist to stare at Bastian Cane with meaning-filled irritation.

"Well, I can' help it if cities give me th' grippe . . . they *stink*." Bastian tucked his chin, sniffed, and blinked reddened, watery eyes. "Plug me right up. An' it weren' my idea to come in th' first place."

"No—it was *my* idea—" Raider Prescott closed his eyes and drew a deep breath that only confirmed the odiferous nature of the otherwise splendid Philadelphia. Despite the unusual refinements of paved streets and brick footpaths and surprisingly soot-less streetlamps, there were still the smells of wastewater in gutters, the residue of horse traffic, and the crowding of unwashed bodies and greasy cooking fires. Raider's straight, incisive nose curled in sympathy. The longer he lived with Bastian's cursedly delicate sense of smell, the more he seemed to develop one himself. As soon as this unsavory business was done, he'd be only too glad to get back to the sea.

"I don't like it any better than you do." He opened his eyes to find several women, stopped in small clumps, watching him as he stood in the street with his booted legs spread, his hands on his narrow waist, and his broad, muscular shoulders jutting forward. He was used to the strange effects his appearance had on women and dismissed it, giving Bastian's arm a swat to urge him along. But Bastian doffed his gold-rimmed tricorn and smiled winningly at their feminine audience as he was led away. His fierce, blocky strength was visible in every inch of his seaman's frame, and its contrast to Raider's lean, muscular grace made the pair the subject of admiration everywhere they went. But unlike Raider, Bastian never got enough of the female adoration they inspired . . . and was known to exploit it whenever possible.

Raider halted at the next street corner and stopped a portly fellow with an open baker's cart full of fresh-baked loaves and rolls to ask directions. The fellow scowled and crossed his arms over his chest, staring pointedly at his wares. Raider breathed out patiently and produced a few copper pennies. The fellow shoved a dark, fragrant loaf into Raider's hands and pointed down the street and indicated three blocks to the east and another north . . . the way to Woolrich Mercantile and Freight. Not knowing quite what to do with his unplanned purchase, Raider tore the loaf in half and shoved it down into his ample, gentlemanly coat pockets. He had other things on his mind; his long, sinuous stride said so. He beckoned Bastian along with a nod and they struck off in the direction they'd been shown.

"I don't like it. *Wool*rich." Raider shuddered as they halted at another busy street corner to wait for a passing carriage. He didn't like dealing with anything or anyone that smacked of *wool*. It was utter bad luck for him; he was convinced. And their present venture needed all the good luck it could get.

"There be plenty of other merchants," Bastian offered testily, sniffing futilely and shaking his head in bewilderment at his highly selective ailment.

"Not ones with wagons." Raider crossed his muscular arms over his chest and stared coolly at his partner. They'd discussed this little point in their plan before and Raider wasn't about to resume the argument now. "We have to have wagons."

"We wouldn' have to have wagons to cart th' stuff if we'd jus' sail on up th' channel into dock . . . like proper traders."

44

"And face the har—" Raider realized where they stood, on a busy street corner collecting stares, and lowered his voice, "the *harbormaster* without the proper papers. We'd be volunteerin' for the triple tree . . . you know that as well as I do."

In spite of Raider's resolve against it, they *were* having the same argument as they had last night . . . and last week . . . and for the last month as they'd planned this expedition. They were in search of a merchant with a ready coin, wagons for hauling their wares overland, and a willingness to overlook some of the bothersome details of commerce . . . like bills of lading, shipping manifests, and bills of sale. And the stableman where they'd left their horses had assured them that Neville Carson was their man. So much for business references given by a fellow who mucked out horse stalls for a living . . .

"A bit o' coin would take care of a fussy harborman," Bastian grumbled as Raider pointed down a narrower street and struck off in that direction.

"We don't have a bit o' coin," Raider reminded him. "That's what this is about . . . turning that hold full of luxury into something useful."

"Coulda sold 'em in Sain' Thomas . . . an' had a fine old time spendin' it after . . . wenches and brandy an' rum till ye were blind . . ."

"For a tenth of what it's worth, you mean . . . and nothing more'n a banging head to show for it, after." Raider was trying not to get angry, trying to remember the years they'd fought and sailed and wenched and drank together. Bastian was ever a man for a quick reward and a fast squeeze of pleasure . . . even if it meant forgoing the hope of much greater gain, later. With all the ships Bastian had plundered, all the booty he'd taken, he should be a wealthy man by now . . . and so should Raider.

"What's wrong wid you, Raider?" Bastian pulled him back by the arm with an expression of growing horror on his square features. "Are you goin' respec'able on me?" The question struck a spark in Raider's penetrating green eyes.

"Respectable?! God—you take that back!" He towered over Bastian with a sudden flash of ire. "You know exactly what I think of the *respectable* squats of this world . . . who have all the money and make all the bloody rules. They see to it other folks

45

live by their rules while they do what they will and take what they want. The slimy, two-faced . . . The only thing I ever intend to do *respectably* is die . . . in bed . . . at a very old age." He turned on his heel and strode off, glowering at the brick buildings that crowded in on the narrowing street and searching for some sign of the Woolrich Mercantile Company.

Bastian watched him go, matching his dark look when he realized Raider hadn't completely denied it. He jolted into motion, hurrying to catch up with Raider's long stride and worrying that they were making a great mistake in coming here . . . in seeking out new markets for their commandeered goods. Never before in the history of their unusual partnership had they stooped so low . . . forced to truck with the likes of respectable businessmen. He had a very bad feeling in the pit of his stomach and promised himself a romp with a ripe tavern wench to steady his nerves, the very minute this unholy business was done.

Some minutes later, Raider Prescott and Bastian Cane stood across the street from the door to the Woolrich shop, eyeing the place with understandable confusion. It was a huge, dark brick building, inset with two large, leaded windows for the display of goods . . . except that the windows seemed empty just now . . . and in need of a good washing. The letters spelling out "Woolrich" were barely legible on the signboard hanging above the door on a wrought-iron bracket. And both the sign and the door were in dire need of a painting.

"This be it?" Bastian frowned and lifted his eye patch to get a clearer, two-eyed view. He caught Raider's look of equal puzzlement and straightened, dropping the leather swatch back into place. "Don't look very prosperous to me."

"Carson warned us Woolrich is a skinflint." Raider pulled down his waistcoat as if stiffening his determination. "Likely he won't even spend a coin to keep the place up. Stinginess is a very *respectable* fault. Come on; let's get it over with." He jerked his tawny head toward the door. "And remember . . . I'll do the talking."

The Woolrich shop was no more impressive inside. The impact of its surprising size was cancelled by its air of vacancy. The bell on the shop door had long since quit functioning and only the muffled clap of wooden door striking wooden frame announced their arrival.

"Well, it's about time, Mary!" came an irritable voice from above, and they looked up as one man to find a curvy female bottom dangling on a ladder that was propped against the ceiling high shelves. A wench in green woolen was stretched far to one side with a feather duster in her hand, swatting at the dust on a few glass lamp chimneys that were poised precariously near the edge of the topmost shelf. When there was no response to her chiding, she cast an irritable glance over her shoulder and at the same moment managed to dislodge one of the fragile chimneys with a jab of her duster and it went crashing to the floor.

"Oh-h-h!" The crash startled her and her foot slipped and she swayed on the tipping ladder. And the sight of a wriggling, swaying bottom just at eye level was more than Bastian's ever-ready impulses could withstand. He jolted forward to steady her, managing to fill both hands with her curvy bottom. And what started as a gentlemanly gesture of support soon became a lusty, exploring squeeze that elicited a furious squeal and a kick from the wench. Bastian laughed as he avoided her heel easily, then grabbed it to set her foot on the rung again. He gave her a smart whack on the rump for good measure as she sputtered outrage and hurried down the ladder to confront her molester.

Blythe hit the floorboards and wheeled, crouched and furious. The anger she'd bottled during the morning's calamities suddenly exploded inside her. Two male faces bore in on her, one laughing lustily, one merely smirking at the absurd picture she made . . . a disheveled and indignant "shopgirl." And before she thought, before her sensible, respectable nature could interfere, she launched herself at that smirking face with her arm in full swing. The slap clearly caught him off guard, for he made no move to defend against it and his head snapped gratifyingly.

"How dare you lay a hand on me, you . . . lout!" she snarled, grabbing her stinging hand and quelling the urge to wreak further mayhem on his very large person before he recovered fully. It never occurred to her that beneath the shock of that undeserved punishment, he might be gathering force for a bit of mayhem himself.

"Here now—" The odd, laughing voice to one side sobered enough to clutch at her arm, "no harm's done—" But Blythe jerked her arm away savagely and backed toward the wooden counter.

"Get out!" she commanded, her cheeks stained crimson, her full bosom heaving.

Raider dragged his big hand from the hard plane of his stinging cheek and stared at it with astonished eyes. "Since I've already paid . . . I think I'm entitled to a bit of play," he growled, his voice so deep and furious that it set the remaining lamp chimneys vibrating on their high shelf. In a flash, he sprung at Blythe and dragged her stunned form against his iron-hard frame, pinioning her dangerous arms at her sides with his. When his mouth swooped down toward hers and she shrank from it, he followed her, bending her backward over the wooden counter and molding his lean body against and over hers.

She wriggled and protested, feeling dizzy and starved for air as his firm lips crushed over hers. But with her arms pinned at her sides and her body bowed and stretched backward over the counter, she had too little leverage to effect any movement, much less real resistance. Alarm spread through her at the realization of what was happening . . . *for the second time today!*

But close on anger's heels came treacherous tendrils of warmth, curling through her. His lips were strangely both hard and soft on hers . . . unlike anything she'd experienced. The command of his body over and against hers stunned her, and as she struggled for breath, the scent of him filled her. He was like . . . a fragrant loaf of new-baked bread. And she was starving, reeling with a new kind of spreading hunger she'd never known until now. It seemed to be coming from somewhere below her stomach . . . somewhere she hadn't realized existed until now. Her blood was humming and her weakened limbs slowly relaxed. He seemed to be melting her, like warm butter, against him.

Raider felt Blythe's softening and instinctively his mouth gentled over hers. The kiss that was meant to punish deepened with a sudden rush of more urgent and primitive need. She was soft and curvy and her mouth beneath his was fragrant and yielding. His arms clamped harder around her, though it was impossible for their two bodies to be any closer. Lord, it was delicious—bending

48

her pliant flesh to his, invading that sweet-velvet mouth of hers. She startled when his tongue stroked hers and that innocent reflex inflamed him sharply. He must have groaned, for Bastian began coughing, insistent and raucous enough to penetrate the pleasurable haze enveloping his senses.

But it was the warning throb of his own body that finally pounded the futility of the situation through to him. Only the fiercest of disciplines broke that bone-melting contact with her honied mouth and peeled him from her warm body. His legs shook as he backed away and his lips and arms and loins screamed in protest. What in holy heaven was happening to him?

Blythe felt him loosen about her, felt his arms withdrawing and was powerless to stop it. Her bones and muscles had all turned to butter. It was a long moment before she realized she was free and another one before she could manage to push herself up onto her elbows, then upright again. Her knees were weak and her blood seemed to have drained from her head to more exotic parts of her body, leaving her dizzy and confused.

Bastian's final "harumph" snapped the trance she seemed to be under and again her eyes registered the two men who'd barged into her own shop and set hands to her . . . and lips. Good Lord—she was quaking all over! She backed quickly toward the passageway that led to the office and the warehouse and covered her naked, throbbing lips with the back of her hand. She scavenged every scrap of indignation she could find inside her, but her voice was strangely hoarse as she ordered, "Leave this shop at once! Get out!" And she whirled and ran down the passage into the warehouse.

Raider stood in the middle of the shop, stunned, then bewildered by his unthinkable reactions to the wench. He felt Bastian's questioning eyes on him and began to redden like a stripling.

"That was bloody stupid," Raider managed to say before Bastian did. And it was a minute before he recalled that it was Bastian who started it all and turned to glare at his partner. "You and your randy hands—"

"I jus' give 'er a little pat. It weren't *me* what kissed her—" Bastian glared back with a bullish attitude. But a moment later, their mutual accusations faded under a new reality. "What'll we do?"

Raider turned his back and stalked away, running his hands over his face as if to rub away the clinging memory of her soft skin and honeylike taste. "Old Woolrich will likely toss us out on our ears," Raider rumbled irritably. And he knew it would be his own fault, this time; letting his passions get the better of him when he had such important business to attend.

Blythe ran into the warehouse and through the shelves and the cavernous main floor, searching high and low for Carrick and calling frantically. She found him nestled atop an overturned barrel in the upper loft, snoozing peaceably. She roused him and dragged his disoriented person down the steps, raving about having been mauled and insulted in her own shop . . . and not standing for it.

In the pasageway beside the office door, Carrick turned to his employer and blinked away the last of his sleepy fog. "What's this? Miz Blythe . . ."

She hissed softly, releasing some of the steam inside her. "I said . . . there is some riffraff in the shop. I want you to go and clear them out—get rid of them, do you hear?" With a furious nod, she turned and sailed into the office, slamming the door behind her.

Carrick sighed raggedly and straightened the spectacles on the ridge of his nose. He was in no hurry to traverse that passageway and confront "riffraff" of any sort. And so it was several moments before he emerged in the shop to find it mostly empty. Two fine-looking gentlemen stood in the open street door, engaging quietly in an argument of some sort. One gentleman was clearly a fashionable man about town and the other wore a commanding nautical uniform. Carrick craned his neck for a glimpse of the objectionable "riffraff" and was vastly relieved to find it no longer present. He straightened his rumpled waistcoat and cleared his throat discreetly as he stepped around the counter.

"May I be of assistance, gentlemen?" he intoned in his most dignified voice. The two silenced and turned to stare at him, casting glances at each other from the corners of their eyes.

"Undoubtedly you can, my good man." Raider sauntered back inside with admirable cool. "We've come to see Woolrich, on a rather important matter. If you'd be so good as to announce us?"

"Certainly sir," Carrick mustered all his businesslike presence and inquired, "Whom shall I say is calling?"

50

"Mr. Gideon and Captain Cane, of the good ship *Windraider*."

"Indeed. Be so good as to wait a moment, sirs." A ship's captain and an agent, Carrick surmised, allowing himself a smile of satisfaction. This was just like the old days. There was a time, not so very long ago, when the Woolrich office had teemed with the likes of these fine gentlemen, all itching to do business with the shrewd Jebediah Woolrich . . . and his son Walter. There was a jaunty spring in Carrick's step as he retraced the passage and knocked on the office door.

"Yes . . . what?!" Blythe looked up from her oversized chair with her cheeks aflame from the heat of her angry humiliation. The shock of that dastardly assault had jarred the numbing fog from her senses and she was quite herself once again.

"Gentlemen here, miss," he intoned, quite pleased with his news, "to see you . . . from the ship *Windraider*. I think they've come to do business."

"Business?!" Blythe scowled confusion, then startled. Lord, someone was actually here to do business—and with her in the state she was in. She sprang up, her hands flying about her person and finally landing on her apron strings. "Give me a minute, then show them in. What do they want, Carrick?"

But the clerk was already gone and she just had time to rip the apron from her and stuff it into a desk drawer before she heard him returning. Her hands tugged at her bulging bodice, then slid over her work-mussed hair as the door opened again and Carrick entered, followed by two figures that widened both her eyes and her nostrils.

"You?!" Her jaw loosened briefly as she heard Carrick introduce her as Miss Woolrich and them as "Gideon" and "Captain" . . . somebody. And shortly two irate camps were turning on a very puzzled Carrick; one demanding to know why he hadn't chucked them out in the street and the other insisting that his little joke could cost him dearly.

"We came here to see old Woolrich himself," Raider proclaimed furiously, trying not to look at the heated little wench with the tumbling hair and cherry-red lips, ". . . not to waste our time on wasp-tongued females!"

"Wasp ton—? *I'm* Woolrich!" Blythe declared angrily, turning inescapably to that towering figure with the tawny hair and that shockingly memorable face. Lord, he was tall and his shoulders were broad as an oak . . . and every bit as hard. In fact, the realization drilled through her, he was hard all over . . . even to the jadelike stones of his eyes. And just how she knew his density humiliated her very respectable sensibilities. Her blood seemed to be rushing to her lips and breasts with appalling eagerness and to counter it she allowed her shamed anger full rein.

"I've run this business for my father for the last three years and I've *never* stooped to do business with the disreputable likes of you!"

"This is absurd—" Raider protested, shooting a harsh look at Carrick, who had backed toward the door and been blocked by Bastian. Carrick met the demand in Raider's stare with a sickly nod of his head.

"Miss Blythe is in charge, here, sir. Ye must deal with her . . ."

"You're wrong, Carrick," Blythe corrected the aging clerk, "They won't be dealing with me at all. Show them out!" Her veiled eyes were heating dangerously and a noise came from Carrick that might have been a groan. Her arms crossed defiantly beneath her uncorseted breasts, unconsciously emphasizing them, as she adjusted her stance, bracing determinedly.

"See here, Miz Woolrich." Bastian stepped forward, inserting himself between Raider and the indignant Blythe. "We meant no harm . . . jus' saw ye about to fall and meant to give a shop wench a bit of a hand. We'd no way of knowin' ye were a proprietor. We come wi' a fine bit of business to propose . . ." And before Blythe could object, Bastian launched into an explanation of their various cargoes.

Blythe heard only one word in three; something exceedingly odd was happening inside her. She felt this "Gideon's" eyes on her and responded as though they were his hands. That strange sliding and emptiness recurred in the middle of her and she felt unaccountably lightheaded. The tantalizing scent of fresh bread began to fill her head again and set her mouth watering. It was the same delicious and bewildering scent she'd inhaled when *he* had spread all around her, pressing her, holding her.

She was just hungry, hadn't eaten all day, that was all! She was conjuring up things. She clung to her rational processes desperately, even as her hands moved to cling to the edge of the desk.

Her face flushed becomingly as she tried valiantly to avoid staring at the tall brute. Her reddened lips parted and she could scarcely stand still . . . much less listen to the captain's description of where his ship was located and what he was saying about wagons and a day's ride . . .

Wagons? She didn't have any wagons, she realized dimly. And he was going on about very reasonable prices . . . money? She didn't have any coin, either! And the third word that caught her notice was a name.

" . . . so, Mr. Carson were good enough to send us on to you," Bastian finished genially, expecting the name to work a bit of magic with her. It worked a bit of mayhem instead.

"Carson . . . sent you? Neville Carson?! I wouldn't entrust a coin to the likes of you if my life depended on it!" she heard herself declaring. And in spite of her long years of habit and warning impulses to the contrary, she lifted her blazing golden eyes fully to the one called Gideon and was gratified by the jolt in his angry composure. Blythe meant to scorch him properly with the heat of her contempt . . . before she tossed them out on their ears. "Out . . . *Out!* I've no time to listen to your tawdry little schemes!"

Bastian sputtered shock at her virulent order and shot an angry look at Raider. What he saw jolted him. Every line of Raider's lean, graceful body was rigid and his face was darkening dangerously. Bastian clapped a hand on Raider's arm to pull him along, but Raider seemed to have been turned to stone by her stunning, golden glare and wouldn't move. Bastian realized he had to get his partner out of there . . . quick. "Then we'll not be troubling ye further . . ."

Suddenly, Raider came to life and the unaccustomed fury in his face turned it into a sculptured bronze mask. His big fists clenched and Bastian strained mightily to hold him as his jadelike eyes raked Blythe's haughty stance.

"You—you'll regret this, you . . . *Wool-witch!*" His rolling-thunder voice set the hairs on everyone's necks on end as he allowed Bastian to drag him from the office and toward the exit at the front of the shop.

Carrick shook his bewildered head at his youthful employer and at Blythe's irate order, he startled and followed the seafarers to be sure they found the street this time. That left Blythe alone, wilting behind her father's desk, trembling and unable to move. Icy relief was trickling through her legs even as dread tingled up her spine. Gooseflesh appeared all over her skin and her fingertips still vibrated from the echoes of his harsh words.

For the second time that day, she'd been kissed, then threatened. Her trembling fingertips came up to touch her very sensitive lips and for perhaps the first time in her sensible, responsible, dutiful life, Blythe honestly didn't know what to do. Confusion welled inside her, battering her eyes in waves that finally broke through her stalwart defense. A salty warning trickled down her cheeks and she flew to slam the door. Everything was a blur of misery as she crumpled into her father's worn leather chair and laid her head on the ink-stained blotter. And for the first time since she was a child, Blythe Woolrich began to sob.

By the time they reached the street, Raider Prescott was at full boil. The unaccustomed turmoil inside him blinded and deafened him to nearly everything around him and Bastian just managed to pull him down the street and into a narrow, deserted alleyway.

"Damn and blast!" Raider finally thundered, his fists clenched and his broad chest heaving. Bastian stepped back and flipped his eye patch up to watch this rare venting of Raider Prescott's wrath with two very widened eyes. For all his dangerous and violent profession, Raider Prescott was a man who never lost his temper and seldom even lost his composure. It was one of the things that made him memorable to his enemies and inspired pure devotion in the men who sailed under him.

"Who in hell does she think she is?! Damned arrogant little witch!" He stomped and slammed the bricks of the nearby wall with his open palm, and Bastian could have sworn he saw mortar dust fly. "All on account of a little feel . . . a paltry squeeze— that's a *respectable female* for you! God, they haven't got the sense God gave a turnip! Wouldn't even listen . . . *listen* to us! Just stood there glaring like the Almighty on Judgment Day . . . a vision of pure hellfire in her eyes! Did you ever in your life see such eyes?! A witch, for sure—"

He went on stomping and snarling, and twice more that brick

wall shuddered under his blows. And each furious curse, each hair-raising metaphor, lifted Bastian's incredulous brows another notch. He'd only seen Raider like this one other time in their decade-long association and that was little more than a month ago, when the leader of that unholy Caribbean pirate "League," Long Ben Harvey, delivered his vicious ultimatum . . . via the bloody back of one of their crew. Then, as now, Raider Prescott's usually imperturbable cool had utterly deserted him and his crew spent two very uncomfortable days as he roared and raged.

But this wrath was from a different source altogether, and after the initial venting of its explosion, mercifully, it began to clear. When his steam was mostly exhausted, Raider leaned a shoulder against that battered wall and closed his eyes, struggling to reassert some control over his volatile behavior. His volcanic responses baffled and somewhat embarrassed him, for this time they were caused by a woman . . . a woman he'd kissed. No woman, ever, had rebuffed Raider Prescott's kisses . . . much less a woman who'd responded to him like that little witch had done.

"Sweet Morgan's Blood." Bastian shook his head, clearly awed by the latent potential for rage that Raider carried within him. Bastian had always admired a clean bit of fury.

"It's what I get for trafficking with the likes of so called *respectable* folk. And *females*. Gawd . . . they're the worst. Treacherous, conniving, unpredictable . . . There's nothing lower than a respectable female, Bastian . . . and there's the living proof!" He thrust a righteous finger toward the end of the alley and that Woolrich witch . . . wherever she was.

"She ain't got her sails full-hung, Raider; it be a fact." Bastian was vastly relieved to see Raider regaining a semblance of rationality. There was a long pause. "I wonder how she knew . . ." Raider frowned at him quizzically and he completed it, ". . . that we was disreputable. I wonder how she knew we was pirates." He looked down at this stunning, royal blue officer's garb with a frown. "Ye suppose we forgot somethin'?"

Raider's eyes closed, and fortunately the last of his control dropped back into place just then. "We're *not* pirates, we're privateers . . . colonial privateers . . . a distinction that could conceivably save our necks someday." They'd had this argument before, too.

55

"Hoistin' a striped jack don't exactly make us 'sons o' liberty,'" Bastian objected. "We sail fer ourselfs and ain't never paid no percentage . . . that makes us *pirates*, old son!" Then he was back to his original question. "How'd ye think she knew we ain't got letters o' marque?"

"We prey on British ships only, because I like these brawling colonies — we're *privateers* . . . and she didn't know," Raider declared sourly. "She was referring to your lecherous attempt on her precious bottom when she called us disreputable. Respectable females measure everything by its relation to their blessed virtue. God . . . who'd want hers, anyway . . . a prune still on the damned bough!" He pushed off from the wall and strode purposefully for the street.

They argued all the way back to Market Street, then beyond, Bastian Cane insisting they go back to their ship and set sail immediately and Raider Prescott more determined than ever to make a deal for their cargo and itching to skin a bit of "respectable" hide in the process. They retraced their steps to the Gaff and Garter, only to find Neville Carson conveniently gone. They followed him to his offices and found him absent from those premises as well . . . and not likely to be reached until the next day.

Bastian watched Raider's intensity deepen as they made rounds of various merchants, making inquiries as to possible buyers. Their goods were welcome, for dismally low prices . . . the sale always contingent upon delivery, which was out of the question. Over and over they were told that if they had lead ballast that could be melted for shot, or powder, blankets, boots, or muskets . . . they'd be wealthy men, posthaste. Those items were at a premium on both sides of the War for Independence and it was no secret that some "very respectable" merchants of Philadelphia gouged exorbitant prices from whichever side was willing to pay.

It was dusk when they stopped before the open door of the Man Full of Trouble Tavern and Raider snarled something under his breath, then ducked inside. Bastian followed, eager to wet his whistle and to rid himself of the foul taste respectable commerce left in his mouth. The place was decent enough to eat in, but both ordered only liquid refreshment.

"It ain't fer us, Raider, truckin' and tradin' with these respec'able sorts." Bastian leaned close and insisted after he'd quaffed a full pint of stout ale, "They ain' nothin' but trouble for the likes of us. Ye give it a good shot—"

"It's that Wool-witch," Raider muttered, seeming not to have heard Bastian. "Damn bad luck, *wool*. Always has been. I should have known . . ."

"Another round an' we'll start back for the ship." Bastian waved over the serving wench and clamped his arm about her friendly bottom as he ordered a noggin of good rum. He turned back to Raider just in time to hear him say, "The hell we will. I came to do business . . . and it's business I'll do . . . if it kills me."

Bastian's square, ruddy face washed crimson. He stared at Raider's finely sculptured face and glittering eyes and a new determination seized him. "A body'd think ye were cozyin' upta these miserable hypocrites—"

"It's them or it's Long Ben Harvey . . . the devil or the deep blue sea," Raider's stare was cold indeed. "I choose the sea . . . and if you don't like it, Bastian, come up with something else."

Bastian's scowl deepened and his burly shoulders puffed with irritation, but he made no rebuttal. There was none to make. He knew Raider was right. They'd been given an ultimatum from the lethal pirate "league" that operated from Caribbean bases. To market their privateered goods in Charleston, as they had for several years, they'd have to pay a bounty—a very stiff bounty—to the pirate league that controlled that traffic. Raider had boldly refused their blackmail, declaring he'd find new markets for their prizes. That was what this clandestine trip was about . . . securing those new markets. Only the markets they'd found here were far from lucrative and nearly as closed, in their own way, as Charleston's black market.

The rum arrived and Bastian was annoyed indeed to have Raider grab it first and bury his nose full in it. Raider was a sipping man, normally, a tenacious habit from his earlier, gentlemanly life. Bastian was about to snatch the flagon back, but the sight of Raider's tawny, aristocratic head tossed back in abandoned indulgence struck a spark in Bastian that warmed the cockles of his piratical heart. It would do the lad good to get a tootfull . . . maybe burn this notion of dealing with "respectable" sorts out of his mind altogether.

But, as he watched Raider's unusual indulgence, Bastian began to worry again about this new determination of Raider's to ensconce them in trade with the respectable element of commerce ashore. Raider had a most respectable background himself, born a gentleman and educated fine . . . at Oxford . . . some Mary-sounding college or such. Always in trouble with his noble family for his lusty ways and strong-headed opinions. Since Bastian rescued him from arrest on a king's revenue cutter, nearly ten years ago, he'd secretly feared Raider would someday revert to his gentlemanly respectability on land. Despite Raider's professed contempt for the ways of respectable society, every extended stay they made on land made Bastian a bit more nervous.

There was but one thing for it, Bastian realized, ordering another round of that potent golden brew. He had to get Raider back to sea immediately. In his volatile state, there was no telling what he might decide to do. And he'd put up less of a struggle on the way back to the ship if he was soused proper.

"Come up with something else," Raider had said. And as he sat, watching Raider determinedly drinking himself into a royal fog, Bastian determined to do just that. He'd see they got coin enough to run on a while—and he wouldn't be so particular about how it was done. It needed to be something sufficiently lucrative to give them operating capital and piratical enough to ensure they wouldn't be exactly welcome anymore among Philadelphia's respectable contingent. The things he knew best . . . spiking and boarding and pillaging and burning . . . stealing and ransoming; they were all serious pirate work, for which he needed a crew. But wait—*ransoming*. That was fairly profitable stuff . . . and not overly strenuous, depending on who was taken and what ransom was demanded. A light went on in Bastian's crafty gray eyes and he scratched his square chin thoughtfully. If he planned it right, a certain abduction he had in mind might net them a fat ransom . . . and inoculate Raider against all desire for the "respectable" in one fell swoop!

Bastian's wicked grin registered as rather strange with Raider, but the rum had taken firm hold in his empty stomach. When Bastian suggested taking a room in the tavern for the night,

Raider nodded numbly and swayed to his feet. He could use a bed . . . had to get some rest . . . had to find . . . a buyer . . . first thing in the morning. . . .

Chapter Four

When the last rays of the setting sun crossed the horizon, on
that tumultuous day, the celestial bones were snatched up to begin
the game anew. It was just at that moment that Blythe looked at
the waning light from the window and at her wilting clerk and
sent faithful Carrick off to his lodgings for some rest. She vowed
she'd finish the sad business of the papers they'd been working on
and she'd lock up afterward.

Now, two hours later, she was just too tired to think straight
anymore . . . too tired to even worry properly. She rubbed her
burning eyes and quit her desk in the Woolrich office, rolling her
aching shoulders and massaging her tight neck. There was only a
stub of a lighted candle to see her toward the street door of the
shop, where she'd left her short cloak. She didn't usually travel
afoot after dark in the city, but it was either that or spend the
night in the office chair. Her own soft bed at home was all her
mind could think of. It was the one comfort she could still count
on, and if she had to brave the Philadelphia night to reach it, so
be it.

She slid her dark cloak over her shoulders and fastened its worn
clasps. Her fingers were rough and stiff from her day's hard work
and tension. She was hungry in the extreme, weary to the bone,
and utterly at a loss for how to explain her lack of lavender soap

to Nana, her lack of a husband to Mrs. Dornly, and her decision to sell the Woolrich shop and warehouse, to her father . . . whose cooperation would be required.

The little candle flame flickered and snuffed, leaving her in a moment of darkness until her eyes adjusted. She set the tin candleholder on the bench by the shop door and went out, pausing to lock the door behind her. A painful smile pulled at her moon-paled features. What was there inside that might be considered worth stealing?

The narrow street was dark, but around the corner there were streetlamps. She could see their yellow glow and could make out the distant drone of hooves on cobblestones and foot traffic. She'd just keep to the lighted streets and keep her head down. She'd done it before . . .

Suddenly there were footsteps and a rushing from either side of her, and by the time she could heed the warning of her fatigued senses, she was already seized . . . by each arm! She twisted and wrenched in that punishing grasp, and as she sucked air to cry out, something was stuffed into her mouth . . . and she was being hauled off her flailing feet and trussed around with a binding of some sort. Her world careened and she screamed, only to find the sound trapped mostly inside her own head. Her thrashing produced muffled grunts and curses from her abductors, but hindered them little. All went menacingly black as something was thrown over her head—a heavy blanket of some kind. Then she was lowered roughly onto the damp cobblestones while that awful shroud was wrapped tight around the rest of her.

Blythe's struggles ceased abruptly, for she was occupied fully trying to breathe between the cloth stuffed in her mouth and that suffocating mantle of darkness. She felt herself being hoisted and carried along over the uneven cobbles while she gasped and fought for breath with each bump and jostle. And shortly, the street was dark and silent once more.

Bastian Cane waited just outside a darkened, smelly livery stable on the far south side of Philadelphia. He sat on the seat of a horse cart, his shoulders hunched and his coat drawn up against the chill. The moon was full up now and he scowled forbiddingly at its sly face as if daring it to interfere in his plans.

He took another pull from the bottle at his feet and let the liquid fire of the uncut rum seep through his chilled frame. There was a moan and a shift in the back of the cart and Bastian leaned over the seat to check on a blanket-clad form, nestled in the hay. He sighed with deadly patience at Raider's blissful oblivion; Raider had the best end of it tonight, corked proper and sleeping through what would be a miserable, several hours journey back to the ship. He raised his head to search the darkened outlines of the nearby buildings, wondering what could be taking his hired henchmen so long. He had no doubt they'd make good their work, for he was a fair judge of men; he knew the hunger for coin in a man's face when he saw it. But he still wished he had his own men for the job—Sharky and One Tooth or Clive.

It was a few minutes yet before a stealthy figure crept around the corner of a nearby building and waved, catching Bastian's eye. He jolted upright and snatched up the reins, slapping the horse into motion and just managing to turn the cart around to bring it up beside a narrow foot alley between two ramshackle buildings. Shortly, two figures emerged into the dim street at the rear of the cart and hoisted a long, rolled object into the straw-filled cart with a thud. A bit of silver flashed in the moonlight, followed by the flash of three moon-wicked grins, the kind that can only be seen in the dead of night.

The jostling of being dumped into the cart had loosened that suffocating shroud around Blythe's head and she managed to get her nose to the edge of the blanket and gulped fresh air. She struggled desperately against the tight ropes that bound her and against that torturous gag that wicked up all the moisture in her mouth and throat. But all her thrashings only burrowed her deeper into that scratchy bed of straw, intensifying her helplessness and despair into true panic. She was being forced—taken away. Oh, please—someone help—

But in the long night ahead, no help came. There was only the lulling sway of the cart for comfort and her beleaguered mind and body finally surrendered, then embraced it. She slid into a merciful darkness, a deathlike sleep without dreams.

In the gray of a murky daybreak, the cart reached its final destination at the head of Delaware Bay. Through the mist steaming off the bay waters into the cool air of early morning, a prearranged signal was exchanged between the cart and the watch on a ship anchored offshore. Soon a longboat was launched with a three-man crew, pulling silently for Bastian's lone figure standing beside a cart on the weedy shore. There were murmured instructions, nods and stealthy movements through the rustling grasses.

That heavy blanket was again draped over Blythe's exhausted, unconscious form and she was lifted from the cart with great finesse and transferred to the longboat. She roused a bit as they lowered her into the bottom of the vessel, but as soon as she stopped moving, she settled back into oblivion. She did not feel the thud of a second form, dumped unceremoniously into the bottom of the boat. Nor did she feel it roll to lodge against her. And soon the boat was in motion and the hushed slap of the oars in the water were the only hint of the silent conspiracy unfolding around Blythe and her partner in oblivion, Raider Prescott.

Toughened hands untied and lifted Blythe to fasten a coil of rope around her and she wakened with a jolt in the damp chill of dawn. Panic galvanized her responses, but her scream reverberated only in her own head as she was hauled, flapping and flailing, over a railing onto the deck of a ship. Then leering, snarling male faces were pressing close, all around her. She thrashed and wriggled in their grasp and the order came from below to "bind 'er up . . . good an' proper."

Forthwith, she was bound again, hand and foot, and at somebody's order she was tussled below decks and dumped onto a bunk in what appeared to be a large cabin. She wrestled against her bonds. This time someone had tied her hands behind her and it was excruciating! Muffled croaks of outrage were all she could manage as she rolled onto her side to spare her beleaguered arms. Shortly a face appeared above hers and she fought to turn her head to match its orientation.

"There ye be. Safe harbor wench . . . for now." Bastian's square, genial face lit with the most wicked of grins as he took in the fires leaping in her unusual eyes. He swung away, but her muffled mewls and groans caused him to turn back and he flipped up his eye patch to stare at her. "Be there somethin' wrong, Miz Woolrich?"

Blythe croaked again through her gag and was rewarded by its removal. Her jaws ached, her mouth and throat rasped like sand on wood. "Wa-ter—" She lay helplessly on the bunk as he moved around the cabin and returned with a tankard of cool water. Raising her easily on one burly arm, he helped her down the precious liquid. As soon as the last drops salved her parched throat and dried vocal apparatus, she opened her mouth and screamed for all she was worth—right into Bastian's unsuspecting ear.

He dropped her on the bunk like a hot coal and clapped his hand over his ear in mute agony. But a split second later, he had recovered her cloth "stopper" and shoved it into her open mouth again. "Damnation, woman! Ye near deafened me! Ye'll wear that plug till we're well at sea, see if ye don't." And a long, harrowing moment later, Blythe heard a door slam.

Her heart beat in her ears for several minutes and she managed to wrestle onto her side and raise her head enough to see something more of where she was. It was a ship's cabin, all right . . . but nothing else seemed to make the least bit of sense. Through one wall jutted a huge, terrifying horned beast, as though it were charging into the cabin, and on another, above an ordinary-looking writing desk, hung a huge striped animal skin with a catlike head and murderous-looking fangs still attached. There was a huge ebony-wood table in the middle of the floor—held up by carvings of four voluptuous, naked women at the corners. In the middle of the table was a huge beaten-brass tray and a tall, exotic-looking vessel that might have been a pitcher . . . with sculptured human arms for handles.

There were numerous shelves built into the cabin walls on three sides. They were lined with all manner of oddities: ivory carvings, unusual vases, stuffed lizards, giant sea shells. What appeared to be a large, ostrich-feather fan on a pole was leaned in one corner, its bottom braced by an ornate carved chest. A large chair near the writing desk was made of huge, curved spikes, that reminded her of teeth, with leather strung between them. And Blythe was at a loss to explain just how she knew it was a chair . . . It was all so bizarre, so bewildering that she slammed her eyes shut and moaned. She was going mad . . .

But a moment later, her uncommon sense came to her rescue. When she reopened her eyes and it was all still there, she decided it was as real as the feel of rope on her wrists and that cursed wad of cloth she'd been choking on for . . . who knew how long. Lord. She'd been abducted . . . carried off . . . kidnapped! She tried frantically to reason out what had happened to her, beginning with her leaving the shop . . . was it the night just past, or was it even longer ago?

No, she reasoned desperately, it started before that. Bastian's face suddenly recurred in her mind. That pair . . . that disreputable twosome that had assaulted her in her own shop and then threatened her. She went utterly weak. They'd threatened her, said she'd be sorry . . . just like— Her mind reeled. Just like Neville Carson!

Chills ran up her spine as the thought settled into her beleaguered reasoning and refused to be dislodged. Neville Carson. Who else? He'd sent them to embroil her in some nefarious scheme and when they failed . . . he ordered them to abduct her! It certainly had the markings of his underhanded scheming. She sniffed automatically for some trace of his rank, oniony scent and was surprised to smell something altogether different. It seemed to be coming from the soft sheets and comforter on the bunk beneath her. It tickled and teased her nose, defying definition at first because it was so faint. But as she snuggled her face closer into the covers and concentrated, she began to recognize it. The faint, but unmistakable scent of . . . *coconut.*

Coconut. Lord! her long-ignored stomach growled irritably. She was near starvation . . . near to expiring totally from lack of food and water . . . and the heinous blackguards put her on a bed that smelled like coconut!

On deck, Bastian Cane ordered sail hoisted, anchor raised, and the ship made ready for a hard run. The motley consortium of humanity that served as crew aboard the *Windraider* snapped to with near military precision. All of them had seen the spectacle of the boarding and knew they now carried a ransomer . . . an especially toothsome female of a ransomer. They set to their arduous labors with her wriggling image in their minds and a glint in their worldly eyes. There would be time later to hear the full story of what happened ashore, but for now it was enough to have crafty old Bastian Cane again in charge, to see their handsome captain, Raider Prescott, snoring unceremoniously on a wet

65

coil of anchor rope, and to recall that delicious scream that had issued from the captain's cabin earlier. It wasn't hard to surmise that they were again embarking on a venture that nestled in the shade of the law. And there were many in the crew who were gratified indeed by that realization.

Bastian craftily negotiated the maze of French ships poised at the mouth of Delaware Bay just at sunset . . . when officers would likely be below decks, taking their dinners and brandy, and crewmen on watch would have the setting sun in their eyes. He raised a "striped jack" to identify them as colonial partisans and answered all hails with a suitably jaunty curse of British tyranny. They had seemed just one more of the fleet of private vessels enlisted by the colonial congress as privateers in the war against Britain.

The *Windraider* broke into open sea joyfully, unfurling her voluminous sails as if stretching, relieved to escape confinement in that landlocked stream. She was a sleek, copper-clad frigate, black in color, all the way to her bulwarks, which were white and trimmed liberally in gilt. Her austere and elegant colors matched the sleek way she caught and rode the wind. Some older sailors might have called her overrigged, but in the skillful hands of her captain and mate, her illegal, movable bowsprit and extra canvas gave her a marked edge in engagements with other ships. She danced the wind, nimble and facile, and easily claimed that coveted "raking position" across an enemy's stern for her crew. Massive running backstays helped her withstand the driving strain of her sails. Whatever hadn't been thought of in the laying of her keel had been reinforced and added after she was acquired by her present owners, Raider Prescott and Bastian Cane. She was as dangerous a bit of bark as ever was launched from Plymouth's shipyards and Britain's navy was much the poorer for her loss.

Her prow was overseen by a gilded carving of a particularly voluptuous female in dishabille. Her hair was flowing and the expression in her eyes was defiant and purposeful. She was the embodiment of the spirit of both men and vessel and her tough crewmen spoke of her as though she were part mistress, part sister, part prophetess. In her honor, the crew never brought "female companionship" on board. Bad luck, they believed, to rouse her jealousy.

Female "ransomers," however, were another matter altogether. They could rightly be classed as "spoils" and housed and transported for gain without disturbing any superstitious pirate protocols. Over the last few years they'd taken several significant prizes and ransomed numerous prisoners back to their homes. Blythe Woolrich was "spoils" and, to Bastian's way of thinking, the only real danger she posed was to Raider's hopes for a respectable outlet for their commandeered cargoes . . . and perhaps his own hearing.

Throughout the day, Bastian watched Raider's saturated sleep on the deck and tried not to worry about Raider's reaction when he awakened. After all, it was Raider's own fault he got soused proper and challenged Bastian to come up with something else . . .

The sun had blown its last fiery breaths into the aging day, spewing hot crimsons and molten golds across the skies, when Raider roused for a second time. The first time, Bastian had advised him to stay put and let Ali, their ship's physician, bring one of his famous herbal mysteries. But by the time Ali arrived, Raider was sleeping heavily again and Bastian waved the puzzled Ali off with a satisfied expression. Now, several hours later, Raider's head was banging and his stomach felt like someone had dropped live coals into it. He pulled himself up to a seat on that cold, miserable coil of rope and propped his throbbing head in his hands. His burning eyes were mere slits as they opened on the sight of his own deck, his own crew going about their normal "under sail" duties. Finding himself on his own ship seemed completely reasonable, though he had the odd feeling that it wasn't quite right, somehow. Suddenly all he could think about was getting below to his own soft, dry bunk in his mercifully quiet cabin.

One squinting glance at the wheel revealed Bastian in charge, and that seemed utterly normal, too, thought not altogether expected, for some undefinable reason. He heaved himself up and made his way, unnoticed, to the hatch. Twice, his feet deserted him on the steps and he banged harshly against the passage wall because he was holding his lean belly as if afraid something might fall out if he didn't. The rectangle of his cabin door loomed ahead of him in the gloom and the beckoning comfort of his bed gave him that last bit of strength necessary to achieve his target. He threw the door open and, in the dim light, he lurched across the cabin to his bed and flung himself into its waiting arms.

It was Blythe's waiting arms that absorbed the shock . . . and her chest, her shoulders, and her mind. She'd been drifting in a troubled half sleep and hadn't even heard the swing and muffled bang of the door and the footfalls. But in a flash, she was wide awake—her heart thumping furiously. She'd expected this for hours . . . had braced on the far side of the bunk on her side, watching the door through exhausted eyes and praying for deliverance . . . until the vigil became too much for her. Now the hour had finally come and no clarion of salvation had sounded. She had only herself to account. And desperately she vowed to make wretched Neville Carson rue his mortal birth!

But as Raider's body descended, it had pushed the pillows back against her head and it was a long moment before she could reclaim enough breath to begin even a modest resistance. And in that moment, she realized he hadn't moved. He just lay there, wedged against her with something thrown across her lower parts. Even with her eyes closed she knew it must be some hideous part of him . . . She could feel its pulse. She gulped air and opened her eyes, fighting to raise her head past the pillow that had been pushed up against her face and threatened to suffocate her. A broad male shoulder was pressed into her breasts as she lay on her side. He was face down, his head obscured by the pillow, and his narrow hips were turned slightly toward her. One long, lean leg was sprawled across her— *Lean?!* This wasn't Neville Carson!

A curious mixture of relief and outrage coursed through her. If it *wasn't* Neville Carson . . . then who was it?! She wriggled and moaned and croaked her displeasure in no uncertain terms. And as she wriggled and jerked, her anger grew to almost supplant her fears. Whoever he was, he was going to deeply regret trying to ravish Blythe Woolrich!

Raider felt his bed, his pillows—everything—moving, and it was a long moment before his fogged thinking made sense of it. Another body occupied his bunk . . . squirming and thumping around. He pushed up and squinted, finding himself face-to-face with what appeared to be a rag with a face around it. It made no sense at all, so he closed his grainy, reddened eyes and tried again. This time he recognized the feel of something wriggling rather familiarly against his pelvis and the inside of his right thigh. That brought his eyes open fully and this time he saw a female face with a rag stuffed in it . . . dark, tumbled hair and bared, creamy shoulder and most of one voluptuous breast. Good Lord . . . there was a female in his bed! He never brought females aboard the *Windraider* . . . nobody did. He squinted closer. Ye gods! It was . . .

Him! That other one . . . that "Gideon." Blythe stared up into a pair of bloodshot eyes and a set of striking, angular features that had taken her mere seconds to memorize at their first tumultuous meeting. He was the one assaulting her! She stared at his straight, finely arched nose, the hard, smooth planes of his cheeks, the strength of his brow, the ripe, firm-bordered fullness of his lower lip and was hardly aware that her wriggling resistance had all but died. He was so close . . . she could feel the heat from his face. Then the smell of stale ale and rum engulfed her as he panted softly, frowning at her in what she could have sworn was bewilderment. And to her surprise, he reached up and pulled that wretched cloth from her mouth. Her aching jaws closed and she moaned with relief. She swallowed hard several times, nearly hypnotized by his fascinating lips and, inexplicably, her mouth began to water.

Raider looked down into that heartlike face, with its fascinating little dent in the chin, its sweetly bowed lips that beckoned him to relieve their dryness with the moistness of his own. But it was her eyes that finally captured and focused his reeling attentions. The little wench had eyes the color of bright, fresh-minted dubloons. Gold, they were pure *gold* . . . the color every pirate's heart craved. And they were set in a feathery whirl of long, dark lashes that seemed to sweep his excitable skin every time she blinked. She'd blinked several times just now, as though she were having trouble believing her eyes, too. He raised one lead-weighted hand up his side to touch her face, brushing her breast, her shoulder in the process. The dark poollike circles in the centers of her eyes pulsed as if the movement shocked her and her lips parted.

The scream that split the air very nearly split Raider's head as well. Her aching body, her starved lungs, her parched throat, her burning pride; they were all screaming, too, and the unholy din belted Raider back like a fist. He thudded onto the floor with his hands clamped over his ears. The impact of the fall from the bunk sent waves of pain crashing through him and the scream vibrated in his head until his nerves seemed to combust spontaneously. He was on fire!

He moaned and rocked in agony until it occurred to him to put distance between him and the source of that demonic screeching. He lurched to his knees and half crawled, half staggered toward the door. He pushed himself up on the edge of the writing desk and turned, still clutching his ears, staring with horror at the screaming female in his bed. Her screeching was moderating into a hoarse, half-hysterical croak, and in counterpoint, his own deep voice raised.

"Bastian!"

His big hands came up to hold his head together and he roared again, setting the timbers around them vibrating. He staggered with the pain of his own volume, but called a harrowing third time, *"Dammit, Bastian Cane!"*

There was a banging and a thudding outside, and the door flew open as Bastian charged into the cabin. His eyes were wide as he took in Raider's heaving, red-eyed fury and the Woolrich wench's blanched face on the bunk.

"So, ye've found her, have ye?"

Raider straightened furiously, forgetting to watch his clearance and banging his head on a ceiling beam. He crumpled and grabbed his head again, snarling, "What in hell is *she* doing here?"

"Then I take it ye remember her . . . and we don't need no fancy introductions." Bastian's face was the very picture of deviousness and just as Raider opened his mouth for a virulent response, Bastian spoke the word that both explained and confused everything: "Ransom."

"Ransom?" Raider blinked, then glared again. "Good God."

"She be hostage, Raider." Bastian stuck his thumbs in his wide black belt and his jaw turned to stubborn granite. "Her cagey old skinflint of a pa'll have to part with a good bit of his riches to ransom back her juicy little hide."

Raider and Blythe's eyes both widened at this bold declaration, though from entirely different reactions. Raider was appalled that, on his own, Bastian had embroiled them in something as drastic as kidnapping and Blythe was stunned to hear her father described as a wiley old coot—and a rich one at that!

"Have you taken leave of your senses?!"

"You said—" But Bastian stopped. From the corner of his eye he could see the wench glaring at them and found it galling to be grilled in front of a mere captive. Pirates had more pride than that.

Raider saw his look and read its sentiments . . . sailing men didn't stoop to arguing in front of mere females. "Not here," he growled with a furious glance at Blythe. He grabbed Bastian's arm and pulled him toward the door. "Outside!"

The door closed behind them and Bastian was hurtling up the passage steps to the deck before Raider could pull him back. He had no desire to air their impending argument in front of the entire crew, and he sensed that that was precisely Bastian's game. Soon they were standing on the mizzen in the last bit of sunlight, face-to-face, scowling at each other. It was an instant invitation to the *Windraider*'s crew, who were steeped in the democratic tradition of real piracy and felt fully entitled to take part in whatever row was spawning between their leaders.

Every man-jack not currently involved in a function critical to sailing collected on the hatchcovers and nearby deck and in the rigging to witness what would undoubtedly be a major policy-making session. Clive with his blade, One Tooth, Ali in his turban, One-eyed Harrison, scar-faced Sharkey, Old Willie with his wooden leg, and at least forty more; they glued themselves to the taut, irritable forms of their handsome captain and his impetuous partner and watched with abject fascination.

"You *said* to come up with somethin' else," Bastian proclaimed heatedly. "We couldn't sell our cargo for bilge nor ballast—" the crew murmured and commented aplenty on that, "so I found a way to make respectable old Woolrich pay our freight . . . all clean and neat-like. We got us a fat pidgeon for ransoming."

"We got a ticket to the gallows, you mean!" Raider's voice vibrated even the belaying pins in their slots around the mizzen-mast. Lord, but the man could bellow—The crew exchanged proud nods. "Good God, Bastian . . . kidnapping, ransoming . . . that's out-and-out *piracy!* Hanging offenses!"

"Ye're getting to be an old woman, Raider Prescott . . . We risk hangin' every day we draw breath!"

"From the British." Raider stomped closer, his face a mask of cold bronze, ". . . not from the colonies!"

"But one be same as t'other—"

"Like hell it is!" Raider boomed. "We trade with the colonies . . . we sail under their rebel colors. They're linked now . . . one congress, one government. If we pirate against one, they'll consider us pirates against them all."

"Well, hell, Raider, we *are* pirates . . ." There was a round of murmuring, both pro and con, at Bastian's declaration, "That's what we're supposed to do!"

Raider's ire came alive on the air around them and a hush fell over the men. Even the sea seemed to hold her breath in the silence. When he spoke, Raider's voice was ominously quiet. "We're *not* pirates. We're privateers . . . a private warring vessel, raiding only on *British* ships."

Bastian took a step back, and several of the crew followed his example. When Raider Prescott went quiet, he could be a very dangerous man indeed. There was a long, crackling silence in which Bastian scrounged every scrap of determination he possessed, but his voice was still unsteady when he spoke.

"Not now, we ain't. We got the Woolrich wench and th' ransom note be already on its way to her pinchpenny pa. In three weeks time, we'll be *rich* pirates. And there ain't a damned thing to be done about it."

The irrefutable logic of Bastian's assertion pounded through Raider Prescott like a cannonade and ignited the crew like fired pitch. They'd kidnapped a wench, sent a proper ransom demand . . . just like proper pirates. What was done was done. They were already beyond the pale of the law once again . . . and the crew was none too dismayed by it, judging from the raucous bravado and bawdy humor erupting all around. Not even Raider Prescott's volcanic ire could quell it once it had started.

"Dammit, Bastian!" Raider seethed, feeling that unsettling raw anger roiling in the middle of him again. How dare Bastian presume on his leadership and their long comradeship like this?!

His powerful biceps flexed, his ironlike fists clenched; he was within a hairbreath of bashing Bastian senseless. It was times like this he wished he could just shove all reason aside, as Bastian so often did, and just let his guts and muscles take over. But his reason declared that he was partly to blame himself, this time . . . getting blind drunk and passing out like that.

"You've got what you wanted, you old sea dog. We're bloody well pirating again. But I warn you . . . this is your mess. I wash my hands of the whole thing. The Wool-witch is your responsibility. Get her out of my cabin and keep her out of my way!" He pivoted and started for the hatch.

"Count on it, Cap'n." Relief poured through Bastian and a crafty spark bloomed in his eyes. "I'll jus' be movin' the little piece straight inta me own cabin. And ye'll not have to see her again until she's been bought back proper." Lusty insinuation had crept into his voice and the crew responded with volunteering for duty on the wench as well.

Raider stopped dead, his hand on the polished frame of the hatch opening. He turned slowly and beheld Bastian's lecherous grin of anticipation. Bastian's carnal appetites were famous in their Caribbean ports of call. And in his younger, wilder days, it was told, he'd never let a little thing like a wench's unwillingness hinder him. It seemed he meant to revert to all his old habits at once.

Raider took a ragged breath and ordered harshly, "The wench will go back in the same state of virtue in which she came . . . whatever the hell that is."

"Ye can't mean ye'd deny me a bit of the spoils, when it was me brought her on board in the first place?!" Bastian was insulted mightily. "Dammit! It's inhuman! You don't want 'er . . . tossin' her out of your cabin. Or maybe you're thinkin' of bunkin' her in with the lads! One Tooth and Clive . . . they'd be pleasant bedmates for a well-born wench, them two," he spat, clearly outraged by Raider's gentlemanly edict. He knew, as did each crewman, that violation of a captain's order meant a severe flogging . . . or worse.

Raider tightened in the pause and looked at the eager faces of his hardened crew. One Tooth licked his lips lustily and Clive fingered his ever-present stiletto blade in open anticipation. No well-born woman deserved such a fate, no matter how damned "respectable" she was . . . probably not even the Wool-witch. Raider's dilemma showed in his face.

"Dammit, Raider, she'll be no worse for the wear," Bastian prodded, ". . . might learn a thing or two to take back to her 'respectable' beaus!"

Raider pounded a furious finger at them. "She'll stay in my cabin, dammit . . . and you're all to keep away from her . . . you hear?! And if aught goes amiss with this insane scheme, Bastian Cane, I'll know just who to take to account." And he stormed through the hatch and below.

Bastian rubbed his barrel chest and smiled his wicked best at their puzzled and somewhat disappointed crew; he hadn't lost his thespian touch. He knew Raider well enough to predict where he'd be vulnerable . . . his gentlemanly code of honor. And Bastian was still enough of a rogue at heart to use his friend's own standards against him. The first part of his plan was going off splendidly; it seemed they were back in the pirating business. And as for the second part, ensuring Raider's antipathy for the "respectables" of the world, that part should begin any minute now if the "Wool-witch" was half the woman Bastian thought she was.

Raider strode back into his dimly lit cabin and crossed it in three long strides. Blythe shrank back on the bunk and opened her mouth for another of those ear-splitting wails, only to have him lunge at her and clamp a big hand over it forbiddingly. His other arm clamped around her waist and he dragged her wriggling form to the edge of the bunk and held her there, against him.

"Hush silly woman, I'm not here to ravish you," he bit out caustically. Then his dry, aching eyes narrowed and his deep voice dropped to an irritable rasp. "But, any more of that ungodly screeching and I'll be forced to drastic measures. You're aboard my ship and we're at sea. There's not a soul to come to your aid, witch. Reconcile yourself to it and I'll set you free."

Blythe was panting, quivering, aching. His deep tones vibrated through her in a frightening way and they were followed by waves of heat emanating from his powerful body, so near hers. She searched his determined jade eyes and realized he expected some agreement. She swallowed and made herself nod. She'd agree to anything to be free of those merciless ropes on her wrists and ankles.

Chapter Five

Raider slowly removed his hand from Blythe's mouth and blessed silence reined. He moved slowly, watching her wide eyes, feeling the tension in her panicky breathing. He sent both hands round her waist to work the bonds at her back, reasoning that having his arms around hers would make it easier to stiffle any resistance she'd raise. Never mind that it brought his chest against her breasts in a delicious parody of an embrace.

The feel of the knot was familiar; it was Old Willie's famous "special hitch." And the feel of Blythe against him was disturbingly familiar, too. She was soft and curving . . . fitting against him in all the right places. It was a minute before he realized the knot was loose and her hands were coming up to push frantically on his chest, which was now pressing down against her soft breasts. The pressure finally halted him, making him realize he had pushed her back on the bunk with his body and that his arms had wrapped possessively around her waist. Her fingers were splayed over the mounds of his chest, and at that moment he couldn't have said whether she was resisting or caressing him. It was the second time he'd had her in such a position and her reaction was strikingly similar; melting confusion, quickly replaced by hot sparks of anger.

"Get off me, you oaf!" she rasped, now pushing earnestly and struggling against his hard, muscular body. Her reaction was equal parts of outrage and humiliation at the way she was treated . . . and at the way she responded. He was so big and so hard— "Don't you *dare* set a hand to me, you . . . low-life!"

Raider reddened and jerked upright. No woman ever spoke to him the way she did — much less in such an intimate posture! His tall, gentlemanly strength and striking face had secured him an amorous welcome wherever he'd cast a memorable jade-green eye. From Lisbon to Madagascar, the Gold Coast to the Barbary Coast, it was agreed that Raider Prescott was fluent in a sensual language that women understood and appreciated universally. He bent and reached for her dangling feet and she kicked at him — *kicked!*

"I said —" she screeched hoarsely, "don't you touch me!"

"I was going to free your bloody feet," Raider gritted out just as the door banged open and Bastian burst inside. He and some of the lads had obviously been listening at the door; on pirate ships, there was no such thing as privacy. They were vastly disappointed by the scene they'd invaded.

Raider slanted a nasty look at Bastian and his mates, then glared at Blythe and announced to them all: "Believe me, Wool-witch, nothing could be further from my mind than taking liberties with your . . . precious person."

They watched her struggle to raise her feet back onto the bunk beside her, then watched as her stiff fingers worked clumsily at the ropes. Raider finally growled and muscled her hands aside to work the stubborn knot himself. The rope came away from her trim ankles with a flourish and he was knocked back as she sprang off the bunk and staggered away.

"You'd better not touch me . . . any of you." Her legs were unsteady from both hunger and their long confinement. She stumbled against the wall and clung to one of those shelves, turning to confront a raft of male faces, leering at her. Long harrowing hours of fear and uncertainty crowded in on her, but she was determined not to let this mangy pack see how weakened she was. She always managed . . . always held her head up. "Where is he?" she rasped. "I want to see him . . . I *insist* on it!"

"See who, witch?" Raider demanded irritably, watching her pale face and her stubborn chin with its luscious little dent, and her trembling shoulders.

"Neville Carson, of course."

"Neville Carson?" Raider was surprised.

"Surely you remember your employer . . . Neville Carson. I assume he's on board. I insist you let me see him, now!"

"Carson? You think he hired us to kidnap you? Why on earth would he do that?"

Blythe's golden eyes blazed with the very last of her precious reserves of energy. "He thinks he can force me to marry him. But he's wrong and I intend to tell him so."

"Why on earth," Raider snorted disbelief, "would he want to do that . . . force you to marry him?"

"I should think that was obvious." Blythe lifted her chin and tried to combat the ominous ringing in her ears.

"Not hardly, Wool-witch," Raider sneered. "In fact, I find the prospect that any man might want to marry you entirely baffling."

"He . . . wants Woolrich mercantile . . . and Freight," Blythe was struggling against a narrowing tunnel of darkness that was constricting her sight. And there was that frightening ringing in her head that was becoming a roaring. "And he wants . . . revenge because . . . I hate . . . his . . ." She could hardly make herself speak; everything seemed so cottony and spongy around her suddenly. The sparks in her eyes were dying, burning out, just as she was.

". . . naught to do with Carson," Bastian had stepped forward to interject menacingly. "Ye've been taken fer ransom, wench. And ye'll not see Philadelphia again until yer old father hands over a hunk o' his gold."

"Wha-at? . . . I can-n't . . ." She heard a roaring rumbling as his mouth moved and she knew there should have been words. But all sound seemed to be coming from miles away and she clutched frantically at the shelves behind her back. She had that cursed sliding sensation in the middle of her again . . . only this time, it seemed to be carrying the rest of her body with it. "Y-you work for Nev— You mangy l-lot . . . you-u tel-ll 'im—" She lost both the struggle to keep back that closing circle of darkness and her grip on the shelf behind her in the same instant. Her eyes slammed closed and she slid ignominiously down the shelves to the floor. She honestly tried to rise and managed to think how humiliating it was to faint from a silly thing like hunger . . . then everything went dark.

"Lord!" Bastian started toward her and was restrained by Raider. "What happened?"

"She's fainted," Raider studied her limp form with mounting irritation. "It's just a 'respectable female' trick. They do it all the time." He felt several pairs of eyes on him in question and calmly

responded, "It's nothing to worry about. That's just what they want
. . . somebody fussing and worrying over them."

"Well, should we do . . . anythin'?" Bastian was willing to accept
Raider's interpretation since Raider had actually lived amongst
respectable females, but he still didn't like the wench's ashlike color.
He frowned quizzically at the lads in the doorway and they shrugged
and shook heads, disavowing such knowledge. Respectable females
were a breed they'd had no dealings with. They all turned back to
Raider.

"I guess I could put her on the bunk . . . till she comes to," Raider
huffed in disgust.

"You do that." Bastian was relieved to deposit the responsibility in
Raider's hands and tugged at this belt and sniffed as he strode out.
"Just be sure you don't touch nothin' you don't have to."

The door closed and Raider's lean jaw flexed visibly. He was stuck
with her . . . a conniving, treacherous, *respectable* female. He let his
eyes drift over her sensible green woolen dress, all rumpled and
twisted around her, revealing shapely feet clad in sensible woolen
stockings. He tried not to notice that her breasts were full and barely
constrained by her beleagured lacings. Her thick dark hair was
tumbled disgracefully around her pale shoulders and her pose, on
the floor, was something less than artful. Somehow, just now, she
didn't seem like a haughty, overbred heiress.

He strode over and knelt beside her to pick up her arm. It was limp
as a noodle. He frowned and inhaled to steady his nerves before
slipping his arms beneath her and lifting her up and against him.
She was limp all over and, for some reason, that utter lack of
resistance registered with him. It wasn't in the character of a
respectable faint, or in character for an irascible Wool-witch. He
carried her to the bunk and laid her down gently. No corset to loosen,
he smirked, but a second later that realization alarmed him. Tight
corsets were the leading cause of ladylike faints. What if there really
was something wrong with her?

He lit the two brass lanterns in the cabin and held one close to her
face to have a better look. The angle of the light emphasized the
hollows under her eyes and sharpened the lines of her features,
making them appear thinner, strained. He scowled and turned away.

He meant to ignore her firmly, now that his duty was done. But
something drew his gaze to her heart-shaped face, to those lips he

had tasted and felt respond to him briefly. They were miserably parched and cracked. He braced and turned away, doing battle with a tenacious remnant of the gentleman in him. With long breath, he went to the carved chest in the corner and took out a small, enameled ginger jar. He came to stand beside her and with a lean, bronzed finger, he spread an unguent on her dry lips. Then that same finger soothed his own dry lips and he felt a curious warmth from it, as though their lips met in his touch.

He forced himself to turn away, feeling vaguely unsettled by this unholy urge to touch her. She seemed to have cast some spell on his senses. Maybe she really was a witch . . . she certainly had the temperament for it.

His deepening scowl ached like the devil and his pounding head and parched throat made him recall his own physical duress. Washing thoroughly and changing into his own soft breeches, jackboots, and shirt improved his disposition some. But he still had a thirst the size of the Great Sahara and called for Old Willie to fetch some fresh water. When it came, he drank his fill and turned his thoughts to just where he was going to sleep for the night. He came to stand by his comfortable bunk and found himself staring at those pale lips again. His hand came up to finger his own and it occurred to him that her voice sounded as parched as her lips. Could she be thirsty, too?

She'd been tied up, gagged, for who knew how long. And he knew what that was like. There's been a time, once, in Algiers, when he'd been kept bound and gagged like that for days. When the Grand Dey finally set him free, he drank like a camel and swore he'd never be thirsty again . . .

Raider tried to rouse her, but she made no response when he took her in his arms and held the cup to her mouth. It took a bit of dribbling before she came to enough, but then she seemed to rouse and drank desperately. He poured more and propped her shoulders against his chest and held the cup for her again. Her eyelids fluttered and he noted a twitch of her lips as she sank back into oblivion. When she nestled on the bunk again, he felt her warmth clinging to his chest and arms.

He startled. The little witch. He'd have to sleep on the bloody deck for the next month!

The Philadelphia waterfront was especially lively that same night. Long-awaited French ships had docked and the harbor area was full of well-oiled soldiers and seamen. Both drink and female companionship were at a premium. But for two waterfront regulars, Runyon and Spars, price was no object this night. They'd turned a pretty penny the previous night, napping some female for a sea-faring bloke. And they'd gotten a healthy bonus when they'd agreed to deliver a paper of some sort to a waterfront warehouse office the next day.

It was well on toward midnight when Runyon and Spars came staggering down an alley behind a seedy rooming house. They were supported by two rather blowsy females, who managed to get them up a set of half-rotted wooden steps by promising all manner of decadent delights once they were inside.

But, alas, paradise of that sort is a rather elusive thing. Once they were inside the low, sour-smelling crib, one of the females produced another cheap bottle and insisted they have another sociable little drink first. One drink led to another and soon both blokes were insensible on the floor . . . with rifled, empty pockets. In the small metal brazier lay the charred remains of a note one of the enterprising trollops had found on Runyon's person. She couldn't read, but it didn't seem like any negotiable paper note she'd ever seen . . .

The sun was well up the next morning when a clattering and rustling in the cabin wakened Blythe. When she opened her eyes, a grizzled male face hung above her, just inches away. She cringed, then countered her instinctive reaction and glowered at it. It moved back and pursed its toothless mouth. Dark, ferretlike eyes examined her openly, and a gnarled hand came up to scratch the graying bristles on its chin.

"Jus' checkin' to see ye was alive," the fellow puffed toothlessly. He turned and thumped his way to the door and out on his wooden leg.

Blythe lay for a moment taking stock of her condition. She seemed weak, but surprisingly whole otherwise. That cursed cottony feeling in her mouth and head was gone, clearing sensation's pathways. A horrid thought struck her and she bolted up on the bunk, feeling frantically beneath her cover. Her clothes were intact and just as she wilted with relief, she was stung alert again.

A host of foody smells invaded her head . . . warm, bready smells, rich chocolaty aroma, pungent tealike vapors, and tangy bouquet of cheese. Her mouth watered so, she had to swallow twice as she searched the morning-lit cabin for the source of that olfactory banquet. Her eyes widened on a large silver trays set on that ebony-wood table that was so obligingly supported by those naked ladies.

She hurried from the bed to inspect the silver pots and covered dishes, finding under each a paradise for both eyes and palate. Fluffy scrambled eggs with ham, topped with melting slices of sharp, cheddared cheese; hot, fresh-baked scones made with raisins; pale, creamy butter and thick, sweet chocolate; and a mélange of fresh fruits, pared and diced and served with shavings of coconut. She nearly fainted. Food . . . and such food!

In the grip of pure, primal hunger, she snatched up the fine silver plate and dug into the repast as though she hadn't eaten in days . . . because she hadn't. She nestled in a carved chair with her feet curled under her and began to consume those heavenly eggs and sugar-cured ham. The cheese pulled into luscious golden strings that she sucked joyfully into her mouth, and she poured and quaffed cup after cup of the rich chocolate. She piled butter and orange marma-lade on the scones and shuddered as the concoction writhed on her tongue and slid down her throat. The fruit was sweetened with honey and she finally abandoned all pretense of manners and dove into the serving dish with her own spoon, groaning with pure joy at the delicate mingling of flavors . . . plums, pears, pineapple, and that blissful coconut.

When she couldn't eat another bite, she poured some of that lovely warm tea and consumed it twice, once by inhaling those delicious brown vapors and again by sipping and savoring it. There was marmalade on her fingers and she sat back, licking them daintily and sipping her second cup of tea when the door swung open and Raider Prescott strode in, raking the cabin with his cool, assessing stare.

Blythe would have sprung up immediately, but the leaden, stuffed feeling in the middle of her prevented it. She unwound her feet from beneath her and pushed up, eyeing him warily. For a few moments, in the delirious frenzy of eating, she'd forgotten her untenable situation. Now, in the calm light of day, and feeling quite fortified by her monumental breakfast, she felt she ought to set things straight.

But when he approached the table, she backed away toward the bunk.

This "Gideon" was tall and tawny, his hair was windblown, and one side of his shirt collar was flipped up against his corded neck. His casually buttoned shirt revealed a generous slice of sun-browned chest, furred with tawny gold. His soft woolen breeches clung to his muscular thighs and his lower legs were covered by tall, splendid jackboots. He was . . . intimidating, to say the least.

"You're awake," he observed casually, letting his eyes drift over her rumpled form as he rolled back his full sleeves. After a cold, uncomfortable night on deck, he was starving . . . and even bedraggled and beset, she looked good enough to eat. The hollows beneath her eyes seemed to have filled, her skin bore a peachy blush, and her curvy frame . . .

"No thanks to you . . . and your scurvy lot," she lifted her chin and clasped her hands in front of her. "I demand to see Neville Carson, immediately."

"We settled this last night. He's *not* on board." Raider paused and leaned back on one long, muscular leg and looked pointedly at her ill-constrained breasts, wondering if corsets could have gone out of style for respectable females. If they had, it would be a powerful enticement to bring Bastian over to his views about finding new markets among "respectables." He still had hopes that after this fiasco was over . . . "Your Mr. Carson has nothing to do with your being here."

"He sent you to my shop, didn't he?" she charged.

"Well . . ." Raider startled, "yes, he did, but—"

"And when I didn't cooperate with your little scheme, he ordered you to kidnap me," she asserted, taking advantage of his surprise.

"Not hardly, Wool-witch. That little jewel was Bastian's idea."

"I don't believe you."

"Right now, I don't care what you believe. You're captive and awaiting ransom . . . and you'd better pray your old father thinks enough of your troublesome hide to spend some of his misered hoard. Because if he doesn't . . . by the *Articles* we sail under, you're classed as *spoils* and my crew is entitled to a share of you." His voice lowered and vibrated her very fingertips. "Every man-jack of them."

Blythe drew her chin back abruptly, feeling a little shocked at what he seemed to mean. But her very sensible nature came to her rescue yet again. More threats. He was trying to scare her, intimidate her . . . just like his horrid employer, Neville Carson. Only this time she knew it for the empty threat it was. She knew Neville Carson wanted her for himself.

"I demand that you either let me see Neville Carson or you set me ashore, immediately."

"You're in no position to demand anything, Wool-witch."

Raider dismissed her with an annoyed sweep of his hand, sitting down in the chair Blythe had recently vacated. He frowned and shoved the dirty plate aside with a curl to one side of his aristocratic nose. He lifted the first dish cover, and scowled. A second came off and clanged on the tabletop as he grabbed for the third. Ire etched deep into his brow as he lifted a stony look of accusation at her.

"What in hell happened to my breakfast?!"

"Y-your breakfast?" She saw his fists clenching as he rose and she swallowed hard. The food was meant to feed him? She reddened from the tips of her breasts up. It did seem awfully fine fare for a prisoner and there did seem to be a large amount of it. "I . . ."

"*You* ate it?" he blinked, hardly able to believe the clear evidence of his own eyes. "All of it?"

"I . . . didn't realize. I hadn't ea—"

"Sweet Morgan's Blood!" he thundered, scarcely able to believe this toothsome little wench was capable of it. All the respectable females of his acquaintance picked at their food! But then, respectable females were also known to be greedy as well . . . "You ate my whole breakfast?! That damn well tears it!" He was around the table like greased lightning and grabbed her by the shoulders before she could escape, in her overstuffed condition. "Let's get something straight, Wool-witch—"

"I'm Wool*rich!*" She made a valiant attempt at escape, then surrendered to his corded muscles and braced for his worst. "Perhaps you have the wrong person, after all. I'm Blythe Woolrich!"

"You're whatever I want to call you," he snarled, "while you're on my ship. Get this straight . . . I don't want you here. You're a respectable female and that means you're nothing but a damned lot of trouble."

"Then take me home," she demanded, with eyes that widened at the mention of her home. "My family needs me; I have to get home to them. Set me ashore . . . today . . . anywhere. I'll find my own

84

way back . . . and I'll see you're not blamed. It was Carson—"

"It was *not* Carson!" he gave her a frustrated shake. "Are you daft as well as stubborn? It was my partner, Bastian Cane, that took you . . . and totally on his own initiative. You're aboard my ship the *Windraider* . . . and you'll stay here until you're ransomed."

"That's absurd, my father won't—"

"He damned well better, if he ever expects to see you again." The steely calm in Raider's voice worked its charm on Blythe and her eyes widened even further. He had pulled her against him, and where their bodies touched she felt warm vibrations when he spoke.

"Listen and listen well, wench. I'll not be inconvenienced further on your account. You'll keep to this cabin and when you do go out, you'll stay away from my crew." He saw her reaching for a hot reply and quelled it with: "Oh, they'd like *you* well enough, but I doubt you'd last very long when they started to demonstrate how much. They're a bloody heathen pack; rescued, snatched, lured, and dredged from the meanest, vilest captains in the Caribbean. They come from pirate ships, every one, and they're used to pirate ways."

"Pirates?" she snorted. "In a pig's eye. You're not pirates, pirates aren't . . ." she swallowed back the word "handsome." "They don't—" she almost said, "speak gentlemanly English." Then she seemed to conjure that faint but familiar scent again and stopped utterly . . . Coconut.

The confusion in her face was fleeting, but he noted it and realized it matched his own. When he held her like this, she didn't feel like a spoiled, temperamental "lady." A second later, the thought only served to underscore the treachery of her kind.

"And you're an expert on pirates and their ways, I suppose, you with your lily-white hands and drawing-room manners." He seized her hand and forced it up as evidence, staring at it pointedly. Blood rushed into the skin over his cheekbones. Her fingers weren't lily-white; they were work roughened and there were pale pads of hard use on her palms. And further down was a bracelet of bruised and chaffened skin . . . from the ropes his men had used on her. He tightened angrily all over and released her roughly.

"Stay *in* this cabin and stay *out* of my way!" he thundered, storming out.

Blythe stumbled back against the bunk, stunned by the contempt she'd seen in his face. She clasped one little red hand in the other and shame burst all over her creamy skin. The food in her stomach turned to one great doughy lump and her broad shoulders sagged.

He still wouldn't admit Neville Carson was behind it all . . . when she knew good and well he was. Perhaps they were taking her to Carson, somewhere . . . but then, why keep it such a secret? Or perhaps . . . perhaps Carson wanted her to think they were pirates . . . so he could "rescue" her . . . and claim her undying gratitude and her family business in one fell swoop. Likely, that was it . . . something really devious and underhanded. Her family would be grateful beyond words for her safe return and undoubtedly welcome—

Oh, heaven. Her family. What would they do when they found her gone? How would they get along? Who would give Nana her baths and mix her medicinal powders and fill her foot warmer at night? And who would decide what to sell next to buy food . . . not prideful Mrs. Dornly, surely. And who would watch her father to see he didn't wander off or hurt himself with some crazy scheme, like trying to harness lightning with those silly metal poles he'd installed atop the roof? Who would help with the wash and finish the cleaning when Lizzy was exhausted? Would Carrick know enough to proceed with the sale of the shop and warehouse on his own?

Then a truly devastating thought struck her. Who would fend off Neville Carson if he tried to take possession of Woolrich House? Perhaps Carson didn't want to marry her anymore . . . just wanted her out of the way so he could bully or wheedle her father. What vengeful pleasure he'd take in tossing them out into the street . . . penniless, hungry . . . and all because she retched at his revolting kiss! She couldn't help it if she hated kissing . . .

Blythe sank onto the floor beside the bunk, clinging to it desperately. She felt sick in a way that had nothing to do with the mass of food that was congealing in her ill-treated stomach. She was responsible for it all . . . the whole mess was her fault. She had to find some way to fix things . . .

For their part, the residents of Woolrich House did not mark Blythe's absence right away. And even when they did, there was more irritation than alarm in their reaction. Lizzy was late with her water, as usual, the morning after her abduction. Noting Blythe's bed was

86

made, she had no way of knowing it hadn't even been slept in and left the water on her doorstep. It was nearly two hours later that Lizzy answered Nana's irate calls and found the old woman in a regular snit. Nana alternately pouted and railed against Blythe's unnatural lack of filial devotion, going on and on about viper's teeth and ungrateful children. Nana didn't even ask where Blythe might be . . . and Lizzy was too busy thinking about how much extra scrubbing she'd be left to do in the main hall if Miz Blythe didn't get home in time to help.

Walter Woolrich missed her at breakfast and was both perplexed and relieved to find her gone. It wasn't like her to forget to bid him good night or to miss breakfast. But he had a new idea he was itching to work on; copper coils that drew sick humors from afflicted body parts . . . a most promising concept . . . and Blythe's absence would make it easier for him to acquire the materials he needed. He asked Mrs. Dornly not to reveal his whereabouts to his daughter and was told emphatically that he could count on her silence. The staunch housekeeper, it seemed, was miffed in the extreme that Blythe hadn't appeared last night to inspect the cleared attic and hear the awful tale of what she'd had to go through with Simmons the butcher and the others. Mrs. Dornly was not a woman to suffer interference with her martyrdom gladly.

And so another full day was to go by before any alarm was sounded. And even then, it was faithful Carrick who initiated it. He missed Blythe at the shop that first day, for they were to begin contacting prospective buyers for the warehouse. He waited an extra night for good measure; Lord knew, the young woman had enough to keep her busy at Woolrich House. When she failed to appear the second day, he roused himself and paid an afternoon call on his erstwhile employer, Walter Woolrich.

Walter scratched his frizzled head, bewildered, when Carrick inquired as to Blythe's whereabouts; how was he supposed to know where she would be? They asked Mrs. Dornly, who declared irritably that Blythe hadn't seen fit to appear for meals for almost three days.

Three days? It wasn't like Blythe to miss meals; she loved food. They called for Lizzy, who testified she hadn't had any help with the scrubbing or mending for three days . . . and was ready to give notice. With growing trepidation, Walter braved his mother's lair and learned, in the darkest of terms, that Blythe had certainly followed in his own footsteps . . . abandoning both conscience and duty with regard to one's elders.

"But where is Blythe, then?" Walter asked Carrick with a very befuddled look.

Back in the sparsely furnished drawing room once more, Carrick was about to broach the subject of the sale of the warehouse when a visitor arrived, asking for both Blythe and her father. Neville Carson shoved past Old William when he heard Walter's voice and he barreled straight into the room with a venomous gleam in his eye.

"Good day, Woolrich. I've come to speak with both you and your daughter on a matter of some importance," he proclaimed, turning his back pointedly on Carrick. "Please be so good as to send for her immediately." He pulled a paper from his coat pocket and clutched it meaningfully. It was the mortgage to Woolrich House.

"Well, Blythe . . . isn't here just now. She's gone off, it seems . . ." Boyish Walter was bewildered by Carson's brusque manner.

"Gone off? What do you mean . . . where is she?"

"Well, that's just it . . . she's just whiffed off . . ." Walter caught sight of Carrick's gaunt face contorting frantically behind Carson's back. It took an excruciatingly long instant before Walter realized Carrick was warning him to say nothing. "Off . . . off to her aunt's in Charleston . . . with hardly a bit of warning."

"Well, I am surprised to hear Miss Blythe behaved so rashly. I had always counted her the most sensible young woman of my acquaintance," Carson intoned skillfully. He fingered the folded parchment in his hand and his eyes narrowed as though he weighed something on a mental balance. "I confess I am distressed to find her gone. And how long do you expect her to be away?"

"Several weeks," "maybe months," and "who knows?" Carrick, Walter, and Mrs. Dornly answered at once. Carson cast a suspicious glance at them, but found them quickly united behind Walter's perfectly guileless explanation:

"There's the rub; she was vague about the length of her stay. You see, my sister, Felicity, has been after her to come for a long while. Can't think what put the burr under her saddle to go just now."

Carson had a fair idea what had spurred her desire to escape Philadelphia and it did not especially improve his coleric disposition. He intended to savor Blythe's horror when he foreclosed and tossed the lot of them into the street. He wanted to make her wheedle and beg . . . to flex his power and force her to sacrifice her pride and her body to him to save her precious family. And he could be a very patient man, where revenge was concerned. He abruptly stuffed that paper back into his coat pocket and asked to call on Walter in the near future . . . on some business matters. Walter graciously agreed and Carson withdrew.

Carrick wilted and presumed on his long association with the family to crumple onto the settee beside Walter. "That was close." He dabbed at his face with his handkerchief.

"You think it unwise to let others know Blythe is missing?" Walter asked, surprising everyone present with that bit of deduction.

"Especially Mr. Carson." Carrick wiped his spectacles, resettled them on his beak, and stared at his employer with a certain annoyance. "Miss Blythe would most certainly not want him to know. She detests him."

"Does she now?" Walter looked at Carrick and seemed to see the gray hair at his clerk's temples and his receding hairline for the very first time. Good Lord, how the little man had aged. "He seems like an amicable fellow to me."

"Excuse me, sir, but you're not exactly known as a judge of character. Miss Blythe is much better at deciding who to like and who to dislike. I think there are several things that we should discuss, sir. And right away." Stork-thin Carrick drew himself to his feet and gave his frayed waistcoat a determined tug.

"You think so?" Walter looked up at him with cherubic surprise. "Well, indeed. Perhaps over dinner, then." He looked up at Mrs. Dornly and she sniffed with indignation at the thought of the hired help sitting down with "family."

"Perhaps we should contact your sister Felicity in Charleston, first thing, to see if Blythe has gone there," Carrick suggested.

"He don't have a sister named Felicity . . . don't have a sister at all," Mrs. Dornly declared as she turned and sailed off toward martyrdom in the kitchen again.

Carrick stared at Walter, who shrugged, seeming a bit perplexed by that news. "Oh . . . well . . . I always *wanted* one."

Chapter Six

The enforced idleness of her first day of captivity was hard on Blythe. She was used to deciding and doing, to taking things in hand and making them work. She had never had more than a few empty minutes at one time and had no idea what to do with herself. She sat, paced, fumed, and tried very hard not to think what might happen to her when Neville Carson finally arrived on the scene. Inescapably, her mind drifted to her home and she worried how they'd manage without her and wondered if wretched Neville had tossed her family out in the streets yet. That very minute, her loved ones could be wandering penniless and hungry . . .

Every time she heard voices outside the door, she tensed, only to wilt with relief when the door remained closed and silence descended again. The only person she'd seen all day was that toothless old fellow with the wooden leg: Old Willie, he said he was called. He informed her that he saw to "cabin duties" for "The Raider" and his partner Bastian Cane. According to him, there had originally been two ships. Burly Bastian Cane's bark, the *Jamaica Lady,* had been sunk a few months ago in a row with several British ships and they were "on the lookout" for a ship to replace her. The ferretlike intrusions of his gaze made her very uncomfortable and very quiet and he left.

Desperate for activity, since activity always helped her think, Blythe began to examine the oddities that were hanging on the walls and lying on the shelves in the spacious, sunlit cabin. The great beast that seemed to be charging through the polished mahogany panels of the wall, was, in reality, stuffed. It had one massive horn in the middle of its monstrously-shaped snout and a craggy, bristled hide that gave it a ferociously wrinkled and ugly appearance. She went on to the great striped skin on the wall, deciding it must have been a tiger at one time. The size of its teeth and extended claws were enough to confirm the awful things she'd read about the beasts. "Raider" Prescott . . . the name nagged her. What kind of man bore such a name and surrounded himself with such fierce and hideous-looking things? Well, at the very least, he had a bald lot of nerve. He assaulted her, kidnapped her, and now had the temerity to demand her cooperation!

But then she turned to the shelves and found a breathtaking collection of sea shells in wondrous, iridescent colors, and in the most fantastic shapes imaginable. She turned them over and over, marveling at their complexity and fragility. Oriental ivory carvings of great delicacy caught her eye next, and then she moved on to a gilded music box made with enameled panels depicting faraway palaces and exotic gardens. Silk fans on one shelf reminded her of that ostrich feather fan standing in the corner and she fingered its silky plumes gently, wondering how a brute of a sea captain could have acquired such elegant accessories of leisure.

But it was the three shelves of books that baffled her most. Her father had seen to it that she was well educated, but she could only read English and some of her mother's native French. Here were books of philosophical discourses in Latin, histories, books on natural phenomena, catalogs of plates of botanical and oceanic life, and compendiums of literature in English, French, and Italian. Two small, gilt-edged books caught her eye, and though they appeared to be in Italian, she recognized from the form of the print that they were likely poetry of some sort. She recognized only one word in the flowing, feminine script that dedicated them: "Raider." But it was enough for her to surmise the nature of their contents. Apparently this "Raider" Prescott got books of love poems from Italian ladies. And from the way the little volumes opened voluntarily to certain passages, he'd used them . . . often.

The shape of his firm-bordered lips wriggled into her consciousness and she heard them speaking a soft, silibant cadence . . . in that deep resonant rumble of his. She slammed the book shut and stuffed it back on the shelf. Even the wretch's possessions had

91

disturbing effects on her! She climbed up onto the bunk and clamped her hands together between her knees. She had no time for such stuff, she had to think of something . . . soon.

Just at sunset, Blythe stood before the cabin door, running her fingers through the tangle of her hair. She needed to look relatively presentable and sensible. She was going to find that Bastian person and reason with him, convince him to set her ashore. Divide and conquer; it was the best she could come up with under the circumstances. She smoothed the waist of her bodice and ran her tongue over the front of her teeth. The cool feel of the polished floor boards beneath her feet was unsettling; she'd just have to pretend she was wearing proper shoes.

The passageway was empty when she opened the door and peeked out. She saw three doors, a set of polished steps leading up onto the deck, and a much steeper, ladderlike set of steps leading to whatever was below. Stepping out into the passage, she took a determined breath before mounting the steps topside.

Bastian Cane was at the wheel when Blythe stepped on deck and squared her shoulders. He saw her right away, watched the way the light breeze caught her tumbled hair, and heartily regretted the part of his plans that required her to be placed in Raider's exclusive care and housed in Raider's cabin. She was a beauty, the Wool-witch. But she was also Raider's object lesson in respectability. Bastian grinned wickedly at the turmoil such a treacherous blend of beauty and respectable hauteur would undoubtedly create in his captain and partner.

Blythe stood looking around her at the massive sails and the intricate maze of rigging, the smooth deck and sleek railings of the *Windraider*, and a bit of trepidation curled her cold hands at her sides. She'd never been on a ship before, never imagined the impact of seeing nothing but unending water in every direction. It brought home the chilling reality of her abduction at last. There were miles, maybe hundreds of miles between her and her home now. The feel of the crew's eyes on her pulled her from the awful spectacle of the sea, reminding her of her mission. Several scurvy-looking, half-naked seamen were staring at her as though she were sugar cake and she lifted her chin to ward off the vulnerable feeling it produced in her. She quickly located Bastian on the quarterdeck and made her way back to him.

"Excuse me, sir." She heard and felt movement of some sort at her back. "I wish a word with you."

Bastian turned aside to issue orders to a man at the wheel before turning fully to her. His leather eye patch was flipped up against his forehead and she was surprised to find two apparently healthy eyes turned intently on her. "Aye, miz? What can I be doin' for ye?"

"Actually, sir, it may be what I can do for you." Blythe measured her words in her most reasonable tone. "You're in something of a position, sir, having taken me from my home, from my family, by force." Bastian's boyish grin surprised her. "I don't think you realize just how this will seem to the authorities. It will be construed as an act of *piracy* and dealt with in a very severe manner."

Bastian made a show of scratching his chin. "Piracy?! Ye hear that, lads? They'll con-strue us pirates." Rowdy male laughter buffeted her from behind and she stiffened. She'd obviously collected a following; it made her suddenly dread the return trip to the cabin.

"See here, Mr. Cane. I insist that you set me ashore in or near the Commonwealth of Pennsylvania as quickly as possible. I have responsibilities on land . . . a business and a family to attend. I'll be willing to . . . sign documents indicating that I came of my own will—"

"You'd do that, would ye?"

"It could save you from a charge of *piracy*," Blythe insisted meaningfully. But something in Bastian's wide-eyed look mocked the generosity of her offer.

"That be right accommodatin' of ye, miz . . . except we be pirates, a'ready. And it don't matter much what them respectable landlubbers charge us with . . ." That grin turned up on one end, *"till they catch us!"* The rough laughter that elicited rasped against her bare skin and her pride, producing a becoming flush of color in her cheeks.

"You're—" she tightened furiously, "you claim to actually be pirates?"

"You have the great fortune, Miz Woolrich, to be in the clutches of the man known throughout the Caribbean as the Scourge of the Seven Seas . . . Raider Prescott. He be th' boldest, slyest captain from the Gold Coast to the Barbary Coast . . . a fearless renegade, even amongst pirates." Bastian inched closer with every word, savoring the looks of shock and horror on her face. "Don't let them rake's looks and that silky tongue gull ye. He be as true and ruthless a pirate as ever hoisted a jolly roger." There was a burst of raucous affirmation from the bodies closing in behind her, and as Bastian Cane crowded closer, she was forced back toward that unseen peril.

"That's ridiculous." She swallowed hard, only now giving credence to Raider Prescott's warning that she stay in the cabin and away from his crew. She tried valiantly to hold her ground.

"Ye be luckier'n some, I guess. Most of Raider's female captives don' live past the first sunrise," Bastian's expression changed to one of lustful malice, ". . . what wi' all the lads here claimin' rightful shares. Jus' be thankful you got a rich pa . . . and that old Raider's got such a yen fer gold. But even so, beware; he's got a hellish temper." There was a strong current of agreement at that pronouncement. "Ain't made no females walk the plank in a while," Bastian rubbed his chest and let his gaze wander over her, "so I'd say he's about due . . ?"

Blythe scarcely heard it when it came; a low, snarling oath from the back of that cutthroat throng. Her heart was beating in her ears and her hands were icy balls at her sides. She was aware of jostling and squelched oaths of protest nearby, and shortly Raider Prescott broke through that menacing pack that was blocking her retreat.

"What in bloody hell is going on?!" Raider demanded, his vibrating bellow setting the hair on their necks atingle. Blythe managed to tear her eyes from Bastian to look at him. He stood over an arm's length away, his fists planted on his hips and a glaze of ire on his face. Strangely, the sight of his clean, handsome features and powerful physical presence poured hot relief through Blythe. Her waffling wits jolted back to duty and she suddenly felt silly, being taken in by Bastian's overblown menace.

"She be tryin' to—" and "Your partner says you're—" Bastian and Blythe spoke at once.

"I told you to stay in the cabin." He ignored both responses and stalked closer to Blythe, his eyes narrowing. His voice became dangerously quiet. "You've disobeyed and I'll not tolerate it."

Blythe misread his quiet tone and failed to see the distancing of his rough crew. "And what will you do, Captain?" She stuck her dented chin up at him, letting the last rays of the sun set fire to her eyes. "Make me walk your 'pirate's plank'? I hear you've not met your quota of late. Or perhaps you'll toss me to your drooling, ravenous crew so they can each have their 'share' of me!"

"Silence, wench." Raider's voice was even quieter. "Get below where you belong."

"They say you're pirates." Blythe stuck her fists on her hips in imitation of his determined stance. It honestly never occurred to her to be afraid of him . . . since she didn't think he'd try to kiss her just now. That was the direst consequence she could imagine from him . . . Her defiance generated a murmur through the *Windraider's* crew. "But I say they're about as full of wind as their wretched sails. All strut and bluster. And they call you a bloodthirsty, rampaging pirate . . . the Scourge of the Seven Seas. How absurd!"

"You're the one behaving absurd, woman," he gritted out, casting a warning glance at this hardened crew. A pathway to the hatch opened magically; they'd read such dark looks before. "Get yourself below—"

"I'm not absurd! I'm the only sensible, rational person aboard this wretched bucket!" she proclaimed, turning to the wild assortment of faces that watched between herself and Raider. Old Willie stood at the front of the pack, beside another fellow with a noticeable lack of teeth, and she unwittingly chose the two worst men in all Raider's crew to use as her examples.

"Good Lord, just look at them," she gestured disparagingly at Old Willie and One Tooth, "not a tooth in their heads . . . and old enough to be grandfathers. And him—" she turned on Bastian and jerked that upturned flap of leather down over his eye with a flourish, "pretending he's a dangerous, one-eyed jack of a pirate."

"You go too far, wench—" Raider's frame was beginning to tremble as Bastian jerked the thong of his eye patch off his head and sputtered outrage. The cords in Raider's neck became visible and his shoulders thickened; signs his crew knew portended an explosion. They backed yet another step.

"And you with your Italian sonnets and ostrich feathers—" she raved, fully matching his billowing anger. "You'd have me believe your men are hardened and dangerous freebooters, savage and pitiless . . . when in reality they're nothing more than petty pick-locks and riffraff . . . scrounging and scraping at Neville Carson's beck and call . . . doing his pathetic dirty work—"

Raider exploded, lunging for her and ramming his shoulder into her middle. He jerked her off her feet and clamped his corded arms around her bottom and flailing legs, heading for the hatch. Her screams were more outrage than fear as she was tussled through that scurvy crowd and banged several times against the hatch opening and the wall on the way below. She beat at Raider's broad back and threatened every vile and dreadful fate she could summon to mind.

It was quite a spectacle; the usually controlled and commanding Raider Prescott, furious and muscling their delicious little spitfire of a captive. The lads were glued to the sight. They rushed to crowd the top of the hatchway to watch him carry her into his cabin and slam the door.

It was some moments later that they began to recall what had caused the fracus and reacted to it. The wench had stood there, on their own deck, captive and gravely outnumbered . . . and called their lady *Windraider* a "wretched bucket." Then she had the bile to turn on them and cast aspersions on their very piratehood. Called them windbags, toothless and pathetic . . . picklocks and scroung-ers! Lord, it was intolerable! Not a man amongst them would stand for it. Something would have to be done . . .

Below, in the captain's cabin, Raider Prescott was of a like mind. He was going to make her rue very hot, disparaging word she'd just uttered. The nerve of the witch—defaming him and his crew to their very faces! He grappled with Blythe's wriggling form across the cabin and dumped her none too gently on the bunk. She came up snarling, fighting through the tangled mass of her thick hair to face her abuser. In the grip of pure primal fury, she brought one foot up and kicked him—*kicked him!*—in the stomach. Fortunately he saw it coming in time to dodge partway. But the point was scored, and in a stinging red-tide of anger, he fell on top of her, pounding the breath from her.

"O-o-ouff! Get off me, you . . . foul, disgusting—" She pushed and shoved for all she was worth, trying to dislodge him, but he soon caught her wrists and pinned them to the sides of her head. Then her wriggling and struggles only brought their bodies together in rather strategic spots.

"I warned you Wool-witch," he panted, staring furiously into her blazing golden eyes. "I ordered you to stay in the cabin . . . to keep away from my men. I've seen what a female can do to a crew. I'll not have maiming and bloodshed on my ship over the likes of you!"

"That lot doesn't have the guts to maim anybody—"

"Wrong, witch! Every man-jack of them has done his share of slashing and bashing . . . some for his mates, some for his honor, and some just for the bloody fun of it! And they'll not shrink from punishing a female who steps afoul of their code . . . even if it is with her foolish talk. And I won't lift a finger to stop it, if it comes. I'll not be set against my own men over the likes of your precious hide!"

The heat of his big body was flooding into her from all sides, and the heat of her own resistance was subtly being redirected into other channels, new undiscovered channels. Above her, his sculptured features were bronzed and the centers of his jadelike eyes had become dark, dangerous pools that reflected the hot flame in her own. His lips were parted; he panted raggedly in the silence, and that soft rush of air in and out of him reached through the turmoil inside her to capture her senses. She felt his breath on her face, heard the sensual rasp of his breathing, and she began to smell it again . . . that faint, unmistakable scent of coconut.

She fought it with all her sensible, reasonable nature, but it was still there, and growing stronger. The warm, sweet scent of coconut invaded her on the air they shared and for the first time she realized . . . it came from him.

"And just how many men have you killed, Raider Prescott?" her barb took a moment to find the center of him and she felt his belated flinch. He'd been distracted by the sweet-cream texture of her skin and the ripe bow of her lips.

"More to the point," his deep voice made her vibrate beneath him, "ask how many women . . ."

She had no chance to ask anything. In the next moment, his lips crushed hers and all rational thought fled before the onslaught of

97

wave after wave of powerful new confusions.

Blythe was stunned, gasping and pushing at him, trying to break that terrifying contact, but he followed every movement of her head as though he'd willed it himself. The hard pressure of his mouth eased as she slowed and surrendered; he began to really kiss her instead of just possessing her mouth. The sensations were shockingly familiar . . . the hard-soft pressure of his lips, their velvety texture, their gentle flexing that massaged and caressed her. Her constricted senses widened to admit more . . . the strange deliciousness of his body pressing hers, that strange, recurring scent of coconut that made her want to taste more . . .

It was becoming very difficult to remember that she was being punished . . . and that she despised kissing. How could anyone dislike the marvel she was experiencing; his mouth on hers, the delicious tracings of his tongue around her lips . . . Wait— She was supposed to be asking . . . something . . . But when her lips parted, he took it as an invitation and his tongue slipped inside to claim the silky treasures of her mouth. That small invasion shocked her mental processes back to duty and she managed to slide her mouth away long enough to utter, "How many . . . women . . . Captain?"

"Hundreds . . . thousands." His response had to rumble up through her body to reach her ear. His words were slightly slurred, as though he'd imbibed strong brandy. "I've . . . los-st count." And indeed he was intoxicated by her delicious softness, her surprising firmness, the faintly honeylike taste of her mouth.

Blythe did hear it, "hundreds . . . thousands." But she was warming beneath him, yielding to the steamy flow in her veins. She breathed him into her, feeling as though the borders of her body were melting, absorbing him. It was such sweet, delicious madness. Her eyes were closed and she concentrated fully on the sensations he produced in her. Excitement trickled just beneath her skin like rivulets of molten glass that cooled, then splintered to embed in the core of her untried body.

The tips of her breasts tingled as his muscular chest ground against them, and the hard pressure of his body along her stomach, her pelvis, and legs called her to respond, to writhe closer . . . closer. Nothing in her dutiful, responsible life had prepared her for such a bold, uncompromising onslaught of pleasure.

His mouth moved and slanted to possess hers in marvelous, changing combinations and instinct tilted her head to better receive him. Her freed hands came up to touch his hard shoulders and stayed to trail along the ridge of his collarbone and up the corded strength of his neck. His hair was thick and crisp beneath her awed fingertips. She'd never voluntarily touched a man before . . .

Those feather-light brushes stoked Raider's need and he groaned, burying his face in the sweet hollow of her throat and feasting on her skin. He shifted to one side to pushed the rim of her bodice back to bare the point of one hard, erect nipple. A tremor went through his body as he leaned to rub the raspy planes of his face over that sensitive peak. Then his head turned and his mouth reached for her.

She squirmed and gasped and Raider raised onto one elbow and tore at the laces of her bodice to take both her breasts into his hands. He stared at her, opened and bared to his need. Her golden eyes bore a patina of desire, her hair was a warm sable flood over the covers. Her broad, smooth shoulders were perfect, living marble. He bent to take her nipple into his mouth again and something vibrated all the way into her loins with every flick of his tongue. It was pleasure and torture combined, for she had no idea of the source or the goal of these slow-building pressures inside her. She was being pushed, swept into unknown regions of feeling and pleasure . . . she who'd known so few pleasures in her sensible, respectable life. She was drunk with sensation.

But her reeling wits managed to snag on one last, careening thought: "thousands" . . . there had been thousands before her. A chill went through her neated nerves and his hands and mouth on her seemed different somehow . . . suddenly wrong.

"No . . ." she managed, pushing weakly at this shoulders, "Please don't . . ."

He allowed himself to be pushed back and stared fixedly at the cherry-sweet splendor of her lips and the tantalizing tightness of her dark coral nipples. She responded to him, he could feel it, and he intended to have her—now. Never mind how it had begun . . . he wanted her! But as his arms bulged and flexed to overcoming her resistance, his intention circled back to sting him sharply.

He wanted the Wool-witch? Was bent to take her, no matter— The insistent throb of his loins against hers suddenly jolted him.

Good God—what was he doing—losing control of himself like this?! He peeled his hot flesh from hers so abruptly it left them both dizzy. He stood by the bunk, his arms twitching and his face a hot, polished mask of self-contempt. He'd meant to tame her temper, to force her cooperation, and to prove she was vulnerable to him, in one fell swoop. And there she lay, pliant, bared to his pleasure, conquered by his sensual power. But his victory was tainted by his own confusing impulses. He'd made her submit, only by surrendering to his own unthinkable desire for her.

There was only one way to account for so humiliating a lapse in judgment and he seized it guiltily. "Learn this lesson well, Woolwitch."

Blythe pushed up, dazed, and clutched at the gaping front of her bodice to hide her bared breasts from him. She could scarcely breathe. A lesson? He'd been teaching her a lesson?

"That was just a sample of the perils of captivity aboard a pirate vessel. Learn respect, witch, or learn the hard way what pirates do that deserves it." Raider watched the confusion in her luminous eyes being replaced by anger and he felt an annoying twinge in the middle of his broad chest.

"You . . . you wouldn't dare harm me." She tried to summon a bit of disdain, but found it in short supply. The swollen, naked feeling in her lips and the burning in her nipples was too humiliating. "If Neville Carson finds you've ruined me, he'll . . ."

"Ruined you?" Raider stared at her, feeling a odd sinking in the middle of him. "God," he laughed harshly, "that's something I haven't heard in a blessed long time . . . the pleasures of the flesh connected with 'ruination.' That's 'respectable' talk. Only the hypocrite old sows of 'proper society' condemn pleasure as corrupting, wench . . . mostly because they've never tasted it themselves. And they inflict their juiceless existence on the rest of the world by branding young girls as 'ruined' if they lose their maidenhead to a man who hasn't paid a properly negotiated price. But I forget you're quite 'respectable' yourself . . ." He stared at Blythe's ill-concealed breasts, the awful realization dawning on him even as he asked it. "Lord—you don't mean to say you're . . . ?"

"I . . . am." She flushed crimson, trying to keep her chin up, wondering just how close she had just come to a change in that status. Perhaps that was Neville's idea in having her abducted;

100

having her ruined, then returned to his clutches so that she'd be grateful for any offer of marriage, however distasteful. She choked on the thought and stared up at him with wide, shocked eyes.

"Morgan's Blood!" he rasped, stepping back as though half afraid of contamination. Then his irritation bloomed again. His polished jade eyes raked her thoroughly. Every defiant tilt of her head, every provocative little twitch of her bun, every gasp and shiver of her untried body under his confirmed it. She was an innocent . . . in more ways than one. A *respectable virgin*. He took in the luminous allure of her big eyes and shuddered. With a raw pirate oath, he wheeled and strode out, banging the door savagely behind him.

Blythe wilted, angry and frustrated and confused, all at once. What an infuriating beast of a man he was . . . this "Lady-killer" Prescott. "Hundreds," it came back to her, maybe "thousands," of women had fallen before him. Beneath him, she corrected herself weakly. And she had very nearly made "thousands-and-one." She took a deep breath to ward off that now familiar sliding sensation in her middle and hurriedly began to draw her bodice laces.

Every time he came near he assaulted her in some fashion . . . just like wretched Neville Carson. No, a sardonic little voice inside taunted, not like Neville at all. Raider Prescott was hard and lean and his kisses made her melt inside. He was like warm bread and she became butter . . . In his arms, she forgot all about being a prisoner, forgot about her family's dire straits, even forgot she hated kissing . . .

Her shoulders rounded as the horror of it struck her. She forgot herself totally . . . a lifetime of sensible, respectable behavior, abandoned the minute his lips touched hers. Her fingers came up to trace her love-swollen lips and that peculiar emptiness in her stomach grew more pronounced. Lord, she was in more trouble than she realized . . .

On deck, Raider seethed and stalked about in a dangerous mood, barking orders like a veritable Blackbeard. His lads were impressed and exchanged proud looks and righteous nods as they hurried to execute his orders. He finally came to a stop at the bow railing, bracing into the wind, letting it pull the heat from his tortured body. He was furious with himself, letting a mere female undermine his control of things aboard his own ship. She was a greedy, temperamental, conniving little witch, a perfect example of the "respectable female" in all her harrowing glory. She alternately shrieked and fainted, she hogged his food, she scorned both him and his ship before his own men . . . then got him all juiced and primed and turned *virgin* on him! And now, because of his own ridiculous edict . . . he found himself in the untenable position of chief defender of the little witch's virtue . . . against his own men. He'd have to keep his crew a bay for three long weeks. Lord knew that would be enough of a trial. But he had his own volatile cravings to contend with as well . . .

"Well," Bastian interrupted his mental diatribe, "I trow ye taught her a thing or two." There was vicarious lust in his eye and a grin on his square face. Raider met it with an accusing glower.

"She's a virgin."

Bastian shuddered with disgust, then startled. "Still? Ye mean ye didn't . . ."

"I said she'd go back to her people in the same state of virtue . . . and I meant it." The guilty bronzing of Raider's face was hidden by the evening shadows. His honorable observance of his own order was hardly responsible for her continuing virtue, but it was clear from Bastian's disappointment that he believed it was. Raider read disgust in his partner's rigid back as he stalked away. He couldn't see Bastian's satisfied grin.

Chapter Seven

The *Windraider* cut a smooth southerly course, bound for temporary anchorage in the North Carolina cape. Its vast network of channels, inlets, and bays formed a renowned shelter for ships in need of refuge from authority of various kinds. It was Raider's decision to lay over there until the appointed time when they could collect the ransom and rid themselves of the Wool-witch. It would also give them time to send foraging parties ashore to replenish their stores and water supply. A particularly isolated little bay Raider knew could also provide shelter for a minor bit of cleaning necessary on the *Windraider*'s hull. It seemed a most logical course of action.

But Raider's plan was not without some risk. Packs of British ships cruised the area, owing to a new British offensive in the southern colonies. And they itched for a bit of revenge against known privateers, such as Raider Prescott and his lady *Windraider*. Even worse, there was the real possibility of confrontation with "Long Ben" Harvey's scurvy flotilla of pirate ships. They prowled the waters of the Caribbean and the Carolinas for ships of all sizes and descriptions, with no regard for political affiliation. British, patriot, neutral . . . it made them no difference whose goods they confiscated. It was indeed a narrow corridor the *Windraider* sailed, between an imperial navy and a pack of unscrupulous sea dogs. They'd have to be lucky indeed to come out of it unscathed . . . and luck had been in short supply lately.

For two days following their blazing confrontation on the deck and below, Raider confined Blythe in the captain's cabin. He tried subscribing to the conventional wisdom of "out of sight, out of mind." But his entire routine of life aboard his own ship was disrupted. He managed a bit of sleep in Bastian's cabin — when he could bear the snoring; he took meals on deck while standing watch; he hadn't shaved in three days nor changed his shirt. Every daily task and operation aboard the ship, it seemed to him, suddenly required his crew to pass the captain's cabin. And every time a man started down the hatch, Raider was pulled from wherever he was on deck to make sure he was just passing by. Everything, it seemed, focused his thoughts, his attentions on that door to his cabin . . . and on the curvy little virgin behind it.

Increasingly, Raider's crew found him gruff and prone to snarling. They just shrugged and shook their heads. They could handle a bit of tyranny; they'd suffered much worse on other ships. But it irked them plenty to think a mere female was the cause of turmoil aboard their ship. They remembered well her hot remarks on deck that evening and had come to one mind that the wench ought to be taught proper fear and respect for her captors. And it wasn't to be long before they began . . .

The key to the cabin's door lock hadn't been liberated from the British along with the ship and so Blythe suffered the uncertainty of never knowing when Raider or some member of the crew might barge through the door. It was a tribute to the loyalty of Raider's crew and their respect for his orders that Old Willie was the only other human she saw for those two days. Twice daily, Old Willie brought her food and water and by the morning of the third day, she was desperate enough for a human voice that she actually tried to talk with him.

"Wait—" She halted him at the door after he'd deposited her morning tray of oat porridge with brown sugar, griddle cakes with butter and jam, and tea. "I've been wondering . . . about the food." She clasped her hands together at her waist and braced her shoulders. "It's exceptionally fine . . . and fresh-made. I've always understood there was meager fare aboard ships . . ."

"Not *our* ship. Old Raider, he feeds us fine — same as th' officers. We all eats the same grub, even—" he looked as though it gave him no pleasure to relate—"pris'ners."

Blythe stiffened at his narrow-eyed stare. It was clear he recalled her disparaging remarks about his age and dental deficiency. She wasn't especially proud of her rude remarks, however justified they might have been by duress. "How do you manage? I mean, do you cook it yourself?"

"Me?" Old Willie snorted. "Naught me. It be Franco. We got us a full ship's galley . . . took out part of the ferward, b'low decks, fer him. Calls himself a 'cu-seen-eer,' or some such."

"A *cuisinier?*" She cocked her head. "You have a French cook?"

"He be Frenchie, all right," Old Willie declared defensively.

"Unbelievable." She spoke from amazement, but she could see Old Willie took it otherwise. His nut-brown face puckered like a walnut and his mood darkened further.

"Long Ben even tried stealin' him from us, oncest," he proclaimed pugnaciously, ". . . lost three good mates that night. S'where I lost me laig." He thumped his truncated thigh with a gnarled fist.

"You lost your leg in a fight over a cook?"

"Don't believe me, eh?" Willie was really offended this time. "Come on—I'll prove to ye!"

His hand closed over her wrist, and he was dragging her through the door into the passage before Blythe could protest. Then he was pushing her brusquely down that ladderlike set of steps leading farther down into the bowels of the ship. He dragged her through a long, mostly open deck, between two rows of massive, cast-iron cannon on huge wooden carriages. They weaved among stacks of iron balls and water barrels placed in strategic locations and Blythe could see, by the meager light of a square port opening at the muzzle of one cannon, that the planking of walls and floor were blackened. There was a faintly acrid and ashlike taint to the chilled air. It was a gun deck, she realized as Willie pulled her along.

Then another smell intruded on that warlike aura . . . the smell of food cooking. Willie pulled her down yet another short ladder and into a large chamber with slanted walls lined with beaten copper sheathing. Huge bags of potatoes, flour, and onions were stacked all around; barrels of apples and pickled cabbage and cucumbers were stacked to the ceiling; and great sides of salted pork and beef hung from overhead beams, and swayed and bobbled like a thicket of willows. There were huge kettlelike copper crocks set in fire brick and two square iron ovens, set above glowing brick hearths. Pots and worked iron utensils hung from hooks all around the walls.

A flurry of invective French burst from one corner and there was a blur of gray and white and an explosion of movement. Old Willie turned and grabbed Blythe's shoulders, shoving her down onto a mound of burlap bags on their right. A rush of air whistled above them and there was a twanging thud . . . then a second one. And Willie jerked her up and thrust her back behind one of those hanging carcasses just as a third wicked carving knife sang briefly, then found an often-slashed post beside them.

Her blood-curdling scream was perfectly involuntary, though she might have done it consciously had she been capable of thinking. She did manage to scramble up the ladder steps when Old Willie pushed her against them a moment later. Then she found herself on the gun deck again, leaning numbly against a smaller cast-bronze bit of naval artillery.

"Ye see . . . we got us a Frenchie cook, all right." Old Willie's tone was triumphant indeed.

"He might have killed us!" Blythe reacted from pure shock.

"Naw." Old Willie watched her indignation and noted her lack of weak-kneed tears and trembling. A grudging bit of respect was being born in him. "Th' thing to remember wi' Franco he, he alwus throws to the left. Jus' duck to th' right an' ye'll come out alive."

Blythe opened her mouth, but yelling and a thumping rush of bodies from two directions across the gun deck made it impossible to hear her hot response to Old Willie's advice.

"Damnation!" Raider was at the head of the pack, with a blade in his hand and a dusky snarl on his face. He slammed to a halt before her, his head bent to avoid the low ceiling and his big shoulders twitching with the expectation of violence. The sight of Blythe's curvy form pressed tight against one of the forward carriage guns sent a hot blast of steam through his racing blood. "What in hell is going on?" he thundered, as the rest of the lads crowded around, shouting and brandishing weapons. "What are *you* doing down here?!"

"I've just met your cook . . . and very nearly been murdered in the process!" She straightened, trying to match his angry presence.

"I confined you to my cabin—you disobeyed again!" His voice began to quiet as he glared accusingly at Old Willie.

"She wanted to see Franco wi' her own two eyes," Willie stuck up his grizzled chin at his captain, ". . . so I reckoned she oughta."

Raider turned a narrowing gaze on her, only slightly relieved by the unscathed skin of her breasts and shoulders. And he suddenly wanted to throttle her within an inch of her life himself. He thrust the hilt of his blade at the bloke on his right as he reached for her with his left hand.

"No, *stop* — "

But she was jerked off her feet and slung over Raider's shoulder for a second time, to a chorus of guttural and ribald advice on dealing with troublesome females. Raider had to stoop as he made his way the length of the gun deck bearing her wriggling form across his broad shoulders. It was tricky, negotiating the opening to the next level up. But he soon kicked back the portal to his cabin and off-loaded her inside so that she landed on her bottom on the floor.

She skittered back, crablike, as he slammed the door against the prying eyes and ears of his men. She could hardly see him at first through the tangle of her thick hair. She managed to swipe it back and clear her vision just as his tall boots came to rest on either side of her legs. Her attention was forced up the length of his manly legs to his fists on his hips and then up to his blistering glare.

"You might have been killed, Wool-witch." His fierce rumble set her skin atingle. The sight of her below him, caught between his booted legs, was disturbing indeed. "And dead, you'd probably be even more trouble to me than you are now!"

"My blood would be on your head, keeping a lunatic like that about—"

"On your own head, witch!" he countered. "I told you to stay in the cabin . . . to keep away from my crew."

"You can't keep me caged away like this for . . ." It suddenly occurred to her; she had no idea how long her captivity might endure. "How long before you turn me over to Neville Carson?"

"We'll turn you over to *your father,* as soon as we have his gold firmly in hand . . . and only then." But for some reason the only gold he could think about just now was that which flashed in her eyes as they stared up at him.

"And how long will that be?" she demanded, cringing as he reached for her. He pulled her to her feet and held her curvy warmth trapped against his still-coiled and expectant muscles. She pushed at his hard ribs and tussled in his grasp, but her traitorous eyes were drawn upward to his firm, velvety lips. For a moment she stilled and they just stood, bodies touching, breathing, feeling each other. His head began to bend toward that stream of warmth that was escaping her lips and she gave a panicky push that freed her and sent her banging back into the bunk.

"Three weeks' time." Raider stiffened irritably. "Assuming he wants you back, that is. Until then, you'll keep to this cabin, seeing, speaking to no one . . . not even Willie. He's not as old and befeebled as you seem to think; he's certainly still susceptible to a female's treacherous wiles."

"I'll not stand for it." She felt herself beginning to tremble. The rush of adrenaline that had sent her heart pounding and ignited fires in her eyes was gone and without it her knees weakened and her hands grew icy. "I won't be locked away for weeks in this wretched hole without even a breath of fresh air. It's inhuman!"

Her eyes grew darker, luminous before his absorbing stare, and he was suddenly enwrapped by her rapid breaths . . . and the way they made her lovely breasts rise and fall. Her sober woolen bodice was twisted slightly off center, exposing and emphasizing those sweet, forbidden parts of her that he'd enjoyed so briefly. Her skin was like pale satin . . . and he was losing all control of his hungry senses again, just standing in the same damned room with her!

"Wretched hole?" he started, reddening belatedly as his eyes raked his comfortable, well-appointed cabin. There were whole houses ashore that weren't as big as the spacious quarters he'd given up because of her. "You ought to be thankful, Wool-witch, that you're not required to sleep up down in the hold, waist-deep in bilge water! You occupy the captain's cabin without being required to —" He halted; he was about to lose his temper again.

"Now I should be cooperative and grateful for being abducted and held prisoner? Locked up with hideous beasts —" she pointed furiously at that horned creature that inhabited the wall, "— and bored witless without anything to do. Now I'm denied air and sun —"

Raider's jaw clamped like stone. What else should he expect from a snobbish, respectable female . . . who was probably used to nothing but the finest of everything . . . having her every whim met. Silly, ignorant little witch . . . she might have been knifed mere moments ago, and still she railed against the seclusion meant to ensure her safety. Well, he decided hotly, if she insisted on being given the run of the ship amongst his volatile crew, so be it. Let her have a taste of them . . . and see how soon her tune would change.

"Very well." He stepped back rigidly and his volume increased with each word. "You'll be allowed out on deck each afternoon, for an hour. You wait until I come for you . . . and you'll leave the deck the minute I say so . . . without mewling or sniveling. Is that clear? And whatever

happens is on your own head, do you hear?!" He was shouting at her
. . . the whole ship undoubtedly heard.

She nodded triumphantly, but wilted onto the bunk the minute the
door slammed behind him. She was icy and quaking all over. Lord.
That maniac Frenchman had thrown a knife at her! She could have
been . . . But her eminently sensible nature quickly refuted that
possibility; he wouldn't have dared slice up their employer's intended
wife/victim. Neville Carson undoubtedly wanted that privilege for
himself. It was just a cagey bit of blade work, probably intended to
intimidate her into cooperation.

Well, she was far too sensible to be taken in by such an obvious trick,
she decided hotly. And too proud. She'd not let them see her flinch or
cower at such obvious attempts to frighten her, the mangy lot! And if
she was to be his prisoner, kept in this miserable confinement for the
next three weeks, she intended to see that Raider Prescott was every
bit as uncomfortable. He'd rue the day he kidnapped Blythe
Woolrich . . .

Blythe would have been gratified to know her goal was already
realized. Raider Prescott heartily regretted ever laying eyes on her,
much less hands and sundry other parts of him. He was remarkably
restrained when he reached the quarterdeck. His only comment to
Bastian's open curiosity was: "That is the damned prickliest female
I've ever seen in my life. If her old father's got a wit in his head, he'll
pretend he's never heard of her."

The next afternoon, when Raider stepped inside the cabin, Blythe
wasn't immediately visible and he stiffened and jolted farther in. The
sight of her nestled on her knees in the corner poured hot relief
through him. But the heat was quickly appropriated by his very short
temper. The lid to his great sea chest was opened and precious and
costly mementos of his wayfaring life strewn around her on the floor.
There she sat, surrounded by piles of luscious satins, soft velvets,
brocades stiff with gold wire embroidery and whisper-light silks in a
veritable Eden of color. Those great golden eyes of hers raised to him
in surprise and her skin flushed to the color of sweet Turkish apricots.

"What in hell are you doing?" he blustered, raking both her and that

109

disturbing display with his eyes.

"I . . . I . ." She was the color of Spanish peaches now, embarrassed at being caught plundering his things when that really hadn't been her intent at all. "I had to have something for my hair . . . a brush or something and I just . . ." She looked around her at the wild profusion of color and texture and sent a caressing hand over the fabrics. "I didn't mean to . . . It was just so . . ."

"Just like a respectable female, grasping and presuming . . . clamming onto everything that isn't nailed down," he proclaimed, roundly irritated at her bold invasion of his most personal effects. It was as though she'd invaded his very memories themselves. "Put it back . . . every bit of it."

Blythe was stung by his harsh tone and reacted. "I have to have a brush!" She got to her feet quickly. "My hair is horrid mess of tangles already . . ." She jerked a handful of it up as evidence. "It's got to be brushed or I'll soon have to cut *knots* from it." She crossed her arms beneath her breasts and tilted her chin in defiance. *"Never mind* the brush; find me a pair of scissors. I'll cut it off and save us both the trouble. And I'll leave it to you to explain to Neville Carson why I was scalped!"

Raider blinked. She'd probably do it, too . . . just to spite him. And imagine the uproar in Philadelphia when they ransomed back a captive with her hair cut off. Not even Long Ben Harvey, in his darkest, vilest depredations, cut off a female prisoner's hair. He growled and stalked to that richly carved trunk in the corner, rummaged about, and pulled out a carved ivory brush and comb that was inlaid with amber and lapis. He thrust them at her with a command to, "Get it done!"

He saw her turn the elegant pieces over in her hands, examining them with widened eyes before sinking onto a chair beside the table and setting to work. He saw three strokes of the brush through that jumbled mass of silk before he had to turn away. Each seemed to rake his own excitable skin and that excitement was quickly being relayed through the rest of him. He determined to ignore her and to take advantage of the opportunity to change his shirt and wash a bit. But when he'd stripped off his shirt and poured water into the basin to wash, he caught sight of her, sitting taut on the edge of the chair, biting her lower lip and clutching the brush handle tightly. He found himself in front of her with his hands stuck on his hips.

"What now?" His growl was decidedly softer.

"It's just so tang—" She held her breath. His muscular, sun-bronzed chest filled her vision. He was hard and smooth and tanned, with occasional lighter streaks on his chest that registered in her mind as scars. Light blond furring trickled from his throat all the way down his stomach, tucking neatly into the wide black belt at this narrow waist. She swallowed. "I . . . need a mirror . . ."

He tightened visibly, and after a pause, swung away to rummage in the drawer of the washstand for his shaving glass. He thrust it into her hands with a caustic, "I'm surprised you hadn't already found it."

Blythe refused to give in to the turmoil inside her. There they were, shut up together and pretending to ignore each other while going about the intimate duties of toilette. But she couldn't keep her eyes from seeking him, nor her shameful desires from lodging in her throat. She was thinking like a pure hussy . . . wanting him to notice her, wanting him to . . . Her hard thoughts made the brush grab even harder in her snarled hair.

And as if her thoughts had called him, Raider came across the cabin and grabbed the brush from her fingers.

"Wait—" She thought he was taking it from her. "You can't—"

"Be so good as to *batten your lips!* If I left it to you, we'd be here all day." He dragged the brush through her hair several times, gentling markedly when she flinched. His knowledgeable fingers began to work magic on those stubborn tangles and the precious brush soon clattered onto the table. Blythe braced, for his fingers lingered on her hair. She was very aware of the not-yet-buttoned shirt he wore and of that warm, unsettling scent of coconut that emanated from him. She could scarcely breathe for the expectation rising in her. Was he going to kiss her again?

Raider stepped around her, his eyes glowing with fresh heat. "Anything else, *my lady?*" His sarcasm nettled Blythe in warm and very sensitive places.

"Yes." She stood shakily, determined not to let that peculiar melting inside her weaken her proper defiance. "I must have a change of clothing . . . I've been forced to live and sleep in this soiled dress for days." She managed to make it sound the vilest fate imaginable. "And . . . I need water . . . for a bath."

His jaw dropped and he began hurriedly stuffing his long shirttail into his belt. "A bath!" he growled furiously. "Like hell!"

111

He grabbed the top of her arm and propelled her toward and through the cabin door. He released her the instant they made topside, with the guttural reminder, "You're on your own."

Raider strode angrily back onto the quarterdeck, feeling Bastian's quizzical gaze on his black mood. "Ye were a bit of time fetchin' her topside." Bastian observed suggestively. But Raider's scathing look squelched Bastian's urge for a bit of nettling. It appeared the Woolwitch had already done a fine job of it anyway.

"She had to fix her hair." Raider was pure male indignation. "God — do you believe it? About to confront God-knows-what peril at the hands of the toughest, ugliest pirate crew in the Caribbean and all she can think of is fiddling with her hair." He thumped the arm of his bosun, at the wheel, to get him to step aside and surrender the wheel. And he saw the way Bastian was chewing back a grin.

"Not one damned word out of you, Bastian. I'll run you through, I swear it."

But a second later, as his eyes searched the deck for her, his irritation boiled over afresh. She was near the railing, staring out to sea, with her long hair lifting and spreading around her on the breeze. "That's a respectable female for you, Bastian." He pointed derisively in her direction. "Take a lesson. The greedy little witch . . . she eats like a field hand, sleeps in my damned bunk . . . *alone*. I just caught her going through the things in my cabin like a dose of salts. It's intolerable. And she had the nerve to demand a brush. I had to give her the one I got from the Rajah of Maripoor. And clothes, she's suddenly got to have clothes . . . been sleeping in her bloody dress, she says." His voice dropped to a menacing snarl as he leveled an accusing look on his partner and announced her final outrageous demand, ". . . and a bath. She wants a bath."

"Henry Morgan's Spleen!" Bastian swore with a judicious bit of outrage. "A bath. God, Raider, she couldn't demand no more of ye if'n ye was proper married!"

Raider shivered as though someone had stepped on his grave and turned on Bastian with full resonant force. "Don't ever . . . *ever* let me hear such foul language on your tongue again!" He handed the wheel back to Bosun Deane and headed for the comparative peace of the gun deck, hoping a whiff or two of gunpowder might steady his nerves.

Blythe wandered along the sleek, polished railing, all too aware she was collecting stares from the *Windraider*'s crew. She was determined to have a bit of fresh air and determined not to be intimidated by their crass, leering stares.

Fastening her concentration on the ship itself, she realized it was really quite impressive. The masts were huge and the rigging that had seemed a fragile net from afar was comprised of ropes nearly the diameter of her wrist. Everything was surprisingly neat and scrupulously clean: cables carefully coiled, every spar and lashing in place, the deck well scrubbed, each spare inch of canvas meticulously folded and lying in readiness. She stopped just up the steps to the fo'c'sle where two seamen sat mending a bit of sail and watched them. Their supple fingers worked long, wickedly sharp needles in and out of the thick canvas sheeting as though it were gossamer silk. The stitches they made were as regular as marked time and appeared sturdy indeed. A faint smile of bemusement curved her lips and she soon found herself looking into the narrowed eyes of one of the sailmakers.

"I was just . . ." she felt the need to justify her staring, "watching. Your work is quite remarkable." Both blokes just looked at her with a hint of resentment. One reached for a wicked-looking blade and ripped into a piece of patching canvas without taking his eyes from her breasts. The sounds of the tough fabric ripping and popping seemed utterly menacing, and she lurched into motion again, crossing her arms protectively over her chest.

When she approached the bow, trying to catch a glimpse of the ship's gilded figurehead, another figure intervened in her line of sight. This one was shirtless and broad-backed and covered with myriad scars that gleamed ghostly white against his swarthy skin. He turned to face her and, instinctively, his hand went to the knife in his belt. She swallowed hard as her eyes flew to the strings of great, triangular teeth he wore around his neck. Her heart picked up its pace.

"My . . . are those . . . fish teeth of some sort?" she managed politely, gesturing to his savage adornments.

"*Sí,*" Sharkey eyed her from a squint and introduced himself, "I be Spanish Sharkey." His English was thick with the accent of his namesake, but Blythe had no difficulty making out this next. "See dese, *senorita?*" He pointed to the maze of whitened scars creasing his broad torso and explained eloquently, "Shark." He raised two fingers on one hand and a knife in the other. "Two times." The knife came

113

down in savage, lightning thrusts on the air, again and again. "I keel
. . . two times. Hees teeth, my teeth now." He eased and replaced that
savage blade in his belt, pleased by her widened eyes. "Sharp teeth . . .
ver-ry sharp."

Blythe watched, frozen, as Sharkey reached for one of her hands,
then thought better of it and brought his own up to demonstrate the
razorlike edge of those huge triangular teeth that lay in deathly rings
about his body. She watched the crimson flow freely from the cut he'd
made on the back of his hand by merely drawing the edge of a tooth
across it. Her throat began to close.

"Sharp . . . ver-ry sharp, sí?" His dark eyes glittered as he thrust his
hand at her for her to admire. Blythe blinked, feeling a strange,
cottony feeling in her head, and prayed she wouldn't faint again.

"Sí, Senor Sharkey. Ver-ry sharp, indeed," she managed, pulling
her chin back and steeling herself as he leaned closer. His grin was full
of gleeful menace. It was also full of large white teeth . . . that had
been filed to shocking, sharklike points. Blythe hoped she wasn't
gasping and cringing.

"So good to have met you." She nodded politely and stepped around
him, to continue her tour of the deck, praying that her knees still
functioned and that her bladder wouldn't. She paused, feeling the
weight of eyes on her, and clutched the port railing to steady herself.
She was suddenly regretting the freedom that only minutes before
she'd been relishing.

Get hold of yourself, Blythe, she commanded. It's obvious the poor
man is half crazed from being attacked by sharks. Her eyes closed and
she drew deep breaths of the warm sea air, feeling steadier with each
one. After all, she told herself, she knew the lengths to which a mind
could be driven by a severe shock. Her father was a prime example.
Some folk probably thought him crazy, too, but he certainly wasn't a
danger to anyone, except possibly himself . . . and their livelihood.

Reassured by her very sensible reasonings, she resumed her stroll
along the deck and paused to watch the hands clamoring up into the
rigging to kick loose something that seemed to be stuck on one of the
main sails. She soon found herself surrounded by shirtless crewmen,
some standing, some kneeling; all watching her like a spider watches a
fly. A bristled, burn-scarred face thrust into hers. "Ye be in our way,
wench."

Blythe recoiled only to bump into another hard, naked shoulder and grizzled face. This one's glare drew her eyes down toward the deck and only now did she realize she was standing in a puddle of water. The cold and wet finally relayed through her stockings and her fear.

"What's holdin' ye up, ye lazy sons of—" A voice pierced that tense conclave like a blade. A fellow with a short, dark blue jacket over his customary shirt and knee-length pantaloons shoved his way through the tangle of shoulders to glare at her, too. "They be swabbin' the deck . . . and ye be in the way."

"It looks" she swallowed hard, "perfectly clean to me."

Bosun Deane regarded her through slitted eyes for what seemed an eternity. Then he raised the short, knotted whip he carried and cracked it on the air just above the heads of the crewmen. They fell on their brushes and scrubbed furiously. Blythe saw that several of their backs bore whitened lash marks and her horrified gaze was captured by the menacing instrument of discipline that the deck officer held. She had to concentrate all her faculties on lifting her chin and making her legs work, so she didn't see the grins and the righteous nods the lads on their knees exchanged with their whip-wielding bosun.

Raider Prescott suddenly bore down on her with a cool stiffness to his gait and expression. "It's time," he uttered, reaching for her.

She was frozen, ashen, and the feel of his warm hand on her arm was like a warm blast of reality. A dozen crewmen stood watching her with disturbing intensity. She flushed as she read the hungry looks in some of those faces and was relieved not to be able to read the dark, shrouded looks in others.

"Now." His command had a finality to it that Blythe felt no compulsion to defy. Raider pulled her into motion and they were halfway to the hatch when a bloody bellow of a cry rang out on deck, a cry that sent chills up Blythe's spine. There was a sudden rushing from all over toward the source of that unearthly sound and she heard Raider snarl a curse and felt his hand tighten on her arm. He jolted into motion, headed for the center of the ship and dragging her along.

In a quickly assembled ring of crew, stood a seaman with a wicked knife in his hand, his face purpled with rage. He was crouched, ready to spring, spitting what sounded like curses in a slurry of languages. The object of his fury faced him in a slightly modified crouch, owing to his wooden leg. It was Old Willie, knife drawn and crinkled eyes burning. Both men had more than a smattering of gray in what was left of their hair and she realized she'd seen Willie's opponent before.

The other night, on deck . . . he was that other toothless fellow . . .

He seemed to be accusing Old Willie of something and from the shouts of encouragement all around them, she gathered that the accuser's name was One Tooth. She stared up at Raider, whose eyes had turned to cold, polished stones. He halted at the front of the circle, keeping a savage grip on her upper arm.

"You bloody flux . . . you stinking dung heap—" One Tooth's flaccid lips flexed as he snarled, and Blythe made the odd discovery that he wasn't completely toothless after all; he had at least one tooth, visible in the front of his head. "You thievin' spawn of a pox-eaten whore—I'll kill ye, I will!"

"What the hell's doin' here?" Bastian bolted partway between them, keeping an eye peeled for any sudden lunges. "Take yerselfs off and be done—that's an order!"

"He stole me teef!" One Tooth charged, digging at the air with his blade as if to show Old Willie what he had coming.

"He what?!" Bastian took a step back.

"Me wood choppers, what I liberated from 'at fat English feller . . . he sharked 'em clean outta me kit . . . an' he don't e'en deny it!"

"Well, he don't need 'em!" Willie charged defensively. "He wouldn' sell ner trade 'em proper! He gots teef of his own!"

"I be savin' 'em . . . fer when me other teef go . . ." One Tooth snarled.

They were fighting over a set of wooden teeth?! Blythe was incredulous. These two balding, toothless old coots were ready to knife each other over something like false teeth? She looked around and saw an odd mixture of blood-lust and amusement in the crew's faces, especially when they turned on her . . . as if absorbing and savoring her reaction.

Blythe felt Raider's grip on her slacken, and he rustled slightly against her skirts, coiling. She looked up just in time to catch a small jerk of his head and suddenly he was launching across the deck at One Tooth at the same time Bastian and two others exploded into the fray. In short order, they had both combatants restrained and Raider was glaring at them, his shoulders heaving as he expressed raw displeasure in graphic terms the old salts were sure to understand. Then, with obvious restraint, he promised them a night in chains while he decided between the lash and more sinister fates.

Blythe had seen enough. "The lash?" She jolted forward, and

116

Raider spun to face her, taken aback by her audacity. "You can't be serious. Why, the whole thing's absurd . . . fighting over wooden teeth! Good Lord . . . *teeth!*" She caught sight of Spanish Sharkey's malicious leer nearby and waved an irate hand in his direction. "He's got plenty of them . . . why don't they just borrow some from him!"

Before Raider could lay a furious hand on her, she wheeled and shoved her way through that ring of crewmen and disappeared through the hatch.

The lads stared at each other and at their white-lipped captain and turned away to their regular duties with shrugs and shakes of head. This female captive of theirs was a tough one indeed. It would take more than a nasty little knife fight to send her shrieking and scuttling. Still, it was a shame they didn't get to witness what promised to be a fine bit of mayhem; Old Willie and One Tooth would have made a helluva fight. A fellow didn't get to be an *old* pirate without being fairly dangerous.

Raider didn't trust himself to follow her right away. He saw the antagonists safely manacled and stowed below decks and laid a stern round of orders that spent some of his ire. But by the time he burst into his cabin, he was still at a slow-rolling boil.

"Of all the stupid, idiotic—" If you value your neck, don't you *ever* intrude in a situation involving my men again!"

"The whole 'situation' was absurd. You can't really expect me to believe *pirates* fight over wooden teeth." She managed to face him.

"It was serious enough, witch. They'd have drawn blood, maybe killed each other if I hadn't stopped it. And you're responsible!"

"Me?" She stood up to his towering anger, feeling his heat crowding her as he stalked closer. "You dare blame me?"

"Willie never worried about his bloody teeth until you came along, calling him toothless and pathetic." His voice went quiet and was all the more intense for it. "He's got a pirate's pride, whatever his age, and he's earned the respect of every man-jack in my crew. I'd rather have him at my back in a fight than any man I know, except Bastian." His hands came up, itching to throttle her. But he didn't trust his volatile impulses where she was concerned. He wheeled and stalked out, slamming the door with typhoon force.

Blythe stood looking at the door, hearing the savage quiet of his words, feeling for the first time the deep anger that rode beneath them. In all the world of words, he'd found that one that never failed to go to the heart of her: *responsible*. The horrible charge settled in the middle of her like a stone. She'd caused it, he said. She'd scorned Old Willie, and his injured male pride demanded he do something to recoup. So he stole a set of teeth. But surely he knew that in the close confines of a ship he'd be found out . . . The realization trickled through her. He knew, all right. He provoked a fight to prove himself!

Blythe slumped into a chair and clasped her hands between her knees. Her first outing among the men of the *Windraider* had been a total disaster. What a ghastly bunch they were—leering, snarling, knife-crazy. Every single one of them had an audacious blade in his belt and brandished it at the slightest provocation. They used whips to make the men swab the deck, gloried in the sight of blood, and looked ready to cut a throat, hers especially, at the first opportunity. She'd never seen such an ugly, scurvy-looking collection of humans in her life! But no amount of contempt, no shock or fear, not even a recitation of the wrongs committed against her could alter the fact that Old Willie and One Tooth were in trouble . . . and she was *responsible*.

Above, Raider was once more stalking his quarterdeck, his hands clasped behind his back. "It's just like I feared," he fumed. "The little witch has trouble brewin' amongst the men already."

"Old Willie . . ." Bastian chuckled. "Lord, Raider, ye shoulda let 'em have at it. Woulda been right entertainin'." Raider's frown deterred him little. "Well, it's been a week since we had a proper floggin'. If we go too long, the lads get testy."

"I tell you, Bastian, the woman's bad luck. *Woolrich*. Wool has always been cursed luck for me."

"But not fer me." Bastian pulled the knife from his belt to scrape a ragged fingernail. An ambiguous grin lurked around his mouth. "It was on account of 'wool' I got you fer a partner. And I reckon wool will make me rich this time around."

Chapter Eight

A young lad of about seventeen replaced Old Willie at cabin duties the next morning. He was lanky and awkward and his large brown eyes dropped shyly whenever Blythe looked his way. As she ate, she learned his name was Richard and that he'd been brought on board the *Windraider* at a very young age. Bastian, it seemed, had known his mother in Charleston, and when she died of fever, he and Raider took the boy with them. Blythe was surprised to find him pleased and proud to be sailing with Raider Prescott and Bastian Cane.

"An' not jus' me, miz. The other lads, too. Why, whenever we make landfall by other ships, we has to anchor out a ways and post watches to keep blokes from jumpin' ship to join ours."

"Really. I find that rather hard to believe," Blythe declared testily, "what with floggings and knife-play the order of the day here."

"Oh, no, it's true, miz." Richard shifted his lanky frame and his face broke into a boyish smile. "It be on account of The Raider, true enough . . . but mostly, it be the food."

"Food?" Blythe frowned.

"We all eats the same food, officers an' men, aboard the *Windraider*. We got us a Frenchie fer a cook. Well, ye been eatin' his cooking . . . it be a damn site better'n knocking yer bread agin the deck to shake out some of the worms before ye eat. That be a tar's fare on most ships, be they navy, merchant, or pirate." He lowered his voice and leaned closer. "We et like that when we wus in prison

119

in Algiers. Ye can feel the buggers squirmin' agin yer throat whilst yer trying to swaller 'em . . ."

Blythe shuddered and looked at the boiled sausages on her plate, and felt her stomach heave. He laughed a Bastian Cane kind of laugh and set about straightening the bunk in a rather clumsy fashion. Blythe watched him, then rose and waved him aside, claiming she needed something to keep her busy and it might as well be work of some sort. He looked at her with mild surprise, nodded, and began to clear her tray away.

"What . . . what will he do to Old Willie and One Tooth?" The creases she smoothed from the soft coverlet migrated into her brow.

"Floggin'. Already been sentenced and carried out. Got fifteen, Willie did. Took it like a man. One Tooth, he got seven."

"Good Lord." Blythe paled and covered her mouth with her hand.

"Coulda been worse." The lad turned to her with earnest eyes. "Stealing from a shipmate be a capi-tal offense on a pirate ship. Most captains slit a bloke's nostrils, if they let 'im live . . . or cut a piece out of his ear. That way, everybody's warned the bloke can't be trusted. But, The Raider, he just flogs mostly, like a navy man."

Blythe shivered. Raider Prescott just "flogged" . . . "like a navy man." This tough, brutal world of men was foreign to everything Blythe had known in her life. She looked into Richard's guileless brown eyes and realized he accepted it as a routine part of daily existence; maiming, knife-fights, flogging. He actually seemed to *admire* Raider Prescott . . .

But the lad's veracity was upheld by his comments about the wonderful food. Old Willie had said something similar . . . She stopped with a pillow in her hand and a picture of Willie, beaten and bloody, reared in her mind's eye. She paled, feeling the weight of responsibility for his plight settling on her broad shoulders afresh. She was responsible. And somehow she had to make things right.

"Richard?" She turned to the lad, who was heading for the door with the food tray. He paused and she asked, "Where is he? Old Willie. Is he hurt badly?"

Richard frowned. "He be down on the berthin' deck, below guns. He prob'ly ain't feeling so good."

"Could you . . . take me to see him?"

Richard drew back and Blythe had to both charm and bully him to get him to agree to show her the way. And in the end, he only agreed because he was "goin' that way meself" and he "couldn't help it if'n ye were to follow me."

He led her out of the cabin, down those ladderlike steps onto the gun deck, then down a second ladder to what he called the berthin' deck. Every available nook and cranny was stuffed with barrels, bales, and crates. Here and there, a hammock was strung up between beams, and there were other signs of habitation, an occasional sea chest or kit bag. Floor space was limited to narrow walkways and the piles of blankets atop bales and stacks of burlap bags testified to where the men slept, when off duty.

Richard paused at each juncture of paths to make sure the coast was clear and then hurried on to the bow end, where Old Willie lay, face down, on a cot. His only comforts were a coarse blanket and a generous layer of herbed grease on his flayed back. He startled when he heard them and whirled, his knife in his hand. His defensive snarl muted to a puzzled scowl.

"What're *you* doin' here?" he demanded roughly, looking past and around Blythe as if expecting someone else. He glared at Richard and the lad hurried off toward the galley.

"I . . . just came to see . . . how you are." Her face was pale even in the dim light of the open port nearby.

"Why?" Old Willie scowled deeper, a bit flattered and a bit suspicious at the same time. He'd never had a respectable female take an interest in him before.

"I . . . you're one of the few people I know on board . . . and I wanted to see if you were all right." She glanced at the ugly red weals on his back and her voice dropped to an awed whisper. "Does it hurt very much?"

Old Willie saw the sympathy in her luminous eyes and decided it hurt like the very devil. "It ain't hardly bearable." His fist clenched around the blanket. "But I had worse," he looked up into her worried, heartlike face with its quivering chin, "when they cut me laig off. They jus' took a saw to me wi' six blokes holdin' me. Bit th' leather so hard, it busted all me teef out."

Blythe swallowed and nodded, kneeling on the deck beside the cot. "Is there . . . anything I can get for you?"

"Get fer me?" Willie's feral brown eyes widened, then narrowed on her, then closed as if in pain. He wasn't a man to pass up such an opportunity. "Well—we be striking land. An' if I was to have me some of Franco's special clam chowder . . . Clams has got a healin' power . . ." He peeked at her from the corner of one closed eye and saw consternation in her face. He groaned pitifully, and pursed his sunken lips.

"I'll see what I can do . . ." Her voice quivered, and for some reason she thought of Nana and her unrelenting pain. He groaned again and she blurted out, "I'll get you some, I promise." She touched his gnarled hand briefly, then stood to go.

Willie watched the tenderness of her cool fingers on his battered hand with such amazement that he almost forgot to wince again for good measure. No female had ever touched him like that. But as her skirts disappeared around a stack of bales, his awe evaporated and a wicked grin spread on his wiley maw. He licked his lips. If she survived old Franco, he'd have clam chowder.

Blythe stood on the gun deck, staring down at those ladderlike steps that led down into the gaping jaws of Franco's inferno. She swallowed hard, screwing up every bit of courage she possessed. Old Willie needed clam chowder, her thinking ran; it was her duty to get him some . . . she'd promised. Only after she left him, did she realize what the keeping of that pledge required. She felt a little sick, thinking of her last encounter in the galley. But she had to try.

She climbed down the steps, watching scenes from her brief life passing before her eyes, and threaded her way through the hanging sides of meat, hoping they weren't an omen. Her heart was beating in her throat when she emerged into the scene that had been etched into her memory by adrenaline. There were the pots and iron ovens, the bags and barrels of foodstuffs . . . and in the middle of them, with his back to her was a squat, dark-haired man wearing an apron over a pair of gray seaman's breeches. His head was covered by a floppy, baglike hat, and as he moved, Blythe made out powerful muscles beneath his fleshy shoulders. He hefted and transferred a huge iron kettle of stew toward an odd-looking dolly, and when he was through, Blythe cleared her throat to speak.

The savage speed of his turn galvanized Blythe's flight response and sent her diving onto the bags of potatoes at her right. A half instant later, the air hummed above her. She lay there in shock, unable to move, wondering crazily if she'd remembered the right direction to fall. Was it *left* he always threw? She was scarcely breathing when he came to stand over her, his dark eyes flashing and his French thundering off the walls.

"Non!" she breathed, *"je vous prie . . . arrête!"* When he didn't lunge for her, she managed to raise her head and look at him. He stood with a scowl of surprise on his face and a wicked cleaver in his hand. "If you don't mind . . . I think I'd rather die standing up." She'd spoken that in French, too. It wasn't very good French, to her own ears, but it had a marked effect on the volatile French *cuisinier.* He backed a step, and she managed to push up with trembling arms and made it onto her weakened legs.

He scowled at her and spat a swirl of rather nasty insults that she could scarcely translate with her ladylike knowledge of the language. But she managed to gather that he was insulted to have his realm invaded. And after a pause, he wanted to know how she dared set foot in his domain.

The frantic heat in her blood primed her for either flight or fight . . . and with a hot rush of righteous anger, she chose the latter. How dare he, she demanded, toss knives at a lady who had come to praise his artistry and beg his aid?! He behaved like a common brute — no better than the savage swine he fed . . .

The look on his face stopped her tirade. He seemed shocked, in turmoil. In the silence that followed, Blythe realized what she'd done and felt a little dizzy. She'd be lucky to get out of there alive. She backed a step, clasping her icy hands and praying she made it to the steps before the cleaver did.

"Mam'selle!" He halted her in her tracks and she turned with her heart in her throat. *"Mon Dieu!"* His fleshy face was full of emotion as he clutched his wicked blade. "Where did you learn to speak my lovely French?"

Blythe blinked. She *had* spoken in French. "My . . . tutor," she explained, feeling like her mouth was lined with wool. "And my mother . . . she was French . . ."

"But no one speaks to me in my tongue — except the Raider! Say something more . . ." he asked, a wistful light appearing in his fierce countenance. And in that moment, an understanding was born between Blythe and the *Windraider*'s vituperous cook. She diplomatically revealed her delight in the wonderful food he'd sent her and praised his culinary skill . . . in her best schoolroom French. He revealed a fierce pride in his cooking and a surprisingly boyish loneliness for his homeland—especially the sound of his native tongue. And it was only a matter of a few moments before *Françoise*—he *hated* the name "Franco"—was warming to the possibility of clam chowder.

The *Windraider* dropped anchor that afternoon in a snug little cove with a fine sandy beach and plenty of grasses. Some of the crew were dispatched inland to forage for supplies, the rest immediately set about cleaning and maintaining their lady *Windraider* like a hoard of busy house fraus. That same afternoon, Blythe looked up from washing her soiled petticoat to behold a ruddy face pressed against the window glass, staring at her. She startled, then flushed, and ordered him to take himself off and not come back. Soon there was only a rope visible and she relaxed, but only until a second face appeared with the same leering expectation. She sent him off, too, but realizing that something was going on outside her window and went to see.

Below, the men were scraping and tending the *Windraider*'s hull, suspended from ropes hanging from the deck. They obviously viewed such duty as a golden opportunity to get an eyeful of their prisoner. Sputtering outrage, she cast around the cabin for something to block the window and her eyes fell on Raider's great sea chest. She'd sworn not to touch another of his wretched things . . . except out of necessity. She managed a quick glimpse at the window where a shadow heralded the arrival of yet another curious face and decided that this was certainly a necessity.

She threw open the trunk and drew a deep breath at the dazzling array of garments and fabrics. Her fingers danced over their marvelous textures and, for some reason, Raider Prescott appeared in her mind's eye. They were his . . . and every one of them reminded her of something about him: the sleek satins were like his lips and the velvets were like his tongue, the silks were the smoothness of his hard skin and the crisp brocades were the surprising texture of his tawny hair . . . She shivered. This was no time to think about her enigmatic captor's very memorable features.

She selected a length of translucent silk in a jumble of butterfly-bright colors, thinking it would admit some light, but would disappoint curious eyes. She climbed up onto the bunk to stretch it across the window just as Richard knocked on the cabin door and she asked him for a hammer and some sharp tacks . . . and a bit of thin rope or line. Richard scowled, but hearing Blythe's very sensible explanation, finally consented and fetched them for her. He watched her clamber onto the bunk and gather and swag the precious silk across the windows so that it could be drawn down to provide privacy or pushed aside to provide light and a view of the faraway beach.

Blythe sent him off, relieved of his scrub brush and bucket, and proceeded to finish washing her petticoat and stockings. It was a pity she couldn't do her chemise as well . . . but she had nothing to wear while it dried. But the more she thought about it, the itchier it became and, in final desperation, she loosened her laces and removed her soft cambric chemise as well. She'd never felt so utterly naked as she did beneath that scratchy woolen dress and she threw herself into dusting the shelves and scrubbing the cabin floor to take her mind off it.

Raider opened the door some minutes later and stepped inside his cabin, scowling at the odd rosy light permeating the place and scowling even deeper when he saw what caused it. "What now?!" he growled irritably, searching the cabin for her. She heard his rumble and her head popped up behind the ebony wood table. She was obviously on her knees and he strode across the cabin, determined to catch her in whatever she was up to.

There she stood, on her naked knees in a puddle of wash water. Her skirt was tucked up under her waist to bare her shapely calves and ankles, and she was positively falling out of her bodice. His eyes were riveted on a creamy vertical line of flesh visible behind her lacings. The rounded edges of her breasts were visible from two directions now, above her neckline and through her straining laces. He flushed hot, staring at her unconsciously displayed loveliness, and his voice dropped.

"What in hell do you think you're doing?"

"I'm . . . I'm—" She lurched to her feet, clutching the scrub brush with both hands, "just cleaning the floor. It needed a cleaning and Richard—"

"—was supposed to se to it! I'll have his hide."

"No!" Blythe stepped forward hurriedly. "I told him I'd do it. He's not shirking. I . . . just had to have something to do . . . while my clothes dried." The mention of her clothes sent a lightning bolt of shame through her and she dropped the brush to jerk her skirts down over her bare legs and cross her arms over her chest.

Raider tore his eyes from her disappearing skin and jerked his head aside . . . just far enough for his gaze to catch on her undergarments hanging on a line stretched across a corner of the cabin. He turned to follow his head and his eyes lit with indignation. The cord was strung from his rhinoceros horn to the back of his elephant tusk chair. His trophies . . . the result of his great hunting and trading expeditions . . . and she had hung her laundry on them! "What in hell is this?!" he demanded, sweeping a muscular arm at them, then at the windows, "and that?!"

"I . . . had to wash my clothes; I have nothing else to wear! And as for the window, I had to put up some curtains to keep your men from watching me. They were dangling over the side on ropes, peering in—"

"And little wonder, with you stripped naked right before their eyes—" He growled, closing the distance between them, "like a shameless hussy—" Then his hands closed on her warm shoulders and he ceased all semblance of rational thinking. His pride, his desire . . . everything in him was suddenly on fire.

"No— I wasn't naked . . . I didn't." She pushed against his chest, knowing he was going to kiss her and knowing if he did, she would probably kiss him back. The quiver in her plea was some part excitement at the thought. "I'm not a hussy. Please don't touch me. You have no right—"

His mouth was mere inches away; she could feel his breath on her burning face. His arms around her were warm and vital; his hands caressed her back in that massaging, mesmerizing way. Every bone in her body seemed to be melting. He did have a right, she realized dimly, the right of desire. She wanted him to

126

touch her, to kiss her, to make her forget he'd kidnapped her for another man.

No right. The words rumbled through Raider, resurrecting memories long buried, memories of another woman, another respectable female he'd held to his heart. Only she had surrendered to him, given him what he wanted . . . until he made to claim her fully and take her to his life and name. Then she'd spoken of rights . . . and claimed he had none with her. And when he meant to press his case, she'd betrayed him to the custom's officers. Her greed, her ruthless quest for higher station in life sounded the final knell of his demise in respectable society. And even now, nearly ten years later, the harshness of that lesson made him pause in his quest for Blythe's treasures. "No right . . ." It echoed in his head.

Blythe felt an unreasoning disappointment as his arms loosened and left her. He stalked away, leaving her trembling and stunned by the swift rise of her own desires. The scent of coconut clung to the air around her and she was confused by the heat in her loins and the burning in her breasts. Her lips felt absurdly bare. When he turned on her, his eyes were hot with an old ire that Blythe couldn't have understood.

"Since when do ladies scrub floors on their knees, wench?" he bit out. "What are you up to?" he retraced his steps and snatched up her hand, glaring at its water-reddened skin. For some reason it bothered him that her hands weren't soft and white like the rest of her. "You plan to complain of our horrible treatment of you when you return to Philadelphia . . . is that it? Display your poor hands and collect sympathy while you blacken our names a bit more?"

"No, I . . . I just had to have something to do. I'm not used to being idle." She was bewildered by the sudden change in him. It made all the warmth he'd produced in her collect in her chest, so that she felt a burning there. "I needed to wash my clothes and I just wanted a bit of privacy . . ." She pulled her hand from his and pointed at the windows irritably. "And privacy is difficult to come by aboard your ship, Raider Prescott."

For some reason the sound of his name on her lips surprised them both. Raider felt a curios twinge in the middle of his chest and Blythe tightened all over as though she'd just made a terrible

127

gaffe. It felt ridiculously intimate to actually say his name aloud . . . in his presence.

"Damn!" he muttered, taking a giant step backward and searching her furiously for some flaw that could rally his defenses against her. But her eyes were big and very gold and her delicious little body was barely clothed in that absurd little dress that seemed to belong more on a serving wench than a spoiled, wealthy society chit. His eyes flew to her plain chemise, simple petticoat and stockings, so neatly laundered and hung. No highborn lady he knew voluntarily washed anything . . . even herself. His hot gaze dropped to her reddened little hands, and he thought of those calluses. No "lady" worthy of the name lifted anything heavier than a needle. And what the hell kind of father allowed his daughter to be seen in a place of business, much less let her participate in it? There was more here than met the eye, and he suddenly had a very bad feeling about Bastian's half-baked scheme . . . and about the effects the Wool-witch was having on him.

"Well, I have to have something to wear," Blythe saw him staring at her smallclothes and spread her arms over her exposed breasts. She was reddening to the roots of her hair. He watched shamed color spreading through her and felt an unholy urge to do something to relieve it.

He stalked to his great sea chest and flung it open. "Here," he growled, setting her fingertips vibrating with his intensity, "find something to wear."

"I can't wear any of those," she tried to lift her chin. "They're . . . strange and . . . unsuitable. I wouldn't even know how to put them on. Besides, it would be unseemly for me to wear things left by . . ." She swallowed hard and lowered her eyes. His paramours . . . the hundreds and thousands of his conquests. But she couldn't make herself say it. It made her ache inside to even think it.

"Good Lord, aren't we the prim little thing?" He took her meaning well enough. "Then can your proper little fingers wield a needle?"

"Of course, but . . ."

He hissed a bit of steam and bent to rummage in the bottom of the chest to come up with a silk-covered box and tossed it onto the table. "You'll find what you need in there." He saw her consternation and clarified it for her. "Stitch yourself something suitably 'respectable,' then. Use whatever you need from here." He went to his carved chest in the corner and pulled out a blue glass bottle with a wide, corked neck and brought it to her, shoving it into her hands. "Here. Use this on your blessed hands; they look like bloody boiled lobsters."

He watched her eyes lower to her hands around the bottle and saw that shamed heat in her face again. "Damnation!" he uttered, mostly at himself. "And no more scrubbing. I'll not have you playing martyr at my expense."

On the way to the door, he passed his beleaguered trophies and turned back, pointing savagely at her small clothes and blustering, "And get those damned things off my rhinoceros!"

The door slammed behind him and Blythe just stood there, her lip quivering, her eyes watering. He certainly knew how to humiliate a body. Something inside her chest swelled painfully. She could still see the disgust in his eyes. He hated so-called "respectable" women, though, they were greedy and troublesome and conniving . . . But she couldn't help being respectable . . . she certainly never tried to be . . . it just sort of came naturally. She looked down at the bottle in her reddened hands, thinking he must really hate her . . . and wishing she could return the sentiment. But he was too interesting and too strong and too handsome and too puzzling . . . and she liked his kissing. She never ever expected to like anybody's kissing . . .

She hurried to his monstrous stuffed beast and slipped her laundry line from its great horn to retie it around a knob on the back of one of the carved chairs. At least now she knew what it was called, a *rhinocerust*.

She sniffed and stared at the bottle in her hand, working the cork free. A potent blast of scent filled her head. Coconut. *His* coconut. Raider Prescott always smelled good enough to eat. And as she poured a bit of the oil into her hand and worked it into her thirsty fingers, she blinked and let the tears roll down her cheeks.

Bastian strolled around the empty deck of the ship beaming satisfaction in the warm autumn sun. Down the beach he could see some of the lads foraging for driftwood, and the strains of an

129

old sea chanty drifted up from where the lads were working on the hull. It did his spleen good to see everything rolling along so smoothly. The sight of Raider, standing with one foot propped in the top railing, staring out to sea completed his pleasure. He strolled over, reveling in the turmoil present in every line of his partner's striking frame. When Raider rubbed his face miserably and spoke through his hands, it was all Bastian could do contain his glee.

"She hung curtains. She's hung up a bloody clothesline . . . and *curtains*."

Raider waited until near sunset to brave his cabin again and was relieved to lead a fully clothed Blythe on deck. He deposited her on the quarterdeck without a word and went to join the lads who were lined up to take their daily ration of grog. They stood at the barrel, drinking it down, each in his turn, and when Richard appeared at her side, Blythe asked him about it. He explained that Raider wouldn't have any swapping of grog rations, because the practice caused frequent fights among the men. So he followed the navy practice of making the men consume their daily ration at the barrel, where it could be duly monitored and recorded by Bosun Deane with his roster.

Blythe watched as the line dwindled and heard Raider say something to the grizzled deck officer that spread through the lounging, drink-warmed men like a contagion. There was shuffling and noise as they got to their feet and swarmed the mizzen-deck. The excited calls finally became audible on the quarterdeck. "Almonds!"

"Hot damn!" Richard forgot all about Blythe as he raced on bare feet for the mizzen. Bastian watched the consternation on her face and sidled over to explain.

"We took almonds off'n the last British merchantman we plundered . . . bags of 'em. And the lads has been itchin' for 'em. Looks like Raider's feelin' a bit bountiful this evening. Now I wonder what could have put him in such a *givin'* mood?" His slanting look and suggestive tone raked Blythe like cats' claws.

"Certainly not your example, Mr. Cane." She stared up at him with flashing eyes. "I suspect the only thing you've ever given anyone is *trouble*." She removed herself to the far side of the deck and Bastian chuckled to himself.

It was some minutes later that the great burlap bags of the nuts were hauled topside and set up for distribution. Each man received a grog cupful in his hands and hurried off to a spot along the railing to crack and feast on them, tossing the shells into the water. Unfortunately, rail space was limited and the lads squeezed in, elbow to elbow, and soon the inevitable occurred. Shouting and shoving broke out, a dispute over whose nuts were whose.

Raider cut through the throng of his crewmen like a knife, reaching the core of the trouble quickly and bellowing an order for them all to "stand to." There was almost instantaneous order. Only the two combatants themselves dared move a muscle, and that because both had already abandoned good sense.

"He's got mine—" and "You lyin' maggot!" came charge and countercharge. Tall, lanky Stanley and quick, wiry Clive faced each other with blades drawn and all knew that Clive's familiarity with blade work made him odds-on favorite to survive, if the contest ran full tilt. Raider thundered an order that brought the antagonists up straight, facing him. His voice was low and whatever he said was inaudible from the quarterdeck where Blythe stood. But both blokes could be seen eyeing each other and nodding and a frenzy broke loose around them.

"Sweet Morgan's Blood!" Bastian spoke at Blythe's elbow. She turned and found his eyes glistening with expectation. "He's gonna walk the knife."

"What's that?" Blythe frowned.

"Captain's justice—" Bastian grabbed her wrist and pulled her toward the steps down to the mizzendeck. "He learned it from me!"

The men were swarming around the circular, tablelike capstan, mid-deck, as Raider bounded up onto it and stood with booted legs braced. He called for grog and his blade and was soon handed both. He stood and belted down the entire tankard without a breath and then called for "hands!"

Bastian dragged her through the men, to the edge of the crowd. Raider's back was to them, but they had a clear view of the two men, Stanley and Clive, placing their hands side by side, fingers widely splayed, onto the polished wooden surface at Raider's feet.

Raider drank back a second tankard as it was handed to him and wrapped his lean fingers around the knife handle, pointing it down. And before Blythe's horrified eyes, he began to stab the top of the capstan between the blokes' fingers, walking it from one end of their hands to the other and back.

"Good Lord!" she breathed, paling as she grasped Bastian's sleeve. "What is he doing?" She could scarcely hear his reply for the roars of encouragement, the jeers, and general melee around them.

"A contest is to decide an undecidable dispute. The cap'n walks the knife till one of the blokes pulls out . . . or loses blood." Bastian held up his left hand to show his ring finger missing at the first joint. "I learnt it from my old cap'n an' I taught Raider. Ye see, after each round old Raider'll toss back a stiff grog to woolly his head a bit more—so's to keep his personal feelin's out of it . . . and steady 'is hand . . ." Bastian saw the horror blooming on her face and laughed wickedly. "It's pirates' justice, Wool-witch."

"No—" Blythe gasped. And just then, Raider paused for his third gill of grog and turned a bit as he squatted on his heels above them. He caught sight of Blythe's whitened face at the edge of the crowd, and for a long moment, their eyes met and held. Raider read her fear, her horror at his actions in her luminous golden eyes. It was as though she were seeing him as he truly was for the first time. And oddly, it was as though he saw himself for the first time in a long while, reflected in her gaze.

There was a pause as his eyes roamed the hardened faces of his crew, reading their expectation, their mood as clearly as he'd read hers. He jerked his head back to pour the grog down his throat. He had to finish this bloody business . . . and finish, he would. At the side of his vision, he saw Blythe wheel and fight her way through his noisy crew and away. And in short order, he'd downed two more tankards and managed to draw blood from one of Stanley's fingers without doing it any permanent damage. The lads were somewhat disappointed as they turned away, but the tension had been defused and there would be a peaceful night ahead . . . for everyone except Raider. The grog was just now really setting in on him.

He checked with Bastian, who clapped him on the shoulder and congratulated him on a fine, manly performance of duty, then headed below for a bit of rest. He paused by his cabin door and started in. But the door was blocked, stopped by something. "Wool-wish! O-pen this-s door! Wool-witch!" But the door remained closed against his halfhearted pounding, and he snarled and swayed off toward Bastian's cabin, having already forgotten just what it was he wanted to say to her.

Blythe sat on the bunk with her hands clasped between her knees, watching the washstand she'd shoved in front of the door. Her heart was beating in her throat as the sounds of Raider's pounding died on the air. The fierce set of his features as he walked the knife through his men's fingers was burned into her brain. It came as a shock to her. In so many ways he was gentlemanly; his speech and his learning, his aristocratic looks, and especially . . . his gentle touch.

But even as Blythe was warming helplessly to him, the gulf between them was widening. He was every bit as dangerous as the rangy, menacing crew he led. The hard, flinty quality that sometimes invaded those jade eyes was chilling. It reminded her they were strangers and adversaries, from entirely different worlds. Blythe wrapped her arms about her empty middle and wondered why the realization had the power to make her feel so very desolate and alone.

Chapter Nine

Clam Chowder. The words had the ring of magic on the *Wind-raider*. The deep, beguiling sea was like a tempestuous mistress that a man loved and feared and could not bring himself to leave, though it could cost him his life to stay with her. And like a haughty mistress, the sea gave up precious few benefits to the men she ensnared. Every gain came allied with peril . . . except for clams.

Clams were delicious, nutritious, and blessedly docile. But only in periods of leisure and safety did a crew have the chance for so placid an undertaking as clam-digging. And leisure and safety were hard to come by on a privateering ship. Thus, on the *Windraider*, clams had come to mean more then mere gastronomic indulgence; they meant plenty and safety and good times all around. Thus when Franco made the suggestion to the Raider and Raider had Bastian assemble a work detail early that next morning for the purpose of a clam-dig, word spread through the ship like wildfire.

The lads romped up and down the beaches and set to with spades and picks, whatever they could find. Their mood was light and, like playful boys, they chucked sand at one another and dunked each other in the water. And they returned to a chorus of cheers, for the soft-shelled clams had been plentiful.

Soon the empty shells were heaved over the side and the mouthwatering smells of butter, garlic, and herbs wafted up from the galley. The crew settled in to wait. But it was to Blythe that the first tidings of the ripening delicacy were sent, midafternoon. François sent Richard for her, inviting her into his domain for the first tasting of the dish she'd inspired.

He held a wooden spoon of the precious golden concoction up for her to taste and Blythe rolled her eyes in an exaggerated, very French manner. *"Magnifique, François!"* A boyish smile lit his forbidding countenance and she asked to carry the first bowl to Old Willie, who was bunked not far from the galley. François scratched his head in confusion, but agreed.

"I promised," she smiled hesitantly, holding the bowl near Willie's nose so he could sniff. "François's clam chowder. If this doesn't fix you up, nothing will."

Willie pushed up jerkily, his crinkled eyes wide with astonishment. She'd done it . . . she'd gotten him Franco's clam chowder. He lifted his face to her as she settled the bowl for him and produced a hunk of François's dark, fragrant bread to accompany it. Her sweet face was grave, expectant. She'd braved Franco and kept her word. He was too surprised to eat . . . almost. He slurped and moaned from the pleasure of it, scarcely able to hide his curiosity about how she'd managed it. Finally his question came blurting out: "How'd ye get Franco to do it?"

"I . . . remembered which way to fall." She lowered her eyes and settled on a nail keg beside his cot. It made her uncomfortable to think about the weight of conscience that sent her to Franco in the first place.

Willie nodded, knowing there was more to the story than that. This prisoner of theirs wasn't like any female he'd ever known. He talked between bites, telling Blythe about his early days with Raider and Bastian; how they picked him up from a wreck near the Azores and how he'd done everything from gunnery to carpentry to rigging. It was a contest as to which he relished most, the chowder or the attention. But at last, he finished the bowl and sopped it clean, then sank back onto his bed with a lidded sigh. He declared he didn't know when he'd felt so satisfied . . . except . . .

"Except?" Blythe sat forward on the little keg she occupied.

"Well . . ." Wiley Old Willie was loath to see this special treatment end. "I be used to an evenin's grog . . . alwus helps me sleep." He grimaced and wrested about on the cot. "An' what with this lot," he glanced over his shoulder at his healing stripes, "I be hard-pressed to rest proper . . . wi'out me ration." His sunken jaws seemed especially hollow just now and his eyes had a listless expression that made Blythe think of Nana again, for some reason. A horrible sinking feeling came over her. Nana was hundreds, maybe a thousand miles away . . . but she could see to Willie's needs, and offer a fervent prayer that somebody, somewhere was caring for her precious family as she cared for him.

"Well . . . I'll send your ration down to you this evening." She couldn't imagine that no one else had thought of bringing it to him. But then, after that calloused display of inhumanity by Raider Prescott last night, it should be no surprise that consideration was in short supply aboard his ship. Her cool fingers stroked Willie's hand and she rose to hurry back to her cabin before Raider Prescott realized she was gone.

The sun was sinking low and the sky was hung with rosy silks and gossamer strands of spun gold when Raider appeared in his cabin to escort Blythe topside. He took her elbow firmly and frowned at the way she stiffened and avoided the merest glimpse of him. He directed her up the steps and through the hatchway, examining her icy mood.

"Did you enjoy your dinner?" he finally asked, thinking Franco's famous clam chowder would prove a safe topic. He rather expected her to be impressed and had planned to relish her surprise.

"It was . . . tasty," Blythe responded in clipped tones. Silence descended as he steered her toward the quarterdeck. He scowled, nettled by her casual acceptance of their extraordinary cuisine.

"You're sewing, I see."

"Just one dress." She glanced at him defensively, thinking he already regretted his generosity. "You needn't worry . . . I'll try to use as few of your things as possible."

"I said you might use whatever you needed . . ." He tightened irritably and reached for her hand, inspecting it. "You used the oil. I'd say there was already some improvement. Coconut oil . . . an old native woman in the islands showed me how to use it on my skin to salve the dryness. The sun and salt are hard on the skin . . ."

Blythe's tongue seemed padlocked as she pulled her hand back and stuffed it through her other one, around her waist. All she could think about was the incongruity of a calloused rogue of a sea captain going about smelling like her favorite ladies' cakes. But at least now she knew where that bedevelling scent came from. And she hoped it might be easier to withstand . . .

Raider's own irritation at her icy mood annoyed him even more than her reaction. Why should it bother him that the little witch accepted his best as if it were her due, disdaining his largess and even his exceptional concern for her? After all, wasn't that exactly what he'd come to expect from fancy-bred, high-strung, *respectable* females?

She stopped by the railing, looking out at the sea, and Raider's gaze was captured by the way the evening sun set fire to her long, thick hair. Her skin was dappled like fresh summer peaches and her long lashes formed feathery crescents against her cheek as she shielded her gaze from him. She seemed determined not to look at him, not to give him the pleasure of beholding the burnished disks of her eyes. And suddenly he was furious with her . . . and especially with himself for wanting her to look at him the way he looked at her. God and the devil! He was acting like a bloody "gentleman caller" . . . hanging on her words, aching for a glance, a nod, a smile. He backed a step and, without another word, he wheeled and headed for the comparative sanity of the below decks.

Blythe was relieved to be spared his scrutiny and his disturbing presence. Her eagerness to see him, to hear him, to feel his eyes upon her in that tactile way of his, was appalling.

She leaned on the quarterdeck railing and watched as Bosun Deane supervised the raising of the grog barrel and the distribution of rations. She was soon joined on the quarterdeck by Richard, whose face was cheerful indeed from his watered rum. He explained that Raider had generally decreed a double ration tonight . . . probably in celebration of the chowder.

Blythe thought immediately of Old Willie and how pleased he'd be to learn of their good fortune. "Do you think they'd mind if I slipped to the head of the line to get Old Willie's ration? I promised I'd bring it to him." She turned those great golden orbs on Richard, who stammered a bit.

"B-but you can't, miz. Grog's a seaman's right . . . only when he be duty-fit. A bloke has to stand in line himself to get it . . ."

"That's absurd, Richard . . . and uncivilized. Willie needs a bit of grog to help him sleep. He's still mending. And I promised." Blythe was heartily sick of these barbaric seafaring traditions and snatched Richard's empty tankard from his hands and started for the steps. But Richard pulled her back.

"Ye can' do that, miz." His calf-brown eyes were wide. "It ain't Willie's right, and . . . the lads won't like it."

"I honestly don't care what they like and don't. I've given my word and I'll not go back on it. Though I'll go to the back of the line . . . if it will make you feel better." But Richard's surprisingly strong grip still detained her.

"Ye can't do this, miz. It'll cause trouble . . ."

The tension in his face made her realize he was genuinely concerned. "Richard, they wouldn't dare harm me . . . Neville Carson wouldn't like it." But still Richard held her fast by the arm.

"Well," he swallowed hard, "if'n ye're determined . . . I'll go for ye." When she eased, he advised her to stay put and took his tankard from her hand. Quickly, he was down the steps and heading across the mizzen for the end of the dwindling grog line.

Blythe watched him, thinking what a fine young man he could be someday; courteous, helpful, unafraid of hard work. And she noticed the stares he collected as he presented himself at the back of the line. The stares quickly became glares that heated furiously as more of the lads turned to see. A rumbling started somewhere and even the lads that were lounging about were soon at attention and glaring at Richard.

"Damn and blast!" the scrawny bloke named Clive spoke for their growing number. "We caught us a rat tryin' to *double the tub!* One extra ration ain't enough for the young prince, here. He thinks he be entitled to more!" There was an ugly outpouring of agreement that pulled Blythe to the quarterdeck railing.

"He been gettin' uppity o'late!" came a harsh charge. ". . . since he took up wi' fancy female company" came a rejoinder. And suddenly he was being shoved out of line, to fall against a burly bloke, who pushed him hard against another, who shoved him around further. Soon that mangy pack was closing in on him,

138

some drawing knives.

Good Lord, they were attacking Richard! Blythe stood frozen, watching from above . . . scarcely able to fathom the depths of their ire. A panicky glance around revealed that neither Raider nor Bastian was topside. The ranking officer was the hard-handed Bosun Deane.

"It's not fer me," Richard was protesting as they grabbed his arms and held him, "it be for Old Willie!"

"Like hell it be!" Clive snarled as he waved his nasty little stiletto blade. "Willie ain't duty-fit and he ain't entitled . . . He knows it, too! You be takin' privileges because ye got cosy wi' our fancy pris'ner . . ." He turned to his mates, ". . . follers her about wi' a moon-calf face . . ."

"Well, we ain't standin' fer it! Methinks the whelp needs a lesson, mates—" came another ragged growl.

Blythe watched, horrified, the proud defiance of Richard's stance and heard his protest being drowned in calls for his punishment, and a hot bolt of outrage burst up her spine. Acting on pure impulse, she jolted for the steps and was quickly down them and shoving her way through that heaving mass of hard male bodies.

"No-o-o—*stop!*" she demanded, pushing through to the front of the pack, mere feet from where they held Richard's straining form. "Stop it! He's done nothing wrong! It was me—I promised Old Willie his grog ration, and I'd have stood in line myself—" Blythe turned to face that deadly circle, her chest heaving, her golden eyes blazing, ". . . except Richard volunteered! You scurvy lot—he was trying to help a mate, not to break one of your precious rules. And he did it to help me keep my word—to one of you!" Her hands were icy and she could hardly breathe as she lunged forward and grabbed Richard's arm to yank him free and pull him beside her. The lads who held him were too surprised to resist.

"It's me you dislike . . . though God knows why, since I've never done anything to any of you, except speak the truth. But I'll not let you punish an innocent boy because of it." She pulled Richard's sleeve and started for the edge of the circle nearest the hatch, but they wouldn't part to let her pass and she backed one step . . . then two. Those grizzled, hardened faces began to inch closer.

"Well, well." Clive fingered his blade and his bilious eyes narrowed as he stalked closer. "We got the fancy wench to ourselves, lads. She thinks her wishes be commands hereabouts. *Her Highness*. Well, we ain't all green-bearded boys, chit. We got ways of dealin' wi' troublesome females . . . ain't we, lads?" There was a wave of ugly laughter all through the pack, and Blythe was sick to realize exactly what they meant.

She raked a panicky gaze about for some sign of help, some sign of Raider Prescott. But in another harrowing instant, she recalled every warning he'd given her about his men . . . and how she'd fare under them — *all of them*. He said he'd not lift a finger to stop it, if it came. And it had finally come.

She swallowed hard as they backed her toward the railing, closing in around her. Some were snarling about "the plank" and others were laughing nastily about seeing whether a Wool-witch would float. She had the presence of mind to push Richard behind her, shielding his dumb-stricken frame as they neared that polished railing and that long drop to the sea.

"I don't care what you do to me, but I swear — if you harm him because of me —" She choked on the last part, knowing there was precious little she could do to any of them, overwhelmed and unarmed. What she saw in their eyes convinced her her end was near and she could only think of young Richard . . . of getting him away. She turned and pushed him along the railing, yelling, *"Run!"*

Her cry and her shove exploded his benumbed responses and he scrambled through the blokes along the railing. They were so intent on her furious, defensive form that they didn't hinder him seriously. And suddenly she was alone, in that awful closing circle.

Clive stepped forward flicking his slim, wicked knife back and forth before her terrified eyes, and several other blades appeared. And suddenly she could move no further; her legs refused to work. And with the fatalistic acceptance with which she'd approached her short, hard life, she raised her chin and refused to cower anymore. If this was to be her end, then she'd prefer it to be quick . . .

"Then do it —" she choked. "Do your worst while you have the chance! Finish me — end my misery here and now!" Fires leapt in her huge golden eyes as she turned them first on Clive, then on one after another of his mates. Some spat muffled curses, some glowered. None moved.

"You'd best use those wretched blades. For if you don't —" She had no idea what to do if they didn't carve her up. "I . . . I'm drawing a double ration . . ." was all she could think of. "And I'm taking it to Willie. And the lot of you can go rot . . ."

Her hot words and her queenly, broad-shouldered stance were impressive, in the face of their collective threat. But it was the scorching heat of her unearthly eyes . . . *golden* eyes . . . that made them halt and stare at one another in confusion. The little wench stood there, alone and unarmed, blazing defiance at the lot of them. It was truly something to witness . . .

Scrawny Clive's blade lowered first, then another went down, then another. Blythe felt a harrowing tunnel of darkness threatening at the edges of her consciousness and fought it with every ounce of her strength. She saw them easing back and made herself put one foot before the other in the direction of the grog barrel. Her movements were stiff; she was walking inside the shell of herself, horrified by her own actions. All around her she felt their movement, but they parted to allow her access to the barrel. The bosun said nothing as the "dipper" handed her a full tankard of grog. Her hands were shaking so violently she could scarcely keep from spilling it, but she turned to the hatch and was allowed progress to it as well.

They trailed her down to the gun deck, then to the berthing deck where Old Willie malingered on his cot. Several who crowded in after her were witnesses to Willie's shock when she handed him the tankard without a word and turned to make her way back to her cabin. She mounted the ladders and crossed the gun deck under scores of watchful eyes. Crewmen littered her way like stones scattered to mark a trail. She moved with fatalistic grace, her head held high, her shoulders back, for she expected at any second to feel the bite of a blade.

By the time she'd reached the door of Raider Prescott's cabin, the tension and fear frozen in her were beginning to thaw. She slumped back against the closed door, quaking, scarcely able to believe she was still alive. Challenging them like that; she must be half mad! They had knives and they itched to use them . . . on each other or on her; it made little difference to them. They were

141

fierce and ugly and cruel; stealing, brawling, kidnapping . . .
living savage lives by a savage code . . .

Good Lord . . . *they were pirates!* She swayed as the chilling
realization swept through her. She'd really been kidnapped by
pirates! She staggered to the bunk and collapsed on her hands and
knees atop it.

Lord! Then she really had been in jeopardy of life and limb, not
once but several times! At least twice with Franco . . . then on the
deck with Sharkey . . . and the knife-fight . . . and probably every
other time she set foot amongst them. She hadn't believed it;
always found some reason not to take their overblown menace
seriously. But this time she'd been too sensible for her own good!
They'd been pirates all along . . . dangerous and violent men.
And she very well might have been killed . . . several times over.

The horror of it gripped her as she sat there on her knees,
staring out at the darkening waters. There was no place to run, no
way to escape in the midst of that relentless, heaving sea. And
even within sight of the beach . . . she might have been a
thousand miles away, for she could not swim and there was no
chance of taking a boat by herself. The sea, she realized, was but
one more agent of the vengeful fates that had beset her and her
family at every turn these three years. Why? Why was all this
happening to her? Why was she singled out?

Once the mechanism of thought was roused, it proceeded in
relentless, methodical fashion with a will of its own. Awful realiza-
tions clunked into place, one after another, like the tumblers of a
lock that had guarded a secret from her. And the secret was all the
more devastating for having only been a secret to herself. Blythe
Woolrich was a young woman, essentially alone. She had no
family capable of protecting her . . . her social position and
connections had dwindled to nil . . . her finances were desperate
and she had no marital prospects. She worked like a scullery maid,
ate only the cheapest fare, wore frayed and outdated clothing, and
she couldn't even manage the means to heat and light her home in
the cold winter months ahead. Simply, she was "easy pickings" for
men like Neville Carson . . . and Raider Prescott.

She was, she faced the awful reality of it squarely for the first
time in her life, *vulnerable.* Capable, responsible Blythe Woolrich,
she who had decided for and provided for her family these past

several years, was in reality a lone, defenseless female . . . on the shelf . . . unwanted. It was undoubtedly her chief allure for a vulture like Neville Carson. She wrapped her arms around her hollow, chilling shoulders and began to rock. She suddenly didn't want to think anymore . . . but somehow couldn't stop. All this time, all these long, lonely years, she never saw it. She'd convinced herself she was capable and responsible . . . able to manage things, to see to her family's welfare . . .

But just look how she'd managed things, a sardonic little voice inside crowed; just look at how things had turned out. She believed that someday she'd be able to help her father, that he'd come back to her, back to reality . . . and it hadn't happened. She kept believing that she could hold the family business together, that things would get better someday . . . and that hadn't happened, either. She kept believeing that someday Nana would be well and they would be a family again . . . but that would never happen. And against all odds, some stubborn little part of her had kept believing that she might someday have a bit of love, a bit of joy in her life that would make all the work, all the effort, worth it in the end. And now she knew beyond a shadow of a doubt that would never happen. She would never have a life, a family . . . a love.

It was the killing thrust. That stubborn little flame of hope in the middle of her that had weathered endless, grinding work and hunger and overwhelming odds . . . finally surrendered. Her short, hard life had reached its final, degrading conclusion. She'd been abducted by pirates, men who would as soon snuff out her life as they would barter her like a sack of flour. She was destined to suffer under Neville Carson's vengeful hand and, she shuddered, probably under his revolting bulk as well.

Blythe couldn't even breathe. She tried desperately, but everything in her chest seemed to be swelling, blocking it. Her vision went next; everything blurred and hot tears began to scald her cheeks. Small, snubbing gasps of air were all she could manage. There wasn't a single person to rescue her, no one who might even care enough to search for her . . .

Raider Prescott came exploding up out of the cargo holds, raw fury blinding him to things like hand-holds and ladders. Grim-lipped Bastian followed, making use of at least a few ladder rungs, and Richard panted and clambered after them both, at a safe distance. He'd managed to find his captain in the deepest, murkiest hold in the stern of the ship and gasped out the lady's peril in such explicit terms that Raider came up snarling and cursing both himself and his own men.

Raider landed flatfooted on the quarterdeck, with his naked blade in his hand, and visions of the Wool-witch trapped in a raging mob . . . perhaps carved up a bit . . . in his head. Everything on deck was awash in crimson and, as he stomped savagely down to the quiet, mostly empty mizzen, it was a long moment before he realized that the red he saw everywhere was the blood in his own eyes. He blinked and glared about him at his skittering crew, demanding, "Where in hell did they take her?!" He grabbed Clive by the shirt and gave him a savage shake.

"Berthin' de-e—" was all Clive managed to gasp before Raider dropped him like a limp rag and tore down the fo'c'sle steps and ladders to the berthing deck. He found a good number of his men crowded around Old Willie and their subdued mien confused him momentarily. This was not the grisly scene he'd anticipated . . .

"Where the hell is she? What have you done with her?!" he demanded, itching to lay into the lot of them. Frustration was fanning his ire to dangerous proportions.

"She . . . went up to yer cabin, Cap'n." Old Willie rose. "She jus' brung me a ration . . . then went straight up to th' cabin . . . honest." They flinched when Raider's cold-jade eyes narrowed furiously.

"If she's been harmed in any way . . . I swear I'll hang the lot of you myself." Raider's deep, quiet rumble unsettled even the most hardened nerves amongst them. He wheeled and stomped up the ladder and across the gun deck, feeling a small trickle of relief through his cramped middle. They hadn't assaulted her or carved her up; she was back in his cabin, probably in one piece. That was good, he thought . . . for he wanted the privilege of killing her himself! Taking such a fool chance with her safety . . . and scaring him like this!

His anger was hardly mastered when he burst through his cabin door and found her on her knees on the bunk, her shoulders rounded. She didn't even rouse when he slammed the door savagely behind him, nearly flattening Bastian's nose. Relief at her apparent safety poured through his frame, followed by a jagged bolt of ire.

"Of all the stupid, idiotic females in this bloody world . . ." he thundered at her, "why did I have to get stuck with *you?!* God . . . you're more trouble than you're worth!"

In all the world of words, he had managed to find the very ones that would be like hot pitch on her torn and aching heart. Why was he saddled with a stupid, useless, defenseless female, he demanded to know! The insults seared through her, cauterizing her damaged sense of self and melting the last restraint on the anger she had denied and suppressed through years of toil and disappointment.

It boiled up from her loins, fiery and foreign, seizing her frame and trembling it. She wheeled on the bunk to face him, her eyes hot with new flame at fate's calloused treatment of her. And as the instrument of fate in her wretched life, he was now destined to bear the brunt of all her stored and bottled anger.

"Worthless, am I?" She shook with the power of volcanic steam. "Isn't Neville Carson paying you enough for your troubles?! How could a single, defenseless female like me make the slightest bit of trouble for a vicious, desperate bunch like you and your crew?" She slid from the bunk and stood, coiled and quivering, her golden eyes now molten, sunlike in intensity.

"They didn't finish me off when they had the chance . . . the cruel wretches," she blazed, striking a nerve with her next charge. "Is that what you're here for? Well, you can kill me or beat me—it doesn't matter to me anymore—but I won't bear your insults . . . I *won't!*" Then everything exploded inside her, showering hot, molten lava against the underside of her skin.

She wheeled and jerked up the huge bronze pitcher from the ebony table and heaved it at him. It clanged against the wall and floor and thumped and rolled to a stop at Raider's feet. The little embroidered sewing box was next and it crashed open, scattering silver pins and sending bobbins rolling. She turned and began pulling things from the shelves, and at first he was too surprised to do anything but duck.

"Dammit, Wool-witch!" He just missed being grazed by a huge

clam shell. "What's wrong with yo—"

"I didn't ask for Neville Carson or a crazy father or the cursed British . . ." she raved, heaving a large pink conch shell at him with her other hand. ". . . or Nana's illness, or Indian attacks—not any of it! And I didn't ask to be kidnapped! It's your own wretched fault you're stuck with me and I'll not bear your foul abuse anymore! I'm the one who was wronged . . . and you say *I'm* responsible?! Just get out! *Out* . . . and leave me alone!" She reached for the music box, but her frantic fingers grasped a carved ivory tusk first. She hurled it with everything in her, and there was a satisfying "Uff-f—dammit!" when it slammed into his shoulder.

A stuffed lizard, a jade Buddha, a book—she seemed bent on destroying his cabin and him in the process. The sheer volume of her unleashed fury stunned him temporarily. "Dammit, Woolwitch—come to your senses, woman!"

Her aim improved and his surprise abated at the same precipitous rate, and suddenly he was in motion, lunging for her, dodging foreign objects and her flailing fists to grab her waist and one arm. They wrestled and struggled furiously, body against body, Blythe kicking and spitting fury and Raider determined to stop her.

"Get your hands off me!" She pushed and pummeled with all her might. But it wasn't enough to overcome Raider's tightening hold on her waist. Her nails came up. But his lightning reflexes caught her hand snaking for his cheek and snatched it back. And while he had to sacrifice his grip on her waist to save his skin, she bucked away from him and delivered a nasty kick to his knee . . . that had been aimed higher. The jab of pain cleared a part of his faculties that had been fogged by the steam of his temper and he began to feel the desperation in her struggles. Somehow this wasn't the same as their earlier clashes. He managed to force her chin up and the anguished fury of her beautiful eyes shot bolts of alarm through him. Suddenly he was no longer just defending himself. Something *had* happened to her . . . and he had to know what it was.

He had to constrain her first, to somehow reduce the threat of those dangerous hands and nails. His gaze landed on the bunk and he tussled with her toward it. He lifted her wriggling body against him and wrenched about, flinging her onto the bunk and managing to fall on top of her.

"Ouf-f-f!" His weight pounded precious breath from her and she bucked and twisted beneath him, struggling for air. "Go on," she choked, her gaze focused somewhere beyond him, somewhere that filled her voice with pain and pleading, "beat me or kill me and get it over with! It couldn't be any worse than . . ."

"I'm not going to beat you, Wool-witch, for God's sake!" He grappled afresh with her frantic hands. "Calm yourself, wench! What is wrong with you?"

"No—just get off me and leave me be . . ." The pain in her chest was killing. Her whole life, her whole being was shattering around her. "Please—*oh, please!*" Her panicky hands defied his to grasp his sleeves and push wildly. But she couldn't move his hard warmth any more than she could dislodge the relentless fates who'd ravaged her life. And with a ragged, shuddering sob she surrendered. The fiery brilliance of her eyes drowned in a flood of hot, stinging brine. Her lashes shut against the blurred sight of his face, sending hot tears rolling from her eyes back into her hair. She struggled against anguished sobs for breath . . . for life.

"Wool-witch—" Raider's square, lean-fingered hand came up to her cheek, and she flinched from its brandlike heat that burned all the way to her tortured heart. "God, Wool-witch, they hurt you somehow. I swear, I'll kill them with my own bare hands—" His righteous ire, his manly disdain, had drowned utterly in that first anguished tear. Something akin to the ache of battle-fear crushed through him as he watched her inner struggle in her streaked face.

"No—" she sobbed, "please—"

This time when she pushed at his sleeves, he flushed hot with shame at his brute use of power and raised on his arms to move his weight from her. Below him she was pressed like a rag doll into the soft mattress, so small, so hurt. Her fingers still clutched his sleeves. Then her golden eyes opened and, through the liquid crystal that clung to them, he glimpsed pain. Raw male protectiveness surged through him in powerful waves.

He dropped to sit on the bunk beside her and gathered her impulsively into his arms, holding her soft frame fiercely against his heart. She wriggled for one brief moment, then her hands clasped his corded arms and she clung to him, burying her face and her sobs in his shirtfront. His hand came up to stroke her hair

147

awkwardly and lingered to cradle her head against him.

"Tell me, Wool-witch—" He felt her shudder and could have bit his tongue. After a long minute, he took a deep breath and started over. "Blythe," her name had a painful sweetness on his lips, "tell me, what did they do to you? Are you hurt?" It was an agonizing moment before he felt her head move against his chest and realized she was responding in the negative. Something oppressive lifted from his shoulders.

She was too dazed, too confused to resist when he pulled her fully onto his lap and cradled her in his arms. His warm fingers stroked her back, her neck, her arm, for a long time, making gentle, reassuring spirals that reached into her beleaguered heart. "I tried . . ." she snubbed, breathing in gasps as her arms slipped around him to hold him desperately tight.

"Tried what?" His deep voice rumbled all around her. Had she tried to escape?

"My father . . . he just likes candles and magnets . . ." She sobbed quietly for a moment, then released her panicky hold on him long enough to wipe at her tears and nose. "Nana's still sick . . . but she has to have red yarn . . . and lavender soap. And Mrs. Dornly can't show her face to Simmons . . . but I tried . . . I really tried."

"I'm sure you did," he murmured in a shushing monotone and pulled her head against his chest. She wasn't making a bit of sense, but it didn't seem to be entirely his crew's fault. There seemed to be something more to it.

"Somebody had to be sensible . . ." Fresh tears squeezed from her closed eyes and she shivered as he caressed her shoulder, "somebody has to be responsible . . ." She turned a red-nosed, teary-eyed look up to him that would have melted a block of granite. And Raider Prescott was only made of flesh and blood.

He felt warm and spongy inside. Her lips were stung cherry red and her great golden eyes were magnified by prisms of lingering tears. Her skin was flushed like rosy peaches and that enchanting little dent in her chin was quivering. "Why?" she was asking, and he was suddenly all too aware of her curvy little body fitted tightly against him.

"Why did I have to be the one? Why me?" she whispered in a small, faraway voice, replacing her cheek against the hard mound of his chest and nuzzling gently.

All that fluid warmth was flooding into his loins and his eyes widened. He was instantly aware of every inch of contact between their bodies. He was trying to console her, trying to understand what had set off such a huge eruption of anger in her. But his own feelings were perilously near his surface . . . a surface she was pressing and clutching and rubbing . . .

A tantalizing trickle of coconut made its way up her puffy nose and she moved her head and turned her face to follow it. That warm slice of hard, vital skin at the neck of his soft shirt; she breathed deeply of it and opened her eyes to stare up at him. His jadelike gaze was warm indeed and his tawny hair hung over his forehead in that way that made her want to brush it back for him.

"And why do you have to smell like coconut all the time?" she asked, hardly realizing she spoke aloud. "It's . . . my very favorite . . ." Her cherry-sweet lips parted, her golden eyes glowed. A man would have had to be a bloody saint to resist her . . . and Raider Prescott was not precisely a saint.

Blythe saw his head bending, saw his eyes fastened on her lips, and she made no move to avoid the inevitable. And when his firm, satiny lips moved over hers, coaxing, exploring, she responded like parched ground absorbing the gentle rain of his kiss. Slowly, she blossomed under the warm, spring shower of passion that invaded and nourished the empty reaches of her.

Raider pressed her to him, clasped her against his heart, giving her his strength, his assurance, the gift of his desire for her. And in that swift and stunning rise of passions, Blythe found her old, stunted, sensible self crackling and splintering around her like a shell grown too small to contain her any longer. And from beneath that restrictive cocoon of duty and respectability, a woman of earth and warmth and desire began to emerge.

His hands on her body were a balm, his kisses drove the hurt from her mind and replaced it with stunning new delights; shivers of icy heat, sweet burnings and strange, wondrous hungers. His kisses trickled downward to find her breasts even as his hands raised her skirts and searched the satiny curve of her bare thigh and hip. She gasped and arched and whispered the truest longings of the unfolding French half of her heart, "Kiss me, Raider Prescott . . . touch me . . ."

Raider heard her with more than just his ears. He heard with all his senses, all his being, in a way he'd never heard a woman before. Every part of him rallied, allied to give her what her very heart entreated. He would love her joyfully, pleasure her . . . He raised his head to let his kiss tell her so and her golden eyes fluttered open to meet him, warmed, trusting, glowing. And as he lost himself in the welcome of her fragrant mouth, it was that look that lodged sideways in his mind and refused to merge and flow neatly into the stream of his desires. That look spoke of loving and meant more than just the pleasurable joining of bodies. That look spoke of comfort and giving and surrender . . . and a host of other things that suddenly collected in Raider's chest and throat so that he couldn't breathe.

He raised his head and saw her wriggling, kitten-like, against his warmth. Her eyes were feathery crescents above passion-blushed cheeks and her lips were parted, ready to receive him, primed to respond. Her hip undulated shyly against his stilled hand and that provocative little movement managed to shock his libertine senses. She wanted him. It was all coming back in jarring clumps of reality. The Wool-witch wanted him. She was opened to his desires, vulnerable . . .

Alarm blasted through him, rattling every nerve and fiber of his being. Lord, what was he doing?! Making love to a vulnerable captive under his own protection . . . and a *virgin*, no less! Morgan's Boiling Blood—what was happening to him? Muscles that had been invaded by a languor of sensual preparation now coiled as though he was under attack. And indeed he was being assaulted—by treacherously respectable impulses he thought long subdued.

Blythe felt his pause, his tightening, and opened her eyes to look at him. He was tightening and his hands had stilled on her. She could feel him pulling away and was confused by it. She reached up to stroke his cheek and her fingertips stayed to trace the bold curve of his lower lip . . . the way she'd often longed to do. "Please . . ."

"God . . ." she heard on an indrawn breath and the raw turmoil of that single syllable sent her heart into a panicked retreat. Then he was rising, setting her aside firmly and sheer disbelief numbed her responses against unseemly protest. She wanted to hold him

150

back, to beg him not to leave . . . to ask him to love her . . . to make her forget. The words rose no further than her constricting throat, but the pain they caused rose into her eyes.

Raider strode across the cabin, breathing raggedly as he retucked his shirt in his wide belt. He paused and drew a hard breath before turning to face her. But he still wasn't prepared for the sight of her, sitting in the middle of his tousled bunk, looking tousled herself . . . and utterly defenseless. Her bodice was awry, baring much of her creamy breasts, her lips were lightly bruised from his kisses, and her eyes . . . Her eyes were huge, luminous, and full of confusion and fresh hurt.

"Please" was all she said. But it spoke volumes and every line was an indictment of his treatment of her and his own unthinkable weakness of her. There was but one outcome for such a yearning and that was pain. And from the riot in his loins and the searing ache in his gut, he knew it was already too late. His mouth worked and no sound issued forth. There was nothing he could say to her, no apology to make, no word of comfort to recompense what he had promised and not given. He had no right to promise . . . or to give. *He had no right.*

He backed to the door, misery like a taste on his tongue and like a weight on his broad shoulders. And with a last painful look at the tousled beauty he craved like the air he breathed, he turned and left her there.

Blythe sat there, stunned, feeling as though he'd torn some part of her away . . . a part she couldn't afford to lose. He'd warmed and comforted her, touched her with gentle hands that reached into her sore heart to bind it up. And she'd responded with all she had to give . . . herself. And Raider Prescott had turned away.

He didn't want her. The tears rolled down her cheeks again, silent tears, the kind that come from the deepest grief. Now Blythe Woolrich was truly alone.

Bastian saw Raider step into the twilight on deck and hurried to inform him of the results of his inquiry into the incident. "It seems Miz Blythe Woolrich took it upon herself to change the *Articles,* single-handed. She were dishing out grog to the weak and afflicted," Bastian snorted, contemptuous of such blatant virtue. "To Old Willie, of all the blokes. And when the lads called her to account, she near laid *them* flat. Nobody touched her precious

151

hide . . ." he watched Raider's grim control, "unless . . . you, maybe . . . ?"

Raider turned a simmering glare on Bastian, who drew his chin back sharply. He didn't like this mood of Raider's; it was subdued and troubled in a way Bastian hadn't seen before. "We heard the ruckus . . . bashin' things was she? Got a nature like a banshee. Blythe, that be her Christian name, don't it?" He grunted disgust. "Never saw a female so mis-named in me life—"

"Dammit, Bastian—" Raider grabbed his shirtfront with quiet rage that was only a whisper away from mayhem, "keep your bloody mouth shut!" He wheeled and stalked off, battling the urge to really thrash Bastian within an inch of his cavalier, hedonistic life. He slammed against the bow railing, facing into the wind, tortured by the mingled heat of confusion and need. The worst of it was, an hour ago he'd have agreed with Bastian . . . would have called her the prickliest, most troublesome female God ever put on this earth. Then he'd braved and conquered her anger . . . and found the vulnerable, irresistible woman beneath it. He'd tasted her passion, comforted her pain—and made a horrifying discovery about himself in the process. Raider Prescott, erstwhile gentleman and privateer, and currently pirate, was vulnerable, too.

Chapter Ten

Bastian Cane wasn't the only one who'd heard Blythe's eruption. The lads had watched Raider slam the cabin door in Bastian's face and they scrambled to press their ears to walls and floors beside and below the captain's cabin. According to the *Articles*, they were entitled to a share of everything aboard the *Windraider* and they took that to include things like brawls, excitement, and a good spectacle now and then. Their eyes widened at the way the wench railed and steamed at their captain and they exchanged righteous nods when it was clear The Raider had taken her in hand physically. The Raider knew how to handle females, all right.

Then everything had gotten quiet, and their grins and ears began to burn from imagining what the silence meant. The Raider knew how to enjoy a female, too, even a prickly one. They turned away with heated faces, not able to swallow properly or to meet each others' eyes as they headed topside for a nip of cool air.

They were surprised indeed to see Raider emerge from the hatch shortly after them. And they read his dark, pensive mood as a sign that whatever passions had built had certainly not been spent. They wagged their heads in awe at The Raider's self-control. He said she'd not be touched and it appeared he meant it. Not many captains felt bound to abide by the orders they laid down for their crews. So, being red-blooded males themselves, they wouldn't have really held it against him if he had bedded the wench.

And what a wench she was! Lord, they'd never seen a female

with such grit! To stand up to their collective menace they way she did, she had to be the bravest female alive! Anne Bonney herself couldn't have done any better. Dared 'em to finish her off, she did, then stared 'em down with those dubloon-gold eyes of hers. And all over a gill of grog . . . that she'd promised to one of their mates. It showed she had an admirable set of priorities; she prized both liquor and loyalty. Remarkable sense for a "respectable" sort . . . and a female at that . . .

Raider spent a very long night on deck, trying to shake off the harassment of his own arousal and berating himself for the inconceivable stupidity of protecting the little witch's virtue . . . against her own desires! He shuddered. It was downright chivalrous of him, pulling away like that when his real desire was to plunge into her delectable little body and pleasure her straight into paradise. The longer he was around her the more gentlemanly he behaved toward her. It was a bad sign that he felt this strange ache in his chest and was so dead set on protecting her when he knew damned well that respectable females always landed on their feet . . . just like cats.

It was that unholy anger of hers that had thrown him off his stride, he decided . . . that and the way she had seemed so girlish and vulnerable and irresistible, all at once. She'd had a scare with his men, but she'd given as good as she'd taken. There was more to it than that. Her anguish had seemed deep and fermented, as if from a hurt a long time building. It had something to do with her life on land . . . her father and some other people . . . and Neville Carson undoubtedly figured in somehow. She obviously still believed they had abducted her on his orders . . . the stubborn little witch.

This unprecedented need to know what was going on inside her tumultuous person annoyed him royally. She made him want things he hadn't even thought about in years. He wanted to talk to her, to tell her things, ask about her. Lord, *talk* to her?! See how treacherous they were . . . these respectable females. A little fainting, a few respectable tears and they got you all softened up and talking . . . and next came understanding them and . . . God. He couldn't wait to get her off his ship!

Blythe was in no mood for company when Richard brought her tray the next morning, but she managed to apologize for drawing him into so desperate a situation. She was little relieved to have his moony-eyed assurance that he'd have braved far worse to be of service to her. She sent the tray back to François later with a very French apology that her appetite wasn't quite the usual.

She'd never felt so alone, so abandoned in the world. The odd thought struck her that if the revelations of the previous were true, being alone was not exactly a new condition in her life. It was a state she'd managed to endure these last several years and she'd survived.

But somehow this loneliness was different. She groaned and wrapped her arms around her waist. It had to do with Raider Prescott and the new kind of closeness and delicious sensual promises he had introduced her to. Knowing now that such man-woman delights existed, and that she'd never have them, made her feel achingly alone and deprived. All he had to do was turn his probing, tactile gaze toward her or invade her with that deep, startling voice of his and a fierce longing swelled within her. She wanted to touch him and talk to him and satisfy her curiosity . . . and this shocking need for physical contact he'd awakened in her. His tenderness confused her, his magnetism puzzled and excited her, and the casual fierceness of his ways frightened her. Why of all men did she have to be kidnapped by the sensual and enigmatic Raider Prescott?

That was how Raider found her; sitting on her knees with her hands in her lap, staring out the window. He cleared his throat and she turned and slid from the bed.

"I . . . wanted to be sure you were . . . unharmed," he began, searching her face and finding a slight puffiness about her eyes and nose. She'd apparently done a bit more crying. The thought settled harshly on his stomach.

"I'm . . . fine, Captain." She couldn't bear to look at any part of him and so selected a point on the wall just over his shoulder to focus on. "I must ask you to excuse my behavior of last night. I think . . . I was not quite myself. I shall try to behave better from now on." The flatness of her tone and the way she veiled her eyes

155

and avoided looking at him pricked him sharply.

"The apologies should be mine," he rebutted, feeling stilted and defensive. "My crew's behavior was inexcusable, and if you'll give me the names of those involved . . . or describe them, I'll see they're punished fully."

"No—I believe you warned me, did you not?" She reddened noticeably, embarrassed by her need to look at him, when he'd made it excruciatingly clear he wanted nothing to do with dull, respectable her. "In any case, I couldn't be responsible for anyone else being punished on my account."

"What do you mean, *anyone else?*" He stepped closer.

"Old Willie . . . I was responsible, remember?" Her fingers slipped behind her back to wind themselves into knots. He was scowling fiercely at her and she turned away, feeling a little sick.

She couldn't have known that behind that scowl he was in turmoil. She felt responsible for Old Willie's lashes . . . and braved the rest of the crew to carry him his grog ration? Lord, she was making it up to him! Raider suddenly felt like a prize fool, for he knew exactly where she got the idea she was responsible for Willie's absurd behavior . . . him! But he certainly hadn't expected the Wool-witch to take it to heart. Then it hit him. The *Wool-witch* hadn't; curvy, vulnerable little Blythe Woolrich had.

"You have my assurance that you'll be returned to your father unharmed." For some ungodly reason he had a compelling need to reassure her. "Somehow you've gotten the idea that Neville Carson is responsible for your abduction, but he had nothing to do with it. I'd never have put the *Windraider* at the disposal of such a man . . . nor for such a purpose as forcing a female into marriage." His involuntary shudder validated his claim. "It's a simple bit of ransom, that's all. We'd gone to Philadelphia to search for new markets for the cargoes we've privateered. And my partner decided on one of his infamous 'shortcuts' to riches."

Her better sense surrendered and she turned to him, searching his finely sculptured features, his straight, perfect nose, his high cheekbones, and his full, firm-bordered lips. And finally she could avoid the pull of his eyes no longer. The openness of his gaze spoke several things to her, but most importantly, it said *he was telling the truth*. It struck her like a fist in the stomach, and she turned to the table and began to fumble with the lid to her little silk sewing box.

"Neville Carson . . . asked you to marry him?"

Blythe swallowed hard and tried to sound calm. "No, he ordered me to."

Raider watched the sudden rigidity of her shoulders and the stubborn set of her jaw. He could imagine his Wool-witch's response to Carson's apparently graceless proposal and it pleased him in a perverse sort of way. He meant to ask more, but her posture and fierce concentration on winding a bobbin of thread said she was now as closed to Raider Prescott as she had been to Neville Carson. And he turned to the door with that gnawing, unsettled feeling in him still unsettled.

Blythe sank into a nearby chair, clutching that bobbin so tightly it hurt her hand. They were holding her for ransom. *They really were pirates and they really were holding her for ransom.* And Neville Carson had no part in it! A bright bubble of irony worked its way up from her stomach into a giggle, then a chuckle and then a laugh. Her shoulders soon shook with soblike tremors of cleansing laughter and she couldn't seem to stop. The absurdity of it. They were holding her for ransom . . . thinking her a spoiled, rich man's daughter . . . she who didn't have a spare corset-lacing to her name!

By the time her laughter finally slowed to occasional tremors, her cheeks hurt and her sides ached. The thought of a ransom note being delivered to her home sobered her slightly. Mrs. Dornly would probably think it was a dun of some sort and tip it into the cookfire, post haste. And if it happened to survive the housekeeper and made it to her father, he would probably stuff it, unopened, into one of his several pockets, where it wouldn't see the light of day for years.

Blythe's last laugh caught and congealed in her throat. Her vivid imaginings assumed that her family was just as she left them . . . at Woolrich House, going on with their lives. And if they were still at Woolrich House and if someone did manage to read the ransom note, who amongst them would have the sense to believe it, much less do anything about it? Her stomach cramped. Even if they read and understood . . . and worried about her . . . there was nothing to pay a ransom with. Nothing at all.

She was being held by a desperate bunch of men who had threatened her life while they expected she would make them rich.

Lord, what would they do to her when they learned she was penniless?!

"Carrick?" Walter Woolrich saw the loyal clerk bearing down on him from the front door of Woolrich House and felt a vague uneasiness, as though he were about to be scolded for something. "My, how nice to see you. What are you doing here?"

"I was to come at two, sir, for the meeting." Carrick handled his worn hat uncertainly and finally chased down Old William and thrust it forcefully into the aging butler's hands. "You don't remember." He stared disgustedly at Walter and pulled him into the scalped parlor. There was only the settee, a small table, and one wing chair left in the great chamber. Even the air was chilled and thin. "Your meeting with Mr. Carson," he prompted emphatically.

"Mr. Carson? What about?" Walter scratched his head in confusion.

"I believe," Carrick huffed, "he has a business proposition to make."

"Oh, bother." Walter plopped down on the settee like a recalcitrant boy, "Business of some sort. Why can't Blythe—"

"Miss Blythe has disappeared, sir, more than a week ago!" Carrick turned a turnipy shade and his sallow cheeks puffed. "Good Lord, man, can't you even recall your own daughter's disappearance?!" He jerked off his spectacles and fished in his pocket for a handkerchief to wipe them. "See here—your daughter is missing, in God knows what peril, and the least you can do is fear a bit for her safety and well-being . . . like a proper father. God knows she's taken care of you long enough . . ."

Carrick would have said plenty more, but the ponderous Neville Carson was just arriving and he bit off his scolding to assume his place behind the settee where Walter sat. Cool greetings were exchanged. Walter called for sherry; Mrs. Dornly brought barley coffee. And after a taste, both Walter and Carson set their cups aside with a shudder.

"It came to my attention, sometime back, that Woolrich Mercantile could do with an infusion of capital, sir." Carson launched directly into the subject of his visit. "Of course, I spoke with Miss

Blythe on the subject and we were near to reaching an arrangement of mutual benefit when she . . . took herself off to her aunt's. Bye the bye, how is dear Miss Blythe enjoying her stay?" His fleshy hand laid over his heart as though to steady it, a parody of wistfulness that sent Carrick into a fit of coughing.

"Oh," Walter's guileless face beamed, "she's doing splendidly." He suddenly began to search his coat pockets vigorously, persuing and discarding vintage pieces of paper onto the floor and settee. "We've just had a letter . . ." He paused and frowned, "Can't think what I've done with it. At any rate . . . she's got a new beau. All atwitter—"

"A new beau?" Carson blanched and rolled forward. "A suitor?"

"Yes." Walter felt the pinch of Carrick's hand on his shoulder and shook it off, "isn't it splendid? Well, I suppose it's not totally unexpected . . . she looks so like her mother. Elise was French, you know, and very blond. Blythe took my coloring . . . except for her eyes—"

"Lovely indeed," Carson said tightly. "But I pray she will not do anything so rash as to accept a proposal before coming home . . . to the bosom of her family. For I, too, long to see her again." His expression did indeed contain longing . . . for a bit of mayhem on her stubborn little neck. "Did she speak of when she'll return?" He pulled a sheaf of papers from his voluminous coat pockets and unfolded them, more determined than ever to entrap the Woolriches in a web of indebtedness.

"Six weeks, I believe . . . or did she mean she'd begin the journey then," Walter murmured as though recalling. "Well, you may be sure she'll be home by Christmas. Blythe wouldn't miss Christmas . . . we always have special jellies and coconut cakes . . . They're her favorites, you know." His smile was as earnest as an altar boy's, and Neville Carson had to accept it.

"Now as to my proposition," Carson glared about for a place to spread his papers and, finding none, spread them on his own knees. "What I propose is something in the order of a loan, Woolrich . . ."

Some time later, after the signing of the papers and the exchange of hands and Neville Carson's departure, Carrick melted into the chair opposite Walter and mopped his beleaguered brow. He'd done his best to influence the terms, but the "loan" Carson had foisted upon Walter Woolrich was clearly one-sided. He reviewed the terms with Walter, insisting that Walter come to the shop himself each day to oversee the business.

"And another thing . . ." He shook his finger at Walter. "Whatever possessed you to say that about Miss Blythe having a beau? Good Lord—of all the things to say to him!"

"Well, I thought . . ." Walter frowned, puzzled. "It would seem a natural thing for a young girl . . . off visiting her Aunt Felicity in Boston."

"Charleston!" Carrick corrected irritably. "Felicity's in Charleston."

"Are you sure? When did she move?"

"Oh, for God's sake, Walter, there isn't any Felicity! Sharpen up, will you? And don't mention 'beaus' to Neville Carson again. He entertains hopes of Miss Blythe himself, and it's not politic to enrage a man you're in debt to."

"He hopes for Blythe?" Walter was surprised. "Well, how splendid!"

"It's *not* splendid; it's terrible!" Carrick was ready to shake his employer soundly. "She loathes him, remember. And the lout has tried to . . . *foist* himself upon her."

"*Foist* himself?" Walter's unlined forehead finally creased with understanding. "Why, the wretch!" Then his puzzlement returned. "Then why are we doing business with him?" Carrick took the question as a hopeful sign that some of this was getting through to Walter.

"Because we're desperate. And desperate men sometimes do foolish things."

"Oh." Walter nodded sagely.

Carrick wiped his face with his hands and made Walter promise to be ready for the shop at eight the next morning. And he warned Walter to wear something suitable for working . . . and to have Mrs. Dornly pack up an extra biscuit for his dinner, since they'd be working all day to prepare the shop for new goods. Walter agreed stoically and pouted when Carrick made him repeat it back, word for word. Walter was ever so glad to see his bossy clerk depart.

When the front door closed, he brightened and started up the stairs to his attic. It was Tuesday and Lizzy was cleaning in

Blythe's bedchamber, having shoved some of the meager furnishings out into the hall. Walter caught sight of himself in her long cheval mirror and turned irritably, thinking it was his clerk dogging his steps.

"Now see here, Carrick—" But the face didn't seem to be Carrick at all. And for a moment, Walter stared. The face looking out at him was familiar. But it had gray hair, a dented Woolrich chin, and a whorl of wrinkles around each eye. Good Lord . . . the realization dawned as he touched himself and saw his action reflected the glass . . . it was *him!*

When in heaven's name did he get to look like this?

The *Windraider* nestled at bay for the next week, reprovisioning, mending and hull-tending while they waited for the appointed time for the ransom rendezvous. It was blessedly dull and achingly dull for a crew used to hard work and frequent danger. More and more their thoughts turned to their extraordinary female captive. When the word went out amongst the lads that the Wool-witch was "off her feed," the lads mumbled amongst themselves, wondering what could be wrong with her. Their concern was piqued by the way she kept to her cabin exclusively, refusing to appear on deck either in afternoon or evening. By the evening of the third day, Raider was tired of being pulled from his duties to monitor the way his men were traipsing past her door on every routine errand below decks. It was as if they were lusting—or *pining*—for a glimpse of her, and it reminded him all too pointedly of his own unsatisfied itch for her.

When he could stand it no longer, he invaded her cabin, intending to haul her up on deck bodily, if need be. He found her curled on his bunk in the sun-heated cabin, with her lacings loosened partway, her hair tied up, and a torn shirt in her lap . . . *his* shirt. Several others, already mended, were laid out neatly beside her and his eyes widened incredulously.

"What's this? What are you—" He strode forward, snatching his shirt from her and trying not to notice the satiny sheen on her breasts, her tantalizingly loosened laces, and the moist tendrils of her half-raised hair that clung to the nape of her neck. "That's Richard's job—mending."

161

"I was only trying . . . Richard needed help and I'm not used to being idle. It's very hard . . ." She paused, veiling the confusion in her eyes and clasping her hands. Actually, she'd noticed the sad state of his shirts while searching for something to sleep in and suggested to Richard that she mend a few . . . to make up for the inconveniences Raider suffered on her account. But she knew Raider wouldn't take such news kindly.

"I'm sure being a 'respectable' lady is taxing indeed," There was an edge to his voice.

"I mean . . ." She absorbed the barb and lowered her gaze to her oil-softened fingers. His unconsciously followed it. "I've always worked . . . in my home and in my father's business. It was Nana's way of seeing that I learned responsibility." The smallness of her voice lodged in his chest.

"Who's Nana?" He put his hands on his waist. "You said something about Nana the other night . . ."

"Nana? Did I?" She glanced at him warily and he thought he saw a flicker of strong emotion in her eyes at the mention of their heated encounter. "Nana's my grandmother. She's been ill for the last year and a half . . . a stroke, they said. She raised me after my mother died."

"And your father? Why isn't he running his own concern?" Raider's challenge unnerved him as much as it did her. Hearing his pondering put into real questions made it seem all the more important. Why indeed would a gentleman, however miserly, let his well-born daughter work her fingers red in a tumbled-down business?

"My father has . . . other concerns." She worded it carefully. "He's never been much interested in the mercantile and he's always hated the mules that our teamsters drive . . ." She shrugged as if to say that was reason enough for anybody.

"Lord, it's stifling in here." An icy trickle down his spine warned that his volatile responses to her unconscious sensuality were churning again. He was appalled at the way she seemed to take hold of his responses whenever she was near. First she took over his cabin, then his crew . . . and now his very self-control. "I'll not be accused of roasting you alive. Up on deck with you, Wool-witch." He reached for her wrist, but she pulled back quickly enough to thwart him.

"No, really, I can't. I . . ." She looked frantically about, realizing he was reaching for her again and that he looked very determined. "My stockings . . . I washed them."

"Again?" He looked down just in time to catch sight of her bare toes being swallowed up by her skirts. "Then go without."

"They get soiled quickly, going without shoes. I can't possibly go barefoot." The tantalizing rub of her loosened bodice made her cover her breasts with her arms. "It wouldn't be proper."

Not a week before, she'd been raving and demanding freedom of the ship and now she wouldn't leave the cabin. The change was so drastic as to be mildly alarming. Coupled with the way she kept her eyes lowered, it betrayed the low state of her spirits and Raider didn't like it at all.

"It's proper if I say it's proper. This is my ship, remember," he growled. "You're going on deck!" He was mesmerized momentarily by the tops of the creamy mounds she was trying to shield from him. Both his throat and his hands on her shoulders tightened. "For God's sake, lace yourself up, wench!" He managed to rip his eyes and his hands from her and to wait by the door. But his gaze drifted back to watch the way her shoulders rounded as she turned and began drawing her lacings tight. Then she pulled a bit of cord from her thick hair to let it fall about her shoulders.

"About time," he muttered irritably when her lagging steps took her to the door at last. He seized her wrist and pulled her along and up the hatchway.

Blythe took every step as if it led to the gallows. She had no desire to confront his snarling, resentful crew again, or to feel their hot, hungry looks pressing her from all sides . . . especially in her bare feet.

But the deck was awash in warm, dusky light and there was a cooling breeze to kiss her flushed skin. There were few crewmen topside, at first, and, seeing that, she calmed a bit. She didn't think they'd try to slip a knife into her with Raider Prescott watching. A few of them did manage to confront her . . . with curious looks. Among them was Spanish Sharky, who gave her a toothy leer that was remarkably like a smile.

But, shortly, word spread that the Wool-witch was out and about, and the lads began to scramble up onto the deck in numbers. They all had excuses for being topside . . . though the

163

sight of grown men snarling at each other over the rights to a scrub brush and bucket strained credulity a bit. They scrubbed and mended and climbed into the rigging to check lashings they'd checked a score of times already. All the while, they watched Blythe's subdued, womanly form . . . and Raider's pensive mood.

Bastian came topsides, too, but mostly to watch Raider watching Blythe as she wandered about the quarterdeck. The burly pirate was discomforted by what he saw. Raider studied and absorbed every nuance of the Wool-witch's posture and mood with a subdued hunger. And Bastian had the worrisome intuition that it was not merely physical. He sidled over to Raider who barely took his eyes from her beguiling shape to acknowledge his partner's presence. And when Raider spoke, his softened tone gave Bastian's vague anxieties a stiff boot.

"She's mended my shirts."

Over the next several days, Blythe was required to present herself on the deck both afternoon and evening, and Raider would accept no excuses, not even when the late September rains came and he had to lend her an oilskin for protection. He never failed to take her arm or clasp her waist to physically impel her topside, but as soon as she reached the deck, he peeled his hands from her and kept a telling distance.

She dreaded each outing, thinking it could prove her last. But she was both surprised and relieved to find a noticeable absence of malice in the crew's attitude toward her. They began to nod or wink in her direction, as if acknowledging her presence on the quarterdeck. And as she relaxed a bit and began to venture further, they sometimes paused in their tasks to offer explanations of their numerous seagoing duties — sailmaking, gun-tending, rigging. It was unnerving to find herself standing in a ring of grizzled, overpowering sea dogs who, only days before, had been eager to slit her throat. She tried not to flinch or cower, but an occasional burst of raucous laughter stopped her heart and sent blood flooding into her lovely skin.

At such times, the lads watched her lift her chin and square her shoulders and were pleased with the way she braved their gruff ways. She had grit, the Wool-witch. That's why they took it to heart when she was occasionally seen on the fo'c'sle, leaning against the railing, staring off to sea as though wishing for a glimpse of her home. Her long hair billowed around her like a maidenly cloak and she had a wistful expression that softened the most grizzled hearts aboard. There was a bit of sadness in the Wool-witch, they realized. It touched a harmonic bit of sadness in each of them, for there wasn't a man amongst them who didn't have a few long-buried hurts himself.

Old Willie returned to duty and he and Richard glowered and shouldered each other aside to escort her and introduce her around. Every man-jack in Raider's crew had a specialty and was eager to show it. Gradually she met them all: Ali, the ships' physician, with his dispensery and herbal stores; Stanley, the ship's carpenter, who demonstrated his carving ability and let her try her hand at his gouges; Fawlkes, the brawny stoker; Black Jimmy, the sooty chief gunner; and Oars, the local lifter whose specialty was "heavy things." The lads grinned and blustered under her straight-forward looks and generally decided she wasn't a bad bloke, for a female with a dry keel.

Even quarry-faced Bosun Deane, whose responsibility included the ship's lines and cables, warmed enough to demonstrate the tying of a variety of seamen's knots and let her try her hand at hauling and tying off a bit of cable. Raider caught sight of her as she strained at the rope and came storming up behind them just as she straightened and shrugged ruefully, saying that it was much harder than it looked.

"Dammit, Deane!" he snarled, just as a capricious bit of wind blew her long, unencumbered hair back into his face. He sput-tered and managed to disentangle the silky web, collecting the eyes of quite a few of his men in the process. "Will you do something with that mane of yours . . . it's a bloody menace!"

Crimson and steaming, she jerked her tresses from his hand and stepped around him irritably, heading for her cabin. Raider was left alone under the puzzled gaze of his men and he scowled and barked at them to get back to doing . . . whatever they were doing.

The next morning, after the lads tried to explain to her the joys of the view from the top of the rigging, Raider caught her climbing up into the netting with them for a glimpse and roared at her, ordering her down. "I'll not have you breaking your silly neck on my ship—and be blamed for it!" He reached up to grab her waist and pull her down, then towered over her, his muscles coiled, his chest heaving. She just managed not to cower. The heat of his ire radiated into her face and she wheeled away, making straight for her cabin.

The lads frowned to themselves. It wasn't like The Raider to get angry . . . much less storm over such trifles. *He* was the one with the gentlemanly past. It baffled them, the way he raved and bellowed at their plucky little captive.

That afternoon, Richard appeared at Blythe's cabin door with an effete, sharp-nosed fellow he introduced as Harry, the ship's barber. Harry had at one time dressed the wigs of the Duke and Duchess of Malmsey . . . before he was snatched from their employ to barber one of Long Ben Harvey's pirate crews. Blythe reddened to realize they were offering her assistance with her hair, but she was not too proud to accept it. And soon, she reappeared on deck with a simple, ladylike coif that pulled her tresses up to the crown of her head, then let them fall in a mass of natural and augmented curls.

The lads commented aplenty on her new look, even Bastian, who was all smiles now that Raider was back to being surly and irritable again. But, if Raider noticed, he gave no sign. Blythe's heart thumped dryly in her chest. He went out of his way to avoid her, she realized, and when he couldn't, he nearly always lost his temper. It was undoubtedly caused by his professed contempt for her respectable status and maidenly state. She lifted her chin and told herself the opinion of a brute pirate shouldn't matter a whit to a respectable young woman. But full brute pirates didn't collect sea shells and love poems and they didn't concern themselves with their captives' hair tangles and work-reddened hands. The thoughts made her feel even more hollow inside.

But, Raider had noticed her hair . . . just as he noticed her every word and every movement. He watched his men gravitate to be near her and watched the way her sensible brand of courage and her unflinching pragmatism charmed their hardened sensibilities. She blushed, but then shrugged off her embarrassment when someone mentioned her bare feet . . . and a pair of roughly crafted slippers appeared outside her door the next morning.

When the bright glare of being on deck constantly made her scowl with a headache, she apologized, assuring them it had nothing to do with their rough company . . . and a ladyish hat with a broad, sheltering brim was produced from amongst their plundered cargoes. And even the other lads stopped stock-still to see the volatile Franco climbing out onto deck with a plate full of chocolate-dipped almonds . . . meant to perk up her flagging appetite. And, as was typical of her, she smiled a salt-melting smile and insisted on sharing them all around.

Their overt courtship of her rare smiles annoyed Raider. Every little kindness they did her grated on his nerves like a steep rasp. But her own gracious and seemingly genuine responses were the worst. They made him snarl and want to shake her . . . mostly to get her attention himself. She ate his food, slept in his bunk, used his things . . . all under his protection . . . and she never bothered to smile at him like that. A shudder went through him. He recognized this awful gnawing feeling in his guts; he'd felt it once before in his life.

It was jealousy. Pure unadulterated envy. The recognition of it made him irritable as the devil himself. Jealousy was a gentle-manly bane, born out of the "respectable" practice of considering women, and their favors, as property to which exclusive rights were bought and sold with marriage contracts. Jealousy was a sickness on a man's soul that put fever in his blood, and Raider had sworn never to suffer its violent chills and sweats again. The women in his world were free agents, encouraged to take their pleasures and seek their fortunes as their charms and cunning allowed. And over the last decade he'd come to appreciate the freedom that their freedom gave him.

Now the Wool-witch was changing all that; dredging up old urges for possession and protection and all the irksome baggage that went with the code of the "gentleman." The worst part of it was, she didn't seem to do much of anything to cause it in him. She didn't simper or flirt or tease, and there didn't seem to be a lazy or deceitful or manipulative bone in her delectable little body. He groaned at the direction of his thoughts, realizing the tension in his loins was worsening.

Dammit—he was supposed to be a privateer, was stuck being a pirate, and was behaving like a cross between a gentleman and a jackass!

Things came to a bit of a head inside Raider several days later, during the issuing of evening grog ration. Old Willie thumped up the quarterdeck steps to Blythe and thrust his own tankard into her surprised hands.

"I figger I owe ye one, Wool-witch," Old Willie grinned wickedly.

"Oh . . . I c-couldn't . ." Blythe stammered.

"Shure ye can," Willie puffed, his eyes alight. "A double fer a double." And quickly Blythe realized he was offering her more than just a noggin of potent, cut rum. The lads quickly gathered on the mizzen below, their faces beaming expectation as they watched this rite of acceptance. They began a drumming chant that demanded a response. It was Raider who provided it.

"Don't be absurd." He strode over and declared above their good-natured thrum, "She'll not drink it. Now take yourselves off." Their drone faltered and was replaced by hushed expectation as Blythe turned to him and lifted her chin boldly. She held her breath and tilted the large tankard to pour every drop of the fiery rum down her throat. When she finished and came up coughing and sputtering, a cheer went up from the lads. Raider snarled something about wasting good rations and stalked away, burning under Bastian's taunting amusement.

But minutes later she swayed and grabbed the quarterdeck railing and Raider, who had been watching for it, muscled between Willie and Richard to spin her around. Her eyes were unfocused and her face was flushed, and before his very eyes she began to slide to the deck. He caught her and lifted her up into his arms. "She's a lady . . . they don't ever drink anything as strong as grog," he growled accusingly at Willie and pale-faced Richard. "Let this be a lesson."

He carried her below under the watchful eyes of his crew and deposited her on the bunk in his cabin. She sat there, weaving and utterly fogged, as he shut the door against curious eyes and came to stand before her with his fists on his hips. "You're drunk, Wool-witch."

"B-b-bly—th-he," she corrected.

"Go to bed, Blythe, and to sleep." He watched the glowing vulnerability of her eyes and the languor of her sweet body and he was suddenly hot everywhere his clothes touched his body.

". . . to bed," she nodded, pulling at her bodice laces and staggering off the bunk, bumping into him. "Haf to get m-my night . . . sh-h-irt." She leaned into him as he supported her and she pointed toward the small stack of things she'd collected on one shelf.

He set her back on the bunk firmly, ordering her not to move while he fetched it. And when he went to get her "nightshirt," he found himself holding one of his own. Lord, she slept in one of his shirts.

She clearly wasn't herself, for she began to remove her dress without the slightest hesitation. Raider was furious with his gentlemanly urge to turn away and so made himself watch like a proper pirate would. But the sight of her body emerging from that worn green woolen and cambric petticoat was pure torture. Her thin, short chemise hid few of her curvaceous delights. His throat closed and his blood began to pound as the outline of her erect nipples drew his gaze and then her curvy hip and the longest, silkiest legs he'd ever seen . . . He was suddenly beside her, without having willed it, and his hands reached for . . . her nightshirt. He tightened all over and forced his trembling hands to cover her creamy shoulders. She snuggled into his shirt, clinging to him for support and gazing at him with a fuzzy, worshipful look that made sharkbait of all his petty resentments toward both her and his men. She couldn't help it if she was irresistible . . . and they couldn't help it if they adored her.

"Th-thank you."

His jealousy and anger melted and slid toward his knees in unison. It left a dangerous void in the middle of him. Until this very moment, he'd never realized the relative potency of small, simple words. Those particular ones had the force of a tidal wave inside him. He had to get out of there. "Go to sleep, Blythe."

But Blythe didn't release him. Quite the opposite; her arms slid around his waist and she rested her cheek against his lean ribs. She wanted so much to touch him and feel his hard warmth and kiss him again. "Ra-aider?"

"Yes?" He was struggling desperately against his erupting need for her.

"I'm not a Wool-wis-sh . . . reall-ly."

He swallowed hard and set her from him firmly.

"I know."

He made himself lower her to the bunk and pull the comforter up over her sweet body. Then he made himself leave her there.

By the time he reached topside, he felt like roiling hot lava inside. He wanted Blythe Woolrich more than anything in his life. And it was clear she wanted him. And the miserable "fates" had decreed that neither of them would have what they wanted.

Chapter Eleven

Two days later the *Windraider* lifted anchor and set sail for the mouth of Delaware Bay. The weather was fine; bright sun and a fair northwesterly breeze. But the mood aboard ship was overcast by the seriousness of the venture they had embarked upon and by their ambivalence toward it. They were to trade their captive for a ransom in gold and silver coin; they'd be rich. But trading the Wool-witch for gold meant losing her and, increasingly, they were reluctant to see her gone.

She didn't seem especially overjoyed to be going home, either. The lads thought it a bit strange that she was so subdued when she answered their comments that they'd soon have her home safely. They assumed her affection for them was to blame and they were partly right. She had grown rather fond of them in the past fortnight. But the bulk of her distress came from her fears of what would happen to her when no ransom was paid and from the prospect of facing Raider Prescott once he learned she was worthless. When he learned she wasn't a wealthy heiress, that all his trouble and inconvenience had gone for naught, he would undoubtedly be furious. And she didn't think she could bear seeing disgust and hatred for her in his handsome face.

Bastian watched Raider and Blythe avoiding each other and couldn't decide whether it was a bad sign or a good sign. Raider was quiet and intense and Blythe was quiet and appealing. She'd softened disappointingly in the last week or so and Bastian wasn't sure if his plan to inoculate Raider against "respectable" life had succeeded or not. And even the lads were being drawn into their somber mood. Bastian was hard put to keep their spirits up by reminding them they'd be rich in three days' time.

On that last evening, when Raider escorted her below, he stayed to light the lanterns and look through his charts. He carried them to the ebony table and spread them out, bracing above them on his powerful arms to peruse them and measure occasionally. Blythe saw the easy movements of his body and the concentration in his striking face, and her throat tightened. She had to make herself look away and tried not to think about how angry he'd be tomorrow at this time. She busied herself putting the few articles and garments she'd collected into a small leather satchel Old Willie had scrounged for her.

"Where are you heading?" Her voice was rather husky.

He looked it up to see her stopped, clutching the dress she'd stitched and barely worn to her soft breasts. He swallowed and looked down at the outlines and curves on the chart, trying hard to focus his eyes on them. He kept seeing her curves instead. "After we collect the ransom?" He tried to sound businesslike and came across rather gruff. "The Danish Indies . . . the Virgin Islands. We have a home base there . . . if a storm or a raid hasn't wiped it out." He looked up at her and, in spite of him, his deep voice softened. "We don't get home much."

Blythe nodded and made herself turn to the bunk so that he couldn't see the unruly flush of her cheeks and the reddening of her lips. She was aching inside. "Well, I suppose in some ways the *Windraider* is your home. You've traveled a lot, haven't you?"

"Yes." He watched the slender curve of the back of her waist, not realizing she could feel his eyes on her as though they were his hands. "Africa, India, the Mediterranean . . . we've seen it all. Bastian says, 'from the Gold Coast to the Barbary Coast,' and it's true. We've gone wherever the winds of fortune have blown us, I suppose."

"I've never been out of Philadelphia . . . until now, that is," she said with a soft little shiver. The air between them was charging, and she felt expectation raising gooseflesh on her skin. But he had refused more than once to have anything to do with her, and it

172

confused her to have him look at her as though trying to penetrate her body visually. "Where exactly were we? I never did know."

"North Carolina . . . the Cape." He straightened, feeling a strong pull in his chest and loins.

"Oh." She barely breathed it. "And these things." She turned her body in profile to him and gestured around her toward the strange creatures and objects that inhabited his cabin with her. "You've collected them from all over the world?"

"Yes." His aching eyes skimmed the sensual contours of her full breasts and narrow waist, her slender neck and straight, round-tipped nose. He wanted to touch her, to take her beneath him and rouse that fire and spirit that he knew dwelt within her.

"And I suppose you have lots of stories, too."

"Lots."

She nodded and, in spite of her, her chin began to quiver. She turned her back to him and found that the shirt she'd been sleeping in was lying on top of the stack. She picked it up, blinking furiously, trying not to cry.

"You can—" His voice was betrayingly husky as it stroked her back, "take that, too. I have others . . ." Then his boots padded softly across the floor and the door closed. When she turned around, she was alone.

Topside, Raider leaned against the railing, staring grimly out to sea. His stomach was squeezing itself in two. Respectable females could inflict the worst kind of pain a man would ever know. He couldn't wait to get her off his ship.

The ransom meet was set at a point of land on the coast at the mouth of the bay. It was a windswept promontory with enough scrubby cover for the dozen men who would stay in hiding during the transaction, unless needed. The *Windraider* was to stand ready for a diversionary full broadside if the signal was given. Longboats were lowered and rowed ashore just as the sun approached its zenith. They had to climb up the sandy embankments to the flat area just beyond.

Raider waved silent orders to send his scouts ahead and then pulled Blythe up with him. Bared blades flashed in the strong autumn sun and the sound of dirt and stones crunching underfoot and the swish of tall grasses were the only sounds. They could see the distant road plainly in both directions, and after a bit of scouting to secure the area, they settled in to wait. Midday, was the instruction Bastian had given in the note and midday meant different things to different people.

Raider seated Blythe on a large boulder and took up a place some feet away, to pace. She shivered inside her short cloak and clutched the small leather satchel on her lap with whitened fingers. She'd never felt so miserable in her life. She watched Raider pace and toss pebbles and make marks in the sand with a stick. Occasionally he strode over to Bastian and she could see them discussing things. Then Raider would look at her briefly, and stride back to his position to pass a bit more time.

Twice in the long afternoon there were false alarms . . . riders on horseback who continued along the road, mostly ignoring them. Bastian and Raider began to conference more and more frequently and Raider stomped and kicked stones and began to glower . . . at her and everyone else. The gulls crying and circling overhead got on Raider's nerves and his mood did not improve when he checked his men in hiding and found some of them lounging on their backs in the sun like drowsy lizards. By the first red of sunset, he was at a slow boil. He'd had a bad feeling about this ransom business all along and now it seemed every intuition he'd had was perfectly trustworthy.

As the sun slipped below the horizon, Raider stormed over and dragged Bastian farther away from Blythe to vent his spleen a bit. But he needn't have been so delicate about it; the whole county could have heard his shouting. Bastian shouted back and eventually both of them turned to stare at Blythe's wilting form and reddened, miserable face.

She watched them approach and swallowed hard, squaring her aching shoulders. The time she had dreaded was here.

"He's probably . . ." her voice cracked humiliatingly and she had to clear her throat to speak above a whisper, ". . . not coming. My father probably won't come."

"Dammit!" Raider ground out as another of his intuitions was borne out. Her life on land . . . there were problems. Then it smacked him between the eyes; she'd known her father wouldn't pay a ransom! "You knew it, didn't you?!" he yelled. She cringed a

174

bit and dropped her head, nodding. "What the hell kind of father won't pay to see his own daughter returned from a desperate band of pirates?! It's unthinkable—"

"Inhuman!" Bastian added indignantly.

"There's . . . no money." She said it so quietly they didn't hear her for their own bellowing. Then she raised her head and repeated it, feeling like she was confessing a cardinal sin. "There's no money, that's why." She braced on her stony seat for the gale that was sure to follow.

"No money?!" Bastian harrumphed righteously. "Don't be daft, wench . . . we sure ain't. Carson told us how rich your old pa be . . . and how tight wi' it. But don't be thinkin' he'll get away wi' this . . ." Bastian shook his finger at her and went on about how both she and skinflint Old Woolrich would be sorry . . .

Raider fought down his own ire long enough to see the way she bit her lip and the way her pale, icy fingers wrung themselves into knots. Misery weighted her shoulders and her head, and when he raised her chin she flinched as if expecting some pain. The hurt and humiliation in her luminous eyes cut through his angry fog. He realized she was telling the truth.

"Dammit, Wool-witch—*no money?!*" He wheeled and paced away, his entire frame trembling with the strain of controlling his volatile impulses.

"You mean . . . there really ain't no gold?" Bastian halted to watch Raider's acceptance of it and began to fear it might be true. "No gold fer ransomin'?"

"None," Blythe whispered miserably, watching Raider's broad back and knowing when he turned toward her again, it would be with either disgust or fury in his handsome face. She couldn't bear to look.

"God." Bastian looked a little sick, but he didn't stay that way for long. He quickly turned on his partner. "Well, Raider, what're ye goin' to do about it?"

"*Me?*" Raider wheeled on him, eyes blazing. He glanced at Blythe's mortified face and was angry with Bastian, furious with her stupid, penniless father, and outraged at the whole lousy lot that fate had handed a baron's younger son! He was angry with everything . . . and somehow all his wretched misfortunes came into focus on troublesome, desirable Blythe Woolrich. "Me—I'm

175

going back to the ship . . . to sort this mess out!"

He grabbed her leather case in one hand and her wrist in the other and strode furiously for the banks. Lads came popping up out of the bushes; the yelling had wakened them. They looked to Bastian for direction and he blustered and waved them angrily toward the beach, striking out after Raider and their erstwhile ransomer.

Blythe burned, feeling their eyes on her. She heard the shocked muttering of the crew and stumbled as she tried to keep up with Raider's furious pace. He didn't even break stride when she stumbled and she knew it was a bad sign. When they reached the longboats, he threw her leather case into the bottom of one and grabbed her by the waist, hoisted, and plopped her down on one of the hard wooden seats none too gently.

He bellowed orders to shove off and punctuated them with selected oaths and snarls. Soon they were under way and the lads put their backs into it, hauling at the oars while exchanging puzzled, angry looks.

Blythe was withering from humiliation inside. She couldn't raise her head, but she knew they were staring at her and she could even separate the feel of Raider's gaze from the rest . . . It was the one that burned. She bit her lip and blinked furiously to keep from releasing the tears that collected in her eyes.

Raider had said she was more trouble than she was worth . . . and he'd been absolutely right. Thinking she was a wealthy and refined lady of leisure, he'd given up his cabin, his wonderful food, even his shirts to her. He'd insisted she do no work—not scrubbing nor mending. He'd given her oil for her hands and provided clothes for her—after a fashion. In short, she'd fared better as his captive than she had in her own home. Aside from the occasional threat of mayhem or murder, she'd never been treated so well, not by anybody. She'd defied him and gotten into numerous scrapes and generally been a lot of trouble and now he had nothing in return. She was worthless . . . to her family and now to Raider and his crew. They would have nothing to show for three weeks of turmoil aboard their ship . . . and she was *responsible*.

The deck was alive with confusion as Blythe was thrust into a swinglike contraption and hauled aboard again. She couldn't look at Richard or Willie or Clive or the others who pressed close for some explanation of what had gone wrong. Raider was soon beside her, taking her arm and propelling her toward his cabin, out of their sight.

Her leather bag hit the polished floorboards of the cabin and the door slammed behind them, and Blythe still hadn't gotten up the courage to even look at him. She didn't want to see the anger and cold disgust in his face. He jerked her around to face him in the dusky light, clamping his hands on the tops of her arms and squeezing as if to force a response from her.

"I want to know . . . all of it," he commanded in a deathly quiet rumble that rattled Blythe more fully than bellowing would have done.

"There just . . ." her voice quivered slightly, "isn't any money. My father isn't rich . . . and even if he were . . . he probably wouldn't know what to make of your note . . . if he read it . . ." He gave her a little shake to make her go on and she squeezed her eyes together and tucked her chin a bit more, so that he was glaring at the top of her head.

"What do you mean . . . he wouldn't know what to make of it, *if* he read it?"

"He's . . . not very sensible," she admitted in an anguished whisper.

"*That's* an understatement," he growled, "leaving a mere wisp of a girl to run a business—" The full meaning of the weathered door and sign and the empty shelves of the Woolrich Mercantile Shop suddenly became clear to him. "God. A *failing* business! What is he . . . mad?!"

"Yes—*no!*" She finally turned her burning face up to him and the pain in her luminous, crystal-rimmed eyes stabbed him sharply. "He's not really daft—he just forgets where he is . . . and doesn't think about things like food and firewood. But I always managed. I ran the shop until the British came and we'd have been fine if . . . they hadn't been so awful. They kept coming around, promising us trade if I'd let them . . ." Her shamed gaze fled his, but her meaning was all too clear to him. The British apparently had wanted what every other red-blooded male who ever laid eyes on her wanted . . . including him. "And what little trade we had, turned away . . . so I had to sell things . . ." Every

177

word sank into place in his burning brain, adding pieces to the puzzle that had bedeviled him since that very first glimpse of her, dressed like a serving wench . . . and working like one.

"Sell things . . . ?" he bit out as the reality of it sunk into him. "Your father is daft and you were left in charge? Surely there was someone more suitable . . ." All his once-vanquished prejudices and notions of propriety and respectability were rearing their loathsome heads in him.

She shook her head and dislodged a bit of that salty prism from her eyes. She had to catch her breath in gasps. "No—really. Nana is still ill, she can't walk . . . and Mrs. Dornly, our housekeeper, won't even face the butcher, much less a band of pirates . . ." She ground to a halt as her throat clogged with internal tears.

"Well—somebody could have damned well sold a few more things to see you brought back from a band of cutthroats!" Raider barked hoarsely.

"But there . . . isn't anything else to sell. The silver and the furniture and the chandelier in the front hall . . . I . . . its my fault." The tears really began to roll, veiling the unbearable sight of his contempt. "I was responsible . . ."

"Responsible?" He braced, combatting a very liquid feeling in the middle of him. "For what? For having a crazy father? And a sick old grandmother and a lily-livered housekeeper . . . and for having randied up the British army—" He shook her a bit with each incredible layer of guilt he encountered in her. She really meant it—she felt some crazy sense of responsibility for her wretched family's misfortunes.

"I *am* responsible . . . I've always been responsible. Nana taught me to be," she insisted desperately, trying to wrest free. "And I always am. I could have married Neville Carson and had enough money . . . except, I retched when he kissed me—and he didn't like it . . ."

"God."

"So it's my fault we're poor and you don't get your ransom money—"

"Morgan's Bloody Liver!" he thundered, fighting a volcanic urge to either throttle or embrace her. He jerked his hands from her as if she burned him and watched her sway as she shrank from him. She was the most infuriating, confusing female he'd ever had to

178

deal with in his life! His turmoil was completed when great crystal tears rolled down her scarlet cheeks.

"I'm so sorry . . ."

Raider's chest was afire and his ribs were too small to contain the confusion swelling in him. The "gentleman" and the "pirate" in him were enraged in a pitched battle for control of his responses. Rather than do something he'd regret with a vengeance, like taking her into his arms, he turned and stalked blindly out, slamming the door behind him.

He stood in the passage, trembling, on the verge of a cataclysmic eruption. They'd kidnapped her and degraded her and threatened her very life . . . and she was standing there apologizing for being penniless and virtuous!

How in hell was he going to explain this to his men?!

Raider found his crew assembled topside on the quarterdeck and mizzen. From their somber mood, he gathered they'd already been apprised of their misfortune. Before he could open his mouth to explain what he had learned, Willie, flanked by Spanish Sharkey and Clive, thumped forward on the quarterdeck.

"Cap'n," Willie wetted his puckered lips and drew a deep breath, "Bastian Cane been tellin' us about th' Wool-witch . . . that she ain't rich after all . . . that ye kidnapped the wrong wench."

Raider blanched and scoured his crew with a murderous look for sign of his scapegoating partner.

"Me an' the lads," Willie hurried on, seeing a potent calm settling over Raider, "we talked it over. Decided to a man . . . put it to votes, we did." He turned to the others who nodded and muttered agreement. Raider coiled inside as Clive took it up.

"We done *re-linquished* our shares in 'er. Give 'em up . . . that means." He looked to his mates for support and received it universally. "E'en old Bastian Cane—he give his up, too." Clive waved to the railing where Bastian glowered irritably and fastened his eyes on his well-polished jackboots. "We couldn't stand fer no harm to come to the Wool-witch, Cap'n. We figger ye'll know best what to do wi' 'er, seein' ye was respec'able yerself, oncest."

Raider rocked back on one leg and ran his hands up and down his face. Lord, they had it bad . . . the lot of them. He looked about him at the faces of his tough, stringy crew and was torn between pride and alarm. They apparently had a heart, these lads, down deep, and somehow the Wool-witch had found it. It was little consolation that he wasn't the only one she'd managed to soften up.

He muttered something about their decision making things easier, but he didn't believe it for a minute. What they'd done was set all responsibility for her squarely on his shoulders . . . and heighten his already excruciating dilemma. What was he going to do with her?

He laid orders to stand out to sea in a southerly direction and the lads scrambled to get the *Windraider* underway. He braced at the stern, trying desperately to think, while he watched the dim outline of the land growing smaller.

Blythe lighted a single brass lantern and settled gingerly on the edge of the bunk. Life just got worse and worse. She had never felt so low as she did now . . . so utterly worthless. Some secret little part of her had hoped against hope that someone in the Woolrich household might have sense enough . . . or care enough . . . to seek help when they got the ransom demand. But her worst fears were confirmed.

Now she faced an ever bleaker future. At best, she might persuade them to set her ashore where she might make her way home, somehow . . . someday. But if her family hadn't been turned out of the house, and if she somehow managed to go back to the business as it was, what kind of life could that be? She would have Neville Carson to contend with again, if he still wanted her after she'd been held by pirates. Her reputation would be in tatters, and her very respectable name was one of her chief allurements, where Neville Carson was concerned. No one would believe she'd been held by a handsome pirate captain and not ravished. She could hardly believe it herself. Her shoulders rounded and she slipped her arms around her waist, feeling especially empty now that he'd invaded her thoughts again.

In some ways Raider Prescott was the worst thing that had happened to her in this whole unthinkable episode. She would never be able to get the feel of his hard, vital body, his delicious, bone-melting kisses out of her mind. She'd never know the completion of his tender loving or glimpse the fascinating man inside him . . .

Raider came through the cabin door half an hour later, in somewhat worse condition than when he left. All of his clear thinking had just given him an abominably clear view of his wretched problems, thus sharpening his inner conflicts. Logic dictated that Blythe Woolrich had to go; that much was certain. She revealed too much of the man he'd kept hidden inside him for years and she had potentially disastrous effects on his men, softening the hard edges that made them dangerous in a fight, diluting their grittier, bolder urges with the milk of human kindness. She simply made him and his men think and act in ways that were counterproductive to a career in seagoing mayhem.

But, dammit—he was enough of a pirate to want what he wanted and let the consequences be damned! He wanted the Wool-witch. Never mind all this bilge-rot about respectability and vulnerability and being suckered and protecting himself. He wanted to feel her sweet body writhing hot and eager beneath him, wanted to hear her love moans as he invaded her woman's heat, and wanted to feast on her cherry-sweet lips and satiny breasts until he'd had his fill. He wanted somehow to brand her very flesh with his possession, to mark her as his in a way no other could.

This obsession with her was scored deep into his veins; it pulsed in his very blood. Just once he wanted to bash logic and experience aside and to take what he wanted . . . give the heedless, pillaging pirate inside him full rein . . .

"Did you tell them?" She slid from the bunk as he stopped before her, planting his fists on his waist. His jade eyes were intense in a way she hadn't seen before. They sent a hot shiver down her back.

"They know."

"I suppose they were angry." She felt his heat across the short distance between them and it made her heart thud faster. She found herself absorbing the curves and angles of his sun-bronzed features and the striking symmetry of his chest and shoulders, storing them away for when . . . "What will you do with me now?"

"They gave up their shares in you, every man-jack of them." He made it sound like an accusation. "They took a bloody vote and surrendered their 'shares.' " His stormy gaze heated considerably as it drifted over the curvaceous territory they'd just ceded to him.

"Then," she swallowed with difficulty, feeling that peculiar ache in her stomach that she connected unerringly with him, "does that mean I'll be set free?"

Raider looked at her heart-shaped face, the maddeningly perfect curves of her lips, the dark, feathery fringe of her lashes and felt his temperature rise precipitously. Set her free . . . when he was doomed to remain bound in perpetual need of her? "Not exactly," he growled huskily. "There's a little matter of shares still outstanding."

"Someone's shares are still—" she choked, afraid to ask whose.

"Mine." His voice had dropped to its lowest register and vibrated all her peaks and extremities. His jade gaze began to glow with the need she had built in him, but he made no move at all.

"I see," she wetted her lips unconsciously. But she didn't see at all. What did he mean? Her heart began beating painful staccatos. She needed desperately to feel whole and warmed and wanted. Just once, she wanted to shove responsibility and duty aside, to wrench from life's unyielding onslaught some of the pleasure that had been so rare in her life. Just once she wanted to know the deep tenderness and fierce, steamy passion of a man's love . . . of Raider Prescott's love. It would probably be the only loving she would ever know . . .

"You've been put to a lot of trouble, Raider Prescott, with nothing to show for it." She veiled her eyes to hide the turmoil in her. He had avoided her like the plague these last days. But could he look at her like this if he really didn't want her? "A smart pirate, like a smart businessman, would cut his losses, I suppose."

"I suppose," he concurred, sending his gaze down the column of her throat, across her creamy chest to those firm, delectable globes he'd seen every time he closed his eyes to even blink for the last three weeks. Her skin flushed, peach-like, in eager response to his visual caress.

"Then perhaps you should . . . take what booty you can, Raider Prescott." The minute it was said, she made the odd discovery of just how much like her dotty father she really was. It was mad to even think it much less utter it, but she had no desire to unsay it. "There's only one thing of value I have left. It only makes sense . . . that you should take it . . . for your 'share.'"

Raider could scarcely believe his senses. When she raised her head, the centers of her eyes were darkening, her lips were parted and reddened. Her breath came shallow and quick and she sought his eyes with hers. He felt those burnished golden disks turning him inside out, ripping his male urge for possession out by its roots.

"Love me, Raider Prescott . . . love me this once." Her voice was a seductive whisper, buoyed on a current of raw, unabashed hope.

Raider was paralyzed for a moment by a scorching confusion. In her own very sensible, responsible way, she was making the decision for him, for them both. She stood there, flushed and vulnerable, offering him that which his inflamed being craved . . . herself . . . the discovery of her intriguing passions. Flame roared up from his loins, heating and expanding his chest, sending shock waves through his shoulders and trembling his arms.

He came alive and jolted forward, taking her head between his hands, tilting her lips up to his. His mouth came down on hers with the fierceness of his exploding need, but quickly gentled to caress and coax, to claim the reins of her budding passions with firm and tender hands. Then he lifted his head to stare down at her face, and his thumbs stroked the silky skin of her temples. She opened her eyes and smiled, a wistful, desirous sort of smile that made him flush even hotter and beckoned him to claim more.

Hot and eager, he hardly knew where to send his hands first. They slid down the sides of her neck and across the sleek lines of her shoulders, where they paused to caress. Her eyes closed and her lips parted as she absorbed the sensations and swayed against him. His arms flew around her to bind her to him, to press her cool sweetness against his burning flesh. And he plunged into the honied offering of her kiss, tracing her lips with his tongue, stroking the liquid velvet of her mouth as he invited her to explore him as well.

Instinctively, Blythe followed his lead, sensing that what he did to her would also please him. She clasped his lean ribs against her

breasts, feeling her nipples burning with remembrance and anticipation. Her hands molded and slid over his powerful back muscles, exploring, reveling in his strength, his latent male power.
Strange melting weakness invaded her legs as he pressed against
her belly and sent his hands down to cup her buttocks, lifting her
against him, holding her as he rubbed his aching hardness against
her.

Blythe's throat closed as he ground seductively against her and
she suddenly wanted to move against his body that same way, to
press all her tingling, sensitive parts against him and feel him all
about her. That craving for the feel of skin on skin she had felt
before with him recurred, magnified now and unquenchable.

She clung to him, opening to his kisses, wanting to feel his
hands on her. His tremors of eagerness migrated inside her frame,
giving expression to her need as well. Suddenly he contracted
around her, lifting her back onto the bunk, where she landed on
her knees at the edge of the soft bed. He tugged on the cords that
bound her hair into a ladylike coil and unraveled its thick cloud
about her shoulders, running his fingers through it, shivering as
its silky strands coiled about his wrists, claiming, caressing him.

Only then did his fingers trace the rim of her bodice to tug at
her laces. She was perfectly still, nestled before him on her knees
as his bronzed fingers slid between her clothing and her skin. His
hands followed the lines of her body, enchanting her garments so
that they seemed to follow of their own volition. She held her
breath as both her bodice and chemise slid down her shoulders like
a caress that raked the points of her nipples.

Opened and bared to his sight, to his touch, she shivered and
opened her eyes. His broad chest filled her sight, so close she
could feel its warmth radiating into her bared breasts. He reached
for her, cupping her breasts, tantalizing her tight coral-colored
nipples with his thumbs, circling her slender waist and sliding his
hands upward to her breasts, then her shoulders.

"You are so beautiful, Wool-witch," he murmured huskily.

"I am?" Her golden eyes found his and she blushed hotter. His
palms were rubbing over her nipples in erotic circles. No one had
ever applied such a word to her before. *Beautiful* . . . It echoed and
rumbled, then rang through her in celebration. *Beautiful,* he had
said. She was desired, wanted. Raider Prescott really wanted her!

Then he planted a knee on the bunk beside her, pulling her fully into his arms and lowering her beneath his hard chest. A breathy sigh escaped her, infused with the fulfillment of small desires. This was just what she had craved, this divine weight on her body, this blanketing heat that flowed from him into her and came to coil in her depths. He seemed to know just where she wanted to be touched and to caress her in ways she hadn't even known to desire.

With skillful movements, he slid her clothes down over her hips and willowy legs. She gasped when he grasped her ankles and slid both hands up her shapely calves and over her knees to reach the sensitive silk of her inner thighs. His nails raked the contour of her curvy hips and trailed across her flat belly to her waist. Fever rising, he kicked his boots off and peeled the clothes from his body.

His lean, muscular frame came down on hers urgently, melting into her welcoming softness, merging with her surprising strength. Her arms lapped around the taut, rippling muscles of his broad back and she opened to his kiss, stroking his tongue, feeling a primal urge to take more of him inside her. Her woman's hollow throbbed with a strange, hot expectation as he took first one nipple into his mouth, then the other, suckling, teasing them. Shocking hot currents of sensation flowed between their skin, a prelude to more intimate exchange yet to come. He ground his hardened shaft against her hip and rubbed it across her belly as he slid his weight atop her.

It seemed natural for her to meet his arching movements and just as natural for her to allow him to slip between her knees and fit himself against that part of her that burned with exquisite anticipation. He kissed and caressed her, rubbing the peaks of her breasts with the crisp golden furring of his hard chest, making her wriggle with delight. And he rumbled an animal laugh, doing it again and again, pushing her higher on that spiral of pleasure that seemed unending.

His hand reached the satiny warmth of her woman's flesh and she startled at the bold intimacy of it. But soon she surrendered to the swirling eddies of delight his fingers stirred in her and she shuddered and arched against his hand, wanting more.

He saw the love flush of her breasts, felt her body reaching for his and relaxed the reins on his need for her. He crushed her soft breasts to him and sought the moist heat of the entrance of her body with his pulsing shaft.

Breath caught in her throat as he parted her flesh by slow degrees and began the joining that would complete what fate and desire had begun between them. She felt him surge and withdraw, over and over, feeling herself yielding, stretching to accommodate him. Despite his gentleness, the ever-increasing invasion of her untried body caused her to coil with tension. Attuned to every nuance of her response, Raider eased and stroked her face and kissed her tenderly.

"I won't hurt you, Blythe, trust me," he murmured against her swollen lips as he stroked her cheek. "Lovely Blythe, trust me . . ." His deep, mesmerizing rumble continued, pouring endearments into her ear, speaking his desire along the arch of her breast, and dropping adorations into the darkened pools of her eyes.

Her fears dissolved in that tantalizing stream of breath that bathed her body. She had come this far, had yielded her intimate secrets to him, and now she would give him all that remained. She pulled his head down to blend their mouths as he would soon blend their bodies. Enwrapped in the deep passion of her answering kiss, he completed their union with a strong thrust that sent shivers of painful pleasure through her, stopping her heart.

Chapter Twelve

All existence skipped a beat and, with that rest, began again. Pleasurable warmth radiated from the steamy fullness in her loins. She felt him move inside her and held her breath at the burning pleasure it caused. Her hips arched toward him and his hard muscles contracted around her, approving, encouraging her movement.

Their bodies began to move in instinctive rhythm, thrusting, absorbing, giving and receiving. Heat built between them with each stroke and Blythe felt a mysterious pressure building in her loins. She rode astride a tightening spiral of pleasure that carried her higher, faster, toward some unknown end. And suddenly Raider plunged into her, rasping against her tender centers of pleasure and thrusting powerfully, commanding her fulfillment with exquisite finesse. Everything inside her exploded—like Chinese rockets flinging thousands of burning crimson and blue-white sparks—like shooting stars searing through her body. She arched and shuddered, clinging to him, gasping and quivering. He tightened convulsively around her and the awesome spasms of his own conclusion joined him to her in a way neither could have foreseen, nor would understand for a while to come.

Blythe couldn't move, could still scarcely breathe some time later when his ragged panting calmed and he stroked her dewy face, nuzzling her dampened hair from her ear to kiss it. "Are you all right, Blythe?"

"Wonderful . . . or dead," she whispered, turning her face to his and getting lost in the loving glow of his expression. His lips were swollen, his eyes heavy with the languor of spent desire. He was beautiful, enthralling, arousing. And she was a little frightened by what he'd caused to happen to her. It felt like her whole body had burned in a storm of fire and now only numbed, smoldering heat and smoke remained.

"Then you're certainly wonderful, wench, for you're most certainly *not* dead." He laughed softly and caressed her waist, feeling a last pleasurable tremor race through her. He withdrew and settled on the bunk beside her, drawing her tight against him and covering them both with the down comforter that had somehow been pushed aside. Bending to brush her lips and her tightly budded nipples with reassuring kisses, he felt her breathing halt. He raised to stare into the brushed gold of her eyes in the dim lanternlight.

"I didn't hurt you?" he rumbled, a brief doubt flitting through his carnal confidence. His hand caressed her shoulder and the side of her slender throat and she shook her head.

"Am I supposed to . . . Is it supposed to be like that?" she whispered.

When he relaxed against her and nodded with a crooked little grin, she seemed so dazed and astonished that anxiety stirred among the ashes of his cooling passions.

"You . . . didn't like it?" God forbid!

"It was . . . wonderful," she murmured, veiling her eyes.

"But . . . what?" His anxiety mounted as he watched her subdued reaction. "Tell me what's wrong, Blythe."

"It's just so . . . powerful." She'd hit upon the exact word to describe the effects of his loving and the cataclysm it wrought inside her. "I never imagined it would be so . . . earth-shattering. It's like a typhoon inside your very body. Heaven—no wonder everyone tries to protect young girls from it . . ."

Raider melted with relief and chuckled, drawing her into his gentle embrace. "Not every woman experiences it quite like you do, my little wench. Some scarcely notice it's gone on."

"Oh?" She flushed and looked away, frowning and trying to make sense of what he said. How would a woman *not* notice something as potent and earthquaking as that? For some reason Neville Carson came to mind and she thought of his harsh, repulsive kisses and the punishing grope of his fleshy paws. Imagine something as intimate as this with a brute like . . . She turned to look at Raider's handsome face and flushed at her own naïveté.

"Oh." She began to understand. Raider Prescott's loving was probably as different from Neville Carson's, from any man's, as his kisses were. "Then it's you, isn't it?" she declared softly, still too overwhelmed to manage any proper discretion. "You know how to make that happen in a woman . . ." She flushed deeply at the smile in his inscrutable jade gaze.

"Me? I wish I could claim so, golden eyes. But honestly, I think it had more to do with you." He thought of the parade of oddly faceless females through his long, amorous history and of their diverse reactions to his well-practiced loving. None of them had responded to him like his Wool-witch had. There was something different about her touch, her embrace. She reached through her innocence in all trust, to explore, to give herself with an eagerness that enthralled him. And her own special kind of loving reached inside him somehow, deepening and intensifying his own response.

"You mean it was me. I did that?" She seemed a bit horrified by the prospect, and he laughed and brushed her lips with his, grinning

"Lucky you, Wool-witch. There aren't many 'misses' who learn the way to paradise the first time out. But, I'd like to think I helped a bit . . ."

She struggled up onto one elbow and stared at him with very wide eyes. "You've had . . . done this with others . . ." The thought was somehow comforting just now. "They did it, too, didn't they? I mean . . . they felt shooting stars inside and exploding rockets and like they were dying, too . . . didn't they?" He came up onto his elbow, facing her. His grin muted to a tender smile and he caressed her cheek.

"Is that what it was like for you, golden eyes?"

Her throat was squeezing shut and she nodded.

"Well, it was like that for me, too," he murmured. "It was marvelous. And right now I honestly can't remember how it was with any other woman. I don't want to remember. It was something very special, Blythe." He kissed her on the tip of the nose.

189

Her "respectable" upbringing was rearing its ugly head, he real-ized, and he wasn't about to let her sink into a quagmire of guilt over her stunning introduction to physical loving. "Now stop worrying about who was *responsible* and if you did things properly. And just enjoy lying here with me."

He pulled her into his arms and lay back on the pillows, cradling her against his hard body, luxuriating in the softness of her breasts snuggled against him, in the comfort of her cool, satiny hip against him. He threaded his fingers through her hair to cradle her head against his thudding heart.

Relieved by his candid admission, Blythe let the hard warmth of him melt her anxiety. She nuzzled the hair of his chest and the faint but definite scent of coconut teased her, filling her head as the rest of her senses surrendered to exhaustion. "It really was nice, Raider," she sighed.

"Um-m-m," he rumbled contentedly, "I thought so, too."

The first gray light of dawn was invading the cabin when Blythe roused from her dark, contented sleep and shifted lan-guidly in the circle of Raider Prescott's hard-muscled arms. All that had passed between them in the last evening was instantly in her recall and she tensed, thinking of her brazen behavior. But for the life of her, she couldn't bring herself to regret it. Now she knew both the delicious tenderness and the full, soul-jarring fury of Raider Prescott's loving. It was breathtaking . . . and a bit intimidating.

She watched the sculptured male features of his face as he slept, and sighed quietly. He was utterly beautiful and his kisses and his loving made a woman feel extraordinary. No wonder he'd made hundreds . . . *thousands* of feminine conquests. *Thousands-and-one,* she corrected herself, feeling a small sinking in her chest. To ward off further thought, she slipped gingerly from his grasp, peeling her damp, reluctant skin from his by slow degrees. When she was free, she rolled to the side of the bunk and gained her unsteady knees. The cool air brought gooseflesh to her skin, and as she hurried across the cabin to her leather satchel, her lower abdomen ached dully with the movement.

She pulled out her makeshift nightdress and drew it around

her. Raider's voluminous shirt left her lower legs bare, and she glanced down at them self-consciously. She'd hurry and wash and dress before Raider awakened.

But she was already too late. Raider watched her toilette from beneath lazy lids, savoring her graceful movements and brief, tantalizing glimpses of her sweet flesh. The sight of her in his clothing started a familiar warming in his loins. The unbuttoned shirt opening slid over and against her cold-tightened nipples, and as she stretched and bent to wash, her lush bottom was outlined like a ripe peach beneath the fabric. She propped one shapely leg on a chair and then the other, rubbing them thoroughly with her wet cloth, and his body came to life at the sight of them . . . long, tapered, silky. And suddenly he recalled the feel of them, entwined with his own on intimate union.

Pushing up on the bunk, he dragged his fingers back through his sun-streaked hair and slid the comforter from him. With her back to him, intent on her bathing, she didn't hear his soft approach.

"Oh-h-h!" She startled as his arms snaked about her from behind and pulled her back against his bare frame.

"Do you have any idea how perfectly enchanting you are of a morning? I've never thought of bathing in a cold basin as an erotic act before." He dropped kisses and nibbles along her ear and down the side of her neck. In spite of her embarrassment, her head swayed to give him fuller access. And in the process, his gaze fastened on the creamy globes so alluringly half hidden by his former shirt. His hands slid up from her waist to capture them. They were cool, and their pliant weight was delicious against his fingers.

"Please," she had to wet her lips and swallow to speak, "I have to dress . . ."

"Not yet, Wool-witch, it's too early. Come back to bed."

Anxiety began to collect in her throat. "No, really . . . I've rested enough." Why was he touching her like this again, pressing her with his male hardness?

"But you've had a taxing night, wench," he laughed softly as his hands closed meaningfully around her breasts. He turned her with the force of his body and nudged her toward the bed, but she veered stubbornly toward the table. He sat down abruptly in a nearby chair and pulled her between his very bare knees. "Then, come let me see you, Blythe." He was grinning, showing those white, regular teeth in the dim light.

"I would think . . . you'd seen enough . . ." Blythe went crimson, fastening her gaze on the square panes of the nearby window. She could feel his eyes like a caress on her bare breasts. His intimate comments and touches roused a variation of anxiety in her, but something in her didn't want this delicious bit of closeness with him to end.

"Not nearly enough." His hands dislodged her loose shirt from her shoulders, and it floated down her body to the floor, leaving her bare to his hands and his hot regard.

"Do you know how beautiful you are . . . how desirable?" The barely perceptible shake of her head brought a wry smile to his face. She apparently wanted him to tell her. "Well, you are," he assured her. "Lovely smooth shoulders—"

"They're much too broad," she protested with a shiver.

". . . and firm breasts with these tight rosy nipples that beg for attention . . ."

"They're too large . . ." She closed her eyes and tried not to wriggle when he kissed the tips of her breasts gently and gave them a playful lick. ". . . they make my corsets bulge . . . unseemly much." He laughed at her mode of resistance and sent his hands down to cup and caress her buttocks.

"Your rounded bottom, Miss Woolrich, is unparalleled." He paused, watching her, teasing, "What? No protest?"

"I . . . don't know much about bottoms." Good Lord, what was she doing, standing naked, under a man's hands, discussing such things?!

"Well, you should make a study of yours sometime . . . it's really superb. I know all about bottoms, you see." There was a beguiling glint in his jade eyes, and when she managed to glance at his face, he waggled his brows wickedly. It was all Blythe could do to stifle her surprised laugh.

"Where was I? Ah. Your legs. Good God, woman, what legs you have . . . all the way up to your rosy little bottom. So sleek and firm . . ." His hands stroked down the outsides of them and returned up the sensitive skin of her inner thighs until he neared the patch of curls at their tops. When she jolted back, he grabbed her wrists to stay her. She stiffened and went crimson, and even in the dim light he could see the flush of her skin.

"You'll have to give up blushing like that, wench . . . blushing is for maids . . ." She sputtered and he laughed, caressing her bare waist in lazy circles that coaxed her to stay. "And you've a curvy little waist," he continued his excruciatingly personal inventory, "and a sweet little belly . . . with a maddening little button in the middle." He pulled her closer and nipped her belly with his teeth.

She gasped and he turned a mischievous look on her, then buried his nose in her belly and tantalized her navel with his tongue. He stopped abruptly. "I don't suppose you know about belly buttons, either. Well, there are two kinds; those that poke in and those that pooch out." He suddenly stood up pointing at his own belly. "Yours is just like mine . . . see?"

Before she thought, she looked down and there was his turgid manhood, staring straight at her. She sucked a sharp breath and recoiled and he had to catch her yet again.

"Sorry, I forget you're not used to men." He grinned and sat down, pulling her embarrassed frame down onto his bare knees. "It's easy to forget things around you, golden eyes. You set me on fire." He felt her trembling and began to realize that her maidenly blushing was real.

"Come, let me hold you, wench." He pulled her forcibly across his lap and released a ragged breath as her cool, silky bottom settled against his rigid shaft. She stiffened and shrank from it, and he wrapped his arms around her and pulled her back. His eyes caught hers, then flicked downward meaningfully. "Just pretend it's not there."

Blythe stared at him with disbelief, and he smiled a smile so purely adorable, so utterly honorable, that she felt all her resistance sliding. The feel of his strong arms around her, the warm admiration of his gaze, the magic of his touch; all claimed her. And when he turned her face to his and kissed her, it was a wonder of a kiss, as gentle as spring rain and as powerful as summer thunder. Her hands found his shoulders and she embraced him, pressing her cool breasts against his chest as she opened to his kisses.

Heat welled inside her as his hands began to move up her

spine and over her hips, thighs, and breasts. Soon she was turning liquid inside again, feeling that strange burning hollow opening between her legs. Rubbing the tips of her breasts against his chest only deepened these delectable tortures and she was soon directing his hands to her breasts to assuage their eager burning. And then Raider felt the helpless undulations of her hip against his shaft and knew the time had come.

He rose with her in his arms and placed her on their bed, going down beside her, wedging her halfway beneath his chest. Through the mad swirl of her senses she realized where he was leading. He wanted to do *that* again. She could feel her body preparing for it, burning with liquid heat, aching for the delicious feel of his hard shaft inside her, stroking, exciting her secretmost places. But it would mean suffering that violent, overwhelming firestorm that charred her insides and she choked at the prospect.

Raider felt her stiffen and sought her eyes. They were clouded with tension and he paused, caressing her and sifting his fingers through the dark curls at the base of her belly.

"I don't think I want . . . to do *that* again," she whispered, bracing.

"I'm going to love you, Blythe, to pleasure you. Remember how good . . ." Her icy shiver smacked a bit more of pleasure's glaze from his senses and he saw traces of fear in her darkened eyes as well. "I thought you liked . . ."

For all her eagerness and natural affinity for it, Raider realized, Blythe Woolrich was new to pleasures . . . of almost any kind. Intent on introducing her to the full delights of physical loving, he'd unthinkingly led her into a maelstrom of desire and release that she was totally unprepared for. He should have seen it, felt it . . . reined his need and proceeded with care. And instead he had behaved like a bloody pillaging pirate . . .

Raider stiffened as he felt her drawing away. He cursed the wretched casualness with which he'd come to approach sex and cursed himself for planting that fear in her . . . fear of her own stunning sensuality. What a clumsy bastard he was, not to have seen it. He knew more about women than that. It suddenly stung him; he hadn't wanted to consider her a woman . . . at least not like the others he'd known and pleasured . . . and he didn't want

194

to think about why. Now there was nothing for it but to lead her down those same harrowing paths again, to prove to her that loving wasn't fearsome or fatal . . . even if it meant seducing her trust.

"You don't have to do *that*, if you don't want to," he refused to release her. "Loving can be done in many ways, Blythe. It's like music . . . many tempos and volumes, no two exactly alike." He caressed her firm-tipped breast and kissed her gently. "And I'll stop any time you want, golden eyes."

Blythe was lost. Music . . . it was like *music*, he said. It was true; the way it flowed and trickled and built inside her, it was like music in a way. He seemed to want it . . . to want her like that . . . and his desire for her seemed enough to compensate whatever turmoil he wrought inside her. When his mouth lowered to hers again, she gave consent in the sweet yielding of her kiss.

This time, Raider accepted the reins of her passions with great care, kissing and caressing her body, leaving no part of her unadored. He nibbled her knees and hipbones, caressed her small waist, and nuzzled her elbows and nipples. By the time he braced and slid his weight atop her, she welcomed it, craved it.

"Open for me, golden eyes." He breathed so softly into her ear that the meaning seemed transferred without words at all. "Spread your silky legs for me . . . let me touch you."

Soon his big hands were tantalizing, rousing her to frenzied heights of longing. She writhed and arched against him, wanting more, clasping his buttocks boldly, seeking the completion of his hot shaft within her.

"Do you want, me Blythe?" He arched above her, trembling and straining for control. Her eyes closed, and she nodded helplessly. He kissed her gently and obliged with breathtaking slowness. When he had finally embedded his full length in her sweet, steamy flesh, it came as no surprise to him that she wanted even more.

With white-hot eyes, Raider watched Blythe undulate beneath him, around him, reaching for him, and he allowed her to initiate the rhythm that brought them together over and over. A rosy flush of response invaded her breasts and face and his muscles quaked, burning with the need to hold back.

She whimpered and gasped, tortured deliciously by the mounting surges of pleasure in her. Out of the churning hot mists of pleasure came that final thrilling rise, that crescendo, bearing her upward, soaring.

"Please . . . oh, please," she rasped.

"Are you sure, golden eyes?" He fought the roar in his own head to collect her tortured response.

"Yes—oh, yes, Raider—*please* . . ." She writhed and clasped him with her thighs, hungry for the release his hard body could give her. In embracing him, she embraced her own sensuality. And in that fierce and tender longing for union with him, her womanhood was completed.

Raider's movements became exaggerations of loving, slow and sweeping. Twice he carried Blythe to the edge of some great precipice and retreated. And the third time, the charm of his loving tumbled her over the edge into a bright, slow-spinning galaxy of delight. She contracted all around him and he buried his face in the hollow of her throat and followed.

It was wonderful! Icy streams of fire licked outward from her center, triggering her muscles, releasing the vast overload of her senses in languid spurts of steam. And she soared, feeling joyfully whole . . . at one with him, with all of existence. Then like the sweet smoke of an applewood fire, exhaustion seeped through her and she smiled into Raider Prescott's sultry gaze.

"It *is* like music," she whispered, reveling in the throb of heat that lingered in her loins. "It was just like . . . a harp." She touched his cheek and brushed his swollen lips with her fingers. In all her life, she'd never felt such joy, such deep, enthralling pleasure in both body and soul. And big, tawny, fierce Raider Prescott was to credit.

"So it is, golden eyes." Raider came to rest on the bed beside her, cradling her dewy form gently and stroking her damp, tangled hair. God, he felt strange inside. He could hardly breathe . . . and it was wonderful!

Blythe hugged him tightly, sated, but somehow still craving him. She wanted to absorb all of him she could in these precious moments. She lifted his hand and kissed his fingertips, one by one, drinking in the musky sweetness of their mingled scents on his fingers and the raspy feel of his legs against her toes.

"You have such gentle hands, Raider." She pressed his palm

against her breast and sighed when his fingers tightened around her. "You collect shells and silk fans and read Latin and love poems and you speak like a gentleman. How did you ever get to be a pirate?"

There was a pause in Raider's breathing, and she sought his eyes. He looked at the warmth in her face and shrugged with a wry, relieved little smile. "Bad luck, I guess. No . . . *fate* is probably more like it. I was smuggling wool across the English Channel to escape the strangling duties the Crown levied on us . . ."

"Us?"

"The farmers and herders on our lands," he explained. "My family . . . had land. Anyway . . . I trusted the wrong person and found a revenue cutter bearing down on me one night. I was arrested and might have hanged but for Bastian. He was pirating in those days and seized the cutter just after the cutter had seized me and my crew. He made me his navigator straightaway and we did so well, we soon had two ships and began a lucrative bit of pirating, operating in tandem. Then Bastian's ship was sunk by the British some months back, taking a healthy cargo with it." He shifted and his eyes came back from those remembered vistas to settle on her.

"I was always in trouble with my father, embarrassed my family. Got sent down from Oxford . . . twice. I was the black sheep of the lot, you see. Never mind that his other sons cheated him blind and gambled and plowed the serving wenches nightly; it was me always got caught. Fate, I guess." There was a lingering trace of bitterness in his acceptance of it, and Blythe stroked his shoulder.

"Your father . . . was he important?"

"He wanted to be," Raider declared, shaking free of his memories. "Ambition is considered a very respectable excuse for doing calloused and even dishonorable things."

"Honor," "ambition," "Oxford" . . . it began to make sense to her. "He was a nobleman, wasn't he . . . your father?"

Raider looked at her, wondering how she knew. He nodded.

She smiled a sleepy smile into his puzzled expression. Anybody with good sense could see he was born at least a prince. Snuggling her cheek against his chest, she murmured, "Don't worry, I won't tell anyone."

There was a long, warm silence as she fought the pleasurable fatigue within her. If she fell asleep, she might miss something with him.

"Raider?"

"Um-m-m?" he was feeling the delicious pull of exhaustion himself.

"Tell me about your rhinosterust . . ."

Raider watched Blythe tumble into oblivion, some time later, and was strangely unable to join her there. He was tired, his body at peace, but he was far from rest. He honestly didn't know when he'd felt so good. He watched Blythe's sleep and pushed the cover down to look at her delectable body again. She was simply the most desirable woman he'd ever seen . . . a notable distinction, considering he'd seen royal-born courtesans and society debutants and whole harems in just such a state of undress. None of them had captured his passions the way Blythe Woolrich had, with a tantalizing blend of innocence and eagerness, of virgin reluctance and wantonness. None of them had managed to raise his wrath and jealousy and passion and tenderness with a single sweep of their lashes the way his lovely, infuriating Wool-witch had.

That was probably the key to it, he realized with the last bit of logic still left to him in passion's burning swath. She made him feel them all . . . all at once. She roused every primary emotion he possessed every time he set eyes on her. Like right now . . . she was stirring his loins, swelling his pride, goading his curiosity, warming his tenderest feelings, and rousing a fierce bit of protectiveness in him . . . and all she was doing was breathing. No, he realized, she was doing one more thing . . . she was trusting him.

Suddenly he felt like jumping and running and leaping and shouting . . . But he slid his arms around her and wrapped her gently in a soft, warm cocoon of covers before he bounded from the bed. He stretched, feeling his muscles humming and his blood racing pleasurably. The sun was up fully, streaming in through the gauzy silk over the windows, and the rosy light seemed a reflection of his own inner state.

He washed and dressed slowly, pausing often to stare down at her dream-brushed cheeks, enjoying this new spot of warmth in the middle of him. He stepped out into the passage and caught Richard going about his morning duties. He ordered the lad to find a large wooden tub and bring it to his cabin, then to fetch fresh water from the galley . . . plenty of it, a whole tub full.

". . . and see that it's good and hot."

"What ye want a big old tub of hot water for, Raider?" Richard couldn't imagine.

"A bath." Raider saw the shock in the lad's face and straightened irritably. "Dammit, if I want her to have a hot bath, she'll have one!"

Richard nodded, wide-eyed, and hurried off. But Raider was left standing in the passage, scowling. That little warm spot inside him was feeling a bit of a draft. He set his jaw and climbed up the hatch stairway, topside, determined to let nothing interfere with his excellent mood.

But from the minute he set foot on the mizzen, he felt their eyes on him . . . Bastian, Old Willie, Clive, Spanish Sharkey, and the rest. They watched his movements, scrutinized the quality of his shave and the combing of his hair, examined the carriage of his shoulders and the manly sway of his sensual stride . . .

To a man, Raider's crew knew where he spent the night. And it wasn't long before they knew he'd ordered a bath for the Wool-witch afterward. A *bath*. He'd gone and done it . . . bedded the Wool-witch. They'd relinquished their shares to him, trusting him to do what was right and "respectable" by her. And he'd gone and bedded her. They honestly didn't know what to think . . . since they hadn't heard a scream nor a whimper issue from the cabin.

But Bastian knew. One look at the satisfaction just oozing from Raider's frame, coupled with the Wool-witch's womanly softening of late, and he knew exactly what had happened. And he was furious! All his hard work, his brilliant planning . . . gone to rotten, stinkin' bilge!

What a bloody disappointment she'd turned out to be, the Wool-witch! Raider was perfectly right . . . a bloke couldn't count on a respectable female for anything . . . except trouble. She'd wrecked a perfectly good ransom scheme by turning out to be damned well penniless. And as if that weren't enough; she'd gotten Raider promisingly riled and outraged and she'd gotten him randy and miserable and she'd defied and inconvenienced him at every turn . . . and then she'd gone and ruined it all by letting him into her bed! Damn and blast! Bastian had his work cut out for him now . . .

"Well, well," Bastian sauntered over to Raider with a gleam in his crafty eyes, "ain't you in fine fettle this mornin'."

"Never felt better," Raider hung one hand on a mizzen tackle cable and leveled an expectant look on his partner.

"Well," Bastian drew a deep breath and set a subtle course as he tugged at his wide black belt, "get 'er outta yer system lad. That be the only thing for it, I reckon. Have at it and stoke 'er up till ye've had˙yer fill."

Raider's eyes narrowed slightly. "It's none of your damned concern, Bastian."

"Now . . ." Bastian rubbed his slightly bristled chin and stared off into the morning, "ye be wrong there, Raider. I got interest in whatever concerns my partner . . . and the good of the crew. When ye bedded 'er, ye made 'spoils' into a 'female companion,' lad. And by th' *Articles* there ain't none of them allowed aboard the *Windraider*."

"She's not 'spoils,' Bastian," Raider's voice was exceedingly calm, "nor a 'female companion.' She's different."

"Well, after last night, I guess you'd know about her 'differences,' wouldn't ye?" Bastian pursed his mouth stubbornly. "Still, she's been naught but trouble—pure *bad luck*—since she come aboard. Ye were right about *wool*, Raider. A jinx, it is . . ."

Raider's face was an unreadable slate as he watched Bastian's maneuverings. He hadn't shipped and fought and wenched with Bastian Cane for nearly ten years without picking up on a few of his tricks. Bastian shifted feet and fiddled with his belt buckle and turned a bit toward the railing, watching Raider from the corner of his eye.

"What're ye plannin' to do with 'er, Raider?" he came out with it. "The lads'll be wantin' to know. They already know ye bedded 'er . . ." A slight pulse in Raider's clenched jaw muscle let Bastian know he'd struck a nerve.

"I . . . haven't decided yet."

"What's to decide? Ye either set 'er ashore at first landfall or ye sell 'er off . . . to recoup some of th' loss—"

"Dammit, Bastian, I'd hate to draw a blade on you." Raider grabbed Bastian's sleeve and his raw, steely whisper sent a shiver up Bastian's spine. His jade eyes were as cold as polished stones.

"Lord, Raider," Bastian took a horrified step backward, "you're thinkin' about keepin' the wench!" Raider's silence exploded Bastian's concern. "Damn and blast . . . it'd be pure madness!" He stomped away and then back, gesturing furiously. "Ye seen what she already done to the lads . . . has 'em steppin' and fetchin' like lap dogs. Come a fight, she'll be faintin' proper or beggin' ye not to. Afore long, she'll have ye turnin' the other cheek with Long Ben . . . an' bendin' the knee to keep the peace. It's what respectable females do, Raider, ye said so yerself! They worm an' wheedle in and start changin' a man . . . *or a crew*. Bindin' ye up, stranglin' ye till ye cain't breathe proper nor think straight. And she already started on you, lad. A *bath*, Raider! Good God— there's the bloody proof!"

"If I decide to keep her, Bastian, I'll keep her, dammit!" His voice dropped to a menacing rasp. It was galling to hear his own long-cherished prejudices spewed back at him. "You bloody well don't have a thing to say about it. Back off!"

"Somebody's got to talk sense to ye, Raider." Bastian's square jaw jutted, itching for combat. "Good God—she stays an' ye'll soon be putting frillies on th' gun ports . . . and rippin' out the magazine fer a damned nursery! Ye said yerself, a drop o' seed never falls fallow in a respectable tw—"

"Dammit, Bastian—I've heard enough!" Raider was trembling with the containment of raw fury. His big hands clenched in front of Bastian's square nose, and it was all he could do to keep from flattening that intrusive feature that was always being stuck where it didn't belong. "I'll decide myself . . . and if I hear another word from you, I swear I'll set you ashore—stark naked!"

Bastian blanched and stiffened, after a seething silence, wheeled and strode forward and down to the gun deck. Raider was left on the quarterdeck, his body braced and quaking. He churned with confusion. All the peace, the joy with which he'd embraced the day were gone. But it wasn't completely Bastian's fault. He was partly to blame himself, shoving away responsibility and duty to take the pleasure he craved . . . consequences be damned.

He'd wanted the Wool-witch so badly that he'd been willing to forget all else. And as he stood there, staring out at the dancing, beguiling waves, he realized that he'd only made things worse by taking her. He searched his big male frame and found need for her curling around every sinew, embedded in every muscle, pumping through every vein. He knew now the sweetness of her yielding, the sensuous joys of her lush body, the startling depths of her response. And he wanted that closeness with her again . . . and again. Lord, he swallowed hard, he might not ever get over wanting it . . .

The possibility was appalling. In her own inimitable way, she'd roused his feelings, gotten under his skin, carved a niche for herself in the middle of him. Suddenly everything Bastian had said to him — everything he'd said himself a million times — came back to him. Respectability meant smothering and stifling under somebody else's rules. It meant duplicity, falseness, in the interest of preserving outward propriety. It meant giving up things . . . pleasures and honesty and freedom . . .

Blythe Woolrich was every bit as "respectable" as she was lovely, and sensual and giving. She had lived by those rules, accepted them, upheld them, even while being crushed under the load of duty and responsibility they inflicted on her. It was just the way she was; earnest and dutiful and oh so vulnerable. And — randy swine that he was — he'd taken advantage of her vulnerable state to claim her in a way no other had, or ever could again. Sooner or later she'd realize that. And no matter how beautiful or enthralling their loving, sooner or later her respectable background would rear its ugly head to proclaim what had happened between them as base and sordid . . . sinful. And the joys he'd introduced her to would only hurt her. The gold in her beautiful eyes would turn to lead. She'd see herself a ruined woman.

Lord. He blanched and his stomach cramped violently at the thought. He'd *ruined* her. And here he was, thinking about keeping her aboard his ship or carrying her off to his island home . . . to serve his wretched need for her delectable flesh . . . his reckless craving for her sweet, innocent loving. And how long would it be before she bore the shame of a bastard child . . . living among hardened, dangerous men . . . abandoned for interminable periods while he was at sea . . . never knowing if he would return. He never knew himself when he would encounter that blade or lead ball with his fate inscribed on it.

"Dammit!" he thundered, wishing some blessed bolt of lightning would part the clear blue sky and end his miserable ramblings. But the sea just kept her timeless lapping and waving, gently mocking his violent wishes. The sun just kept shining, illuminating the darkest corners of his long-shaded heart. And he knew.

He had to send his Wool-witch home.

Chapter Thirteen

Blythe had watched Richard trundle in and out of her cabin, bowed under buckets and buckets of hot water, and could scarcely believe her senses. Yet when he finally nodded at her bundled form on the bunk and withdrew, there really was a large wooden tub sitting in the middle of the floor, steaming cozily into the cool morning air.

She slid from the bunk, gathering her covers about her and tiptoed over to test the water. It sent wonderful eddies of warmth up her arm and her cover slid. She hurriedly collected a bit of Raider's shaving soap and slipped into the hot, soothing water, groaning with raw pleasure. It had been months . . . seemed like years! . . . since she'd had a full tub of hot water for bathing. Oh-h-h . . . it felt wonderful! And as she lay back in the water, feeling it caress her skin, invade her with its warmth, she knew who to thank. The gift was part of the giver, she'd heard it said, and this delicious heat, this pleasurable, intimate flow over her body felt just like Raider Prescott to her.

His eyes, the strong angles of his smooth-sculptured face, the intriguing curl of his sensual mouth—she luxuriated in them as she melted and steeped in his gift to her. The flow of the soap over her pliant contours reminded her of his caresses, of the gentle urgency of his need, of the rousing pleasure of his lips on her skin. And suddenly she was warmed, happy in a way she hadn't been . . . ever.

Raider Prescott wanted her . . . just her. It had nothing to do with duties or responsibilities or even logic. He just wanted her because she gave him pleasure . . . and possibly a bit of joy. To be wanted just for herself . . . it was a marvelous thing. Respectability and obligation, those stern masters had nothing to do with what had passed between them in the night. She had touched him because she wanted to, and he had freely given her pleasure—tutored her gently in the delights of her body. He'd conquered her fears, and warmed and filled both her body and her heart in ways she never expected to know. He had called her beautiful . . . and made her feel that way. And the steamy pleasure of this morning gift to her seemed an echo of all he'd given her before.

Twice she turned Richard away at the door, taking a sinfully long time to bathe and then to dress and to coif her hair. She slipped into her new velvet dress, the one she'd made from the goods in Raider's chest . . . the one she'd somehow felt was too fine to really wear. The beautiful jade color recalled Raider's steamy, admiring eyes, the softness of the velvet was like the caress of his lips. She sighed, giving her front lacings a last tug and then, wrapping her arms about herself in a blissful hug. She was floating . . . like a bright cloud.

Richard brought her thrice-warmed tray again and she accepted it with a sincere apology for having put him off his morning routine. The warmth of her glowing smile would have made him forgive her anything, and he stammered and set about clearing away her bath. The food was wonderful, the tea was divine, and she was soon finished and straightening the bunk, as was her morning routine aboard ship.

It was just before noon when Raider stepped inside the cabin and Blythe rose to meet him with an unmistakable, womanly glow in her lovely face. "Good morning." She sparkled inside. "I apologize for taking so long with my toilette. But I think you're partly to blame. The bath was wonderful, Raider. Thank you."

He merely nodded, trying not to drink her in with his eyes and failing miserably. She was perfectly beautiful, adorable . . . desirable. "That's . . ." he had to clear the huskiness from his throat, "that's the gown you made?" He gestured lamely to her lace-trimmed velvet. His eyes were drawn to the square cut of her fashionable bodice, cut low and rimmed with stiff Belgian lace. Layers of softer lace dripped from her elbows and lapped over her breasts and sleeves in sinuous, painstaking appliqué.

"Yes." She twirled about to let him see it from all sides. "Do you like it? I had to make do for stays . . . but the lace was so lovely, I couldn't help using lots of it." She came to a swirling stop just before him, her eyes sparkling, her cheeks flushed, her lips parted. She was inviting him to touch her.

"You're . . . very talented with a needle." It was a very nice compliment, actually. But, combined with the stiffness of his carriage and the subtle tension about his mouth, it sent a wave of confusion through her. She stepped back, smiling uncertainly, and clasped her hands together.

"Well," she managed, "I've had plenty of practice . . . I suppose." She watched him walk toward the bookcases, pause, and turn back to her. And the aimlessness of his movement spoke clearly that there was something else on his mind. His troubled mood invaded her on the air they shared. Tension and restraint rose inside her. Everything that had warmed and relaxed in her began to cool and coil. He was different, somehow.

Raider stalked toward his chart drawers, then paused and turned back to her again. The pirate in him had absconded, the swaggering coward, leaving the gentleman to sort out the aftermath of his lecherous plunder. Lord how he hated this . . .

He had obviously come to say something and was having a hard time saying it. And suddenly she knew that whatever it was, it would be awful for her. Her heart stopped briefly, then gave a violent lurch and began to pound. Her mouth was drying and her hands were getting colder. This was dread; this awful feeling.

"I've decided . . ." he began, and had to clear his throat again. "I've decided to send you home, Wool-witch." And once begun, he had to continue, to tell her why. "It was all a terrible mistake, your being abducted in the first place. It would be sheer folly to compound the mistake by keeping you aboard any longer than necessary. The men understand and agreed; that's why they

206

relinquished their shares . . ." He saw the darkening of her eyes and the deep blush of her skin and weathered a full broadside of self-loathing.

"Send me . . . home?" She could scarcely say it. "But I don't have—" She bit back the part about having no home. She honestly didn't know whether she had a home or not. She stared at his bronzed face, his closed expression, and all the liquid warmth of the night just past began to freeze within her. A terrible mistake? Loving her . . . touching her in that gentle mesmerizing way . . . that was a mistake? He hadn't really wanted it? Was that why he wouldn't look at her?

"It was all wrong, all of it."

All of it. It hit her with gale force. He regretted it . . . touching her, saying she was beautiful, sharing himself and his past. He regretted loving her. She stood, devastated, unable to even react to the volume of pain that was thundering through her.

"I was wrong to touch you, Wool-witch. If I could take back last night . . ." God help him, he realized, he wouldn't take it back if he could. That's the kind of selfish bastard he was. He wanted those aching sweet memories of her, welcomed the haunting pain they'd cause him every time he closed his eyes.

Blythe's great golden eyes grew luminous and dusky with hurt. It was all he could do to keep from pulling her into his arms.

"It wasn't your fault," she spoke softly. The odd look in his eyes and the scowl that followed just confirmed his displeasure with those revealing and intimate events. She was curling, dying, little by little, inside. "I . . . was to blame. I behaved unseemly. Sometimes I'm not very . . . proper. I didn't mean to make you feel obliged . . ." He watched her taking it onto her shoulders, accepting just one more responsibility for the terrible things that happened to her . . . for his dishonorable treatment of her. And his hands felt for the hole that was blown through his midsection.

"No . . . I should have known better. Dammit, Wool-witch! I didn't mean to do that to you . . . to hurt you or take anything from you." He took one step toward her, and his knees locked and froze, preventing forward movement. "God help me—I never meant to send you home ruined." His fists clenched, his stomach was turning over, pouring hot bile through his lower half.

Ruined? She stared at him, her shoulders rounded as the awful label settled on them. Was that what she was? Ruined? He had touched her gently and loved her body and brought her the first real pleasure she'd known since childhood. Could that *ruin* a woman?

Proper society clearly said so, for "pleasure" and "ruin" were inextricably linked in the standards Blythe had been raised to uphold. By all she had always held respectable and honorable, she had been degraded, ruined. How ironic that it took a pirate who claimed to despise proper society and its false notions of respectability to remind her of it. And how strange that the loss of her "respectability" seemed to matter far less than the loss of Raider's desire for her.

"You mustn't . . . feel responsible for my ruin." When she spoke he made himself look at her, but he couldn't make himself meet her crystal-rimmed eyes. "People would probably think the same of me, even if you'd never touched me. Since I was abducted . . . they would naturally think the worst. At least I'll have . . ." Her voice caught, and she had to look down and swallow to free it. "It wasn't so bad . . . really. Was it?"

The quiver of hurt in her voice was both a plea and a punishment. It cut him like no blade could. He lifted his eyes to the precious gold-and-crystal prisms that were like windows to her soul. She was asking him, needing to know that not everything between them had been a lie. And he had to tell her the truth . . . he had to give her that much.

"No, golden eyes. It wasn't bad . . . not at all."

The pull between them was like a tidal force. Raider took a step forward before he caught himself and his whole body trembled with the need to hold and comfort her. But he dared not touch her. He knew if he did, he wouldn't be able to let her go. And, damn him, he'd done enough cursed damage.

The stiff silk of her new petticoat rustled as she took a step toward him, too. But he made no further move toward her, and his face blurred so that she had to close her eyes. Tears burned

208

down her cheeks and she heard him moving toward the cabin door. She opened her eyes to find him looking at her, his face dark, his feelings in shadows, shielded from her. He nodded and was gone.

Blythe just stood, looking at the door. She had hoped he might kiss her . . . one last time.

That afternoon, the lads watched their Wool-witch step out upon the mizzen, and they paused at their labors to scrutinize her lovely frame, her flushed skin, her lowered eyes. She was dressed in her limp green woolen again, with her hair pulled up into the sweet, womanly coif they'd helped her learn to create.

She smiled tentatively at first one, then another of them. When they scowled at the shame that flushed her cheeks, she took it as a condemnation of her penniless and ruined state and lowered her head, hurrying up to the quarterdeck to be out of their way. She'd already seen that same look in Richard's eyes . . . disappointment . . . tacit censure. She honestly couldn't blame them for it. She'd deprived them of a fat ransom and then had thrown herself at their captain like a . . . shameless hussy.

They watched her trying to make herself small on the quarterdeck, and watched her stiffening when The Raider appeared. They watched the way her eyes seemed glued to the deck and saw the way The Raider towered powerfully over her, and they exchanged irritable shakes of their heads. It was obvious that he'd *taken* his share of her. How else could it have been with a wench as sweet as their Wool-witch?

Bastian watched it all with a keen eye and sauntered over, a welcome intrusion in the strained silence between Raider and Blythe. "Well, Miz Woolrich, ye'll be goin' home . . . I expect ye're right pleased." He stuck his thumbs in his belt and smirked insolently at Raider's dark expression.

"I am . . . grateful," Blythe mumbled, just managing to look up into Bastian's brawny, pleasantly wicked face. His raffish eye patch was flipped up, and Blythe impulsively reached up to tip it down. Her eyes were glistening. "It really does look rather good on you, you know," she whispered.

Bastian looked at her lovely eyes and her strained face and felt a strange downward lurch in his middle that left a yawning opening in his chest. He set a hand to massage his heart and stood a bit straighter to compensate for it.

"I . . . I've given it some thought . . ." She addressed Bastian, since she couldn't bring herself to look at Raider or to speak to him. "Since you're sending me home . . . there might be a way to recoup some of your losses."

Bastian was suddenly all ears, and Blythe could see Raider coming to attention from the corner of her eye.

"You could maybe send another ransom note . . . to Neville Carson. I'm likely going home to him anyway. And if I wrote him myself, beg—asking his help, perhaps he'd pay to see me returned. And you'd have someth—"

"*Damnation!*" Raider flinched as if stabbed.

"Now wait, Raider—" Bastian grabbed his shirtsleeves and tussled him back a step, "the wench be makin' a hogshead o' sense! She be headed fer home . . . an' likely fer the altar wi' him anyways. Why not let him pay what her pa couldn't?!"

"It's the only sensible thing, really," Blythe choked, forcing her crimson face up to Raider's scathing glare. Everything in her seemed to be melting under the heat of his unmerited ire. "He wanted to marry me . . . before . . ."

Before she was abducted . . . she finished it in her thoughts . . . before her reputation was ruined . . . before she asked Raider Prescott to take his "share" of her. She looked up at Raider, and her aching heart climbed into her eyes. Raider felt like someone had fired a thirty-two-pound smasher through his gut.

He shuddered under Bastian's restraint as a quick and nasty vision of Blythe's delectable nakedness wedged under Neville Carson's heaving bulk flashed before his mind's eye. Imagine those greasy, bloated paws squeezing her, his twisted lusts invading Blythe's sweet flesh . . . He growled and broke Bastian's hold, only to seize a deadly grip on the throat of his partner's shirt.

"No, dammit!" he thundered. "I'll not pander her off to the highest bidder—selling her into legal whoredom—" His voice dropped to a graveled rasp. "You've done some low things, Bastian Cane . . . but that's the bilge-filthy lowest thing I ever heard you come up with!"

"I—but, I didn't—" Bastian sputtered, caught in Raider's exploding fury.

"She's going home, dammit . . . home to her family . . ." Raider shook him a bit for emphasis, "on the first damned ship we come across that's northbound! Do you hear?! And I'll pay her passage myself—damn your eyes!"

After a stunned silence, Raider released Bastian and Blythe was already halfway to the quarterdeck steps at a run. He turned to follow her with his eyes and realized half his crew was stopped scowling at her teary-eyed flight. When she was through the hatch and out of sight, they transferred those dark looks to him and he stared them down, sending them back to their duties with pursed lips and clenched jaws. Then he turned away from Bastian's indignant glare to order Clive up into the crow's nest to scout for signs of a sail.

He stood at the stern railing watching the *Windraider*'s wake and feeling big and useless and empty. He'd defied the fates to take a sweet bit of loving to hold inside him . . . and now he'd be made to pay for it. A man just couldn't escape his fate.

The armed sloop *Cherabim* wound her way northward on a packet run from Charleston to New York. Though not a navy vessel, she had been pressed into British service for coastal runs. She carried a contingent of redcoat officers and military dispatches and a bit of "appropriated" goods and stores that were bound for the British commander in New York. She was sailing east of her usual course because of a bank of storms that hugged the Chesapeake and because of the real threat of French ships as they neared the Delaware.

Her quarry-faced captain called for his glass the minute a sail was spotted on the misty gray horizon. It was a lone sail . . . no flag. He watched as the ship seemed to materialize from the gray clouds and black sea, his eyes narrowed and his stance tightened. She was a dark bit of bark with a flash of white. And as she tacked about, he caught her draft and layout. She was a frigate . . . a good-sized one. A lone frigate . . . possibly forty-two guns. Then his eyes widened with recognition.

"God A'mighty!" he roared as she bore down on them, looming ever bigger in his sights, "I know that bark: it be the *Windraider!* Hoist th' mainsheet full—" His barking orders roused the lounging redcoats topside. "I ain't got time fer ye now, gents," he growled, and barreled them aside on his way to unlock his armory, "I got me a fight on me hands . . ."

Raider watched the *Cherabim* unfurling sail and ordered "parley" flags run up the bow jackstaff. There wasn't need for more sail yet, he thought, they could probably run her down with their present sheeting. He turned to Bastian with a grim look on his face and handed him the glass.

"She's a packet, northbound. She'll do." And he sent word to Blythe, via Richard, to gather her things, that her transport home had arrived.

Blythe packed her few belongings and stood in the middle of the cabin, looking about her with dry, sad eyes. She was trying to assert her most sensible self, telling herself Raider was right to send her back. It had been nearly a month and her family needed her desperately. Even if she wasn't respectable anymore, she still had responsibilities. And it was no good wishing them away . . . or wishing for things that could never be. She thought of her home for the millionth time. Heaven knew what she'd find when she returned to Woolrich House—if it wasn't Carson House already.

It was actually a relief to be leaving. These last three days had been terrible indeed. Raider avoided her, the lads watched her with a subdued air of disapproval, and she couldn't make herself eat or sleep. The only one who still spoke to her was Bastian . . . and his delight at her leaving was a bit too open for her to mistake his garrulous behavior for any sort of kindness.

She pulled her short cloak around her shoulders and paused to give the rhino's horn a last, wistful pet. Soon she stood on the gray, chilled quarterdeck with a lump in her throat. She watched the packet ship drawing closer and listened to Raider's deep, resonant orders booming over the *Windraider*'s deck. The gray and damp seemed like walls that caused echoes to linger . . . like memories that weighed on her heart.

Raider wouldn't look at her . . . none of them would, it seemed. And she couldn't blame them. Because of her kidnapping, Raider and his crew were considered pirates now, and they couldn't take the chance on sailing back into the bay to take her home themselves. They had to buy her passage to New York or Philadelphia aboard another ship . . . another bit of inconvenience and expense. She'd brought them nothing but trouble.

Trying not to look at Raider was hopeless. Her eyes surrendered and drifted over his broad back and long, booted legs, absorbing every part of him they could. In a short while she'd be gone, and she'd probably never see him again . . . except every night in her dreams. She squeezed her eyes shut and turned her head away.

"She ain't heelin' to." Bastian strolled over to conference with Raider. "I know she seen us at this range." Concern was etched in Bastian's brow.

"She will." Raider's strong jaw was set at a grim angle, and he ordered a bit more canvas let out. He raised his glass and scoured her for signs of identification. " 'C' — something," he muttered, ". . . no flag."

"How many guns?" Bastian wanted to know, squinting toward their quarry.

"Looks to be no more than eight or twelve . . . and four swivels topside." Raider continued to scrutinize the *Cherabim*'s distant shape, and something glimpsed fleetingly through that strong lens suddenly set his nerves on edge. He scoured the image for some understanding of what had tweaked his sense of alarm, but there was no sign of anything amiss. He lowered the glass and stared at Bastian expectantly.

213

Bastian felt his look and understood it. He raised nis nose to the wind, then turned to Raider with a dusky flush to his now serious face. "Trouble, Raider. I smelt it. Darkness and sulphur on the wind . . ."

Darkness and sulphur . . . gunpowder to be more exact. And whether his uncanny nose actually smelled it, or he had sensed it otherwise, Bastian was right. The *Cherabim* was priming her guns, preparing to defend herself. And when Raider put the glass to his eye again, that unrecognizable flash that had sent a tremor of alarm through him became a steady beacon. Red. The red of coats . . . British coats, a mass of them.

"Redcoats." He lowered the glass. "Damn and blast. It would have to be a bloody British packet." He flicked a glimpse at Blythe's paling face and knew a moment's indecision. Send her off in British clutches? She hated the British. It would be so easy to find fault with the ship . . . to use it as an excuse to keep her a bit longer. But that instant of second thoughts stung him to even greater resolve.

"Run up a Union Jack," he barked to his bosun. "We'll be British, if it suits us."

And as they closed the distance between the ships, Raider took the standard precaution of ordering Black Jimmy and his gunners to stand below at their stations and set his top gunners at the light swivel guns mounted at the railings, fore and aft. Tension ran like a current through the men, and Blythe watched, alarmed, as knives and blades of various descriptions appeared in hands and belts and a few eye patches appeared over healthy eyes.

Raider's graceful frame set firmly by the wheel and he ordered the topgallants lowered and the flying jib run out. Keen-eyed and fiercely intense, he monitored every sway and yawl, every nuance of wind and wave, correcting, checking their progress on the sloop . . . now known to them as the *Cherabim*. She was running from them, there was no mistaking it. Raider barked for Boson Deane to hurry with the flag, and it was soon whipping and snapping in the wind, above their heads.

Whether it was the effect of the Union Jack or simply a surrender to the superior size and speed of the *Windraider*, the *Cherabim* began to slow. There was a palpable easing among the men, and even Bastian's granite block stance softened. Raider ordered the sheets short-hauled and the ship slowed to cruise into a parleying position. When they came within range, he called for his speaking trumpet, and his voice boomed across the two hundred yards of heaving sea.

"Ahoy . . . *Cherabim*! Heave to for parley." There was only the sound of sail flapping, of waves lapping and shushing. Then a bolt of electricity rent the air as the *Cherabim*'s response was seen before it was heard—an angry red flash and a billow of gray smoke. The unmistakable tenor tones of a twelve-pounder's explosion sent a shockwave through the *Windraider*'s deck, hull, and crew. The shot had barely splashed into the drink between ships before a second boom sounded and Raider spun about, alive with fury.

"*Dammit!*" he boomed, "she wants a bloody fight! Bastian—"

But Bastian was already halfway to the waist, just managing to flash a toothy, wicked grin at Raider as he leaped down onto the mizzen. "Guns!"

Another ball fell short, but closer, and Raider shouted orders to his swivel gunners to draw a bead on their man-killing swivels and headed for the mizzen himself. The deck was suddenly swarming with lads rushing to posts, shouting and brandishing their well-honed blades. The smell of burning powder seeped across the murky water setting blood pounding in every head and expectation coiling in every gut.

Blythe stood, ashen, frozen with horror, her heart stopped at the frenzy breaking loose around her. Raider wheeled back and grabbed her arm and dragged her down the quarterdeck steps onto the mizzen. "Get below!" He gave her a none-too-gentle shove toward the hatch, and when she stumbled, staring blindly at him, he took her by the shoulders and gave her a shake. "Get to the cabin Wool-witch and stay there . . . *go*, dammit!"

He managed to penetrate her horror, and she stumbled toward

215

the hatch when he released her. The acrid smell of gunpowder from the gun deck below, filled the passage and clutched at her throat, but somehow she made it down the steps and through the cabin door. She stood in the middle of the floor, staring sightlessly back toward the passage where some of the crew were running up and down the steps, ferrying arms from the armory, topside. Vibrating up through the ship's timbers came yells and curses and pounding . . . and the roaring blast of a twenty-four-pounder answering the tenor of the *Cherabim*'s lighter guns.

Blythe felt the lady *Windraider* shudder slightly with the recoil and other, sharper blasts sounded . . . the baritone of carronade guns, made for mangling rigging and clearing an enemy's deck. "Smashers," they were called and for some reason she recalled the deep current of pride in Black Jimmy's voice when he'd described the short-range, large-bore artillery's function. When he'd fired it on that clear, sunny afternoon to demonstrate its range, he had laughed at the way she staggered from the blast with her hands over her ears. And she had laughed too, after she scraped her wits from the walls of her mind and stuffed them back into order. It had seemed a large and noisy toy . . . all of them had . . . those long, gleaming guns.

Raider ducked inside the cabin, a saber glinting in one hand and a pistol in the other. "Here, Wool-witch . . ." He was gruff as he thrust the pistol butt at her. When she made no move to take it, he reached for her hand and thrust its cold marriage of wood and steel into her palm. His burning jade gaze reached into her pale expression. "We'll take her . . . we've got her outmanned, outgunned. But there'll be boarding and things will be confused. Stay in the cabin, Blythe . . . and if you have to . . ." he squeezed his hands over hers on the pistol, "hold it up with both hands, squeeze the trigger, and don't flinch. Do you hear me?!" She nodded dumbly.

The tension in his face migrated into her as his jaw clenched against the temptation to say things better left unsaid. But his mouth swooped down on hers in a quick, fierce kiss and its bruising intensity stayed with her for a full minute after the door had slammed behind him. She looked down at the cool piece of weaponry that was drawing warmth from her hand, and shivered at the way it seemed to be accustoming itself to her grip. Swallowing hard, she settled on the very edge of the bunk with the piece in her hand. She listened to the frightful roars above and weathered the shudders and quakes from the recoil of the big guns.

Richard and Willie and Sharkey and the Bosun . . . Bastian and Raider and Oars and Ali . . . they were all up there. She could hear it all . . . shouts and the clang of metal and the muffled pops of musketfire. And it was a long moment before she realized the large guns had fallen silent and the din of deck noise had intensified. Boarding . . . Her throat was being squeezed mercilessly. Were they boarding or being boarded? And how many of them would die this gray, wretched afternoon because of her . . . because Raider had tried to send her back to a respectable life?

She lurched up and ripped the lady-cloak from her shoulders, clutching the butt of the pistol more tightly. She uttered a short, desperate prayer and stalked back and forth, staring at the door, listening to the sounds of battle as they were magnified by her own fears. She couldn't just sit here . . . cowering. Her mouth was like cotton, her palms were dampening, her stomach was grinding itself into oblivion as she watched that awful door. What was happening on the other side might be horrible, but the terrors of not knowing were infinitely worse. One Tooth and Stanley and Clive were up there . . . those grizzled and frightening sea dogs she'd come to know and care for in a strange sort of way. They'd accepted her as she was and allowed her a place amongst them. They could be dying . . . while she whimpered and cringed behind a closed door . . .

A hot blast of anger erupted from deep within her broad, responsible shoulders. And her hand was on the doorlatch before a forbidding thought could form in her mind. She jerked it open and the acrid powder-smoke rising from the opening to the gun deck boiled in on her, stinging her eyes, making her recoil briefly. But quickly she was halfway up the steps, hearing shouts and groans and the clang of steel on steel.

217

Stanley came tumbling down the steps, grappling hand-to-hand with a rangy, grizzled tar and gaining some slight advantage as he hit the passage floor on his feet and charged anew, blade swinging. Blythe shrank against the wall, her eyes riveted on the deadly contest, her legs working furiously to force her upward and away from it. Raider . . . she had to find Raider . . .

The deck was smoky and tangled in sagging cable and sheeting and chaotic. Everywhere men were grappling, bodies were sprawled, and more of the *Windraider*'s crew were pouring up from the gun deck below. Violent splashes of red jerked and twisted in furious pairing with Raider's crew. Arms and legs flailed and strained and slashed in savage combat all around the hatch opening. She caught sight of Bastian slashing furiously with a short sword to keep a redcoat at bay. Clive was toppled and grappling on the deck; Oars stood over one slumped form, weaponless, and swung his hamlike fists like a hammer into the spleen of a boarder locked in knife combat with Old Willie. Occasional cracks of musketfire split the din of warfare. Blythe flattened against the quarterdeck steps, her eyes wide and panicked . . . she couldn't tell who was winning or what was happening. Bodies were heaving and grunting and writhing. Panicky and confused, she felt her heart convulse and her stomach heave at the horrifying sights of blood and familiar faces twisted with anger and pain. Her mates, her friends—fighting for their very lives!

A bolt of blinding fury ripped through her . . . a shattering blast like the one that had erupted in her that awful night when the crew had threatened her. Hot blood burst against her skin and invaded her chilled muscles. She had to *do* something! She wheeled and flew up to the quarterdeck, searching for Raider. He was near the wheel, hard-pressed by a heavily braided redcoat; sword-hilt locked against sword-hilt. His face was contorted into a gritty mask, and Blythe watched him straining to heave his opponent back. Out of nowhere came another form, pounding up the steps . . . red and snarling, blood on his blade. The invader hesitated as though startled by Blythe's appearance, then charged to help his ranking officer . . . to help him finish Raider off!

She jolted, screaming Raider's name, and her warning was swallowed up in the confusion. But some shred of it penetrated the roar in Raider's head enough to disrupt his fierce concentration and that British sword-hilt smacked against his head, dazing him enough to slacken his resistance. They broke apart and Raider parried clumsily, shaking his head. And from the side came a new threat . . . a second blade.

Blythe felt leaden as she watched. Everything seemed to move with slowed motion as the second redcoat charged in. Blythe's hand came up as she tried to scream, and the pistol that was still clutched in her white fingers came with it. Raider's voice boomed in her head, surprising her: "Both hands . . . squeeze . . . don't flinch!" She wrapped her second hand over the grip and pointed it at the second redcoat's shoulders. Raider's wild, sweeping parry held him at bay just an instant longer—the instant Blythe needed to squeeze the trigger.

Crack! The redcoat grunted and crumpled to the deck and his commander's instant of hesitation was all Raider needed to deliver a downward slash on his arm, sending both him and his blade onto the deck. It happened in mere seconds . . . all of it, and Blythe was stunned by the effect of her action. But she hurried to Raider's braced, disbelieving form with the pistol still dangling at her side. He shook his head to clear it and stared at her and then at the pistol in her hand.

"Morgan's Teeth, Blythe . . . you?!" His face split into a glazed grin. He shook his head again and his eyes seemed to focus this time.

"Stay put!" he ordered her, glancing around the quarterdeck to be sure it was secured before lunging over the crumpled forms at his feet. He charged down the steps, into the fray, wielding his blade. There was a roar, a flurry of bodies, and a short, fiercely pitched battle. Then, suddenly, it was over.

Panting and heaving and groaning came from all quarters, but the clang of metal on metal died away. Eerie quiet descended as more and more of the *Windraider*'s crew appeared, some climbing

219

up from the subdued deck of the *Cherabim* and some pushing up, gaining their feet from amongst the injured and vanquished. Raider was visible near the waist railing, panting and leaning against Bastian Cane, who was grinning like a barracuda. Bastian tossed back his head and bellowed a triumphant roar that was joined and soon became a deafening din of pride.

Raider found the captain of the *Cherabim* and at last understood why the *Windraider*'s peaceful overtures had been misread. While a crewman aboard a third-rate British ship-o'-the-line two years before, the *Cherabim*'s captain had fought Raider's crew in a losing cause and remembered well both the wily bark and her arresting master.

Raider issued martial orders for clean-up and a casualty report, but his men's response was delayed as he made for the quarterdeck, carrying their eyes and some of their feet with him. Bastian was right behind him, squinting hard at the sight of Blythe rising from her knees in the ragged, gray aftermath of battle with a heap of scarlet at her feet. Her eyes were huge, stunned, and her cheeks flushed. Her fingers still clutched that smoky flintlock pistol.

"You . . . won?" she managed through a cottony layer about her head. Raider didn't seem completely furious with her, though his eyes were heated, glowing strangely. He just stood there, panting, staring.

"Damn—" Bastian lifted the pistol and her hand with it. It was clearly discharged and he sniffed it and looked at the unconscious redcoat at her feet. "You . . . shot him?"

"I . . ." Blythe felt a wave of sickness at the realization, "I . . . he was going to slice into Raider and I . . ." she swallowed, fighting a tunnel of darkness that was narrowing her vision. "I don't think he's dead. I checked . . . I didn't mean to . . . but it was two on one and I . . ." she swallowed, feeling odd and disjointed, ". . . just did . . . what Raider said. Used two hands . . . and sq-quee-ezed . . ." She felt herself going limp and tried to fight it, focusing on the faces that began to crowd around her. There was Old Willie and Clive; they were all right. And Richard—thank God for Richard . . .

220

"She done saved yer life, Raider!" Willie suddenly crowed with a gaping, toothless grin. And chaos seemed to be unleashed afresh around her.

"He-ee's . . . b-blee-eding." She tried to stoop to the fellow at her feet, to see him, but Raider pulled her up, and at his warm touch she went completely to jelly. He barely caught her around the waist and managed to scoop her up into his arms. Her eyes fluttered shut and she couldn't seem to open them, though she could still make out Raider's distinctive rumble through the roaring in her head.

"Well, you were right, Bastian," he growled, "she did faint." He cradled her possessively in his arms and glared triumphantly across her into his partner's tight-lipped glower. "But only *after* she pulled the trigger . . . that saved my hide."

Raider strode for his cabin with her and heard Bastian cracking his verbal whip furiously, getting the men back to the tasks at hand. He carried her to his bunk and set her down gently. He had a million things to do topside, but he stayed long enough to tuck a cover around her cold body and to lay an impulsive kiss on her forehead.

Chapter Fourteen

The lads of the *Windraider* had plenty of experience with the aftermath of battle and set to their grueling tasks with surprisingly light hearts and willing hands. They kept thinking of the Wool-witch's brave stand amongst them and grinned. They checked the wounded and were puzzled to learn there'd not been a life lost on either side, though there were injuries serious enough to take a few men out, if not tended carefully. They returned the *Cherabim's* wounded and set about their customary prize-taking, hauling stores, water, and some promising packets, crates, and bales back aboard the *Windraider*. They hadn't gotten far with their pillaging when a cry came from the rigging: "*Sail ho!* A'port!"

The Raider himself climbed into the rigging, and his glass confirmed his worst expectation: British Navy, three ships. Hearing his booming commands, the men were clambering up into the rigging by the time his own feet hit the deck. They knew well the drill of "strike and run"; often their lives had depended on it. In mere seconds they were heeling away from the *Cherabim* and shortly they had stretched every inch of canvas their lady *Windraider* would bear. The gray, brooding sky filled with whispers and murmurs that filled their sails and sent them slicing through the waves into the sheltering gray from which they'd come.

Two of the navy vessels gave chase, but the *Windraider* was designed for speed and had a good start. They fell off after a few hours hard running, and the lads could continue their cleaning and clearing and tending. The *Cherabim* had been small, but she'd stung like a wasp; two damaged tackles, ripped canvas, a bit of splintered railing. Fortunately, there was no structural damage. Strange, the lads shook their heads at the way of things; it was the little scuffles that sometimes inflicted the most damage. They'd taken whole merchantmen, on occasion, with no more than a few warning rounds fired over a bow.

Raider and Bastian had their hands full assessing the damage, overseeing the cleanup and the patching up, while monitoring their pursuers. Raider had little time to think about Blythe and her reluctant heroism in defense of his life, but there was a renewed energy in his step, a boldness in his eye that had everything to do with her . . . in ways he sensed but didn't fully comprehend. The lads took note of the change in him. The Raider was himself again, they murmured, grinning. His manner was full of that easy control they'd come to respect. A good fight could do that to a bloke, they sagely agreed.

Some hours later, when the unrelenting gray of the sky had become patched with brilliant sapphire blue and began sliding into purples, Blythe awoke in the sunlit glow of Raider's spacious cabin. The familiar scent of coconut made her bury her nose in the covers and breathe it in with a drawn sigh. All was quiet, except for the lulling creak of timbers, the droning sloosh of the *Windraider*'s wake outside the window. Then it came back to her like the revisitation of some terrible nightmare; the fighting, the blood, the shooting . . .

She shuddered and threw back the covers, sliding from the bunk and steadying herself. She had to find out what had happened . . . who was dead. Dread iced her fingers and dried her mouth as she made her way to the door and then made herself open it. She braced, recalling the last time she'd stood there. But this time the air was fresh and a shaft of dusty sunlight sank through the passage gloom to land at her feet. She took a trembling breath and mounted that beam of light toward . . . an uncertain fate.

The deck was cleared of bodies and there was a strong smell of vinegar all around. She spotted One Tooth and Richard on their knees nearby, scrubbing at telling crimson stains on the planking.

They looked up and greeted her with smiles that only partly relieved her anxiety.

"Got to get 'er scrubbed down with vinegar afore she sets too long," Richard panted.

Blythe nodded dumbly and walked about the mizzen to the waist, collecting eyes as she went. She ticked off on a mental roster the names of those she saw, the ice in her heart warming one degree for each healthy body she counted. The crew began to congregate around her, asking after her health and congratulating her on her marksmanship. Relieved, if a bit bewildered, by their lack of resentment toward her, she asked after a few missing faces and was told they were stowed below in Ali's makeshift dispensary, and were being well tended.

Raider muscled through his men and came to a stop in front of her, his fists planted on his hips and his legs braced. His polished jade eyes slid over her in leisurely possession. She was as pale as white sugar frosting . . . and probably would taste just as sweet. Blood surged under his skin and swirled through his lips at the thought. He took her wrist and pulled her along to the quarterdeck, drawing their audience with him.

Bastian watched Raider's controlled ease and his possessive grip on the Wool-witch, and alarm clanged through him like a fire bell. His uncanny nose detected the smoke of smoldering passions clear across the deck. He barreled through the men to reach them and his eyes narrowed on Blythe's peachlike cheeks, fire-kissed hair, and luminous eyes. The same attributes he'd hoped would prove Raider's torment were turning out to be Raider's unabashed desire. It was galling . . .

". . . only eight men." Raider was explaining the slight damage to the ship and their minor casualties. "It could have been a lot worse." Grinning into the sudden flush of her cheeks, he felt his own flaming . . . burning with a bizarre sort of pleasure that the sloop had been British and that they'd had to fight and that she'd defied him once again and saved his cavalier hide in the process. It was a complete disaster, he knew. But right now he was having the strangest feeling that it was a splendid disaster . . . a marvelous muck-up . . . meant to be . . . destined. Fate had tossed his Wool-witch back into his lap, that much was clear. And he was

224

never a man to tempt fate . . .

"There'll be a slight delay in gettin' ye home, Wool-witch." Bastian stuck his thumbs in his belt and narrowed his crafty eyes. "Too bad it come to spillin' blood . . . on yer account."

"I never meant—" Blythe's eyes widened with dismay on Bastian, then on the faces around them.

"Any decent leech will tell you, a bit of blood-letting is good for a body," Raider proclaimed loudly. Over Blythe's head, his eyes narrowed meaningfully on Bastian, daring him to continue that line. "And it does double for a pirate crew, eh, Bastian? Spilling a bit of blood makes a man realize he has to fight hard to keep from spilling it all. And it lets him know who he can count on in a real fight . . . who'll *faint* and who won't."

At the mention of a "faint," Blythe flamed again and lowered her eyes. Bastian stiffened and his square features bronzed. A murmur went through the lads.

"Don't fret yerself, Wool-witch." Bastian spoke to her, but his words were really meant for Raider, who was staring pointedly at him over her head. "We'll set ye aboard the next ship we come across. They can't all be Brits."

Taut silence reigned as Bastian and Raider confronted each other above Blythe's slender form. The lads watched the flint of Bastian's gaze striking the steel of Raider's and felt the scorch of the visual sparks that flew all around. They'd never seen such a deadly serious clash of determination between their leaders before. The Raider had gone stony quiet and Bastian was trembling visibly with restraint.

"The hell we will," Raider's voice issued in a calm, deadly rasp, sending a shockwave through his men. He took Blythe by the shoulders and whirled her around to face him, lifting her shocked face to his. The liquid fire of his eyes sank into hers at the very moment the sun sank into its bed on the horizon.

Blythe felt him reaching inside her, probing her, commanding her response to questions she didn't fully understand. But her heart was thudding, her senses were filling, and her body was coming to life under his touch. She felt the pull of his wanting, the promise of his desire. It was as though he searched her . . . seeking something. His heat invaded her; desire for her erupted

225

in the depths of his ocean-green gaze. Blythe swayed slightly with the dizzying impact of his intensity. There was no disgust in his mesmerizing gaze, no blame, no anger of any kind. Her whole being felt lightened and began to soar.

The lads watched his intensity, saw the trembling of her body in his fierce, possessive grip and began to rumble with confusion. The Raider lifted his head from that scorching, hypnotic contact and his eyes burned with a kind of fire they'd never witnessed in him before.

"She stays." His rumble was ferocious in its deadly calm. He straightened, keeping his tight grip on her as he tossed a smooth, molten glare around him, daring anyone to defy his command.

"*Dammit*, Raider—" Bastian was desperate enough to ignore the warning.

"She's my *share!*" Raider bellowed. "And I'll split the skull of any man who says otherwise!"

Blythe stared up at him, speechless, only now realizing the full impact of what had just passed between them.

"God, Raider—she be a *respectable female*—" Bastian was thunderstruck.

"And I'm a bloody pillaging *pirate!*" Raider thundered, setting both teeth and belaying pins rattling in their sockets. "You conniving old cutthroat, you wanted a pirate for a captain . . . well, you've got one! A black-hearted tyrant of a captain who takes what he damned well wants. And I want *her!*"

He stooped and ducked his shoulders into Blythe's stunned middle and hauled her, sputtering and gasping, up over his shoulder. She squealed and squirmed as Raider pushed through his stunned crew, heading straight for his cabin . . . with the woman he craved with every fiber of his body. And the picture of them that lingered in the lads' shock-blanked minds was that of Blythe beating helplessly on his back and demanding to be set down as he strode toward the hatch.

Raider kicked the cabin door twice; once before him, once behind. His long, sinewy legs covered the polished floor in four strides and he dropped her on the bunk, standing over her as she sorted herself out, tumbling hair, bunched skirts, and reeling wits.

"What do you . . . think you're doing?" she sputtered, wiping hair back from her face. "Tossing me about like a sack of flour—"

"Making up for lost time, Wool-witch . . . *tossing* you." The corner of his mouth quirked up in a lusty curl. Heat shimmered in the depths of his eyes and his breath came fast and hard. "It's what I should have done the minute I laid eyes on you . . . ravished you over and over like a degenerate, lust-crazed pirate. Maybe I'd have you out of my blood by now—" He stood with his well-muscled thighs pressed against the edge of the bunk and speared her gaze with his as he flipped his shirt buttons from their holes . . . one . . . by one . . . by one. Each one broadened the slice of chest that radiated heat like a bronze griddle.

"B-but . . . " she stammered. His declaration of sensual intent held a hint of menace that squeezed Blythe's throat. "Y-you can't—" She saw him rip his shirt from his well-muscled shoulders and fling it aside and she suffered a panicky shiver. "Wh-what are you doing?"

"You learn quicker than that, Wool-witch." He raised one eyebrow as he flicked open the brass buckle of his wide black belt. "I'm going to *toss* you . . . over and over . . . and *over*, until I've had my fill."

His *fill?!* Her eyes widened hugely as she skittered back on her bottom across the bunk so that her shoulder blades hugged the paneled wall. Take his fill of her pleasures . . . make her do *that* until he was sick of her? What in heaven's name had come over him? His features were sleek and sharpened with determination, the way she'd seen them in the throes of battle, mere hours ago. "And then what? Are you going to send me home then?"

"I'll decide that when the time comes," he declared flatly . . . raising one knee, tugging one boot off and giving it a heave. "But don't expect to be going home any time soon, wench. I've got a powerful craving for the taste of you . . . and the feel." His second boot hit the floor.

"You've got a pow—" Everything between her ears seemed to have gone to mush; all she could do was parrot the unthinkable things he said. She shook her head as her eyes fastened helplessly

227

on the flap buttons he was unfastening. Shortly the cause of that great bulge in the tan wool of his breeches flap was uncovered. The thought sent her eyes racing up his lean belly, up the valley that creased his chest, past his parted lips, to his lustrous jade eyes. Then he bent and peeled his breeches down, tossing them aside, without taking his eyes from her.

"Come here, Wool-witch."

Blythe felt more than heard his rumbling command, and confusion erupted in her middle, splintering her very self into fragments. From deep inside her rose a prim little maiden who both cringed and raged at such treatment. A truly respectable young woman would rather die than be used so foully! But the blossoming little sensualist in her stole the floor to demand the release and the unimaginable pleasure he could give her. Perhaps the best way to get him out of *her* blood was to have *her* fill, too! Feeling like a third party in her own skin, Blythe-the-sensible-responsible-female was both tempted and horrified by what was happening. Either he meant to use her, then cast her aside, or he wanted to love her enough for a lifetime because he knew someday he'd have to let her go. And she had no way of knowing which it was.

The things she'd come to know in Raider Prescott were a bundle of contradictions . . . ferocity and tenderness, brutality and even-handedness, callousness and consideration. He was by turns swaggering pirate and considerate gentleman. But it seemed to be the pirate who was demanding a surfeit of her now. Knowing that, how could she surrender to him and live with herself?

"No," she breathed, her senses at fever pitch as she struggled to pull her eyes from his big, fascinating body. "I . . . won't."

"Yes you will, Wool-witch. It's *fate* . . . and there's no escaping fate."

"It's not fate," she tried desperately to make her mind work, ". . . it's your own miserable lusts"

"Then it's my fate to be a lust-ridden pirate," he propped one bare knee on the bunk, "and it's your fate to be the one I lust for . . ."

She wrenched and twisted in his grip, but both of them knew

that his sinewy strength would ultimately triumph. With a fierce tug, he dragged her to her knees and clamped her against his bare, heated body.

"I want you, Wool-witch," he half groaned, half growled. "And I was meant to have you . . . I was fated for it." His mouth came down on hers, sending her senses reeling and her wits into chaotic retreat.

. His tongue plundered hers, invading, stroking, and the heat he poured into the center of her began to melt the hasty fortifications that pride and reason had thrown up around her vulnerable passions. As her resistance gave way, he caressed her waist and back and slid hungry hands possessively over her buttocks. She quivered and tried to withdraw, but her bones were softening, her muscles were melting against him.

"No . . . please." She managed one last rally against the steamy sensations he was creating in her with his hands and lips. He wanted her, she knew, but there would come a time when he wouldn't. That was his avowed plan . . . to get the need for her out of his system! Remember, her protective inner sense begged, remember how it hurt when he left before . . . when he loved you and then turned away? "It'll only hurt . . ."

"No, Wool-witch, it won't hurt. We already established that."

His deep, mesmerizing laugh seemed to originate on the ocean floor of her own being, like an earthquake. And the huge waves of feeling it generated engulfed her half-expressed and misunderstood fears.

"You want me to touch you . . . you want me as much as I want you." His mouth trailed hotly down the side of her neck and his knowing fingers worked beneath the sober woolen of her bodice and the linen of her chemise. The burning in her nipples became an ache of pleasure as he rolled one slowly between his fingers. Her head dropped to one side and shudders rippled through her as his mouth followed his hands.

"No . . . please . . ." Her voice was dry, panicky, and her hands pushed weakly against his shoulders as he suckled and toyed deliciously with her breast. Her hands ceased pushing and her nails dug into the heavy cord of muscles along the tops of his shoulders. He raised his face to hers, desire burning white-hot in him.

"Deny me, then. Say you don't want my loving . . . and I'll stop."

Deny him? How could she? She wanted his loving with everything in her . . . but she wanted so much more. She wanted all of him . . . like the greedy, respectable female he thought her to be. She wanted the wild sweetness of their pleasures and she wanted to luxuriate in his strength and tenderness and to discover all his secrets and hopes and . . .

She didn't want it to ever end.

He moved slowly, giving her time to protest, time to form that small, potent word of negation that he wasn't at all sure he would be able to honor. It was an agonizing gamble. He released her and pulled her gaze into his as he began to loosen her lacings. A devilish, Bastian Cane kind of smile crept over his handsome face. In this particular game, the odds had been weighted in his favor.

She couldn't resist as he pulled her dress, petticoat, and chemise from her and soon she was as bare as he. Her arms lapped up over the sweet globes of her breasts and he pulled them away to wrap them about his lean middle. As they sank back on the bunk, he covered her chilling frame with a hot blanket of desire. Under the masterful play of his hands and lips over her, she began to warm, to respond from the depths of her need for him.

Soon she reached for him with undulations of her hips and welcomed him between her thighs, against her burning mound. He rubbed and toyed and teased her to quivering peaks of excitement, over and over. Her fingers dug into the braided muscles of his back, her teeth nibbled his shoulders and chest, her kisses knocked the breath from him and set his loins on fire. Soon, he was no longer driving events; he was sharing them with her, giving, receiving.

He sank into the sweet cream flesh of her body, kissing her face, her throat, her hair. Over and over he called her his Blythe, his woman . . . his love. And through the blinding steam of her senses, she heard and her heart absorbed those precious ramblings. Out of the delicious fullness inside her flowed whispers of desire and delight that mingled with his murmurs in a litany of loving.

Higher and hotter, their passions built, expanding the boundaries of their separate beings, blurring distinctions between self and other. And suddenly there was a stunning release of pleasure, clear and resonant . . . like the clarion of paradise, it trembled through them. The pure harmonics of that sound were unmistakable, the rightness of it undeniable. They were joined in a way that no mere human had devised and by a bond that no man had ever fully comprehended. It was a bond forged for a lifetime, a bond of love.

Blythe felt the aftershocks of pleasure course through him, answered by her own. She trembled and clung to him, awed and aching. It was so different, each time . . . just as he said. And as languor seeped into her spent body, she wetted her swollen lips and whispered, "Trumpets . . ."

"Hum-m-m?" Raider raised his dusky face to hers and slid to the bunk beside her, turning her with him so as not to separate their bodies.

"Trumpets . . ." she kissed his bristled chin softly, "it was like trumpets this time."

Raider's smile was satisfaction distilled. "So it was, golden eyes."

The tensions of the day now spent, he slid into darkness, still cradling his Blythe against the hollow she'd created inside him. He managed to think that he made a far better pirate than a nobleman . . . and wondered why the hell he'd fought it for so long. Beside him Blythe was sinking, too, thinking that there really did seem to be a sensual "Wool-witch" inside her and wondering how she had gotten there.

Old Willie thumped his uneven gait along the dim passages of the berthing deck, back and forth, carrying the eyes of a number of the lads with him. They might have paced, too, but there was a slow-building charge in their limbs, a static of unspent feeling that might spark and ignite the *Windraider*'s volatile atmosphere if they moved too much. So they sat, huddled and brooding, bearing that prickly resentment on the skin of their necks and shoulders.

"It ain't right," Richard ventured morosely. There were grunts of agreement and lips moved in silent snarls.

"Well, she ain't screamin'." Clive fingered the tip of his stiletto blade with a good bit less pleasure than normal. "Mebbe he ain't . . ."

"*He is.*" Willie halted and glared down at Clive. "Ye can be sure o' that. And there ain't a female born to resist Th' Raider when he makes his mind up."

" 'At be true enough," Black Jimmy sighed heavily from a nearby bale. " 'Member that uppity Lady Sophia-somethin'? Had her on her back and moanin' fer more afore we left Ven-iss. The Raider . . . he's got a devil's way wi' females."

"He be the best, Old Raider," Oars nodded solemnly. It was cold comfort, but Old Willie said it anyway:

"At least our Wool-witch be gettin' the best."

An hour passed before Raider roused and raised his head. His movement wakened Blythe and she stretched lazily, coming to rest just as she was, in his arms with his leg draped casually over her hip. He traced the intriguing dent of her back and the perfect roundness of her bottom, luxuriating in the rare silkiness of her skin. A jumble of feeling welled inside him, and his dark, smoky gaze delved deep into hers, reading her lingering desire for him.

Blythe watched him, thinking there was nothing more important in life than being here with him like this, bodies roused and sated, hearts meeting. It made her feel warmed and wanted. She rippled under his hand and met his eyes.

"You're mine, Blythe Woolrich." As he gave words to the truth that lay between them, his tone was edged with fierce possessiveness.

A shiver went through her heart at the glowing coals of determination visible in him. He had claimed her as his fate, his right, his prize, first with words and then with loving. He was right, she realized helplessly; she was his.

But it was not power, not even the mesmerizing power of his passion for her or hers for him that now bound her to him. In the next instant, between heartbeats, the source of that bond crashed over her like a tidal wave; it was love. She *loved* Raider Prescott . . . that's what all this melting and sighing and burning and crying was about. Sensible, respectable Blythe Woolrich was in love with a pirate! A pirate who'd kidnapped her and taken her virtue and now had made her his mistress . . . against her wishes! Against her wishes, the beleaguered little maiden in her taunted disgustedly, but certainly not against her desires. She'd cooperated fully in his determined seduction. And her hoydenish behavior would be properly punished . . . when he shipped her home, ruined . . . likely with a babe in her belly. She was his all right, but . . .

". . . for how long?"

She said it on a breath, barely audible, but it thundered through her like an eternal judgment. He wanted her body, her pleasures, her surrender. Perhaps he even needed her in that tantalizing physical way. He owned her passion and now laid claim to her future. But for how long? Tears formed in her love-darkened eyes, mercifully blurring the sight of him.

She turned her head and curled on her side away from him, aching. Those tears collected into rivulets, then streams that filled her throat. Her shoulders quaked with silent sobs. Even if she managed to share a bit more than just his bed, even if he came to love her a little, there would still be that "pirate" part of him that was beyond her reach. And that part of him would send her away someday . . .

"Blythe? Wool-witch . . ." He had watched the play of strong emotions in her face and realized she was feeling the impact of his decision to keep her. The accusation in her tears stung him. He tried to pull her back into his arms, to comfort her with the warmth of his desire for her. But she resisted, pushing his hands away and shivering as though she couldn't bear his touch. He stiffened and sat up, then bounded from the bed, staring at her curled, miserable form.

Crying . . . what in hell did she have to cry about? He'd loved her into paradise and back . . . he'd made love to her like *trumpets* — for Morgan's sake . . . and she was sobbing like she'd just been bludgeoned. She hadn't cried like this when he'd taken her vir—

Something in his chest pinched. This time he was taking more than her virtue or her reputation, he was taking her future. The thought settled harshly on him until the pirate in him seized the trend of his gentlemanly qualms and overturned it.

She wanted him as much as he wanted her, he reasoned defiantly. The loving and pleasure they made was rare indeed, as he well knew. Whatever they had together would be better than a life under the likes of a bloated walrus like Neville Carson. And no amount of soggy sentimentalism and maidenly regret would convince him otherwise. He knew the tyranny of "futures" and "expectations" and he was damned well determined not to let them interfere with what he wanted in life . . . with the joy they could bring each other. He'd lost everything once, because of the "respectability" that infected proper society, and he'd not be victim to it again.

She'd come around. Raider's gaze heated on Blythe's quiet sobs. He'd love her until she couldn't resist loving him back. It was their fate.

Grimly, he washed and drew on his clothes and boots, fighting the urge to take her into his arms and burn those respectable regrets from her with the heat of their loving. A subtler instinct told him that she would need time to adjust, and in the interest of their future pleasures, he determined to give her time. She was a bright wench, his Wool-witch. She'd reason it out . . . and come around.

Blythe cried herself literally dry. Then, like the sensible young woman she was at heart, dragged herself from the bunk, lit a lantern, and washed and dressed. She held a cold cloth against her swollen eyes and puffy nose and settled on the edge of Raider's ivory tusk chair, trying to collect her wits.

She was a young woman alone. And in her present predicament, there was no one to turn to, no one to intercede. She had to deal with Raider Prescott herself, in the best way she could.

That made things difficult, indeed, for Raider Prescott, the strong and the stubborn, the bold and the tender, was too much

234

for her to resist properly on her own. It seemed an understandable weakness, considering that the rough and dangerous men he led found it equally difficult to resist him, once he set his mind on something. It didn't seem such a monumental failing . . . until she thought of Philadelphia and her hapless family, and her ruined virtue and the everlasting shame — not to mention *sin* — of being a kept woman.

Massaging the twinge of pain in her heart, she sagged and felt her stomach turning over. Ruined . . . sin . . . hussy . . . *harlot!* She shuddered and managed to squeeze out enough moisture for two more tears. She never imagined when she asked Raider to take his share of her that he would demand it over and over! In point of fact, she hadn't thought at all, only felt. She had needed his tenderness and loving so badly that she abandoned both reason and respectability. She wanted desperately to experience the joy and pleasure that his hot looks and scalding kisses had promised. It would be the only loving she would ever know, she had convinced herself.

Well, she'd gotten a bit more than she bargained for. Raider Prescott was going to see to it that she had more loving after all . . . plenty of it. It was what she deserved for letting the French half of her gain the upper hand, for acting like a brazen, loose-hipped tart! She'd invited this calamity, her prim little conscience scolded. And she deserved to suffer.

Suffer?! The blossoming little hedonist in her laughed. If only she could suffer so for the rest of her natural life; Raider's supple hands on her body, his hard weight engulfing her, driving her into paradise itself. Such torture! came a naughty laugh from deep inside. Lord knew she'd had few enough pleasures in the past few years. What was wrong with enjoying the sweetness and joy of loving Raider Prescott, whether gentleman or pirate?

But there was more to it than pleasures or outraged moral standards, Blythe-the-sensible took over. There would be pleasures, but they would have a price. And the cost would be paid in pain; having loved and lost. It hurt too much already. Her stomach cramped and her eyes burned and her chest ached. She loved Raider Prescott with everything in her.

Then what was she to do? She groaned and jumped up to

235

pace, wringing her hands. On his own ship, among his devoted crew, in the middle of the ocean, there was no place to run. She could fight him and scream and . . . *he'd probably make her surrender anyway*, just as he had mere hours ago. She was too new to such physical wonders, and he was too good at plying them, for her to scorn them convincingly. She could try running away, finding passage home at their first landfall . . . *and likely jump from the frying pan into the fire*. She had nothing to buy a passage with, except that one commodity peculiar to women and desired by men. And the thought of blundering into the hands of another "Neville Carson" was enough to squash that possibility.

She couldn't fight, couldn't escape, couldn't stay . . . Lord, what was she going to do?

Chapter Fifteen

Raider strode the top deck in the cold moonlight, grateful for the sea chill that kept his passions and his temper in check. Bastian wouldn't speak to him and the eyes of his crew bored into him like hot pokers. But he'd made his decision and he'd fight every blessed man-jack amongst them before he'd give her up. When he could stand the pull of wanting her no longer, he made his way to the hatch and ducked into the darkness of the passage.

A single lantern was lit and burning low, casting weary shadows over the cabin when he stepped inside. It took him a minute to locate her curvy form beneath the covers on the bunk. He came to stand beside her, watching the dream-warmed curve of her cheek and stroking her thick night-braid with his eyes. Her breathing was deep and regular. She was sound asleep . . . probably exhausted. The tumult in his blood suddenly quieted and the charge in his loins drained. He wanted to love her again, but his urge to protect her proved even greater. If she needed rest, then she'd have it.

A self-deprecating smile crept over his firm mouth as the tensions of the day throbbed in his muscles. He could use the rest, too. He shed his clothes and slipped under the comforter with her, turning on his side to fit against her back. His hands encountered that familiar green wool and his wry grin masked a twinge of disappointment. Her resistance wasn't completely quelled; that wretched little dress was proof. He sighed quietly, and soon was asleep in his own comfortable bed, for the first time in four long weeks.

Blythe wakened first the next morning, to the oddly familiar feeling of Raider's body beside hers. He appeared to be sleeping heavily and she arched painstakingly across his sprawled frame to slide off the end of the bunk. Her heart thudded strangely at the sight of his broad shoulders above the comforter and the boyish softness of his finely sculpted features. His sun-streaked hair was tousled, and there was a dusty haze on his chin and jaw. He was so long and lean and . . .

She scowled at her wayward musings, making herself recall the dilemma this paragon of masculinity had embroiled her in. Hurrying to the washstand, she washed her face and set about lifting her hair into her proper lady's coif. By the time a soft, familiar knock came at the door, she had smoothed her rumpled dress and finished her brief toilette. She opened the door with her finger pressed to her lips, admitting a solemn-faced Richard bearing a large morning tray.

His dark glances between the bunk and Blythe were telling indeed. Blythe's face flamed and she turned away to fold toweling so that he couldn't see her shame as he laid out the dishes on the table. When he finished, he stood awkwardly a minute, shifting from one foot to the other.

"Two pots," he whispered, and gestured sullenly toward the vessels, "The Raider, he likes his coffee of a morn."

"That's not all he like of a morn" came Raider's deep, commanding rumble from the bunk. They both startled around to witness him, raised on one elbow, bared from the waist up. "He likes a bit of privacy as well." Raider's meaningful glare was not lost on Richard, and the lad tucked his chin and left hurriedly.

Blythe was unnerved to see Raider fling back the comforter and rise, naked as the day of his birth. She averted her eyes and busied herself with breakfast. A soft chuckle reached her ears and her imagination was piqued by the sounds of movement and fabric rustle and water trickling and splashing. Minutes later, he appeared across the table from her, fully dressed and freshly shaved, looking dashing indeed. Her heart gave a queer jump in her chest as he eased his long frame down into a chair.

"I see you've waited for me," he gestured sardonically to her half-demolished plate. "In future, I think it would be nice to breakfast together."

It was the perfect opening and Blythe seized it.

"There . . . can't be a future, Raider Prescott." She swallowed hard. "You have to send me home."

His features tightened. "I don't have to do anything of the sort." He stabbed a piece of salty ham with his knife, flipped it onto his plate, and cut into it a bit too vigorously. He stuffed some into his mouth and chewed determinedly.

"But my family." Blythe came to the edge of her chair. "They need me."

"*I* need you Wool-witch." He swallowed furiously and gestured to himself with his cutlery, "in my bed!" He saw the shrinking in her posture and thought it best to enlarge his declaration a bit. "I want to be able to see you every day, talk with you when I want, watch you and bed you. And I won't be denied."

"But it's not right, keeping me here against my will." Her golden eyes grew amber-dark with shame. "Surely you can see that. It goes against everything I was raised to believe and be."

Her respectable background was rearing its ugly head, and true annoyance bloomed in him. "Well, pleasure doesn't seem to go against your grain overmuch—"

She whitened as if struck and pushed up. She walked unsteadily to the windows and stared out at the smooth, rhythmic waves.

He drew his chin back sharply. That was a stupid thing to say, he realized with an internal groan. He knew more about women than that. Women hated having their passions brought into discussions, even when they were germane to the issues. Blythe obviously had things like respectable qualms and scruples and, like most "respectable" females, she needed to be courted into a surrender. Well, he growled reluctantly, he guessed he wasn't above a bit of wooing . . . as long as it led to what he wanted, in her bed.

He rose and came to stand behind her, but when he reached for her his hand halted midway. From this range, he could see

239

she was struggling desperately with something and he felt an uncomfortable tug of conscience. It could be more than just lack of breakfast that caused this empty feeling that was opening in the middle of him. He didn't like this emptiness, or trust it.

Blythe turned to face him, emotions welling in her lovely eyes and coloring her cheeks like his favorite Spanish peaches. There was only one course left to her, a last, reckless bid for freedom and whatever honor might be salvaged. It was a strategem as old as mankind itself, as feminine and irresistible as Wisdom herself. It was *the truth*.

"I do want you, Raider." Her voice was quiet and oddly husky as she fought being drawn into his mesmerizing gaze. "I want to watch you and touch you and want to learn all about you. And I can't help wanting the pleasure you make for me in your bed. You make me feel . . . beautiful. I've never felt beautiful before . . ."

Raider was dumbfounded. He never expected a confession of her own needs and desires; respectable females *never* admitted such things, even to themselves. Both his strategy and his composure were temporarily undone by her candid revelations. And the unhappiness visible in her as she made them cut into him like a surgeon's knife.

"Lord, you make it sound a dismal state . . . wanting me."

"It will be . . . when you send me away." She didn't mean to look into his stormy green eyes, but she did. And she felt a small part of the hurt she would know when she could look into them no longer.

"Send you . . . ? Who said anything about sending you away?" He swallowed against the squeezing in his throat and sounded gruff. "I plan to enjoy you for a long time, wench. And I'll . . . see that you have . . . whatever you need in return."

"But for how long? Sooner or later something will happen and you'll have to send me away." Moisture was collecting in her dusky golden eyes and Raider suddenly felt himself drowning in it.

Assurances, he choked. She wanted some . . . assurances. God. Just like a respectable female to want a few "assurances" along the way. But when she stood there, looking up at him, turning his loins inside out with those big, sincere eyes and those perfect, quivering lips, he found himself wanting to give them to her. He meant to take care of her, he squared his cursedly respectable urge with himself, so what would be changed by telling her of it?

"You'll find someone you like better, someday, someone really beautiful or someone who's less trouble . . ." she whispered, feeling a knife turning in her heart at the thought.

"I won't." He gave his head a terse shake. "I've never wanted a woman like I want you, Wool-witch. I won't ever want a woman like this again." He shivered and his heart convulsed as he recognized the awful truth of his statement. Her delectable mouth turned up slightly at the corners and she wagged her head in wan disbelief.

"But things happen, Raider. What if I were to get sick . . . people do get sick. What if I was unable to . . . to bed you? Then you'd—"

"Then I'd see you taken care of, dammit! Do you think I'd toss you out while you were sick and miserable? I've got the best ship's physician in the whole Atlantic—"

"But there are other things . . . What if my health was good, but I got . . . I became . . . with child? Then you'd have to send me away. You couldn't have a pregnant mistress or *babies* aboard a pirate ship." Her heart pounded harder with each possible calamity and each emphatic denial.

"In sickness or health, babies or none, Blythe Woolrich, you're mine. And I'll keep you beside me if I have to chain you there."

"But someday you could take a fat prize and be a wealthy man." He was making it very difficult for her . . . refusing to see. "Then you'd want a fancy lady to squire about or even a *wife* . . . and I'd be in the way."

"I haven't got the slightest inclination toward either society or matrimony, Wool-witch! Especially not if I struck it rich somehow—"

"Or poor. If you lost your ship like Bastian did . . . I'd be a burden to you and you'd probably send me away . . . whether I wanted to go or not . . ."

"Richer or poorer, Wool-witch, I'll want you . . . and I won't send you away . . . if you want to stay with me." His face was dusky now, and he flinched slightly at the volume and the content of his denials. She was boxing him into a corner . . . making him say things he hadn't yet thought about, making him want her in ways he hadn't even considered yet. God. *Babies* . . . *their* babies. And sickness and riches and all the "unforeseens" of life. She was talking about a life with him. He couldn't swallow and his head was lightening strangely. God help him, the whole idea appealed to him and, at the same time, it scared the hell out of him!

And then she set the finishing stroke to the roots of his self-sufficiency. "Please . . . I can't stay with you, Raider. I . . ."

"What is it?" he thundered, grabbing her arms and hauling her against him fiercely. "Why the hell can't you stay with the man you say you want?! Because you're damned proper and proud . . . respectable?!"

Tears blinked down her cheeks. He demanded one last truth from her; the real reason she couldn't bear it if he sent her away. She'd revealed so much . . . too much to back down now. If he knew, he really would send her away . . . and she'd have the freedom she feared, yet felt obliged to seek. She had to say it.

"Because I think . . ." but a last craven impulse diluted her confession, "I might be coming to love you, Raider Prescott."

It blew a thirty-two-pound hole through his gut. Love. She might love him. Wanting and needing and desiring he could handle. But she might *love* him. He released her arms slowly and took a trembling step backward. His face registered every single emotion known to man, one after another, after another.

Blythe watched him recoil from her admission and read displeasure and disgust into it. "You've been perfectly honest with me . . . all along," she whispered hoarsely. "You never pretended anything. It's one of the things I admire . . . you're the most honest man I know. And I'm afraid I could come to love you, anyway."

She watched him turn to one side, his expression dark and confused and seemingly angry. She'd been right to tell him. He really would send her away now. He wasn't a man to suffer a love-smitten female's clinging. She never thought of herself as

242

clinging to anyone or anything, except her own self-sufficiency. But sooner or later, her desire for his love would make her seem that way to his roving soul. And, despite his vehement denials, there would be circumstances or feelings someday that would make him regret keeping her.

"Now will you send me home?" she whispered, having to blink away tears to see his response. *"Please?"*

Raider stalked away and stood with his back turned and his shoulders braced, as far from her as he could go. His eyes closed and his chin dropped toward his chest. Muscles in his lean jaw twitched and his fingers clenched.

What if she loved him? Lord, this was a whole new wrinkle. In a total reverse of former positions, his pirate self had a fleeting, panicky urge to do exactly what she wanted — to send her away — and his gentleman self protested strenuously such low, cowardly impulses — avoiding, running from a mere female's power. Besides, his rational self put in, sending her away wouldn't stop this longing for her . . . this craving for her tantalizing flesh and for the intriguing woman that inhabited that curvy body. His eyes opened and filled with the dull white of his shirtfront. A neat little seam of mending ran beside the bone buttons. He fastened on it, beginning a disturbing count of the tiny, even stitches that seemed to blend into the weave. They were the essence of Blythe Woolrich, distilled.

She was a woman who mended shirts without being asked, who carried soup to sick pirates and had more trouble with her own hair tangles than she had backing off a crew of cutthroats who threatened to finish her off. She was strong and soft, responsible and vulnerable, adamant and yet so sweetly yielding. She took responsibility for every blessed thing that befell her, good or ill, and she was oh so delectably eager to experience the full pleasures of life. She was the kind of woman who believed in honesty, even when it was painful, and who kept promises, no matter what the cost.

A woman like that deserved a few promises herself. And a man like him had no blessed right making them. No right at all.

He turned, feeling a queer turmoil of heat growing in the middle of him, spreading outward, reaching for her. He had no defense against the strange combination of lusty and tender urges she produced in him. She stood, braced, at the edge of the bunk, her sweet face a study in contained misery. He took a step toward her and then another, watching the impact of his movements in the pulsing centers of her eyes.

"I can't promise to never hurt you, Wool-witch . . ." His voice was very quiet and all the more potent for it. "But I'll try not to, with everything in me. This need I have for you, I don't pretend to understand it. I don't exactly like it. But it's there. And by whatever honor I have left, I'll give you what I can . . . pleasure and whatever possessions I have. I hope it will be enough, wench. For I can't send you home."

"But what if I do come to . . . ?" she choked, unable to finish.

"With any luck at all," he felt himself quiver at the thought, "you'll realize what a rogue I am and won't . . . come to love me."

Blythe's chin trembled and tears came vaulting down her cheeks afresh. He wouldn't let her go . . . he wanted her enough to brave even the possibility that she might love him. Heaven help her—she wanted him so; it would have to be enough.

"Oh, Raider—" She walked straight into his open arms and molded herself against his hard male frame as though she could absorb him through her very skin. He bound her to him with a possessive hug and gave in to the painful sweetness of her slender arms around his waist, her lush breasts pressed against his ribs.

Through the steam rising in his blood, he felt a thrill of relief. She really did want him. He let out a ragged breath and felt a bit weak in the knees. He had no idea what he'd have done if she hadn't surrendered.

Blythe raised shining, tear-rimmed eyes to him and her cherry-red lips parted as they soared toward his. Their mouths blended, honey sweet and salty from her tears. That hot, liquid joining sent ripples of fire through them both, making hands move and conquer, making skin burn for closer contact.

Raider's smooth-muscled legs were braced and he was panting by the time he raised from the welcoming heat of her mouth. He grinned shakily and set his hands at her lacings, fumbling strangely under the seductive heat of her gaze. When her hands closed over his, he sought her eyes and paused. But she pushed her bodice aside and spread his fingers over the hot tipped mounds of her breasts, covering them with her hands, directing his caress. And she lifted her arms to the back of his head and pulled him down to join them in another bone-melting kiss.

This time when he raised his head, his hands moved swiftly and with joyful ease. Soon her clothing lay in a pool about her feet and his hands and eyes had free rein of his golden-eyed prize. His hands molded to her collarbones and down along her slender arms. He knelt on one knee and kissed her belly and buried his face in the valley between her breasts, nuzzling, drinking in the freshness of her skin and the erotic texture of her nipples. Taking his burning face between her cool hands, she kissed him deeply. And as he came to his feet, he rubbed against her body all the way, clamping his arms around her buttocks and carrying her with him so that he held her off the floor. He pressed her sweet thatch of curls against his bulging breeches and undulated slowly, enjoying her gasps and squirms. But her shocked breaths quickly turned to surprised moans of pleasure and he found himself groaning and moving her to the bunk.

In a flurry of hands and kisses, his clothes were shed. And Blythe kissed his ribs and nibbled his ears and arched against his hot mouth on her breasts. He covered her body with his and sucked breath at the erotic way she wriggled beneath him, her cool skin coaxing his heat, her cloaked heat seeking and setting his aflame.

Drums . . ." he heard her say through the pounding of his blood in his head. "Let's try for drums . . ."

He laughed, free and exultant . . . a lusty pirate kind of laugh.

And drums it was.

The fifth Sabbath after Blythe's disappearance dawned cold and gray on Philadelphia, but rather pleasant on Walter Woolrich. The Sabbath was the one day of the week he didn't find his meddlesome clerk on his doorsteps and on his nerves. He'd been forced to spend long, wearisome days in the confines

245

of Woolrich Mercantile Shop, breathing lint and dust and smiling at people whose names he couldn't remember. Tiresome business, business. He never understood the fascination in it himself. He was only too glad to be shed of its restrictive forms and myriad duties on this one day of the week he could call his own.

He breakfasted alone in the empty dining room, with only his headful of churning ideas to keep him company. He was becoming accustomed to solitary meals and solitary evenings in a cold parlor or attic. But occasionally he found himself addressing his daughter's chair, then turning about to find it empty. It always puzzled him until he recalled that Carrick insisted she was missing . . . or off visiting her aunt somewhere. The story seemed to change sometimes and he could never keep it all straight.

But this morning, he was as eager as a boy for a bit of Christmas gingerbread. He hurried his last sips of barley coffee and suffered his final shudder, then was on his way up the steps to his attic.

In the darkened upstairs hallway, he passed by Nana's partly opened door and a violent flash of movement caught his eye. Drawn to the excitement of motion like a small boy, he hurried into the room and arrived just in time to see the billow of settling covers on Nana's bed.

"Mother?" he scowled and cautiously approached the gloom of her draped and postered bed.

"Walter? Wh-what are you doing here?" The hot flush of Nana's pinched features was hidden by the dimness of her bed. Her heart pounded in her throat. She should have known better than to be out of bed without making sure the door was closed securely.

"I saw . . . I thought someone . . ." He paused, scratching his head. He had absolutely no idea what he was doing there. But it came to him. "I thought Blythe . . ."

"Well, she's not here," Nana frowned. "And don't expect her back . . . ungrateful vixen. Deserted us without a word . . . just like her mother. I told you, Walter, you can't trust fancy French women. Huss—"

246

But Walter had stiffened as if struck at the first mention of his late wife and before that last familiar condemnation was complete, he was on his way out the door. He escaped toward the rear staircase leading upstairs and, like the boy he had become in recent years, took them by twos and threes.

He was panting furiously when he reached the attic door and had to double over with hands on his knees to restore himself. Shortly he flung the attic door back and hurried inside, closing his mind against everything but his latest project, his precious coils.

He worked for several hours, hammering with his rounded mallet, refetching and pulling and wrapping and tapping. It took nearly Herculean effort to finish wrestling the tough copper sheathing into long, spiraling coils that were to be attached to the arms and back of the last wooden parlor chair in all of Woolrich House. His coils, he was convinced, would revolutionize medical practice. They would draw the sick humors from a body, take away all hurt . . . They'd make the world virtually painless. He was busy making the crowning connections of copper wiring when there was a loud scrape and a bustle by the door.

He startled and lost the balance of his squat, tumbling on his rear and instinctively cringing . . . expecting censure . . . or anger in the sound of Blythe's voice. He'd been discovered again—

"There ye be; I knew it." Lizzy came to stand over him with her work-reddened hands on her hips and a petulant frown on her face. "Well, Mr. Woolrich . . . sir. Ye missed dinner again. It be cold as a well-digger's ankle now. Mrs. Dornly be steamin' proper and I come to fetch ye."

Walter wilted with relief and pulled himself to his feet. "Thank heaven . . . I thought you were Blythe . . . that she'd found my coils . . ."

"Miss Blythe?!" Lizzy's pert face blanked, then crowded and contracted with true ire. "Miss Blythe's been missin', sir, for five full weeks . . . and you cain't even remember it?! I seen some low creatures in my time, Mr. Walter Woolrich, but you—" Lizzy stalked forward, coiled like a she-cat. "Miss Blythe, she worked her fingers to the bone for ye and that wailin' bag of

247

bones she calls her grandma. Ye never give her nothin', never even cared she was gone nor what happened to her. I hope she did run off. I hope she did find some feller to carry her away and be good to her. It'd beat stayin' here and workin' herself to the grave over the likes of you! She could be dead . . . and little you'd care as long as you had your crazy 'coils' and doin's! You be the poorest excuse for a man or a father I ever seen!"

The fire in Lizzy's eyes scorched Walter in unexpected places, and when she turned and stomped out, he just stood there, his beleaguered mind reeling from her harsh words. Blythe was gone . . . run off? Maybe dead? *His* Blythe? His mother's harsh words came back to him, echoing Lizzy's; she's deserted them just like Elise . . .

A pain sliced through Walter's chest and both hands came up to clutch his heart. But Elise didn't desert him . . . Elise was dead, they said . . . she couldn't ever come back. And he saw her put into the icy ground . . . his warm, lovely Elise. His legs began to tremble and his hands turned icy. Blythe hadn't . . . wouldn't desert him, not his sweet little Blythe. She wouldn't die, too . . . wouldn't go away. Who would hug him, take care of. . .

Pain welled up in him, crowding his breathing, squeezing his heart, searing through his chest in suffocating waves. Carrick said Blythe was gone, too . . . missing and "who knew why or where?" She was gone, Lizzy said . . . maybe hurt, maybe run off, maybe dead. Oh, God. Blythe wouldn't die, would she? She wasn't disappointed enough in him to die, too, and leave him alone like El— But Elise loved him . . . and Blythe loved him.

He clutched his chest, panting, as cold beads of sweat broke through his forehead and ran down his face. God, it hurt . . . this squeezing, this pain. They were gone . . . both of them had deserted him . . . left him . . . Oh-h—the pain!

He gasped for every breath, staggering, bumping into the edge of the parlor chair. There was a roaring in his head and his vision was blurring. Dear Lord, why was he hurting so badly? Why would they leave . . . his Elise and now Blythe . . . dead?!

Reeling and flailing about, he touched the cold copper of his coils and a last desperate connection was made in his tortured mind. His coils . . . the pain! They'd take away the pain! He groped for the seat of the chair and struggled into it, gasping, moaning aloud, his eyes squeezed shut against the crushing pain in his chest.

He found the split copper coils at the sides of the chair back and managed to pull each half about his ribs like a cold, metallic embrace. Then, as cold sweat ran down his face and back, he shoved his legs into the coils attached to the chair legs and his arms into the coils attached to the arms. Scarcely able to breathe, he laid his head back against the chair and waited, believing.

But the pain continued to twist angry fingers through his chest and guts. God, *please* . . . it hurt so much. Blythe dead, too . . . gone. Maybe he was dying, too. The pain . . . the coils would help the pain. But the pain slithered through his heart and wrapped about his mind, shaking it like a dog does a bone. Tears squeezed beneath his clamped eyelids and burned down his contorted face. His coils, they . . .

He forced his eyes open and was barely able to see the beaten copper tubes he'd spent weeks fashioning. The pain was still there, even worse . . . and the coils . . . *The coils weren't doing anything!* They didn't take away the pain and hurt. He was in agony and the coils wouldn't help!

A fresh volley of pain seized him and he began to snub like a child, ripping his arms from their coils and tearing at the cold copper fingers that bound his ribs. The awful realization crashed in on him; the coils didn't work for him . . . they wouldn't work for anybody. They were a failure!

He crumpled in the chair, sobbing into his shirtsleeves like a child. Not even the pain in his chest could compare with the pain in his long-shielded soul.

It was some time before he managed to straighten and to realize the pain was subsiding. He pulled his legs free and rose, staggering, to stare at the contraption he had been sitting in. For the first time saw a faded parlor chair with nails splintering the wood where crude, heavy copper tubes had been attached. For the first time he saw jagged metal edges and clumsy, boyish dents and uneven turns. With new eyes, he saw the product of his delusions and fancies, a boyish whim run rampant.

249

He'd spent days, weeks hiding it, savoring it, protecting it from his daughter's wrath. All the while Blythe was missing. All the while, he'd been the fool. Copper coils, pieces of metal, just the stuff pennies were made of. He had treated it like a treasure . . . not realizing his real treasure, his young daughter, the last love of his life, was gone. Good Lord Almighty, what had happened to him? Had he gone totally mad?

The attic was cold and dim and the litter of invention on the floor around him suddenly looked like simple refuse. The rafters seemed to close in on him; the attic seemed smaller. The pain in his chest was easing, but the tumult in his soul raged on.

Ashen and drenched with sweat, Walter stumbled to the door, still clutching his chest. His Elise was dead . . . and maybe his Blythe as well.

For the second time in his life, Walter Woolrich was making the painful passage from boy to man. And this time it came too late. His Blythe, his darling little love, was already gone.

Chapter Sixteen

Two changes were instituted in the *Windraider*'s seagoing routine in the first week of Blythe's new status on board; a dramatic increase in the consumption of bathing water and the institution of the deplorably "respectable" custom of knocking on doors. Every day or two, it seemed, Raider was ordering the rain barrels half emptied and the water heated for a bath for Blythe, and the lads frowned quizzically at each other, then scowled. Whatever Raider was doing to her, they mused privately, it apparently made her feel a good wash was in order. And they didn't like the sound of that at all.

But it was the business of knocking on doors that caused the most consternation. It began innocently enough, that first morning of Blythe's mistresshood. Blythe and Raider lay entwined a long while, whispering and touching and ignoring the rest of the world as they discovered each other. The longer they took to appear on deck, the darker the looks that were exchanged by Bastian and the lads. Topside, they were waiting for course corrections, and by noon had struck a good bit of canvas and were losing a near perfect wind, waiting.

Bastian, being the intrepid sort, finally rallied a contingent and tromped down the steps into the passage outside Raider's door. His eyes narrowed at the quiet. Then he heard something resembling Raider's deep, rumbling laugh and went scarlet, glaring at the door as if he could set it alight with the heat of his eyes. His blocky hand was on the handle and shoving the door open before he considered all the possible ramifications.

Blythe gasped and snatched the comforter about her chemise-clad form, but not before Bastian and the lads who crowded into the doorway around his shoulders got an eyeful of silky leg and curvy hip. Raider was caught, flat-footed, in breeches alone, shirtless and bootless, his face half lathered with soap and half shaved. With an aplomb learned from Oriental potentates, he cast a hot glance at Blythe's huddled and crimson form and turned on Bastian and his men.

"Just what in hell do you think you're doing?" Raider was supremely calm. It boded ill.

"We have to be settin' rudder; there be a fair wind . . . and we ain't under orders . . . *yet*." Bastian's blocky chin was out.

"I'll set *your* rudder . . . straight to hell if you ever walk into my cabin again without knocking." Raider's low rasp sent hair prickling on the backs of their necks.

"Knockin'?" Morgan's Balls, Raider—" Bastian was aghast.

"Knocking, dammit! You pound your damned knuckles on the door and *wait* for permission to enter." He stalked toward Bastian, soap, bare feet, and all. He raised a steely fist . . . and set it to the door beside Bastian's head, to demonstrate the proper technique. Whap, Whap, Whap!

The lads watched the seafire in Raider's eyes and swallowed hard. A few of their hands closed and jerked rhythmically, trying out the new maneuver.

"Hell, Raider we got to see you when we got to see you! And we ain't never had to knock on doors before—"

"Well, things have changed." Raider spoke calmly but there was an unmistakable edge to his voice that warned against continuing the conversation.

"They sure as hell have." Bastian jerked his chin back, sounding like the prospect galled him thoroughly. He glowered briefly at Blythe's huddled, shrouded back and turned on his heel to shove his way through the lads.

Raider scorched the others with his glare and slammed the door, narrowly missing the last bloke out. He turned to behold Blythe, settled on the corner of the bunk, her back to him. She had pulled the blanket up around her head so that virtually none of her was visible and he frowned, cursing his crew's untimely intrusion. The luscious warmth of their loving, of her surrender to him was probably forfeit.

He squared his shoulders determinedly and went to her, invading the blanket to lift her scarlet face. "They're used to having free use of my door . . . access to me wherever, whenever they please. Now that I'm sleeping in here again, they just resumed their old habits. But they'll get used to it."

"But . . . will I?" She lowered her eyes and fresh color bloomed in her face.

"You will, Wool-witch," he grinned and bent to brush her lips with his. Feeling her shrink from the contact, her pulled her up and into his arms. "Just think about what a musician you're going to be . . ."

His kiss curled her toes and set off colored rockets inside her head. When he released her, she swayed and blinked and sat down weakly on the corner of the bunk again. He took a deep, satisfied breath and strode to the washstand to finish shaving. As he toweled the last water from his face, he glanced up to find her still sitting there, wrapped in that absurd cocoon with a big streak of soap drying on her face.

"You'd better dress, wench," he laughed gently, enjoying the girlish picture she made. "Some of those chuckleheads may be a bit slow at using their knuckles at first."

Blythe watched him leave and shook free of the spell his lips had worked on her. She dressed instantly, made the bunk and tidied up the breakfast tray. François might be hurt that they'd eaten so little breakfast, she realized, so she downed another biscuit and a slice of ham to make it look better. When a very loud knock came at the door, she felt a little sick and went to open it herself. Old Willie's expression was prunelike as he thumped past her to collect the tray and Blythe had the sinking feeling that it was an expression she should probably get used to seeing. Raider's men wouldn't like it that her presence barred them from his cabin, nor would they like the fact that Raider now kept a "mistress" aboard their ship. She'd learned enough about pirate ways to know that women were considered bad luck indeed aboard ships.

So Blythe postponed her debut as Raider's mistress among his crew. She didn't want to see the speculation and the condemnation in their eyes, the resentment they had every right to feel. She found some mending to do and occupied the long afternoon with a book from his shelves.

The solitude and the shame of her status began to weigh on her nerves. She made herself say the word "mistress" aloud, ten times, trying to get used to it. ". . . mistress, mistress, mistress, *mistress!*" But it still made her stomach a bit queasy. Surely there was a better term. Paramour? Kept woman? Courtesan? Light o' love? She shuddered. Those were the nicer terms for her new status and none of them sounded enough like "wife" to suit her. The domestic trend of her thoughts dismayed her.

She had to leave that genteel respectability behind somehow. Raider Prescott wanted her badly enough to counter his own men and to forgo the possibility of a ransom from Neville Carson. And he promised to take care of her and not to send her away. It was commitment . . . of sorts. And she loved him . . . despite her face-saving talk of "maybe's."

It wasn't precisely what she had dreamed of in the few romantic moonbeams she'd allowed herself to spin as a girl. It wasn't fancy balls and gentlemanly beaus, moonlit garden walks and shy glances, and flowery speeches. It was a hot, sinewy male body reaching urgently for her softer, cooler frame. It was penetrating kisses and worshipful caresses and sensations that shook her very soul. It was stunning, bright pleasures and sultry, stirring murmurs of passion that set fire to her nerves and stripped away all the senseless "should's" of life. It was a woman's primal response to a man's desire. And it certainly wasn't respectable.

"Respectable" fit between cramped little lines society drew to contain and constrain. What she had discovered with Raider Prescott would never fit into society's safe, neat little categories . . . especially not the neat little category of "marriage." It was too wild and sweet and explosive to be "contained," ever.

Well, she told herself, setting her jaw and squaring her broad

254

shoulders, if it was her fate to be the one Raider Prescott lusted for, then she'd just have to deal with it . . . put the most honorable construction on it possible. It just wasn't sensible to pretend he wasn't bedding her. And it would be an outright lie to pretend she didn't want him to. Being the sensible and honest sort she was, she determined to make the best of it. It was her life now, pirate's woman . . . Wool-witch. And she didn't want to think about the rest of what fate might have in store . . .

The lads of the *Windraider* watched Blythe step out on deck each evening and they scrutinized her winsome face and her womanly form for signs of duress. She seemed healthy enough and they were consoled mightily by The Raider's sterling reputation as a smooth and gentlemanly lover. But she greeted them shyly and met their stares with blushes and lowered eyes. Something wasn't right, they decided; she fidgeted and wouldn't say much and withdrew quickly below decks.

It had to be that she was unhappy over The Raider's decision to keep her. Their Wool-witch was a respectable female before The Raider made her his woman. And they had it on Bastian Cane's authority that most respectable females would rather die than bed a man who hadn't said "church words" with them. It seemed a rather extreme preference to them—death before "unchurched" sex. The Wool-witch had always struck them as a more sensible sort. But then, none of them was well versed in the pecularities of the "respectable female" mind. In spite of The Raider's consummate skill, maybe the Wool-witch honestly didn't like being loved up. That possibility and the way she avoided them left them feeling uncertain and more than a little surly.

With each day that passed, they grew more restive and resentful toward their captain. When they learned they were headed for the islands and their home base, rather than prize-hunting, they snorted disbelief. What were they doing heading home instead of getting on with the business of "piratin' "? Then they grumbled about a change the Raider wanted in the blocks of the replacement rigging for the tackle that had been damaged in their skirmish with the *Cherabim*. The Bosun Deane and Flap Danny, the chief rigger, came nose-to-nose with him under the crew's watchful glare and the Raider had to back them down. The lads began to fall quiet whenever the Raider approached and their eyes dulled with resentment whenever he mentioned Blythe or his cabin. And their brand of knocking on Raider's door became more like a full broadside than a request to enter.

Blythe watched the friction between Raider and the lads, feeling responsible and very helpless. It was one thing for them to resent her, she understood that, but it was quite another to see them at odds with their Raider. She would never have mentioned her missing dress if she'd had any idea of the trouble it would ignite in an already volatile situation . . .

That morning, at the end of her first week in Raider's bed, Blythe came topside, dressed in her sea-green velvet awash in Belgian laces. She found Raider on the fo'c'sle with Bastian and asked a word with him. His very warm smile down at her noticeable cleavage sent a wave of heat into her face and she lowered her eyes, a little embarrassed that he should enjoy her so openly before his partner and his men. She wasn't sure she'd ever come to terms with it, but she was trying. Her discomfiture was seen clearly by every man on deck.

"You look like sugarcake, Wool-witch," he grinned. "I do like that dress . . ."

"Raider . . . I'm only wearing it because something happened to . . . my other dress. When I rose this morning, it was gone." She saw the sobering of Raider's face and recalled the strong punishment meted out for stealing aboard ship. "I'm not accusing anyone, but I've searched the cabin . . . and it's just not there."

Raider stroked his chin thoughtfully and flicked a glance at Bastian, who came to attention and searched Raider's inscrutable expression.

"Well, it weren't Stanley," Bastian said irritably, "hers wouldn't fit him . . . and Harry don't do that no more." When Raider stared at him sharply, he waved Clive over to corroborate. A few more of the lads drifted over with him. "Harry don't wear female clothes no more, does he?" Bastian asserted.

"Jus' hats," Clive nodded solemnly.

"See there," Bastian turned a hot glance on Blythe, "jus' hats. Not dresses. It weren't none of the lads what stole her dress." Bastian's assertion produced a wave of murmurs that drew a few more lads in their direction.

Blythe's ears burned as she heard her plight spread from one set of lips to another and felt their collective gaze searching her. Why didn't Raider say something?

"I know it wasn't the lads," Raider finally spoke, setting Blythe's fingertips atingle. She jerked her head up to look at his tight expression. "It was me." A wave of confusion crashed through the lads at The Raider's bold admission. "I gave it a heave . . . overboard. It was the damned ugliest dress I ever saw."

It was hard to say whose shock was greatest, Blythe's or the lads'. The Raider had chucked the Wool-witch's dress overboard? Lord, what was the man thinkin' of, they wondered. Raider callously tossed half of her meager wardrobe overboard?! Blythe was too stunned to hide her hurt and whirled and ran to the hatch and below.

Raider scowled deeply as he watched her go. He'd done it now. Respectable females set great store by their clothes, he knew. It was regrettable indeed that Harry hadn't finished with it before she awakened and found it missing.

"Well . . . what are you gaping at? Get back to your duties," Raider barked, starting for the hatch with long, determined strides.

The lads watched him go and turned to each other, speechless. Tossed her dress overboard . . . They'd never imagined The Raider could be so ruthless! Did he mean to keep her naked?!

When Raider entered his cabin he found Blythe sitting in a chair near the window, staring out at the waves and looking miserable indeed. He went to stand behind her and found his mouth a bit dry.

"You're upset. Maybe I should explain."

"Why should you?" she said with more melancholy than bitterness. "It's your ship. I'm your . . . woman."

He swallowed and made himself say it, hoping it would suffice.

257

"That dress . . . reminded me of things I'd rather forget, Wool-witch. It was from your past." He went to his great trunk and threw open the lid. "You have a different life now. You can make some new things . . . you're very talented with a needle."

It was the second time he'd complimented her stitchery, and it didn't make her any happier than the first time he'd done it. She couldn't look at him, couldn't explain that she wanted that "ugly" little dress for the very reasons he wanted her rid of it . . . for the memories. It was her one physical link with her past, her home. Respectable "sentiment" again. Tears collected in her eyes and she didn't want him to see them. When he came to stand before her, she turned her head away.

"I'm sorry, Wool-witch." He saw her fighting back the tears and quietly hated himself. "I didn't know it meant so much to you. You look so much better in this one." His fingers feathered gently over the puff of her sleeve and then dropped to trace a knuckle up the sinuous appliqué from her waist to her breast. She shivered and he couldn't tell if it was from pleasure or revulsion. He had to know, and he pulled her to him and turned her chin up to test that response.

The minute his lips closed over hers, she was lost in the wonder of his kiss, in the mystery of the tenderness he roused inside her even when she was hurt. When he ended that stunning kiss and raised his head, Blythe glimpsed true regret in his eyes. It was enough.

"Maybe you're right, Raider. Starting over," she whispered. But a tear escaped her lower rim of lashes and Raider caught it on his fingertips.

"Maybe I was wrong, Wool-witch, not consulting you first." The realization jolted him. In the last nine years he'd had virtually no one to account to for his decisions, not even Bastian. He was responsible for his men and ship, and he was careful with that responsibility. Now he found himself responsible in a whole new way . . . both for and to his woman.

"You'll probably need warmer things soon anyway. Maybe some boots." He was feeling a bit unnerved and released her, sliding back into his captain's role. "November can be a nasty month in the Atlantic."

"November?" She looked at him in some confusion, but his withdrawal was only partly to blame. Removed from her land-based routine of cleaning and changing and storing for the seasons, she'd lost track of time. "Don't say it's November already."

"Not quite yet. It's October . . . . the seventeenth, I believe. I could check if you want . . . It's in my log." He watched her face drain of color and saw her shoulders sink as she turned away. "What's wrong, Wool-witch?" He went to stand behind her, trying to decide whether he ought to touch her or not.

"Two days ago . . . I was twenty years old," she finally spoke. "Twenty . . . and on the shelf."

Relief washed over him and he grinned, thanking his lucky stars for a timely birthday that took her mind off their differences. "On the shelf?" He laughed at the sweet absurdity of it. He turned her forcibly and filled his arms with her. "You'll never be on the shelf, golden eyes. There are no pleasures, no joys, no adventures on the shelf. And you've already had more than enough of those to disqualify you from the ranks of 'spinster.' "

She sputtered and pushed against his chest, chagrined afresh by the respectable pitfalls in her thinking and unsure whether she was disturbed or pleased by his insight. When his hands began to move over her velvet-clad back, she shivered and stood still against him.

"I think you need a demonstration of just how far from the shelf you've come."

His mouth crushed hers, and the warmth of his desire for her melted all the confusions that had hardened against him. His well-muscled frame was soon melting her body as well. And in minutes, he was removing her ladyish dress and spreading her lush fall of hair around her creamy shoulders on the bunk. When he lowered himself to her, he shuddered with relief as she welcomed him into her soft heat. Soon they were spiraling into passion's brightest plane, joined in body and touching in spirit.

When her heartbeat returned to a bearable pace, she wriggled from his arms, feeling suddenly free and full of life. "Not on the

259

shelf." She said it over and over in her head. She could never be on the shelf . . . ever . . . not after Raider Prescott's loving. A seductive curl came to her lips as she swayed across the floor to his open sea chest. She bent over the chest, sorting through the feminine exotica he'd collected, fully aware of his eyes on her bare body. She found the things she was looking for, and turned with her hands full of gold wire brocades and sensuous silks, flicking her hair back with a seductive roll of her shoulder.

"I've been dying of curiosity for weeks." Her sultry smile became a grin. "How *would* I put these on?"

He laughed and pushed up on one elbow, luxuriating in the contrast of her dark hip-length hair and the creamy beauty of her bare breasts and curvy hips. "I think . . . those are something like breeches. Come here, I'll help."

She strolled within his reach as he sat up on the bunk, and together they laughed as they fitted her into what appeared to be the oddest breeches imaginable. The top part of them, stiff, gold-encrusted red brocade that was lined with silk, covered her buttocks and fitted indecently between her legs. Covering each leg was a sheer tube of near transparent black silk that ended in a brocade cuff about her ankle. The near perfect fit around her buttocks and against her woman's mound was shockingly like Raider's sensual caresses. When they found and fastened the last hooks, she stared down at her bottom, chagrined by the fruits of her wayward impulse.

"Oh, well . . . I only wondered." She flushed hotly and he laughed and stayed her hands from removing them.

"No . . ." He could hardly speak for the desire squeezing his throat again. He watched her shielding her breasts with her hands and slid his eyes down her silky belly and between her legs. He'd never seen a woman who looked more like the personification of sexual pleasure in his life. "It looks wonderful on you. Try the other part . . ."

"Well . . ." She seemed uncertain and he pulled her closer and held it up to her. It was two shell-like cups of wired broacade linked together by series of fine golden chains. He held the cups in his palms and placed them over her breasts, engaging her

260

eyes.

"What else would they be for? Interesting idea . . ." He mused wicked appreciation for both the garment and the woman that filled it. At this direction she fastened the chains around her, and when he drew his hands away, the gold-encrusted shells stayed in place as though caressing her breasts for him.

"Oh . . . oh!" she breathed, feeling strange slithery sensations under her skin and in her nipples and womanflesh. She made to remove it, and he grabbed her wrists and pushed his long legs over the side of the bunk. "You've seen women really wear these things?" Her golden eyes flew adorably wide.

"In private, or in the company of other women. Certainly not in the street. No place on earth is *that* broadminded."

"Where?" she breathed.

"Persia and Turkey. In harems . . . my harem, actually—"

"A *harem?!*" she gasped, "You had a harem?"

"Briefly. A small one, I had to give it back. The grand pasha's son was very grateful for the fact that I pulled him from a shipwreck and ferried him home. In the East, gratitude has a very tangible expression. I chose to keep this as a remembrance. And now I'm very glad I did." The intensity of his fascination with her body was entrancing. "Walk for me," he asked hoarsely, his eyes glowing white-hot.

She was experiencing a return of those deliciously decadent streams of sensation in her body and she dropped her arms slowly and walked across the cabin. Her buttocks swayed in their golden casing and her legs moved seductively beneath the sliding, shadowy silk. The rasp of the stiff brocade against her hardening nipples was electrifying. She paused and turned to face him, her lips swollen with desire and her eyes shining like Turkish coins. Her full breasts scarcely covered, her bottom caressed intimately by that unyielding fabric, her dark hair tumbling over her shoulders, she was the most erotic and exciting creature he had ever beheld. And she was his.

"Come to me, golden eyes," he whispered raggedly, trembling with an agony of arousal.

The darkening of his eyes and the bronzing of his skin were a revelation to her. For for the first time, she felt her own sensual power in the pull of his need for her. And she explored it as she closed her eyes and wriggled her body, feeling the erotic cling of the garments and the hot probing of his matchless eyes. Something made her want to sway and wriggle, as though in the throes of his loving and, on impulse, she did it. It was a hypnotizing sensation. Desire filled her from head to toes as her bottom undulated and wriggled suggestively, a Salome's dance of pure invitation. She heard his groan and opened her eyes to find him coming toward her.

He went down on his knees in front of her and sent his hands over every inch of her explosively sensual body. His fingers worked beneath the shells at her breasts and toyed with her nipples while he kissed her belly and nibbled the bared skin between her navel and that band of stiff brocade. Then he clasped her body to him and slid his hands down into the pants, cupping her sleek buttocks, then finding the liquid heat of her creamy womanflesh. She writhed against his probing fingers, clasping him to her belly, and soon he was on his feet, lifting her into his arms and carrying her to their bed.

He lay back and pulled her astride his swollen manhood, whispering that he could see her better this way. She was too overwhelmed by the hot flow inside her to object. She lay down on him and wriggled, teasing and reveling in this new sense of sexual power. Soon her hands left him to fumble with her garments and his followed, only heightening the confusion.

"How do I get it off?" she laughed with throaty impatience. By the time they found all the hooks, she was too impatient to remove it all. She just peeled the breeches aside and allowed him to guide her hips downward onto his hot, turgid shaft. Her heart stopped as he filled and expanded her, then began a final thundering crescendo as he moved inside her, lifting and exciting her in new, unimagined ways.

Together they spiraled and shot into the vastness of the heavens, beyond the hottest stars, mingling body and soul. The pure lightning bolts and eruptions of pleasure seemed to peak and subside, then to peak again in her. And when she finally collapsed over Raider, panting and moist and spent, he stared at her in wonder and hugged her to him as though he couldn't let go.

He had never, not in his entire libertine life, experienced anything like that. The whole damn earth moved . . . oceans and mountains and all! And he was left in its quaking aftermath, wrapped in steam and floating in a hazy, delicious netherland of primal satisfaction. Blythe . . . his *hot* little vixen . . . his Wool-witch . . . his love. And as he drifted off to sleep with her in his arms, that last word poured through him, entwining about his roving heart, securing it for all time.

The lads saw none of them that afternoon and glimpsed Raider only briefly that evening . . . when he came out to order the Wool-witch a bath and to check the watch and their position by the stars. They were quietly outraged at this bedding of their Wool-witch in light of his callousness toward her that morning . . . dumping her clothes in the drink!

Despite the smooth seas and gentle wind, only one man on board the *Windraider* got any sleep that night . . . the Raider himself. They could tell he had slept like a babe when he appeared on deck the next morning, bright and early. It soured their feelings toward him a bit more. And soon the tension on the top deck was as thick as chowder.

Raider felt it rising and was determined not to let their resentment over his keeping his Wool-witch on board come to a flash point of eruption. He would accommodate their irritation as far as he could, short of violating his authority and power as captain. He'd seen what arguments over women could do to a crew and knew he'd violated his own common sense where Blythe was concerned. He only hoped the cost he would have to pay wouldn't be too high.

It was the rustle of Blythe's silk petticoat, when she came topside, that collected the static charge of their free-floating ire. Their prickly gaze followed her about the deck and noted the way she avoided them. Shamed to the bottom of her being, they decided, exchanging harsh whispers as she passed. They never guessed she mistook their own fierceness in defense of her for resentment of her womanly presence and disapproval of her purpose aboard. They watched her pause to speak with Bastian and then were drawn with her toward the quarterdeck steps where she sought the comfort of Raider's welcome.

"Lazy wench," he laughed sardonically. "Sleeping the day away again, I see." His words reached the lads, but the sparkle in his eyes stopped with Blythe alone. It warmed her chilled nerves enough for a saucy retort . . . that was completely misread by Raider's crew.

"I was not *sleeping*, Captain." Her eyes flirted covertly. "I had a devil of a time deciding what to wear . . . thanks to you."

"Spit an' thunder!" came a growl from the pack of lads near the steps, and there was a thumping rush up onto the quarterdeck. In the blink of an eye, Old Willie was being restrained between the bosun, and Spanish Sharkey and the quarterdeck was nearly heaving with reined ire as other lads came running and crowded in behind them. Suddenly Raider faced a sea of hostility, with Blythe caught between them.

"Ye went an' throwed her clothes overboard," Willie spat, his face contorted like a walnut meat. "What'd ye expect, but that she can't bear to show 'er face on deck! Ye treat her like a gutter rip—"

"Tossin' her clothes overboard like they was full o' cooties!" came a voice from the back.

"Morgan's Knees—that's low!" Willie charged, lunging against his restrainers.

A hot wave of invective was unleashed, venting frustrations that had accumulated since the minute Blythe first set foot aboard ship. She paled, facing them, caught between Raider and his men, literally this time.

"No . . . please . . ." she uttered into the chaos, her eyes wide and horrified. Their angry snarls and teeming resentments buffeted her physically, and she shrank back toward Raider whose arms drew her possessively against his side.

"Dammit—it's none of your concern," Raider growled irritably, gauging their threat and skimming the crowd and deck for sight of Bastian. "She's my woman and I'll not be answerable to the likes of you for the way I keep her."

"The hell you won't" came Bosun Deane's hot reply, shocking everyone into silence, even The Raider. The flinty deck officer seldom spoke, except to curse, and made it his business to never concern himself with others' well-being. "I had a share . . . I'll have my say. And I say ye cain't keep her naked."

There was a rowdy round of agreement, and Blythe was stunned to realize they weren't challenging Raider because of her . . . but on her behalf! They didn't like the fact that he'd thrown her little dress overboard . . . didn't like it at all. "No, please . . . don't do this," she begged, straining to free herself from Raider's possessive grip. "I don't mind . . . really."

"Well *we* do, Wool-witch." Old Willie strained a bit harder in the bosun's and Sharkey's clutches. "Ye be like one o' us now, an' we won't let nobody treat ye bad . . ." His ferretlike eyes narrowed furiously on his captain, "not even The Raider."

Another wave of determined agreement swept through the two score men assembled. Raider realized full well it wasn't just a dress thrown overboard they were protesting. They were opposing his decision to bed her and challenging his decision to keep her as his woman. It wasn't hard to intuit the strong current of feeling that flowed beneath their rough demands; Raider had felt the same prickly stirrings, the same vengeful needs himself. He understood, all too well. They were jealous, every man-jack of them. They'd relinquished their shares in her body, but not their claims on her heart and her attentions . . . and her welfare. Recognizing that, he felt an infuriating twinge of forbearance and knew it was up to him to defuse the explosive situation.

"Richard!" he bellowed, but without anger; he never yelled when he was truly angry. Seeing Richard's waving response from down on the mizzen, he called, "Go down to dry storage and fetch Harry and Alfonse up here . . . now! Have them bring their work!" He turned his gaze on his men to meet their eyes, one by one, by one. A few stared back, but most could not counter him for long and drew their necks in defensively or

265

lowered their chins.

"Let's get this straight." Raider's voice dropped meaningfully, pulsing with contained threat. "The Wool-witch is mine. I've claimed her as *my* share and I'm committed to her welfare. Some of you have shipped with me nigh on to ten years. Have I ever mistreated a woman? *Or* gone back on my word?"

They murmured reluctant agreement, but a healthy pall of resentment remained, stretched over the strained silence that fell. Finally Clive spoke their collective reservation:

"Aye, but the Wool-witch be differ'n't." And there was a general mutter of support for his statement.

Raider glanced down at Blythe and found her hands clamped over her crimson face as if trying to hide from the humiliation she suffered at this public airing of her worldly status. His arm tightened about her waist, and he stepped forward a bit, shielding her with his body. His next words were chosen for her as much as for his men.

"Yes, she is different . . . more than you know. She's special to you, that's plain. But she's doubly so to me. That's why I've pledged to give her all she needs and to keep her by me . . . for as long as she wants to stay."

Willie eased in the bosun's steely grip, and the anger in his face dulled and softened. All but a few of the lads followed his lead. And shortly a commotion from the rear jostled and parted the tight pack, progressively working his way toward the front.

It was Harry and swarthy Portugese Alfonse bearing pieces of leather and soft cambric draped over their arms and a small pair of boots. "Here they be, Raider." Harry's nasal whine was heard by all. "One of the skirts be finished, but the shirts . . ." He ground to a half under the confused glares of his mates. Raider released Blythe and stepped forward to lift an odd-looking garment of buttery soft golden leather from Harry's hands.

"Blythe—" He turned to her and had to pull her hands down from her face to get her to look. "I was . . . having Harry and Alfonse make you something to wear, something a bit more suitable for life aboard a ship of men. They're only partway finished, but perhaps you'd better see them now." He put the soft

266

leather skirt in her hands and lifted her chin, feeling a twinge of guilt at the disbelief in her eyes. "If you don't like them . . ."

She caught the fleeting uncertainty in Raider's face and fumbled with the garment, realizing it was indeed a skirt, of sorts . . . made like a long and very full pair of men's breeches. Her heart suddenly had wings as she held the skirt up, staring at it. He'd had something made for her — something to wear aboard ship — Then he really did mean to keep her, just as he said! She crumpled the skirt against her, hugging it, then threw herself into Raider's arms, hugging *him* tightly and muttering, "Thank you, thank you, thank you!"

"Wait." He was so startled by her reaction that he pushed her back a bit to see her face. She was beaming, eyes wet and shining. "Don't you want to see the rest?!"

"Oh, it'll be wonderful . . . I know!" She threw her arms around his neck and pulled his head down to give him an exuberant kiss full on the mouth.

"B-but there are boots, too . . ." He reddened, a little shocked by her behavior. Just when he thought he had her figured out . . .

"Oh . . . yes." She saw his surprise and suddenly shared it, coloring violently. But not even the weight of respectable chagrin could make her soaring heart come back to the glove. She peered around Raider to the boots in Alfonse's hands and the other garments Harry held. Over one of Harry's arms was a very familiar splash of moss-green woolen and she bolted forward to snatch it up.

"My dress!" she breathed, holding it to her breast as she turned on Raider with very wide, then very narrow eyes. "You let me think you . . . That really was low, Raider Prescott."

"I *had* hoped to surprise you," he growled self-consciously. She realized he was a little hurt that she was so pleased to have her old dress back . . . when she'd scarcely looked at her new things. It was her first clue that inside Raider Prescott there was also a little boy . . . who just now craved a bit of praise for his efforts. She turned and took the boots from Alfonse, marveling at the fine workmanship and rubbing her cheek against the soft leather.

267

She raised her gaze to Raider's and poured all the depth of her feeling for him into one loving, scorching-hot look.

"It was wonderful of you, Raider. Thank you." She went to him and pulled him down by the arm and planted a kiss on the glowing bronze of his cheek. "I'm going to try them on!" Over Harry's sputter of protest, she relieved him of his work and smiled her way through the lads to race down the quarterdeck steps.

Raider watched her go, still feeling the imprint of her lips on his cheek. He drew a deep breath and turned a righteous and triumphant glare on his men.

"Any more objections?"

The lads wagged their heads sheepishly at Raider's jibe and dispersed in small clumps, across the deck, to wait a glimpse of their Wool-witch in her new attire. It was a walloping relief to know he hadn't given the Wool-witch's dress a heave and that she wasn't pining and unhappy in his cabin . . . or in his bed. The Raider's magic with females had apparently worked on her, too. The way she hugged and kissed him . . . right before God and the whole ship's company . . . made it seem she was downright pleased to be his woman. And The Raider was taking care of her, getting her clothes and such. A fine pair of boots and regular baths . . . a wench couldn't ask any more of a man.

Below, Blythe fumbled out of her dress and into the odd assortment of clothing Raider had ordered constructed for her. The soft leather skirt was split like a pair of loose breeches and Harry had constructed a soft linen petticoat or the same configuration to go under it. The shirt Harry had expressed some doubt about fit wonderfully well, though it was missing a few buttons yet. To go over it, they'd constructed a sleeveless, fitted leather waistcoat, lined with silk, that served as part corset, part coat. It buttoned snugly about her waist and over her breasts, flaring neatly to accommodate her hips. The garments were supple enough to allow easy movement and she dragged on the boots afterwards, admiring their fit below the skirts that stopped mid-calf. She ran her hands down over her clothes, luxuriating in the textures and in the perfect fit. Raider had spirited off her dress to provide them a guide to her sizes.

Raider. She smiled inside, feeling his caress in the very fit of her new clothes. And suddenly she knew. Whatever happened, from this moment on she was proud to be Raider Prescott's woman, proud to share his bed and his life . . . and someday, perhaps, she'd be proud to claim his love.

She twirled about the cabin on her toes, then hurried topside to show off her stunning new clothes. She gave Raider another innocent kiss on the cheek as the lads gathered to admire her new look and The Raider's tastes in seagoing-female attire. But in her rich golden eyes was a glint of promise; she'd thank him fully in the night to come.

Raider accepted that promise with the jade of his gaze and October eighteenth seemed like the longest single day in the history of man.

Chapter Seventeen

Bastian Cane had watched the entire incident of the Wool-witch's new clothes from the waist railing with a jaundiced eye. Look at the pack of them, he snarled mentally, ready to go at each other fang and claw one minute, then all softened up and gushin' like overripe pumpkins the next. Revolting. But of course, when the Wool-witch appeared topside a few minutes later, wearing her stunning new garb, he had to join in the fanfare and hullabaloo a bit to keep from being too conspicuous in his disapproval.

It wasn't that he necessarily disapproved of the Wool-witch herself. She was a right enough sort. And sometimes she was downright charmin', the way she smiled at a bloke and looked him straight in the eye and didn't flinch when he laughed too loud or belched . . . and tried not to wince when he let go a curse. Once or twice in her presence, he'd let himself think just how pretty and how small she was and he'd felt a strange tightness in his chest and a weakness in his feet. Fortunately, he'd been able to recognize those baffling sensations for just what they were: the effects of a respectable female ploy that trapped men into protecting them. One look at Raider and he knew just how treacherous a wile it was, for Raider was now ensnared in the very trap he'd ranted and railed against for nearly ten years. And the poor bastard didn't even seem to care!

And the lads, Bastian watched them admiring, then adoring her as the days passed and got positively sick inside. They argued and muscled each other aside for the privilege of answering her questions and spent their precious few hours of leisure whittling things for her or teaching her to throw a knife, to load a musket, or to deal a hand of cards. The worst of it was, she seemed to realize what they were doing and was positively gracious about it; didn't seem to have a smug or contentious bone in her body. She gave her time and attention generously, with scrupulous equality, except when it came to Raider . . . who always came first.

Bastian Cane kept his grumbles to himself, knowing that to express them would be tantamount to mutiny now aboard the *Windraider*. It was doubly hard for him to contain his resentments, when at Blyth's suggestion, Raider began inviting the crew to share supper in his cabin, a few at a time. Bastian watched the lads sprucing up for it like they were going to church and felt an unreasoning urge to knock heads together. Whoever else was invited to their table, Bastian was always asked and he was hard-pressed to hide his surliness as he watched the lads fumble with cutlery and fancy dishes and say "please" and "yer welcome," following The Raider's mannerly lead. It was just too much, the way they were softening up. She was turnin' a fine-honed crew of sea dogs into bloody useless lap dogs! They wouldn't be worth diddly in a fight!

Bastian's attitude was no secret to Raider or to Blythe, whose woman's intuition sensed the twinge of jealousy that lay at the core of Bastian's grudge against her. But a hundred surly and jealous partners couldn't have dimmed Blythe's bridelike fascination with Raider, or Raider's lusty-pirate obsession with her. They laughed and talked and loved as openly as Blythe's broadening standards of propriety would admit. And in private, Blythe soon came to relish the way there were no standards between them, nothing blocking the indulgence of their passions or their curiosity about each other.

Only occasionally did a cloud appear on their blue horizons. After a very hot bit of loving one night, that left them feeling physically joined well after their bodies had parted, Raider looked deep into the steamy gold of her eyes and glimpsed the unguarded depths of her feeling for him. It rattled him, and when he made to rise from the bunk, he found himself alarmingly incapable of moving.

"Blythe?" he swallowed the knot in his throat and managed to put his fears into words. "You're . . . you don't love me yet, do you?"

Those secret little doors in her heart closed and Blythe shivered at the edge of anxiety in his voice. She swallowed against the squeezing in her throat and managed, "No . . . not yet."

The worst part was the way he seemed to melt with relief as she said it. He gave her a thorough hug and rose from the bunk to dress and check the watch topside. And when he was gone, Blythe sat in the middle of the bunk, still feeling the mesmerizing pressure of his hands on her body and aching for the feel of his love in her heart. How could he love her physically into paradise over and over, protect her and talk with her, listen to her and design special clothes for her . . . and feel nothing for her but raw male need? Were men so different from women in that regard? Could they separate their bodies and their spirits as easily as they unbuttoned halves of a shirtfront?

Perhaps they could, she mused miserably, hence all the respectable cautions to young girls to abstain from giving in to a man's desires before securing their fortunes in his feelings first. Well, it was too late for her to exercise any such caution. She already loved Raider Prescott with everything in her and it was probably becoming more visible by the day. She wasn't a good liar, she knew. Raider believed her just now, because he wanted to believe her. The pirate in him wanted no talk of future, no entanglements beyond the assurances he'd given her. And since those assurances had yet to be tested, she had to hope they would fill the void that the need for his love had created inside her.

She dressed and went topside into the Caribbean night. Raider joined her at the railing, slipping his arms around her from behind and pulling her back against his warm, hard body. He pointed out constellations of stars in the clear southern sky, sharing his wonder at their brightness with her and missing the glistening in her night-darkened eyes.

272

A test of the *Windraider*'s fighting mettle came sooner than Bastian, or anyone, expected. They were three days out from their home base, thinking homeward thoughts, desiring land-bound pleasures they'd been denied for more than four long months. The lads were sea-randy and their tempers sparked and flared over trifles. Blythe worried at first, but Raider explained their sudden edginess to her in rather explicit terms and she colored hotly and tried to stay out of the way as much as possible.

When she carried cups of coffee on deck to Raider and Bastian the next morning, she found them alive with tension, straining their eyes toward the southern horizon. Raider called for his glass and studied the barely visible speck on the horizon for some time before handing it over to Bastian and taking his coffee from Blythe.

"What is it?" she whispered, unnerved by their intense mood.

"A merchant, maybe. She seems to be running alone." He sipped the brew and let his eyes drift over the little creases between her eyes as she frowned. This was a new turn, taking a prize ship with his Wool-witch aboard. Bastian's warnings about her ladyish sensibilities flooded back to him as he watched her eyes widen. With all the questions that were trailing through them, she said nothing.

Suddenly Bastian let out a crow of exultation. "She be a wallowing, ruttin' sow of a bucket! A square, fat bottom just ripe for a good—" he had whipped about and caught Raider's scowl above Blythe's wide eyes, and modified his lusty analogy, "—*raid*."

"Whose colors is she sporting?" Raider grinned at Bastian's open irritation over that bit of censorship.

"Can't see." Bastian flicked a questioning glance at Blythe, then back to Raider. He was asking the question that Raider was asking himself; could they raid another ship with Blythe on board? Would she protest, or faint, or cringe?

If they couldn't take a prize with her on board, Raider realized, then he was a doomed man. Raiding and taking ships, was his living, his life. And if he couldn't do that with Blythe aboard, then there wasn't much hope for him to keep her with him . . . or for him to live without her. He propped his hands on his hips and turned away, staring out over the waist and his lady *Windraider's* billowed sails. He could feel Bastian's poker-hot gaze prodding his back and he could feel Blythe's cooler, softer gaze stroking, trusting him. He had to know . . .

He turned with a hard set to his jaw and took the glass from Bastian's hands, extending it and raising it to his eye. He studied the large white speck and the muscles in his shoulders bunched with anticipation. Still no colors.

He lowered and collapsed the glass and turned to Bastian. "If she's British, we'll take her."

A wicked grin split Bastian's blocky face, for he knew the chances of her being British were good indeed. The British controlled "the eastern Virgins" and had frequent commerce with the Danes who controlled "the western Virgins"—St. Thomas, St. John, and St. Croix. Bastian didn't seem to notice Raider's adherence to his old "privateering" rule about taking only British ships. He began booming orders to "stand to" for action and hurried down to the waist, where the lads were yelling and passing on the good news.

Soon there was a familiar contagion on the top deck of the *Windraider* and lads filled the rails for glimpse of their quarry, before reeling off to their battle stations. In gleeful anticipation, Bastian unlocked the armory and handed out muskets, sending their sharpshooters up into the rigging. Blades began appearing at the men's sides. They were preparing for battle whether she was British nor not.

Raider watched it, refusing to stop it. He knew that this frantic surge of battle preparation served the same primal urge that had been building in them for the last two days . . . It was the same pound of blood in their veins, the same male urgency. He also knew that once it had gone this far, it was an unstoppable tide. And he raised his glass, praying silently for a glimpse of that wretched "double cross," the mingled standards of St. Andrew and St. George, that they called the "Union Jack."

274

And shortly, his prayer was answered.

A hot bolt of fire burst up his back, setting his scalp atingle with anticipation. He lowered the glass and handed it to Blythe, who stood watching him and the lads with an uncertain expression. He went to the quarterdeck railing and leaned on it as he bellowed Bastian's name loudly enough to stir Poseidon himself.

"Aye, Cap'n?" Bastian paused as he was straining on a movable bulwark lashing at the vulnerable waist of the ship. It seemed the whole crew stopped stock still.

"She's flyin' the Union Jack!" Raider bellowed and there was a deafening roar, above which his voice came again. "Then we'd better look British, too!" Blythe didn't realize exactly what Raider meant until she saw the bosun selecting a familiar-looking flag for the pole above the topgallants on the main mast. And shortly, Richard appeared with two dark blue military coats and gold-trimmed British naval officers' hats, red-ribboned cockades and all. Raider slid one coat over his customary shirt and, forward on the fo'c'sle, Bastian did the same.

Looking British, Blythe realized, meant laying a trap. She froze with her hands on the side railing as the furor of preparation increased around her. Her heart began to pound and it was hard to swallow. She smelled the dark odor of gunpowder as wooden buckets of the stuff were carted up to the swivel guns on the quarterdeck nearby. The remembered clang and clash of battle flashed vividly in her mind and trembled her soul.

Raider glimpsed her at the railing, white and wide-eyed as she watched the merchantman growing larger as they approached. He abandoned the waist to come for her and escort her below.

"You'll stay in the cabin, Wool-witch . . . like before." He took her arm and her waist and was surprised indeed when she dug her heels in and refused to budge.

"I won't." She stared up at him, pale but very determined. "I died a thousand deaths down there last time. I have to stay up here, Raider. I have to see what happens . . . even if it's terrible."

"No, Blythe—" He tightened all over at the thought of endangering her.

"Give me a pistol, Raider . . . give me two. I'll try to stay out of the way . . . but I'll *not* go below with you and your men about to fight." The trembling of her chin made it deuced hard to resist her and Raider found himself giving her a fierce, quick kiss and calling for Richard to fetch his pistols.

Shortly they were within visual range and Raider's men stationed themselves carefully, hiding behind the bulwarks so that the top deck appeared somewhat empty. Raider and Bastian stood on the quarterdeck with Blythe, watching the *China Lady* wallow toward them.

Unwittingly, Blythe's presence on deck lent credence to the *Windraider*'s peaceful ruse, for belligerents wouldn't have ladies aboard and the officers of the British merchantmen had spotted Blythe early on. It was a great relief to them to see a British frigate, carrying a lady, probably headed for Road Town in the British possessions. Thus, they made no preparations, except possibly for a few bottles of wine to be exchanged as a courtesy between captains, since she seemed to want a parley.

Bastian and Raider exchanged grins and wags of disbelief as the leisurely pace on the deck of the *China Lady* became quite visible. She was either very trusting . . . or very clever at cloaking her alarm. Tension built to fever-pitch on the *Windraider*'s deck and shortly they were within range and making that last unexpected turn, hard to starboard, to cut across the *China Lady*'s bow at a deadly "raking" angle. The side they'd shown her thus far had been battened and peaceful. But after their hard cut to swing across her path, the *Windraider* showed her teeth; a side bristling with long, gleaming guns that were primed and itching to rip into a fat-bottomed hull. Through his glass, Raider could see the shock on the captain's face and he read fluently the curses he laid on his own gullibility.

"Fire across her bow . . . and take out her bowsprit! Show 'em we mean business!" Raider bellowed. And as his order was relayed below, he issued a second to, "Strike that 'jack' and run up the 'stars an' stripes.' "

The next second, there was an explosion from the center guns, followed by a second and a third. The *Windraider* shuddered eloquently, and shortly smoke boiled up on the wind. Another volley sounded and the deck under their feet rumbled like a living thing. The *China Lady*'s bowsprit cracked and splintered; her triangular jib deflated and dangled uselessly, flapping against her prow. They could see the scrambling on the *China*'s deck and almost hear the rattle of arms being trundled out. Raider ordered a carronade round at her foremast rigging that brought down the top third of the mast and mangled the tackles nicely. The first gunport opened on her side and Raider obligingly ordered a round pumped into it. There was a moderate explosion, a single cannon off-fired, and Raider called for his riggers to strike sail and hailed the *China Lady* demanding she strike her colors in surrender.

Tension was fierce and expectation pounded in every head on the *Windraider*'s deck for the few seconds their response took. When the *China*'s captain's voice came back, announcing compliance, there was a violent outburst of noise from all over the *Windraider*, a stunning release of the energy that had been summoned but not required by battle. In record time, grappling hooks were set on the *China*'s bulwarks and lines were strung and tightened to bring the ships together. Planks were run across, and Raider and Bastian were among the first over, accepting the weathered captain's sword and colors.

Every man in Raider's crew knew his job in pillaging a ship and they set to it with a fierce joy that sent a quiver through Blythe as she watched. They systematically divested the captain and first mate of their keys and unlocked and entered each cargo hold and locked door. Bastian's job was to come after them sending reports back to Raider for his decision on the plunder. Raider himself led the contingent that stayed topside, corraling the crew and stripping them of weapons, separating out the passengers. It was an efficient arrangement usually, and this day was no exception.

Their wretched financial luck of late held. Bastian went from hold to hold finding only bulky raw materials in the cargo holds, and his disappointment with the lot stoked his temper to a true boil. All that priming, powder, and shot, all that expectation . . . for some lumber and few sponges, a bit of copra, and barrels of sugar sap. None of it was likely to bring much of a price in St. Thomas, where it was all too plentiful already.

He stomped up from the cargo holds, determined to find something of worth in the cabins and quarters. Muscular, slow-talking Oars was in the passageway standing uncertainly over the crumpled form of an expensive dressed young man.

" 'E woun't let me pass, Bastian, so I could open the door," Oars pointed resentfully to the cabin door beside him. "I had ta coldcock 'im."

Bastian sniffed vengeful approval and his eyes fell on the door. "What's in there that he was protectin'? Whate'er it be, it's ours now—" He grinned wickedly at Oars and together they rammed shoulders against the thin wooden panels and found themselves flying through a splintering doorframe.

A female scream brought them whirling about and Bastian found himself face-to-face with a young woman with the yellowest cornsilk hair and the bluest Wedgwood saucer eyes he'd ever seen. She was cowering back against the narrow bunk with the back of her hand lapped across her mouth, trembling with terror at the sight of Oar's huge, battered visage and Bastian's fierce, burly strength and one-eyed glower. In the silence that heaved like Bastian's manly chest, they stared at each other, none daring to move or to speak.

Her hand came down slowly and a pair of full, rosy lips moved to utter a deep, breathy plea in a language Bastian recognized, but did not understand . . . Danish. She swallowed hard and clasped her waist with panicky arms under Bastian's steady stare. Her slow movement only drew Bastian's eyes to complete the assessment he'd made of this vision of womanhood. She uttered that same plea again, but Bastian was completely absorbed in the creamy skin of her shoulders, the full mounds of her breasts as they jutted above a stiff corset, and the narrow waist she was hugging as if to contain her vaulting fear. Then his eyes retraced that sinuous path upward and he found himself pulled into the sooty fringe of lashes that rimmed the glorious blue pools of her eyes. Without conscious will, he reached up and removed his eye patch to drink her in with two healthy eyes. It was as though a

278

thunderbolt had seared him to the spot.

The lady's eyes flitted helplessly over Bastian's formidable frame, his strong, square face, and his broad, sensual mouth. Her pouty, petal-soft lips parted to vent short breaths and the centers of her eyes pulsed in confusion at the melting of her initial fears. Then behind those smooth, fright-pinked cheeks, rose a new anxiety that had to do with the way Bastian's eyes were heating on her breasts and the strange excitations she was feeling as the force of his manly presence crowded her. *Du milde Himmel,* she hadn't seen such a man since—

Bastian's curvy blond vision edged slowly toward the splintered doorway and, like a gazelle, turned and darted into the hallway, drawing Bastian after her in a lunge. But as he careened into the passage after her, he found her kneeling over the slender form of the fellow Oars had bashed minutes earlier. She lifted his blond head and stroked his hair, calling him "Gunnar" and starting to weep.

"Well, he ain't exactly dead!" Bastian scowled furiously at the sight of her slender fingers feathering tenderly over the handsome whelp's face. He bolted forward and lifted her by the waist, determined to separate them, no matter what. But instead of the resistance he expected, she turned and melted against his broad chest, letting the tears come. Bastian drew his chin back, startled, but quickly realized this was exactly what he had wanted moments before . . . his arms filled with her buxom blond beauty. He clasped her protectively against him, supporting her as he drank in her fresh womanly scent and enjoyed what he could surreptitiously feel of her.

"He ain't dead, miz. Oars here jus' coldcocked him a bit. He'll be right as rain in a day or so." He shot a dark glance at the lumbering crewman, sounding like the possibility of the bloke's recovery annoyed him. "Do ye understand, miz?"

She nodded mutely, turning those big, teary blue eyes up at him, and Bastian did what came most naturally; he scooped her up into his arms and started topside with her, tossing an order for Oars to bring "her man."

Raider saw Bastian struggling up through the hatch and was

stunned to see the reason for his difficulty. The old sea dog carried a woman in his arms, a blond young woman, who appeared thoroughly frightened and who wriggled in protest. Even more surprising, however, was the grin his partner wore—lusty and a little dazed. He set her on her feet in front of Raider, and shortly Oars dumped a limp body at his feet as well. She fell on her knees beside the body, and began to speak in low, caressing tones as she stroked the fellow's hair.

"Damned bad luck, Raider." Bastian seemed to remember himself as he watched his curvy burden ministering to "her man." "It's a lot of no good ballast; won't hardly pay for powder an' shot. A bit o' sugar syrup—that might fetch something, if we could get it to Boston. But we ain't Boston bound."

Bastian's disappointment entered Raider with a vengeance, magnified. When would their wretched luck ever end?! They could take a million ships at this rate . . . and still barely survive! He planted his fists at his waist and turned his back, staring across the planks connecting the ships. His eyes came to focus on Blythe, standing near the railing on the quarterdeck, watching him. She could see something was wrong and her expression was one of concern.

Bastian came to his side and stared hard at Raider. "O'course . . . we still could make a profit . ." A crafty gleam came into his eye as the possibility took shape in his mind. When he said it, it got an immediate reaction. "Ransom."

"Damn and blast it, Bastian! Not another of your harebrained ransom schemes!" Raider thundered.

But Bastian pulled him off to a relatively empty spot on the deck and they argued it out. And shortly they were rounding up the passengers and deciding who might be worth something to the Danish governor in St. Thomas. There were two sugar planters and a government secretary who seemed promising . . . and, of course, the blond woman. Bastian was all for leaving the Danish "preacher" behind, but Raider watched Bastian watching their curvy prisoner as she tended her young man on the deck, and decided a parson aboard might be just the ticket. When they discovered the preacher to be the Danish governor's cousin,

Raider cast a triumphant look Bastian's way.

They looted the passengers' cabins and the ship's stores, leaving enough to ensure the *China Lady*'s few days' sail back to St. Thomas to deliver their ransom demand. Then they walked the ransomers across the planks to the *Windraider* and Blythe met them with clasped hands and an unhappy look.

Raider paused beside her, giving her arm a squeeze with his free hand. "Sorry, Wool-witch, there just didn't seem any other way. Here, could you see to her?"

He handed their female ransomer over into Blythe's care, and when the young woman saw Blythe, her tear-blotched face wilted with relief. Blythe put her arms around the young woman's shoulders and led her below to Raider's cabin. Blythe sat her down in a chair and comforted her tears, patting her shoulders, then taking her hands, assuring her she wouldn't be harmed. At first, all the woman would say was "Gunnar . . . Gunnar . . ."

"Is Gunnar your husband?" Blythe saw a golden marriage ring on the second finger of her left hand. "Was he with you aboard ship?" The woman said something in Danish, then lifted a pained face to Blythe. It struck Blythe that she was a bit older than she had seemed at first, perhaps in her mid- or late twenties. Faint lines showed at the corners of her eyes, betraying a love of laughter. She had strong, expressive features that verged on prettiness, but were actually more interesting.

"My . . . nephew." She spoke English with a graceful Nordic lilt. "He vas wit me . . . they hit him." She shuddered. "I pray noting happens . . . he iss such good boy. My brother sends him wit me . . . so I don't travel alone. I go home to New York from my brother's plantation . . ."

"He'll be all right." Blythe hoped she spoke the truth. "They sent him back to St. Thomas on the *China Lady*. Why, he'll be home . . . before you are." The woman lifted her face again, and Blythe read her fears and sought to allay them. "They won't hurt you, I promise . . . I won't let them."

Blythe's claim sparked something in the woman's very blue eyes and she straightened, slowly pulling her hands free. She looked at Blythe's lovely face, her striking, sympathetic eyes, and her unusual clothes and seemed thoroughly puzzled. "You . . . who are you? Vhy are *you* . . . here?"

It was the question that Blythe had dreaded most and knew, sooner or later she must face. She took a breath and summoned all the candor and courage she possessed.

"I'm Blythe Woolrich. I . . . was a 'ransomer' once, like you. Only there was no money for the ransom and the captain . . ." she stumbled over her words as she saw the horror rising in the young woman's eyes, "decided to . . . keep me." She'd never realized how awful it would sound, said aloud . . . being worthless and now being "kept." The young woman withdrew slowly, and Blythe could see the awful connections being made in her mind as she realized Blythe traveled with the "pirates" . . . with the pirate "captain," to be exact.

Blythe was one of *them,* her eyes seemed to say, a kept woman . . . a doxy. Worse . . . a *pirate's* doxy! The judgment for that unforgivable offense was clear in the young woman's cooling eyes.

"And what is your name?" Blythe made herself ask, against the tightening in her throat. Being labeled and shunned because of her worldly status hurt every bit as much as she feared it would.

"Signe—" the woman stiffened, "Signe Andersen Thorvald . . . vidow of Jens Thorvald."

"A widow . . ." Blythe didn't know what to say next, and when Signe Thorvald turned her face away, Blythe rose and wiped her damp palms down her skirt. "I'll see to the others now. They're probably worried about you. But there's nothing to fear. Raider Prescott is a good captain and a fair man . . ." But Signe wouldn't look at her and she left with dragging feet.

Once in the passage, she leaned against the paneled walls, trying to calm her breathing and make herself think sensibly about her situation. Sooner or later she was bound to confront someone from the "respectable" world; this just happened a bit sooner than she expected. Signe's reaction to her status was probably no different than her own reaction to those unlucky young girls who'd fallen prey to the light-fingered British during Philadelphia's occupation . . .

But it was different with her and Raider, she argued her case hotly. She loved Raider and he'd pledged her his care and even his affection. He was the only man she'd ever known and he treated her as though she was the only woman he'd ever wanted. Their caring and their loving were very special . . . special enough to bear their own "honor" and to make up for things like "respectability" and "pride." But not quite special enough to make up for the one thing that was missing, the one thing that Blythe craved in the very depths of her being. If she had Raider Prescott's love, she would gladly forgo all the trappings of respectability and purge all desire for a "proper" future from her.

Be sensible, Blythe, she shook herself mentally. You've a man to care for, a home, of sorts, and there's no going back. Whether he comes to love you or not, it's your life now and there's no sense pining over things you haven't got . . . especially when he'd given you so much. And sensible Blythe pulled her waffling self together and made her way topside.

The plunder from the *China Lady* was soon stowed below decks and, at Blythe's request, Raider settled the matter of accommodations for the ransomers. Bastian surprised them by offering his cabin for curvy Signe Thorvald's use. After some rather blunt discussion on the impossibility of his sharing it with her, Bastian was still adamant . . . the lady could use his quarters. Raider didn't honestly trust the glint in Bastian's hazel eyes, but it was the closest thing to chivalry he had ever encountered in his burly partner and so he let Bastian have his way.

Blythe saw the four male ransomers settled below on the gun deck with hammocks and blankets, and Raider appeared to give them the customary cautions of life as a ransomer aboard the *Windraider*. Blythe's mouth quirked up at the corner at the familiar ring of his admonition: "Stay away from my crew . . ." He warned that his men were "a bloody heathen pack; rescued, snatched, lured and dredged from the meanest, vilest captains in the Caribbean!" Four pairs of male eyes fastened on demure, beautiful Blythe as she stood at Raider's side, and Raider's warning was fatally undercut. Fortunately, none of the gentlemen was of a particularly quarrelsome or heroic nature; they were content to suffer as little as possible in captivity and to let the governor ransom them back, posthaste.

The planters and secretary and even the Danish preacher, called "pas-tor" by the others, were a bit bemused by Blythe's efforts to see to their comfort and were surprised indeed when she brought them a very tasty bit of supper. To a man, they intuited her place among these rough pirates, but were gallant or grateful enough to treat her with respect. Her speech and carriage, her charity to them, and her charming manner all betrayed her genteel background and they kept their wonderings about her amongst themselves.

That evening, when Blythe escorted Signe Thorvald from Bastian's cabin topside to join her fellow ransomers for an airing, she felt a twinge in her chest at the way the young widow ran to them and especially at the way they welcomed her with open arms. She joined Raider at the waist railing and he put his arms around her, giving her a hug that warmed her nicely . . . until she glanced up to find five pairs of eyes on her, narrowed in varying degrees of censure and disdain. Apparently Signe Thorvald had lost no time in relating and condemning her disreputable status to them. As was typical of men, they now felt compelled to uphold the standards the proper widow represented and reminded them of. And faces that not minutes before had been filled with gratitude, even admiration toward Blythe, now were cool with disdain. Blythe shriveled a bit inside, and not even the heat of Raider's presence could fully restore her equanimity.

The next day, the ransomers were led on deck twice, and each time when Blythe approached, they stiffened or looked away, sending clear signals of disapproval to her and to everyone else who might happen to be watching. As it happened, Old Willie and Clive and the Bosun Deane were all watching . . . as was Raider. They saw Blythe's cheery expression falter and saw the heat rising in her cheeks as she lowered her eyes briefly. Even not

284

knowing much about "respectables," the lads still knew a snub when they saw it. It baffled them at first, for Blythe had gone to some trouble to see that the "prisoners" were treated well. They began to mutter about it amongst themselves and the word was passed among the lads. It made their blood boil to think anyone would shun their Wool-witch.

Raider, too, had seen it and it explained Blythe's coolness in their bed the previous night. He had thought perhaps it was the female curse, but now realized it was an even worse curse; it was *respectability*. Lord, how he wanted to seize and throttle those pompous, self-righteous, narrow-minded slugs! How dare they pass judgment on his generous, and very vulnerable Blythe?! He came steaming down the quarterdeck steps straight for that treacherous little pack and sent them scrambling below with the lowest, angriest vibrations he could muster. The sight of their pale faces fleeing was gratifying and he barked orders that they be confined to quarters until further notice.

Bastian protested the inhumanity of it and Raider narrowed a furious glance at him and told him in rather succinct, if bawdy, terms to button his breeches flap and keep his 'self' the hell out of it! Blythe had seen the commotion from the fo'c'sle and came running, her face lined with worry. Raider took her by the wrist and pulled her below, into the evening-gray of his cabin.

"What happened?" She clutched his sleeve, flushing. "Did one of the ransomers do something?"

"It's more like what they didn't do." Raider took her by the waist, staring heatedly into her luminous golden eyes. "They didn't behave like decent human beings. They're acting too damned 'respectable' to suit me, and I since I don't have to suffer looking at them if I don't want to . . . then I won't. They'll stay below decks until we land . . . then I'll see they're locked up properly until the ransom is paid."

"Raider!" She pushed back in his arms to stare at his dark, determined expression. "You can't do that. They're human be-ings—"

"They're respectable *squats!* And by acting like it, they've for-feited the right to everything but the mere subsistence aboard my

285

ship."

"But it's not right. I know what it's like to be cooped up and to be—"

"Lord, it's just like you to take up for them after the way they—" He stopped himself, but not in time.

Blythe's luminous eyes widened as she took in his meaning. He had never liked respectable society or the people who inhabited it, but there was more to it this time. He'd seen her hurt over the way they treated her and it angered him. His protective urge sent a flood of warmth through her and she slid her arms around his ribs and hugged him fiercely. His arms tightened convulsively about her and that strange melting occurred in the middle of him again.

"Blythe," his voice was husky as he half kissed, half spoke into her hair, "you're as strong as you are lovely, but you've a tender heart. I'll not have you shamed by what passes between us. It's not wrong, Blythe, no matter what their stupid rules say."

"I . . . it's not their fault, Raider." She raised tear-rimmed eyes to him. "Don't you see—it's mine. They couldn't make me feel shamed if down deep I didn't share some of those same 'respectable' standards you hate so much."

He watched her glistening eyes and felt his mouth drying. She was assuming responsibility again, taking the results of other's failings onto her own broad shoulders. Probably even his own failings, where she was concerned . . .

"Do you . . . are you . . . sorry . . " He couldn't finish it, but there was no need. Her chin quivered as she searched the clean, aristocratic features she'd come to know so intimately and love so well.

"No, I'm not sorry. Heaven help me, were it to do over again, I'd still ask you to take your 'share.' I want to be with you, Raider, always. And I'd brave a thousand Danish pastors and disapproving widows to have your loving."

Raider kissed her urgently, communicating his joy and relief in the most basic way possible. His hands caressed her delectable body, up and down, his tongue plundered her yielding mouth, his need invaded every inch of her skin he could reach. He glanced at the deepening twilight and moved her to the bunk, where he worked her buttons and felt her working his. Soon their clothes were shed and their bodies joined in affirmation of all that was right between them.

No shame, no thought of respectability or restraint intruded in the hot magic of hands and lips on skin, in the splintering climax of passion, or in the sweet, mingled heat of afterlove. Blythe nestled, exhausted, in the crook of his arm and gazed at him dreamily.

"You will let them out . . . won't you?" she sighed.

He had gone completely soft where she was concerned. "Probably."

The next morning, they awakened to a steady, pouring rain. He was fully dressed before he wakened her with a kiss and an apology for the dampened welcome to his island home.

"We'll strike land by late afternoon. I wanted you to see it first in sunshine . . . with palms swaying and bright flowers everywhere. I had hoped it would take away some of your disappointment when you see the house. I'm afraid, Wool-witch, it's not —" Her fingertips stopped him.

"It'll be wonderful, Raider." She pulled his head down and kissed the tip of his nose. "It will be so good to be on land again . . . even wet land."

He sat on the bunk, strangely unable to rise as he watched her slide past him and gain her feet. In the tropic warmth, she'd began sleeping in her short chemise, and as she moved, her hip-length hem flirted with him, winking glimpses of firm buttocks and dark, moist curls. He was suddenly thinking that Bastian could check the watch this morning . . .

But Blythe opened his clothing trunk and came to him carrying his oilskin. She paused before him with an indulgent tilt to her head and pressed a kiss on his forehead as she put his rainwear in his hands. "Don't forget this."

Lord, sometimes she reminded him of his old nurse, he mused, pausing in the hallway to slip the oilskin over his head.

287

Then she became pure Cleopatra, sultry and oh so erotic. Other times she was a hurt little girl . . . or the wizened sage inside his own conscience. There seemed no end to the creatures bottled up inside her. And yet there was a consistency, a constancy to her that turned everything in him right-side up and kept it level, even in the choppy seas of his own motives and feelings. And he knew his nauseatingly respectable prisoners would soon have their freedom back . . . because the woman they had scorned wanted it to be so.

Chapter Eighteen

The sun was out by the time they made the sheltered cove of the island that served as Raider and Bastian's base. It was set like a liquid sapphire, rimmed by white-sugar beaches that nestled at the base of velvety blue-green hillsides. Raider lifted a wide-eyed Blythe from the longboat and carried her through the surf into a rowdy welcome from the local villagers. After introducing her and doling out gifts to the village notables, he led her and a contingent that included their ransomers up the hillside away from the village to the house he and Bastian shared. It was a rambling white structure with thick native-brick walls, Spanish-tiled floors, and louvered shutters that covered arched windows. Numerous porches jutted from the house over the hillside, each commanding a fine view of the sheltered cove and the graceful white beaches beyond. Around a perimeter that included several outbuildings was a stone and palmetto stockade that provided security on three sides, while leaving the view to the sea uninterrupted.

While Raider settled the prisoners in the outbuildings that served as quarters for those of the crew who hadn't made other living arrangements in the village, Blythe strolled around the front garden, looking at the bowers of fragrant blossoms in the walled enclosure just before the front doors. She drank in air heavy with hibiscus and stopped to touch a grapelike cascade of lilac-colored blossoms when the crunch of feet on stone caused her to turn.

Bastian was ushering Signe Thorvald toward her and was carrying a leather satchel Blythe knew to belong to the widow. Signe's face was tight, but Bastian was grinning like a schoolboy when they halted.

"Convinced Raider she'd be best off in the house . . . with us." He seemed quite pleased with his persuasive abilities. "Never know what them no account swabs'll do when they come back from the village wi' a tootful." He turned and waved a gallant arm toward the front doors and the proper Mrs. Thorvald shot Blythe a glance that was part fear and part resentment before she complied with his directions. Blythe was left standing with Bastian's label of his men as "no account swabs" ringing in her ears.

Bastian led a very reluctant Widow Thorvald through a large shady room that functioned as both parlor and dining room. The furnishings were massive and heavily carved—taken from Spanish ships and purchased at various "prize-reckonings" from sundry privateers. As they went toward the bedchambers, he informed her the house was kept for them by a family in the village and that their ship's cook, Franco, always cooked for them ashore as well. He caught the promising sway of her walk from the corner of his eye as he threw back the shutters in the hallway, making it into an airy, open passage. He led her past rooms he pointed out as Raider's and his own, to the end of the hall. There he opened a heavy door into a spacious white bedchamber, sparsely furnished with a large poster bed, a chest, and washstand. "This be your room, for a time." He put down her bag. "Ye got quite a view."

He went to a set of louvered doors that led onto a lattice-sided wooden porch and opened them to reveal a magnificent panorama of the sea. Staring at it, he breathed deeply. Then he turned with a gleam in his eye. "Where be yer husband, ma'am?"

Signe blinked those very blue eyes and realized he was staring at the hand and marriage ring she was rubbing nervously. "My husband iss dead . . . these tree years now." She turned aside to look out on the porch and missed the heavenward roll of gratitude in Bastian's crafty gaze.

"I be purely sorry to hear it ma'am."

"He vas sea captain . . . had hiss own ship. He vas making th' sugar runs . . . New York to islands vhere my brother has his plantation." There was a longing in her voice that broadened Bastian's grin a bit more. So she was a widow with a longing, was she?

Bastian let a low whistle of respect. "Had his own ship, did he? Had me own bark, too, until a few months back. Lost her in a fight with a whole fleet o' Brits. We was privateerin', ye know, Raider Prescott and me; sailed fer the colonies. But since he took that wench fer ransom, he be hell-bent—pardon the expression, ma'am—on gettin' us back into piratin' full-blown. I have my hands full, keepin' him straight." He inched slowly toward the porch where she was standing, half in sunlight. She took a step back and the sun struck her hair, setting it aglow like nothing Bastian had ever seen before. His jaw dropped.

"Excuse my starin' ma'am. Ye got the prettiest damned hair I ever seen in me life," Bastian blurted out, his eyes fixed on the golden halo that framed her face. He was suddenly feeling very strange and liquid inside.

The entranced look on his face was enough to soften Signe's umbrage at his salty language. After all, real seagoing men usually spoke their minds bluntly . . . stated their needs plainly. Her burly, virile Jens Thorvald had been such a man. Signe felt a shiver of fresh regret at the thought of him and smiled a sad, forgiving smile that lodged smartly in Bastian's burly chest.

Her softening mood set Bastian's blood pounding, and his voice was husky like a caress as he sought to prolong this time with her. "Be yer home in the islands, ma'am?"

"New York, in the colonies. I haf lovely house on the Long Island. But after my Jens goes down with his ship—a hurricane it vas—my brother he sends for me; I must come live with him, he says. Zo . . . I come to live with him a while." She turned her head to look out over the sea. "But I go home now."

Drawn by her wistful mood and alluring beauty, Bastian came closer, letting his eyes touch those full, creamy breasts, those shapely arms, those rosebud lips. "You . . . be goin' home?" He could scarcely hear what she said for the roaring in his blood as he neared her ripe, womanly body.

"I do not like tese islands. Oh, at first . . . the sun and the sea. Danes love both. But . . . iss so hot for me," she murmured, her hand coming up to slowly stroke the rim of her square bodice, calling Bastian's aching attention to the creamy globes the fabric scarcely contained. ". . . so hot . . . and I don't like the heat. I cannot sleep . . . it iss always so hot . . ."

Bastian watched, spell-bound, as her hand unconsciously trailed over one breast and down the lush curve of her waist. He couldn't swallow, couldn't move, afraid he'd pounce on her with the slightest provocation. And he intuited somehow that pouncing was not the way to woo a widow with a fierce longing.

She turned and was obviously startled to find Bastian looming above her, big and muscular and radiating the kind of heat not supplied by a West Indies night. His hazel eyes glowed like hammered copper and his broad, sensual lips were parted, drawing her helpless eyes. His face was framed on strong, square cheekbones that complemented a square nose whose raffish cant told of battles . . . undoubtedly won. His neck was muscular and his shoulders . . . *Gud pa Himmel* . . . how broad and thick he was! The kind of man you had to hug twice to reach all of him. Signe flamed at the waywardness of her thoughts and she jolted to the side, then scurried far out onto the porch like a frightened fawn. She could scarcely breathe. This man . . . this "Bastian" . . . what was he doing to her?!

The door flung open and Raider and Blythe hurried inside, relieved to find Signe Thorvald on the porch instead of on her back. Raider scowled at Bastian, who bristled and informed Raider loudly that there was a maneuver he should learn to execute before barging into a lady's bedchamber . . . called a *knock*. He grabbed Raider's arm and ushered him from the room, pausing by the planking door to demonstrate meaningfully several times.

Blythe bit her lower lip with bemusement, then went to check on Signe, who was very quiet and looked a bit strained. Blythe assured her that she had nothing to fear and received a meaningful silence for her efforts. Spirits sagging a bit, Blythe checked the tickings on the bed and promised to bring some linens.

Things were off to a bad start and they worsened through the evening. Blythe went to the crew's quarters to see if their prisoners were comfortable and was answered with cool looks and monosyllables. She found herself apologizing for their Spartan accommodations and inviting them to dine that evening in the house with Raider and Bastian and herself. Under the murderous glares of their guards, Sharkey, Clive, Old Willie, and Oars, they declined . . . oh, so respectably. Blythe flushed at having her generous impulse tossed back in her face, and she exited with as much grace as she could muster. The lads from the *Windraider* watched her go and exchanged hot glares and grumbled curses, vowing amongst themselves that these respectable sods would have naught but bread and water for the rest of their stay.

Then Signe deigned not to show herself for supper, either, and Blythe tried hard not to show her sagging spirits, lest Raider learn of her rebuffed offer and decide to punish the prisoners a bit more. After their leisurely supper, Blythe quietly asked Old Willie to take the curvy widow a tray. He refused until Blythe threatened to do it herself and he relented only because it might save her a bit more embarrassment. Later, he carried the news of the uppity widow's shunning to the lads in their quarters and the grumbling and snarling amongst them grew.

These respectable sorts were totally beyond all logic as far as the lads were concerned . . . shunning the Wool-witch when she was trying to see to their own bloody welfare. But her own behavior was just as baffling. Why would she work so hard to care for a pack of surly, ungrateful wharf-rats like them? They scowled and shook their heads in puzzlement until Clive suggested that it was likely because they were reminders of her old life . . . she'd been respectable, too, when The Raider and Bastian Cane had "napped" her. And Old Willie ventured an opinion shared universally; she ought to be purely delighted to have been rescued from a life among such as them.

It took Bastian Cane to set their thinking on the right track. He came out to the crew's quarters, late, to make sure a watch was posted. He heard their musings and he stroked his square chin sagely, recognizing a golden opportunity when he saw one.

"It be Raider's fault, right enough," he declared judiciously, drawing himself up and shoving thumbs into his wide black belt.

The Raider's fault? They drew back. How could that be?

"I told him it were wrong to keep the wench. 'Send 'er back,' I says. But he's got her under his skin bad and wouldn't listen. He wetted her keel and he beds her regular, ye see. And them respec'able sorts had got a nose for a bit of unapproved pleasure."

"Ye mean somebody has a 'say' on pleasure for respec'able folks?" One Tooth was incredulous. No wonder The Raider hated the respectable life so!

"I be talking 'bout *marriage*," Bastian spat disgustedly. "He ain't wedded up with the Wool-witch and that makes her no better'n a dockside whore to the likes o' the preacher and . . . the widow woman. She be shamed clear to her keel-beam because of it."

"She be disgraced 'cause The Raider ain't wedded her?" Old Willie's feral eyes sparked with indignation. He looked at his mates and saw understanding blooming in their eyes. They didn't know much about respectability, but they were well versed in the intricacies of *pride*. "We give up our shares, trustin' The Raider to do what be right and respec'able by 'er. Morgan's Pizzle! The Raider let us down!"

There was a growing rumble of dissatisfaction through the barrackslike quarters. Several of the lads were back from the village, having spent their passions and drunk their fill, and they joined the impromptu meeting.

"Well, we gotta fix that somehows." Clive looked at Willie and read similar thoughts in his face. "Jus' what does it take to get 'wedded up'?"

"Just a few words said a'fore a preacher," Bastian sniffed, clearly disdaining Raider's squeamishness in the face of mere words. "He already be doin' the rest . . . beddin' her and keepin' her and the like."

"A few words, ye say? That be all?" Old Willie's toothless maw spread in a crafty grin that all present understood. "Then we'll be havin' a few words wi' The Raider ourselves."

The lads did have a few words with Raider, the very next

294

morning. They sent Bastian to lead him to a spot far down the beach, out of view of the house and the village. Raider hardly gave it a second thought when they came across a few of their lads who fell in behind them as they walked. Bastian was keeping him occupied with the details and problems of the ransom exchange and how to make amends to the Danish governor, who was bound to be a bit testy after being asked to ransom back his own kin.

When Bastian stopped, Raider looked up from his boot-toes to find himself in a ring of his men, with Bastian fading quickly to the rear. One look at the grizzled, combative faces around him and Raider began to coil inside. Dammit! he groaned internally. Something was up and he'd been too distracted of late to smell it brewing!

"We got a griev'nce wi' you, Cap'n. And we mean to see it squared." Old Willie acted as spokesman for the lot and got straight to the point. "Ye done disgraced the Wool-witch . . . beddin' her wi'out weddin' her."

"Beddin' without . . . ?!" Raider was struck speechless for a second, then let a half-cursing laugh. "It's none of your concern . . . who I bed, or under what conditions."

"It be our concern when it be the Wool-witch," sallow-faced Clive insisted, garnering a guttural volley of verbal support. "She ain't able to hold her head up for what you done to her. Cain't hardly talk to them respec'able sods nor look 'em in the eye. Shamed her, ye have . . . clear down to her keel-beam!"

The righteous anger and pathos in their hardened faces might have been comical if they hadn't been so deadly serious. Raider drew himself up and his voice got very quiet. "I'll put it plain enough for all of you to understand; she wants me to bed her . . . she *enjoys* it!"

"That be as it may." Willie stuck his shriveled chin up at Raider. "We're of a mind, ye oughta wed 'er. And then them respectable sods won't be snubbin' her no more, nor breakin' her heart. We seen it, Cap'n . . . and we won't stand fer no more of it!"

Raider looked up to see Bastian standing at the edge of their band, his arms crossed over his chest and his mouth spread with a righteous smirk.

"You!" Raider charged toward him, but found the way blocked by Sharkey's and the Bosun Deane's hard shoulders. "You put them up to this, damn your hide!"

"Ye danced, Raider Prescott . . . now pay the damned piper like a man," Bastian challenged, dropping his hands to his sides, where they fell into fists. "Ye had to have the wench . . . wouldn't sell 'er off nor send her away like any *decent* pirate would'ave. Now marry her, dammit, like a respec'able sod. It be just what ye deserve fer fergettin' everything ye ever learned about respec'able folk!"

"The hell I will —" Raider was vibrating with rage when wild-eyed Sharkey and the mountainous Oars pounced on him, grabbing his arms and wrestling him to a stand-still. Raider tried to shake them off but found himself held fast with other lads rushing forward as reinforcements. The flinty Bosun Deane came to stare him hard in the eye.

"Wed the wench or find yerself another ship . . . for ye won't be sailin' the *Windraider* no more."

It splashed over Raider like an icy wave, and his futile wrestling ceased. They meant it. They'd mutiny . . . they were on the bloody edge of it right now! She meant that much to them . . . their Wool-witch. *Theirs, hell!* She was *his* woman! She meant more to him than —

He stiffened and his aristocratic features glazed like hot bronze in the morning sun. He engaged their narrowed eyes, one after another, after another. Sharkey, Ali, Stanley, Black Jimmy, Old Willie, One Tooth . . . this time there was no staring them down, any of them. They were insisting he perform the one act he'd come to despise as the epitome of respectable hypocrisy . . . and that he do it with with his sweet, vulnerable Blythe Woolrich.

Didn't they know what they were asking . . . shackling him and making him chain her to him for the rest of her life? Strangely, it wasn't the thought of his being yoked to Blythe Woolrich that outraged him, for he couldn't honestly imagine ever wanting another woman like he wanted her. But Blythe deserved better . . . and she might someday have the chance to be respectable again, might find a man to do right by her and marry her and *love* her the way she deserved. The possibility pounded the very air from his lungs. His head and heart reeled at the very thought . . . Blythe in another man's arms, loving him, sharing the joys of life and the fascination of her bright being with him.

God help him, he didn't want anyone else to love her . . . he wanted to do it himself! He wanted to love her, to care for her, to be her protector and her mate, and to make and to keep the promises she deserved. He wanted her by his side always and he wanted to give her whatever her heart desired . . . a home, even babies if she wanted them . . . But he had no right to promise things he didn't know how to deliver . . . a love . . . a future. He was a bloody pirate, for God's sake! Icy coldness gripped his heart. What if she didn't want to be shackled to a *pirate?!*

A very long half hour later, Raider found Blythe in the kitchen of his house, helping François prepare a huge grouper for pit-steaming later that afternoon. She brightened when she saw him and wiped her hands and let herself be pulled into the fragrant walled garden. Her skin glowed with a faint blush and her hair shone with a fiery haze of gold. He kissed her first, to steady his nerves, then told her what he wanted:

"I want to marry you, Blythe . . . as soon as possible . . . today." He held his breath, steeling himself, but he was still unprepared for her reaction.

"Why?"

It seared through him like a knife, the way it had ten years before, when that very same question had followed the only other proposal of marriage he had made in his life. He shuddered and lightning flashed in the stormy jade of his eyes. Next would come the laugh . . . that laugh he'd heared echoing in his heart for ten long years . . .

"Why do you want to marry me, Raider?" Blythe was too stunned to take it in properly. "Why now?" It seemed to be someone else standing in her boots, watching the unmistakable swirl of hurt and anger deep in his eyes. Why would he ask her

297

to marry him and stand there looking as though he hated the thought? Instinctively she reached for him, taking his arm, feeling its tension as she dug her fingers into its corded strength. She was fighting desperately to contain the hope exploding inside her.

"A simple yes or no will do," he muttered softly . . . so softly Blythe knew he was serious indeed.

"It's not as simple as 'yes' or 'no,' Raider." She fought the tears that welled in her throat and the hot confusion swelling in her chest. "You . . . never wanted to get married . . . you said so. And I've tried to understand . . ."

Raider searched the flushed heart of her face, seeking the slightest hint of disdain or scorn—something to use in his own defense against her. But in the depths of her burnished eyes he read the hope and the confusion his proposal produced in her and felt his own rising to meet it.

This was his warm, quixotic, vulnerable Blythe, he realized . . . Blythe, who gave herself without conditions, who thought of others' well-being first, even when it conflicted with her own. He sucked a hard breath. That was why she asked "why." She wanted to know if it was what he really wanted . . . if he was sure. And she deserved to hear the truth as he'd come to face it in the last hour.

"I want you, Blythe. I thought it would be enough; I wanted it to be. But the seas are getting smaller and, even aboard my own *Windraider*, it seems I can't protect you from the cruel, stupid prejudices of the respectable world. I'd lay down my life to ensure your safety, Blythe. It doesn't seem to make sense anymore that I wouldn't give you my name for protection as well . . . if you want it."

"Would you really do that?" Her eyes filled so that she had to blink to see him. "Would you really . . . lay down your life?" There was a fierce, painful ache in the middle of her chest. She had to draw breath around it.

"I would," he whispered.

"Why? Why would you do that, Raider?" She watched him through thick prisms of liquid, suspending the release of tears until she knew if they should contain sorrow or joy. His hand came up to trace the precious curve of her cheek and she wanted to curl around it, to find the love she craved offered in its palm.

"I care for you, Wool-witch." He whispered that, too. His extreme quiet was a measure of the intensity of his feelings, Blythe realized. "You've found a place in my heart, wench. And I want to give you all I can."

"You . . . might be coming to love me a little?" Those tears of joy began to stream down her cheeks and she could see his admission shocked him a little as he said it.

"I . . . think I might."

"Then, yes! Yes, yes, *Yes,* I'll marry you . . . whenever—wherever you want . . . today . . . here . . . *now!!*" She threw her arms about his neck and pulled his head down to kiss him with all the passion of her very intense joy. "Oh, Raider—you do want me! You do care—" And she kissed him again, exploding like a rocket in his arms, showering white-hot excitement all through him, catching him up in the delirious, dizzying updraft of her love.

He caught her off her feet, against him, whirling her around and around until they were both dizzy and laughing, hugging and kissing frantically. It was only the threat of air starvation that brought them back to reality. Her feet settled on the ground, though her head was still high in the clouds.

"This evening, then. I have to make arrangements . . ." His heated grin was suddenly pure devilment. "If the Danish pastor won't . . . then we'll go aboard the *Windraider* and make Bastian do the honors."

The lads were waiting in their quarters for word and when they saw Raider striding across the compound with a face-splitting grin, they erupted with cheers and bawdy merriment. Their Wool-witch and The Raider were getting married! Not that they ever had a minute's doubt, once they convinced him of the wisdom in it . . .

Desperate to avoid involvement in such questionable proceedings himself, Bastian threw himself into the task of recruiting the Danish pastor to do the noose-tying. With a crafty bit of flattery to the man's piety and a judicious use of righteous disdain for the tardiness of the nuptials, Bastian soon had the fellow's agreement

299

to perform the rites. And the other arrangements followed quickly behind. The vows were to be said on the beach just before sunset, with the lads and villagers and ransomers present. And afterward, there would be a feast . . . with the best wines and smoked meats and steamed fish . . . and the biggest cake François could manage.

Signe Thorvald had been caught just inside the open doorway into the garden, a reluctant witness to the intensity of Raider's proposal, to the revelation of his tender feelings for Blythe, and to the release of their joy. She had fled back through the house to her room and thrown herself onto her bed, feeling small and vindictive . . . and so very lonely. It was clear as daylight that the captain and his woman loved each other . . . Was that why she'd been so eager to disapprove of their unsanctioned union? Because seeing Blythe's sweetness and happiness made her feel all the more empty inside? She had things to think about . . . curvy Signe Thorvald. And perhaps amends to make . . .

Blythe was surprised indeed to have Signe appear at her bedchamber door that afternoon, with an offer to help her prepare and dress for her wedding. Signe's nose was red and her eyes betrayed the way she'd spent the morning. Blythe was puzzled by the change in Signe, wondering if her own impending respectability were to account for it . . . or if it signaled some deeper change in the widow. Either way, she decided with sensible charity, it was nice to have feminine company to share these hours before her wedding.

Old Willie came for her when the time came, escorting her down the stone path and steps to the beach where everyone waited. She wore her precious sea-jade velvet with its swirls of lace and some flat-heeled slippers Signe had given her. Harry had come to help with her hair, giving her an appealing cascade of ladylike ringlets from the crown of her head, down her back. Clive pressed a bouquet of fragrant native flowers into her hands and she thanked him with a kiss on the cheek.

But from the minute she saw him, Raider Prescott held her attention exclusively. He wore the suit of gentlemanly clothes he had worn in Philadelphia, when he and Bastian had come to her shop. His tawny hair was groomed perfectly, his aristocratic features glowed like a bronze casting of male perfection in the setting sunlight. And when his warm hands enveloped hers she felt his love flowing through her in wondrous waves.

Reverend Rasmussen, the Danish pastor, spoke of the duties of husband and wife, of the conditions of life that required commitment to weather, of the joys of loving and the necessity of giving. And when he bade them repeat those solemn words of binding, not a breath was let, anywhere on the beach.

There was a moment of confusion when he asked if there was a marriage ring. Raider looked at Bastian, who stood beside him, and Bastian winced and shrugged. There hadn't been time to think of such things . . .

Signe Thorvald looked down at her hand and removed Jens Thorvald's ring from her finger. He was a fine man, Jens Thorvald. He wouldn't have minded. She stepped forward and pressed it into Raider's hand with a teary little smile.

With a wry grin of gratitude, Raider Prescott accepted it . . . and used it to seal the vows he'd made to his Wool-witch. And then, with the pastor's permission, he sealed them again with an aching sweet kiss. Pandemonium broke loose around them, hugs and laughter and shouts from the lads and chants from the villagers. Then they were being dragged down the beach to where François had marshaled a wedding feast fit for an island king.

Blythe was floating, giddy from the intoxicating feel of being loved and being married . . . all of it in one day! She ate and drank sparingly, feasting more on Raider's rare, dazzling smiles, on the unabashed love in his eyes. Toast after toast went around the torch-lit circle and each lifted her heart a bit higher, made her blood pound a bit harder in her head . . . made her want to enjoy Raider's loving in this new state . . . marriage. Raider might have read her mind, for shortly he was on his feet, pulling her up and bidding his crew and their guests good night. Halfway up the hill to the house, he stopped and lifted her into his arms, carrying her the rest of the way to the house and to his big, postered bed with its cool linen and its gauzy silk netting.

He stood her on her knees on the side of the bed in the dimly lit chamber and kissed her as though possessing her for the first

301

time. Her hands cupped the back of his neck and she pressed against him eagerly, aching for that steamy, fierce possession she knew would be drums tonight. When he lifted his head, they were both panting, trembling with need.

"I love you, Raider Prescott." She said it aloud for the first time and thought what a nice sound it had.

"I thought maybe it had come to that," he mused.

"And . . . ?" She narrowed her eyes insistently.

"And . . . I guess it's come to this: I love you, Blythe Woolrich Prescott. Love you with everything in me . . . except good sense."

Her head dropped back and she laughed a throaty, exultant laugh. "I'll be the sensible one, then. I've had plenty of practice." She pushed him back and slid down off the bed to stand beside him. "Now be a good pirate and strip my clothes off and ravish me till I can't think straight."

His jaw dropped in genuine surprise, then he laughed, reaching for her shoulders and pulling her against his hardening body. "That's being sensible?"

"As sensible as it gets on a pirate's wedding night." She took his hands from her shoulders and directed them to her breasts, pressing them to her as they closed over her tingling flesh. "Love me, Raider."

Raider did his best to oblige her ravishment request, but as he stripped the clothes from her, his pace slowed to a hypnotizing peel and he showered kisses and nibbles and nuzzles on every part of her warm flesh as he exposed it. She stood, letting his hands take her where they would, feeling them weaving the start of a tapestry of sensation inside her that would take a lifetime of loving to complete. Then she stood before her gentlemanly pirate, naked and glowing, desiring his savage, thrusting heat and craving the gentleness of his caress. She wanted all of Raider Prescott—the tough and the tender . . . everything there was.

He made to remove his own clothing, but she stayed him with a sultry, "Not yet." Her hands began to move over the boundaries of his gentlemanly clothes, feeling him now with her hands, the way she would always feel him with her eyes. She covered the fine broadcloth over his hard shoulders and his stock-wrapped neck with her hands and dipped inside his coat to trace the silky waistcoat over his ribs. She felt his shudder as she knelt before him, caressing his lean hips and glorying in the muscular grace of his hard, shapely legs. Her eyes darkened and she shaded them with lids weighted by desire as her hands came to the hard prominence of his arousal. She touched him lightly, then impulsively pressed and rubbed her face against his hardened shaft, nuzzling, drinking in the warm wool smell of his clothes, the musky male scent of his body.

Raider came to life, pressing her head against him with both hands, groaning with arousal so keen it approached pain. He tried to pull her up and into his arms, but she rose in her own time, rubbing her breasts against his legs, then his hips, and finally his ribs. She arched and molded erotically against his bulging breeches, rippling her nakedness against the raspy wool of his clothes, feeling her body aflame with the pleasures of this wanton play. Her dance of temptation continued, rubbing and tantalizing him, until Raider growled from the roused depths of his soul and clamped her to him fiercely, branding her mouth with his possession.

This time, he ripped his clothes from his body, heedless of their condition, burning with the need to possess her, to take her beyond the boundaries of pleasure to regions he had never explored before. He saw her slide back onto the moon-drenched bed and, as he tossed the last of his clothes aside, he watched the silvery splendor of her body and the dark invitation between her parting legs. He surged over her and spread himself between those silky thighs, pushing into the wet heat of her body, joining them with a power that shuddered her and wrenched a growl from deep in her throat. Then she wrapped him with her legs and arched, seeking more of him, hungry for the feel of him filling her. She coaxed his movement with her own, starting the delicious friction that sent their desires spiraling and soon erupted in a blinding, searing maelstrom of pleasure.

The world took an exceptionally long time to right itself in Blythe's pleasure-steamed senses. She was full from the inside out and from the top down; gorged and stuffed with delectable feelings too delicious to contain. She wriggled lazily under Raider's hot, damp body, luxuriating in the feel of his hard strength,

303

around and still within her.

He smiled and withdrew to collapse beside her, watching the moon-silvered smoke of her eyes and running a hand up her bare side. She quivered like a vibrating string and he slipped his arms around her to turn her onto her side, facing him.

"So that's 'sensible,'" he rumbled in those deep tones that vibrated the very ground of her being. "Heaven help me if you ever work your way up to 'adventuresome.'"

"It was nice, wasn't it?" She grinned with a steamy, satisfied sort of pride and rubbed his raspy shins with her toes.

"Lord, you have a positive gift for understatement. I'll have to remember that in future." He was grinning now, too, teasing.

"Well, I think a pirate's wedding night should be memorable enough . . . to compete," her voice dropped meaningfully, "with Italian noble ladies . . . and Turkish harems." He laughed, feeling light and full inside, hoping he pleased her the way she delighted him.

"It would have been memorable anyway, Wool-witch. I've never made love with a *wife* before."

"Well, of course n—" She paused, catching a deeper meaning in his remark. "You mean, not *anybody's* wife?" A moment passed. He shook his head and Blythe wondered if he were blushing. "Ever?"

"I confess, until quite recently, I've had a sort of prejudice against 'wives.' Women who would make cuckolds of their husbands . . . just never held much appeal for me." He was embarrassed; Blythe could hear it in his voice, could make out the heating in his face with her hand. And she couldn't resist.

"A rather respectable-sounding sentiment for a savage, reprobate pirate, Raider Prescott. You're either the most gentlemanly pirate who ever existed, or you're the most delicious rogue of a gentleman there ever was." She traced his straight, aristocratic nose and his finely arched brows with her fingers. "And I don't care which."

She turned on her back and snuggled her shoulder into his chest and her hip against his groin. She lifted her left hand in the silvery moonlight and moved it so that her marriage ring winked. "Raider—" but whatever she was about to say was swallowed by a sudden recollection, "Gideon . . . when the pastor asked me if I would take Gideon Andrew Prescott for a husband, I almost asked, 'who?' How did you get from 'Gideon' to 'Raider'?"

Raider's eyes veiled slightly. "It was Bastian's fault. He had his heart set on me being a fierce, rampaging pirate . . . and he thought Gideon sounded . . . sissy." He winced for effect at that last word and Blythe laughed.

"It sort of fits you, having two names. Gideon for the gentleman in you; Raider for the bold, pillaging pirate. In fact, I think I rather like it. How many women get to marry two interesting men at the same time?"

His surprise at her rather libertine attitude rumbled through her as he tucked his arms around her. "What a wench, you are."

She turned a supremely satisfied smile on him. "No . . . I'm a *wife*. A pirate wife."

Chapter Nineteen

The Prescotts' wedding celebration proceeded nicely, even in their absence. A bonfire had been lit after a while, both for light and celebration. The lads got gleefully drunk, sang and danced with their village ladies, and not a single blade was drawn, nor was a single punch thrown. The ransomers, as it happened, loosened up nicely with a few rounds in them and became rather chummy sorts to be around. And Bastian Cane had enough of that magnificent Jamaican rum to feel curvy Signe Thorvald clear across the beach.

Through the heat of the fire, her ripe, womanly image seemed to shimmer as Bastian's hungry eyes watched her sip her wine and stare longingly at the dancers, who were cavorting with abandon. Then suddenly she got to her feet and headed down the beach toward the hill and the house. It was the moment Bastian had been waiting for and he seized the opportunity.

He was on his feet, striding after her, drawing virtually no notice from the others, not even the other ransomers. But it was some way down the moonlit beach before he let himself catch up to her. "Ma'am? Ma'am . . ." But she walked all the faster and, in desperation, he grabbed her wrist and pulled her back and around to face him.

"No, please—"

She strained away, but not from fear, Bastian sensed. He reached for her other wrist and she had to face him. In the pale light he could see the bright prisms of her eyes and the flush of her skin. She eased, seeing it was him. "I just . . . walk a bit."

"No, ma'am. This beach be crawlin' wi' pirates . . . drunk pirates. But . . . if I was to come along . . ."

She smiled a wrenching little smile. "I am poor company. I am . . . tinking many thoughts tonight."

So was Bastian . . . and his temperature was rising. "Weddins has a way of doin' that . . . makin' a bloke think thoughts." Bastian grinned his most beguiling expression, flashing healthy white teeth in the silvery light. He felt a thrill of expectation at the way Signe's eyes fastened on his mouth. In an unintentional parody of gentlemanly airs, he released her wrists and offered her his arm for assistance in the soft sand.

She hesitated briefly, hardly trusting herself to touch that hard column of muscle and sinew. She'd seen its rugged muscles bared on the deck of the *Windraider* and had seen it in her dreams for several nights thereafter. But she slipped her hand into the crook of his arm and tried not to catch her breath aloud at the jump her stomach made. When they began to walk, she felt an alarming warming in her womanly places. And the gentle crest and break of the waves in the nearby surf set a growing beat of expectation between them.

"I be purely sorry, ma'am—"

"Signe," she corrected him. "My name iss Signe." His smile broadened at the familiarity she offered him and the small seduction of her smile made him forget what he'd been about to say.

They walked together down the moon-brightened expanse of beach, each feeling and testing the effects of the other's presence. Before they realized it, they were well down the beach, out of sight of the celebration and nearing a grove of coconut palms that jutted toward the water. The mounting pulse of the nearby surf made Bastian remember the bit of wooing he'd planned for just such a moment.

"I be purely sorry, Signe, that ye was caught up in a ransom. I hope it ain't been too hard on ye."

"Not so hard, really. No harder than . . ." She stopped and looked up into his strong face, absorbing the warmth of his arm through his handsome, sea captain's coat. She lowered her burning face, and turned to walk on. Here in the moonlight, having

307

finally laid Jens Thorvald to rest in her heart, she had such a need to talk. "No harder than being a-lone."

Bastian's senses suddenly came alive. He could have sworn her hand caressed his arm briefly as she said it. The rustle of her skirts was loud in his ears and he had a brief, hot vision of shapely legs and rounded hips working beneath them. She suddenly withdrew and veered off to the right toward a palm log lying at the edge of the beach. Bastian jolted after her and found himself settling close beside her on the log and wishing he were closer still.

"My brother iss angry with me." Signe lowered her eyes to her moon-paled hands in her satin lap. "I mourn my Jens a long time. Iss hard to love so much . . . and then no more. You are sailing man . . . perhaps you understand . ." She lifted a softened plea of a look to him and all his manly cunning collected in his throat and he had to swallow it. His arm went around her waist to steady her, but it drew her against him as well.

"My Jens vas gone for long, lonely months . . . then he comes home to me. And, *Gud pa Himmel,*" she melted against Bastian's side and her lashes fluttered as though she might swoon, "it iss like the first time all over again. Always it iss so good between us, so . . . exciting . . . like tunder and lightning. I do not mind the vaiting." She shivered in the night breeze and Bastian pulled her tighter against him, groaning internally at the feel of her small waist under his hand. And just when he thought he had his vaulting desire in hand, she turned, still leaning against him, and her breast rubbed his ribs . . . very slowly.

Bastian's growl was perfectly involuntary, and the way his other arm snaked up to grasp her shoulder to him was a long-standing carnal reflex. But when he lowered his mouth over Signe's startled lips, he knew full well it was the lush, desirable Signe Thorvald he was kissing. And his vast and varied carnal experience told him that she wouldn't resist for long. Signe Thorvald was his for the taking.

When he wrapped her in his steely arms and slid them both down into the warm sand so that they leaned against the log, Signe made no protest. And when Bastian's tongue parted her lips, she opened eagerly to his burning kiss. She was melting inside, glorying in the desire she had despaired of ever feeling

308

again, luxuriating in the overpowering strength of Bastian Cane. He filled her arms, filled her empty being, as he pressed down on the burning mounds of her breasts. Slowly they slid down on the sand, Bastian covering Signe's body partway with his. The rest of her, he covered with his big, blocky hands, intent on securing the pleasures promised in that first, steamy look aboard the *China Lady*.

Soon her bodice was open and Bastian deftly loosened the laces of her corset to free her full, hard-tipped breasts. He kissed them in preparation, then fastened his mouth on them, suckling, producing a rapturous moan deep in Signe's throat. She arched against him, pulling at his shoulders, gasping his name as rivulets of liquid fire spread from her burning nipples downward, into her tingling womanflesh. It had been so long and he was so strong and virile . . . and he knew exactly what she wanted . . .

Indeed he did. He lavished attention on her taut, hardening breasts with his hands and lips, always returning to her lush, pouty lips and grazing her throat, her shoulders, and the valley between her breasts. She began to move her pelvis against his in small, exploratory movements, and Bastian read fluently the state of her desires. His hand raised her skirts and dipped beneath them, finding the warm satin of her thighs and the pleasurable rounding of her buttocks. And as she wriggled under his touch, his hand came to the liquid heat of her proud womanflesh and he felt her startle and shiver at the intimacy of it. He stroked and toyed, tenderly, leisurely, watching the effects of his well-practiced loving flickering through her body like living flames. Then she gasped and arched against his hand, rubbing against him, then stiffening and quaking with the eruption of pleasure inside her.

The shock caused by her spending was nearly as great as the release itself. Signe's heart pounded erratically, she gasped for breath, clasping, holding Bastian to her . . . panting softly, luxuriating in the steamy joy Bastian Cane had made for her.

Bastian Cane . . . not Jens Thorvald! But she had no right to such pleasures with the mesmerizing Bastian Cane! Panic seized her; the crashing shame of her wanton, unforgivable behavior. She was behaving just like . . . a harlot . . . like . . . the captain's woman, a woman she'd condemned and shunned! She pushed Bastian back, surprising him, and sitting up quickly.

"*Gud pa Himmel* . . . vhat have I done?" She scrambled to her feet, reeling, just avoiding Bastian's surprised attempts to retrieve her. "No—please—" she begged, "I beg you to forgive—I am not a loose woman. Only you are so big and strong . . . I am so tempted! But iss wrong . . ."

The need pounding through Bastian hampered his reactions, and she turned and was fleeing back down the beach toward the celebration before he made it to his knees. And in his wrought-up condition, he wouldn't be much good at running—

"Damn and blast!" he dragged himself to his feet, in agony from the aching and pounding in his loins. His whole body trembled for release, craving the softness of her beneath him. "Henry Morgan's Achin' Balls!" he thundered, clenching his fists and shaking them skyward. He'd loved her up, got her all primed and willing . . . and she'd soared and peaked, then pulled away from him like he'd ravaged her! Leaving him heaving and roiling—

He stomped this way and that, jerking his shoulders furiously at every turn to avoid seeing the confusion, the horror in her face again. Then he began to rip his fine, gentlemanly clothes from his body, heading for the soothing crystal relief of the water. It was what he got for aping the gentleman: a harsh lesson in the treachery of respectable females. He dove, naked, into the oncoming waves and swam like a man possessed to drain the charge from his body.

But when he staggered from the water, nearly an hour later, there was still a hard lump in his chest and Signe Thorvald's love moans still whispered in his blood.

"Don't you dare, Raider Prescott—oh—*oh!* Stop that!" Blythe struggled futilely to keep her shirt on her shoulders. Raider's lean, nimble fingers were suddenly everywhere with rapierlike speed, stripping her clothes from her, while her own hands parried like clumsy wooden blocks. It was a startling change from the last few days; Blythe struggling to keep her clothes *on*. More often, since their wedding four days ago, Raider had found himself hard-pressed to keep her in them until he could be sure they were alone and would be uninterrupted for a while.

But now, on his private, secluded stretch of white, palm-rimmed beach, he was having a devil of a time getting her clothes off. "Come on, wife—" He managed to get boots off and her leather skirt and split petticoat down over her bottom. He was panting from the excitement their battle generated. "You've not suddenly gone priggish on me, have you?" He caught her by the shirttail when she made to run and he hauled her back, enwrapped in the play of muscles in her shapely legs as they dug into the soft sand.

"I will not take my clothes off here in the open, Raider Prescott . . . in the middle of the beach!" she hissed, trying unsuccessfully to counter the way he was lifting her shirt up to pull it off over her head.

"Yes you will, wife. You're mostly there already." Raider's bronze features became positively satyric as he wrestled to draw her nearly naked form to him.

"Raider, somebody will see us—" She felt his rock-hard male-ness pressing her unbound body and felt her proper resistance to such wildly improper behavior sliding.

"No they won't." Raider waggled his brows lasciviously. "I posted guards . . ."

"Guards?" You mean somebody knows we're here . . . like this?" She really was shocked, blushing furiously.

"Just a few of the lads. I told them I was going to teach you to swim. They got the idea . . ." He laughed at her sputter. "Well, they know you can't learn to swim in a leather skirt and boots."

Blythe stared at him. Was he serious? "But . . . I don't want to learn to swim!"

"You can't be a pirate's wife, live on a pirate ship, and not know how to swim," he declared determinedly. "If we sank, I'd be stuck rescuing you instead of going down with my ship the way a good pirate's supposed to. Now come on, off with—"

"No!" Her eyes narrowed and her arms cradled her breasts defensively. "If you're determined to drown me, you'll have to do it in my chemise."

Raider decided to leave well enough alone and released her to strip off his own clothes. "Well, you can't expect me to teach you without getting wet myself?"

311

"Just where is gentlemanly 'Gideon' when I need him?" she mumbled, glancing balefully at the water, then at Raider's manly magnificence.

Shortly he scooped her up in his arms and carried her toward the sapphire blue of the lagoon. The shallow water was warm in the morning sun, swirling around and between them, reminding them of other liquid pleasures, and it was difficult indeed for Raider to concentrate on her lessons. She floated easily in his arms and her implicit trust of his directions meant she progressed nicely. After a while, he sent her to the beach and waded out chest-high in the water, ordering her to float to him, kicking her legs as he'd shown her.

But she paused with a moment's uncertainty, standing in her wet, clinging chemise, unconsciously displaying the dark, hardened points of her breasts, the sleek curve of her hips, and the dark triangle at the base of her belly. The gentle surf swirled about her knees. She was Venus, rising from the sea. Fire exploded in Raider's blood, and by the time she'd executed her float and came up sputtering and clinging to him, their lesson was over for the day.

He surprised her with a deep, longing kiss and she snuggled against his warmth in the cooler, deeper water. Soon he was carrying her from the water to the blanket where they'd left their clothes, and he laid her down . . . pressing her into the warm sand with his own weight, shielding her from the tropic sun with his own bronzed skin.

They loved slowly and sweetly, with sinuous harmonies in their kisses and caresses. The full range of strings, violins, cellos, and basses, was present in the final climax of their loving. As their love deepened and broadened, the music they made in loving also broadened, growing fuller, more resonant, ever more satisfying. As they lay together on the warm sand, Raider watched her, thinking how beautiful she was, how responsive, and how lucky he was to have claimed her.

"Do you know you have the most beautiful eyes I have ever seen?" he uttered softly, pushing up on one elbow for a glimpse of them. She turned a drowsy smile on him and lifted her lashes. Gold. He melted a bit more inside. It was his favorite color in the entire world.

"They're too light." She flushed a bit. "They're not proper brown or blue or even green. Nana always hoped they'd get darker, but they never did."

Raider's laugh was puzzled. "You're a tough woman to compliment, Blythe Prescott. Will you at least let me assert that your hair is without parallel in the Western world? Streaks of red and gold fire in it, especially in the sunlight. I've never seen anything like it." He brought some of it to his nose, inhaling the sweet, sun-warmed fragrance of it.

"It's not really so wonderful," she demurred. "Though when you say it's so, I almost believe it." She sat up and looked down at him, sighing with a wry bit of acceptance. "Nana called it a *hussy* shade . . . so it's probably very appropriate for me now."

Raider's laugh engulfed her before his arms did. There was that irresistible little girl again, his little girl. He held her close and looked down into her eyes, the depths of their gold making him feel as rich as Croesus.

"By any chance, does this 'Nana' of yours ride a broomstick?"

In love and in play, the first week of their marriage became a grand dalliance for Blythe Woolrich Prescott and her gentlemanly pirate. They slept and ate and loved by the internal rhythms of their deepening love, oblivious to celestial time and the convenience of others. When it was time for mundane mortal necessities, like meals, they were likely to be closeted in their bedchamber or out romping on Raider's private beach—learning to swim, he called it. Or they were net fishing in one of the lagoons or climbing up the lush hillsides to explore the island—and each other a bit more. Poor François was torn between applauding their devotion to the national pastime of his native France and decrying their neglect of his marvelous cuisine.

Unfortunately, François was not the only one affected by their willful truancy from duty. Bastian went about in a ripe snit half the time, irate at being left to see to the ship and shepherd the ransomers and make sure the lads didn't get into too much trouble with the locals. Worse . . . they left him alone at a very big, very empty table with curvy and reluctant Signe Thorvald and he had to invite the rest of the wretched ransomers in to eat with them to keep himself from doing something impulsive and disastrous . . . like ravishing her. She would hardly raise her face to him and seemed eager to escape her fellow captives' company in the evenings as well. She retired to her room or to the walled garden after supper, leaving Bastian to suffer through long chess matches with the pastor and the planters . . . while he imagined what she was doing and conjured torturing images of what he would like to be doing with her.

To be fair, Signe was quite as miserable as Bastian. She only had to watch his square, blocky frame through the veil of her lashes and echoes of the pleasure he had wrought inside her body shivered through her again. He was so bruisingly, stunningly male and physical that she could not trust herself in the same room with him. And his anger and contempt for her were so hard to watch that she escaped his presence whenever possible. She had never known such bold and unrequited passion before . . . not even with Jens Thorvald.

As the days passed in the shadow of Blythe's and Raider's blossoming love, Signe grew more and more unhappy. The other ransomers began to notice her listlessness and lack of appetite and grew solicitous of her health, asking after it during supper one evening. Bastian startled at their comments, staring at her, cut to the quick at the thought that something might be wrong with her. But she tucked her chin tighter, feeling Bastian's hot gaze on her, and waved aside their concerns, blaming her obvious strain on lack of sleep and . . . the night heat.

Bastian took an after-supper stroll that evening, escaping the obligatory chess match. He managed to catch Signe in the twilight-shadowed garden when he returned and maneuvered skillfully between her and the door, planting himself firmly. He was a daunting sight indeed, voluminous sleeves, a leather waist-coat snug over his very broad, blocky shoulders, tall boots, dark red-brown hair that was grayed slightly at the temples. She began to tremble.

"What be ailin' ye, Signe?" He came straight out with it. "Any fool can see yer not farin' well."

"Iss nothing . . . really. The heat . . . I do not sleep well . . ." She would not look at him and Bastian had the surprising insight that what happened between them the night of Raider's wedding might have something to do with her languishing. Sick with remorse, likely; it dawned on him. Respectable females would rather die that suffer "un-churched" pleasures, he recalled. Well, he wasn't about to let Signe die . . .

"It's what happened t'other night . . . between us," he asserted, taking a step closer that sent her skittering back with widened and very blue eyes. He wasn't sure, but she seemed so full of nerves just now, his assumption had to have struck one of them. She turned half away, then back, clasping her hands until her fingers whitened.

"Please . . . forgive me. I did not mean to . . . leave you so . . . un-zatisfied." Her eyes dipped boldly to his breeches front in spite of her, and Bastian was stunned by her bluntness. "You are right to be angry with me. A voman who takes and does not give . . ." She choked and turned her face away from the shame and Bastian found his tongue had turned to cotton in his mouth. She composed herself briefly, then turned tear-rimmed eyes to him.

"I vas wrong to let you touch me . . . to take your loving. And wrong to leave you. But iss the smaller sin, I hope, to leave you wanting. It is wrong to give myself to you, Bastian Cane. And it will hurt too much when I must go." Her hand came up to clasp and massage that tantalizing valley between her breasts, above her heart. "Already it hurts."

Bastian felt like a thirty-two-pounder had ripped through him. Lord—he hadn't felt this strange, shocky kind of hurt since he'd taken two lead balls at one time and had to fight for another hour in that condition! But Signe was hurting, too, he could see it in her lovely face, could read it in the jerky movements of her hands and the rigid control of her shoulders. What did she have to hurt about—unless . . . she really wanted him?!

He honestly didn't understand it. She seemed to think it would somehow hurt her to have his loving. Why deny themselves pleasures now just because they would have to end after a bit? Respectable females made no more damned sense than a sponge! Give them a scrap of pleasure and they're already tallyin' up the cost in future pain! The glower on his face was fierce indeed and Signe trampled on a few blossoming canaria trying to bolt around him for the door. But he lunged quickly and spread himself in her path. She jerked back as if scorched by their brief brush. Tears rolled down her fair cheeks.

"Please . . ." she begged with eyes that turned what was left of Bastian's middle inside out, "please don't touch me. I can't bear it." He stiffened, unsure of her meaning, and she read his reaction as the disgust she expected. When she slipped by him a second time, he didn't try to stop her. He stood, listening to the sounds of her feet on the tile of the main room of the house. Was she afraid of him? Of herself? How could she say she wanted him and his loving and not be able to bear his touching her? Henry Morgan's Spleen—respectable females were a study in madness! He stormed down to the beach for what was becoming a nightly habit . . . a hard, exhausting swim in a cold ocean.

The approaching "meet" for the exchange of payment and ransomers was a source of mixed emotions for all of the principals involved. The male ransomers had grown rather attached to their island paradise, with no business or theological or governmental worries, wonderful food, stimulating happenings—things were never dull around the crew of the *Windraider.* Bastian was itching to be shed of the lot of them, especially Signe Thorvald, who confused and roused him in ways he didn't ever want to experience, much less explore. Signe dreaded leaving, for it meant never seeing Bastian Cane again and having to suffer her brother's stern lectures about the dangers of being a widow, alone and adrift in the world. But staying, so near the temptation that Bastian Cane presented, was torture, refined.

Raider did not look forward to the intrusion of his "business" into his newly married life, and Blythe sensed it and dreaded it as well. And there was the business of the ransom exchange itself . . . on a rocky islet in midocean. It could prove rather dangerous with only one ship. They might have to run hard after collecting the ransom . . . or fight for it.

On the day they were to sail, Blythe insisted on going along, and much as Raider fretted about taking her, he relented. They set off with full crew in a freshly provisioned ship for the long

316

day's sail to the rocky islet called 'Bishop's Nob.' The mood on deck was subdued indeed as they neared the low, barren island and the scout in the crow's nest spotted a lone ship on the horizon, headed toward the "nob." Tension came alive as they made final preparation for anchoring and deploying two long-boats.

Blythe stood by Signe and watched the pain in the young widow's face, wondering at its source. Surely she didn't expect to be harmed by the very people who were buying back her freedom? No, it was not quite fear she read in Signe's contained hurt. She and Raider had watched Bastian's ogling and maneuvering where Signe was concerned, but didn't think he'd managed to penetrate the cool shell of propriety the widow carried about her like a shield. No doubt they would have heard plenty about it, if he had. Blythe prayed that such unhappiness in the face of going home had nothing to do with anything that had happened to her on their island.

When Signe raised tear-filled eyes, Blythe couldn't resist hugging her reassuringly. And when they made to lower Signe to the longboat on the swing, she clung to Blythe's hands wordlessly, and Blythe offered to go ashore with her if it would comfort her. Raider carried Signe through the low surf, deposited her on the beach, then returned for Blythe. Bastian was busy deploying the shore party like a careful tactitian, claiming the high ground and positioning the ransomers. He was exceptionally gruff, it seemed, when he came to Signe. He growled and told her to stand "somewheres damned obvious" so they could see she hadn't been harmed. She lowered her head and Bastian cursed softly and stomped off.

The opposing shore party came ashore in much the same fashion and in similar strength, though they had to array themselves mostly on the far-side beach, since the high ground was already taken. The governor of St. Thomas, a dignified, brown-haired man in his fifties, led the contingent, that included two British naval officers in full regalia, and Signe's nephew, Gunnar Andersen. They paused some distance away and called for the governor's cousin to be sent over first, to verify the well-being of the hostages. The Reverend Rasmussen glanced at Raider, who nodded, and he went forward into a hearty handshake and a clap on the back. There was a bit of conferencing and some dark looks tossed Raider and Bastian's way.

One of the British officers then picked up a heavy metal box and brought it forward, depositing it on the ground near Blythe's feet, then raking her with a contemptuous look. Raider jerked and Bastian put a restraining hand on his arm, warning him. The ransomers were called forward and they glanced about them at Raider and his men. To a man, they turned to Raider and nodded gallantly in recognition of their captors' generosity before going across to the other side. The officer went to Signe, picked up her leather case, and offered her his arm, which she accepted.

But as they neared the rescue party and Gunnar came forward to receive his aunt, she whirled and went running back across the rocky ground, straight for a very startled Bastian Cane. She threw herself into Bastian's arms and the only reaction he was capable of was the very one she wanted. His mouth swooped down on hers in a stunning, sensual kiss as he crushed her to him. Signe molded herself against him, memorizing every muscle, every angle, every line of him, absorbing every sensation into her drought-stricken heart. Not a muscle moved, not an eye blinked on 'Bishop's Nob' for the small eternity that their kiss endured.

But then it was over and Bastian loosened his hold on her and she pushed back in his arms. Her cheeks were wet, her eyes were blue pools of despair. Wordlessly she reached up to stroke his hard cheek and his lips. Then she stepped back and turned, leaving him there to make that very long walk back across the rocks to her shocked rescuers.

"Raider Prescott!" the governor assembled his wits enough to call out. "I'll have a word with you!" He motioned for the ransomers to be taken to the boats, and by a prearranged signal, the British officers came forward with him to parley.

Raider exchanged glances with Bastian, whose blood was finally draining from his crimson face back into his body, and they, too, approached the center of the islet. Raider had met the governor under more favorable circumstances, when they traded in the free port of St. Thomas, and knew from the gravity of his expression that whatever he had to say would be bad news.

"I harbor you no personal ill will, Raider Prescott, for the taking of my cousin," he began, though his face did little to lend credence to it.

"It was purely business, Governor. We privateer against British ships . . . your cousin happened to be aboard the one we took. I regret the inconvenience to you personally." Raider nodded a gentlemanly nod, which was accepted in kind by the governor.

"Nor must what I have to say be taken personally. Until this last act, you have behaved honorably toward our government. But times are changing, Raider Prescott. This pirate league is forcing changes upon us . . . new alliances. We have made a pact of protection with the government of the British Virgin Islands; we shall act in concert to rid our waters of pirating and privateering ships, dangerous to either territory. You privateer against the British and now must be considered our enemy as well."

Raider's jaw clenched and he had to force himself to ease and straighten. It might have been a mistake to take the governor's cousin . . . but this would likely have occurred without that little irritation. The Brits and the Danes, operating in concert now . . .

"Five days." The ranking Brit, a beagle-faced fellow with bilious eyes, took a half step forward with an ugly sneer on his face. "In five days our combined ships will round the point on that pest hole you call your base . . . and if we find that bloody bucket of yours in evidence, we'll blow you right out of the water. After which we'll level the whole damned island. Nothing would give me greater pleasure than to find you there," he spat, "and to send you and your whole damnable crew straight to hell. I'd have done it already if you hadn't had the governor's cousin and a Danish lady in your camp. You have them to thank for your worthless lives."

The governor snatched the fellow's arm back irritably, making him ease his belligerent stance. He stared gravely at Raider and Bastian. "Go, Raider Prescott. Be gone in five days' time. You've been warned."

"I'll . . . take your warning under advisement, Governor." Raider nodded stiffly and turned, pulling Bastian with him back toward the longboats, collecting Blythe along the way. The lads melted back toward the boats from their positions, keeping a sharp eye peeled for trickery and sails on the horizons. But none were forthcoming; it appeared the governor had just come for ransomers, as required . . . and to deliver his warning.

Chapter Twenty

Word of the governor's ultimatum spread through the *Windraider* like wildfire. Reactions, predictably, ran the gamut from indignation to pure, raw bloodlust, with Bastian vacillating between the extremes. Raider, however, seemed to withdraw, freezing his own reactions, submerging them in the stark business of getting canvas and anchor raised and laying down sailing orders. The lads hurried to get underway, keeping an eye on The Raider, watching for signs of an impending explosion. But everything they saw reassured them that he was firmly in control and already planning their proper course.

Blythe watched him, too, and felt the ache of hurt and anger he wouldn't allow himself to feel. They were being evicted from their beautiful island home and from the thin but sometimes useful protection of a gentleman's agreement with the Danes. Though they usually made it to their home base only once a year, it had been a form of security for both Raider and his men to think of its shorebound privileges and comforts awaiting them. And now that comfort, that bit of stability in their brutal and dangerous world, was gone.

Several times, Blythe approached him as he stood on the top deck, staring off into the lowering night sky. He gave her terse smiles of recognition that contained the clear message that he was not willing to talk about it. She simply slipped her arms about his waist and looked out over the moon-brightened waters, feeling his silence invading her, too. Their brief, idyllic honeymoon was over and they were plunged harshly back into the gritty business of life . . . pirate life. And Blythe prayed that the vows they had spoken and the love they had made would help see them through the troubled times ahead.

The crew and village were hurtled into a numbed preparation for the *Windraider*'s final departure. They sorted their collected trappings of shorelife, taking what might be useful aboard ship, giving the rest to the villagers or just leaving it behind. A handful of the men had women and familial attachments in the village and decided to forgo the sea, to stay on the island. Raider heard their quiet desperation and nodded compassionately, releasing them from the *Articles*. Blythe watched Raider's grimness at such times and wished with all her heart she could do something to alleviate it. The best she could do, it seemed, was to be her most sensible, responsible self, to see to the details and the packing . . . and to be there in his bed each night, burning the worries and the doubts from his mind and body as only she could.

On their last night on the island, she stood in the candlelight, dressed only in her chemise, staring at the big, postered bed where Raider Prescott had claimed her as his wife and declared his love for her.

"I wish we could take it with us," she murmured fondly, hugging to her the shirt she had just removed. Raider looked up from the papers on his writing table. A light frown creased his face and he rose, following her gaze to the great, polished posts and gauzy silken hangings. "Our bed. I just wish we could take it with us."

"Carry it in your heart, Blythe," he murmured softly, coming to stand behind her, wrapping his arms around her waist. "Everything worth having can be carried in your heart."

Blythe turned in his arms and kissed him to keep from dissolving into tears. He moved her to the bed and together they made a farewell melody, a sonata so rich and complete, there was no room for regrets.

The *Windraider* lifted anchor and put to sea with a strong morning tide, with one day to spare on the governor's five-day allowance. The lads kept up a viable pretense of going about their duties . . . until the island began to fade on the horizon and then many of them stopped at the railing for a last look at their erstwhile home. Bastian was difficult indeed, growling and snarling at the slightest provocation, stomping about the crates and barrels stowed on deck and declaring the *Windraider* was overloaded and wallowing like a fat sow.

"Ships an' women—" he declared vehemently. "Cain't get neither to respond worth a damn when they be overloaded!" Blythe smiled for the first time that day, and Bastian caught her indulgent expression and stomped off toward Raider, growling irritably. "Well . . . where be we headed, Raider?"

Blythe and several of the lads in the vicinity turned to collect his response: "Port-au-Prince."

From the grins and relieved nudges that produced among the lads, and from Bastian's suddenly beatific countenance, Blythe deduced that 'Port-au-Prince' was something akin to "pirate's paradise." And she wasn't far from wrong; Bastian volunteered that bit of information. The French had created a flourishing sugar-based economy in the colony of Saint Dominigue that was hungry for both commerce and the trappings of civilized life. And being French, the island officialdom would have no grudge against the *Windraider*, who had only taken British-flagged ships. Most important, Port-au-Prince was an easy, libertine sort of city that accepted cargoes from pirates and privateers and then gave them plenty of opportunity to "reinvest" the proceeds in fleshy pleasures of taverns and in the reprovisioning of ships. The lads would have a bit of pleasure and off-load a bit of their cumbersome cargoes in the process.

It was a temporary measure, Blythe realized, a chance to regroup and reassess resources. That night in their cabin, she dressed for bed and watched Raider sitting at the ebonywood table, studying his charts and tallying their negotiable cargoes in his ledger.

"What will we do after?" She finally put words to her worries, coming to stand near him. "After Port-au-Prince?"

He lifted his head and stared straight out the cabin window before turning and pulling her against his side. He had to be honest with her and hope it would be enough. "Then . . . we'll

323

have enough coin to ensure our provisions and secure us a welcome in a port or two . . . while we look for ships." He read the concern deep in her eyes and sought to allay her fears about their future. "And we'll keep an eye for a small island with a secure cove . . . and a good swimming beach."

Blythe melted, sensing that last part, about another permanent base, was motivated in part by her presence in his life. He was admitting to a need for some stability in their life together . . . agreeing to it. It answered a lot of questions she had been wondering how to ask . . . if she should ask.

"Oh, by all means, a good swimming beach," she laughed, locking her arms around his neck and teasing his nose with the tip of hers. "And while we're at it . . . we'll look for a prize ship carrying furniture."

When he looked a bit pained at the domestic trend of her larcenous impulses, she laughed again and clarified her desire: "Carrying beds, big stately beds . . ."

Port-au-Prince had a wide, perfectly situated harbor, and on the day they sailed into the French harbormaster's venue, Blythe and the lads poured out on the deck to stare at the city, set like a multicolored jewel in the morning sun. For the last fortnight, the lads had regaled and scandalized her with tales of the doings and darings that abounded in the famous port. By the time they arrived, she was almost as itchy to gain port as they were. The harbormaster sent a force on board the *Windraider* to tally and exact duty and soon they were permitted to approach the docks and quays, having been assigned a good berth.

A strict system of liberty was enforced on the *Windraider*, to assure a viable, protective force would remain aboard at all times. The lads were all assigned numbers and a lottery was conducted. The first wave would be loosed on the city's pleasuring districts only after the first agreements for the sale of wares and goods were made. Fortunately, the harbormaster had suggested several merchants who would be interested in acquiring the *Windraider*'s varied cargoes. Unfortunately, Bastian spotted the presence of three ships anchored off the quay that spelled potential trouble for the *Windraider*. He hurried to Raider's side as they cruised under partial sail toward their berth and pointed across the bay. Raider sighted down Bastian's arm to the unmistakable yellow-and-red ships, anchored in the bay. His gaze narrowed and heat welled up in his stomach.

"Long Ben," Raider uttered as if it were a curse and his face became like ruddy granite. "Damn and blast. He would have to be here." He turned away as though the sight nauseated him and found Old Willie and Blythe staring at him expectantly. "Long Ben and his cronies are here," he informed Willie through tight lips. "Tell the men liberty will have to wait."

Willie's face wrinkled like a veritable prune and he hurried off to spread the word. Blythe frowned and shook her head in bewilderment. "Who's Long Ben . . . and why no liberty for the men?"

Raider opened his mouth, but closed it, feeling raw, unbridled fury rising in him and not trusting himself to relate that bit of history. He swatted Bastian's arm grimly, insisting Bastian tell her, then stalked down to the waist with his thumbs shoved in his belt and his body rigid.

"Long Ben's head of the pirate league what issued Raider an me an invitation to join 'em a few months back," Bastian tore his eyes from Raider's scarcely controlled ire and glanced briefly at Blythe before fastening a dark look on those hideous yellow-and-red barks anchored menacingly in the bay.

"You declined. I remember hearing something . . ."

"After a fashion." Bastian's blocky jaw went rigid for a moment. "Didn't much like the way he made his proposal." He turned and scoured the lads teeming up onto the waist for a glimpse of Long Ben's ships. He searched for one face, and when he caught sight of Stanley, he pointed to him. "There be Long Ben's 'invite.' "

On the waist below the quarterdeck, mild-mannered Stanley was ripping the shirt from his back, baring himself to his mates with a hatred burning in his face that rattled Blythe thoroughly. But it was his back that made her gasp. Into the white of the back, the letters *J-O-I-N* had been carved viciously . . . as if to ensure the maximum in pain and scarring. *JOIN,* cut into Stanley's flesh; the scars still gleamed that evil message, written in the blood of one of Raider's crew. It was hardly an invitation;

it was a threat. That was why Stanley never removed his shirt like the other lads, while working on deck, Blythe realized distractedly. And she was suddenly sick.

"What kind of madman would do such a thing?" She tore her eyes away to fix them on Bastian.

"Long Ben's mad a'right. An' clever and treacherous. He's brung a score of ships under his thumb, wi' just such doin's. He controls the traffic of goods into Charleston now. 'At's why we don't trade there no more. It's why we come to Philadelphie, lookin' fer markets. He won't like it that we're here, no more than we like the sight of him. He don't want no 'independents' working *his* territory . . ." Bastian stopped, feeling his own righteous ire rising and he turned away to join Raider and the lads on the waist, to decide on a bit of strategy.

Blythe shuddered, looking across the sunny bay to the gleaming yellow ships with blood-red strakes running along their sides just above the top rows of their gunports. Three ships . . . out of twenty or more. The balmy tropic air took on a sickening chill.

Raider and Bastian laid plans, posted watches, and made their first foray ashore, feeling all the while as though the very mooring posts and stones had eyes trained on them. A confrontation with Long Ben was inevitable, they knew. And they knew their only chance was to choose the time and the conditions of that confrontation themselves. Like careful military strategists, they moved as a group, selecting a defensible spot for a "meet" on a market square, not far from the offices of a merchant with whom they were likely to strike a deal. It was a tavern with rough tables and benches set along a stone Spanish-style covered archway that rimmed the square. That first day, they secured their agreements with the merchant and faded back to their ship, planting men in the nearby warehouses to watch the ship through the night.

The second day, as the agreed cargo was off-loaded, Raider and Bastian went to the merchant's office to collect payment, taking Blythe and a small contingent of men with them. Bastian balked at the idea of including Blythe in their party, but Raider overruled his objection with sound reasoning; Blythe would add credence to their "unsuspecting" ruse, she could wield a firearm if necessary, and would likely be safer in their armed escort than left aboard ship. Bastian was outgunned and surrendered with a characteristic grumble.

They did not have long to wait for an approach. Long Ben's spies were efficient, indeed. No sooner had they left the merchant's office near the square than they sensed a stealthy movement around them in the unpaved street. Expectation swirled up around and within them like the dust their boots made. The noonday sun was bright as they paused on the edge of the busy square and Raider shaded his eyes and looked for signs of his men concealed around the square and the tavern. Satisfied with their cloaked presence, he looked to Bastian who read his look and raised his nose, breathing deeply.

"I be plugged up . . ." he growled with a nasal rasp, "but it'd be hard not to smell that much bilge scum."

Raider nodded and took Blythe's arm, leading her forward slowly with a terse, sideways warning to stay calm and to shoot only as a last resort. "A pistol wields a lot more power *before* it goes off."

Blythe swallowed hard and nodded, sending her hand to the primed and loaded pistol that hung from a strap at her side. Its cool metal had a foreign feel, and she could hardly credit that she'd actually used it once to draw blood from another human being. That was her last thought before being absorbed in the scurry of dust and bystanders and the squawking escape of chickens and parrots from overturned cages reached them from the street at the far corner of the square. From that sweeping wave of confusion, a frightening wall of male flesh materialized, arrayed like a Greek phalanx behind the chilling figure of Long Ben Harvey.

It had to have been him, Blythe realized as she moved rigidly in the direction Raider pushed her. Long Ben was just that: long of frame, long of face, and long on memory, from the way his eyes burned when they fell on Raider Prescott. He came on, stalking a slow, almost painful gait. He was dressed in a crimson officer's coat, replete with tarnished gold naval braid that had once graced a more noble frame. His heavy jackboots were untended and his stained breeches were held to his gaunt body by a worn belt with a gaudy golden buckle. His shoulders were narrow, his hair hung in long, greasy tangles, and his eyes were touched with a half-mad gleam as they stared out of his long, pockmarked face. He was a man whose body was infested with the plagues of dissipation. And the rot had clearly claimed his soul as well.

Raider halted at the edge of the arched portico, with Blythe and Bastian at his sides and Oars and Sharkey and seven more of his men visible at his back. Long Ben stopped a few yards away, looking them over carefully, letting his eyes linger insultingly on Blythe's curvy, leather-clad form before dragging them back to Raider.

"Raider Prescott," he spat through yellowed and decaying teeth, "I didn't expect to be seein' you agin . . . until we met in hell. This calls for a drink." He motioned toward the tavern tables, and after a moment began to ease toward the nearest one, motioning to his men to follow. A bull-necked fellow hurried to pull a chair out for his leader, but Long Ben waited until Raider Prescott approached the table as well before he occupied it. He pounded the table and summoned the tavernman and his black serving wench, calling for the finest rum in the place. And as the quaking tavernkeeper scurried to do his bidding, Long Ben turned his intrusive gaze on Blythe, examining her hair, her lovely skin, her curvy form . . . and the pistol at her side.

"So . . . ye be sailing wi' a woman now." His mouth curled in an ugly bit of speculation. "A fine-lookin' bitch she be . . ."

"She's my wife." Raider spoke for the first time, very calmly. Long Ben threw back his head and laughed, a roiling evil kind of a laugh.

"Damn, you alwus was the gentleman, wasn't you?" Long Ben's face sobered with alarming speed, the way his moods always changed. "It be one of the things I despise about you, Prescott . . . always the damned gentleman." He looked Blythe over again and saw her eyes drifting to his men, two of whom had settled onto stools at the table just behind him. His eyes darted sideways and he snaked about, lightning quick, lashing out with the short, metal-studded whip that dangled habitually at his side. He caught the bull-necked fellow who had pulled out his chair across the face with those metal-studded strands, cutting deep into his cheek and lacerating his forehead and jaw. The fellow howled and grabbed his face, staggering up and staring at his leader through a haze of blood and pain.

"Whoreson!" Long Ben spat, "The likes o' you don't sit in the presence of *ladies*." The other bloke was on his feet before an eye could blink. Long Ben turned back to Blythe with that evil gleam in his eye. "Raider Prescott ain't the only man about who knows what ladies like."

Blythe did her best not to cringe or let her shiver of revulsion be too obvious. She longed desperately for the reassurance of Raider's hand, but sensed that to seek it would betray a weakness Long Ben would enjoy seeing. Her eyes turned from the wretched Long Ben to his men. They were a dirty, smelly lot with plenty of muscle in evidence beneath their motley, ill-fitting garments. Every one carried a wicked blade and several of the ten or so men also carried the ravages of the pox on their faces . . . as well as scars from the kind of lashing Blythe had just seen demonstrated. More than one bore visible notches in his ears and one had huge, gaping slits ripped in his nostrils that had been seared so they could never grow back together. They were staring at her, disrobing her with their eyes, ravishing her with their eyes.

The brown-skinned serving wench brought the rum by herself on a huge platter. She jumped skittishly when Long Ben snagged her arm, squeezing it harshly, demanding that she pour it for them as well. She swallowed, and her large brown eyes flitted with fright toward Long Ben's slavering pack as she obeyed. Seeing her obvious fear, Long Ben's men fastened their attention on her. And as she finished and meant to slink away, one of the pack grabbed her arm and pulled her toward them, laughing at her squirming protests.

Blythe's throat closed as she watched them set rough, punishing hands to her. They relished the girl's screeches, Blythe realized; it excited them. How could Raider and Bastian sit there and do nothing?! She lifted a pleading glance at Raider, who cast a hard, warning glance her way. She stiffened and felt raw anger rising inside her as she turned on Long Ben and found him studying Raider's reaction with a taunting smirk. She was stunned. This display of barbarism was no accident. They were trying to provoke the "gentlemanly" Raider into something impulsive. And he could not afford to rise to the bait, whatever the

329

wench's fate. But she could . . .

"Tell them to stop!"

Long Ben slid his eyes to her, taking in her anger, the molten gold heat in her gaze. His mouth curled into an ugly sneer that refused . . . taunting her to back up her demand.

Blythe swallowed. She had to do something. In plain sight, she removed the pistol from its straps at her side and gripped its handle carefully with both hands. She felt Raider's startle at her side and watched Long Ben's snap and coil across the table. But when she raised the pistol, it was pointed at the wench's abusers and her voice lowered to a furious growl.

"Let her be, you mangy curs!" And when their guttural laughter faded and they turned lust-riddled faces on her, she pulled back the hammer and raised her arms. "Let her *go!*"

Tension prickled on the backs of necks in the long moment that followed. When their grip began to loosen, the wench wriggled free and ran hard for the tavern door. Blythe could feel their eyes hot on her and met them with all the heat and bravado she could muster. Then she lifted her chin and uncocked her piece, laying it across her lap. There was a general easing of both sides and Long Ben's mouth twitched as he reached for a tankard and held it up in her direction.

"To women." He acknowledged her grit, tossing back a healthy draught of the potent rum. Raider and Bastian slowly joined him and he watched her scorn the tankard sitting on the pockmarked table near her. "You ain't drinkin' to yer kind?"

"I . . . don't drink rum, thank you."

Her calm, ladylike answer brought a devious smile to his decayed mouth and he downed the remainder of his tankard before turning on Raider. "Down to business. Ye had your time, Prescott. What be your answer? Do you join up . . . or be hunted down?" Long Ben's bilious eyes narrowed on Raider, searching him and then Bastian.

Raider let the silence speak first and as Long Ben began to redden, he added words to it. "My ladies run as independents, Long Ben." He spoke calmly, but with a rail of steel underlying his words. "Both the Wool-witch," he cocked his head briefly toward Blythe, "and the *Windraider.* I won't sail with you." He saw the heat in Long Ben's eyes beginning to shimmer and continued. "But I need your markets, in Charleston and the Bahamas . . . and you could use the bounty from the ships I take. I think we can come to an agreeable . . . working relationship."

Long Ben studied Raider's cleanly sculptured features, and a mask of geniality closed over his own ravaged face. "My bounty be high, Prescott . . . it's gone up."

"How much?" Raiders voice was stifled, and Blythe looked at him to find that certain muscle in his jaw jumping. Long Ben saw it, too.

"One half!" he proclaimed, pounding a fist down on the table, then breaking into a maniacal leer.

"That's robb—" Bastian made to rise, and only Raider's savage grip on his arm kept him in his seàt.

"That's too high, Harvey, and you know it," Raider uttered tightly, barely maintaining his grip on Bastian and himself. Long Ben's men were at full attention, spreading out and facing off against the *Windraider's* lads.

"It be the price of *independence*, Prescott. Take it or leave it."

There was a long, heaving silence in which the old adversaries studied each other, testing each other's mettle, assessing each other's relative strengths and weaknesses. A cold breeze wrapped around Blythe's shoulders, invading her chest, at the hatred she saw embedded in Long Ben's eyes.

"I'll take it." Raider's voice came forth strongly. "You have a new partner, Harvey. Your man in Charleston . . . he still taking your cut?"

"He is."

"Then he'll have your share of my prizes, one by one." Raider pushed up with his hands on his thighs, in plain sight.

Long Ben's spare, loose-jointed body collected itself to rise with Raider. He extended a long, blue-veined hand and Raider clasped it. "Drink then . . . to our new partnership," he insisted, reaching for the pitcher and sloshing more of the brew into both his and Raider's tankards. Bastian joined them, standing, to raise his tankard aloft. But Long Ben paused, staring hard at Blythe who was red-faced and tight with ire. "You, too, woman. Drink to your man's pact."

It was an order Blythe intended to defy. How dare Raider throw in with the likes of this scabby, pox-eaten . . . But she caught the meaningful glance Raider shot from the corner of his eye. He was warning her not to interfere or object to this unholy alliance. In the agonizing interval that followed, she made herself recall all the reasons she had for trusting Raider Prescott, both gentleman and pirate, and made herself act on that trust. She rose and took her time relacing her pistol in its straps before reaching for her drink. She glanced at Raider, then at Long Ben, and raised the mug to drink the rum like a good pirate wench. Her eyes teared and her shoulders jerked, but she managed to get some of it down.

When he slammed his tankard down on the table, Long Ben looked at her reaction and laughed with something akin to real humor. "Have supper with me, Prescott . . ." his eyes never left Blythe as he spoke, "we'll celebrate."

"I've plans to sail on the tide," Raider declined, adding, "The Danes and Brits have a pact now in the Virgins. I thought you ought to know. They have combined their fleets to protect their sugar ships. It means I'll have to range farther north to find the kind of prize I need. I'll be leaving shortly. So I must decline."

"Disappoint my hospitality, Prescott," Long Ben's gaze was now as brittle as his precarious self-control, "but never disappoint my purse. I'll have what's due me from you." He allowed his gaze to drift to Blythe, and Raider responded in a very quiet tone.

"That you will, Long Ben. You have my word on it."

Then as quickly as it had begun, the "meet" was over, both camps fading to their respective corners of the square and exiting to make for their ships. The skirl of confusion and dust soon settled and Port-au-Prince had narrowly escaped a bloodbath in one of her main squares.

Raider strode hard for the ship, his men slipping ahead and covering the rear, checking the way and assuring that none of Long Ben's men doubled back on them. He pulled Blythe along at his long-legged pace, allowing her little time to catch her breath at corners. By the time they reached the wharf she was steaming. Raider Prescott had a lot to answer for . . . swearing in with that scurvy, revolting wretch!

Raider began issuing orders the instant his feet hit the gangway. Sharkey answered Raider's summons and was told bluntly to go be a shark . . . with teeth sharp enough to sever an anchor cable. Willie and Franco were given orders to see to the stores and to take what coin was necessary to finish them out from the nearest vendors. Black Jimmy was to take his gunners below, break out the powder, and stand by for action. The other lads were collecting fast to receive their orders, pulsing with the charge generated by Raider's bottled fury.

"You can't be serious?!" Blythe planted herself in front of him, interrupting the continuous fire of his orders. "You're actually going to lift anchor and sail off to do Long Ben's bidding? To pay his *blackmail?!*"

"Not *now*, Blythe—" Raider took her shoulders to set her aside bodily, but she struggled and balked.

"Yes, *now!* You actually intend to throw in with that madman—" she charged. "How could you?! You gave him your *word* and your hand on it!" The lads stared between them, wide-eyed and rumbling consternation at the possibility. Raider grabbed her shoulders tightly and gave her a shake.

"I *said* . . . not here!" Raider's face was glowing like hot bronze and his voice was dangerously calm.

"You agreed to give him half . . . *half* of every prize! To do his dirty work—"

"I *lied!*" he thundered. "I lied to buy us enough time to make open sea." He stopped and drew back, quaking and hoarse with scarcely contained rage. "And Long Ben knows it."

He released her slowly and called for Clive and the Bosun Deane to follow him into his cabin. He left her standing there, confused, and unable to react to his revelation properly.

Bastian barked the lads back to their presailing duties and cast a dark look at her paling face and glazed expression. He took her by the arm and pulled her up onto the quarterdeck, out of the way. He turned her to face him and she moved like a puppet, obeying.

"Look, Wool-witch, Raider be doin' what's best for us all. It were the lip service he give . . . or bloodshed on the spot."

"But he said—"

"Ye're the bravest damned female I ever saw, Wool-witch, but ye got bilge fer brains sometimes. Raider bought us time. Long Ben's gonna let us sail outta port . . . then he's gonna come after us . . . hard. I seen what he does to a crew he takes. A bloke'd be better off cuttin' out his own liver. An' he wants you, Wool-witch, in case ye hadn't guessed. All the more reason to come after us . . ."

Blythe paled fully now, and her knees went weak beneath her. Bastian was right. The way Long Ben had looked at her . . . talked about claiming what was due him. She shivered, recalling her fear as they handled that serving wench. They would handle *her* the same . . .

"Shape up, Wool-witch," Bastian ordered gruffly but without real heat. "Raider, he needs you—" Then he realized what he'd said and jerked away, starting for the waist, snarling, "God A'mighty knows why—"

Chapter Twenty-one

The wind was fine and the *Windraider* absorbed the strain of her voluminous sails nobly. She had successfully negotiated the Canal de Saint Marc and slowed near the harbormaster's quay to allow the lads to pluck a wet, exhausted Sharkey from the water. He had grinned his toothiest grin and held up his knife and two fingers . . . for two anchors that would never leave the murky bottom of the harbor. Sharkey's extraordinary ability to stay submerged under water for long periods had probably bought them some time. Even Long Ben's desperate captains knew better than to give chase and sail without a proper anchor. And the third ship was not likely to come after them alone; Long Ben's mongrels always moved in packs.

Soon the sights and sounds of Port-au-Prince were fading in all but the lingering tension of expectation . . . and memory. Blythe stood on the quarterdeck, not yet ready to face Raider again and staring out to sea. She turned to find Bastian settling at the railing not far away, and she was drawn to his side.

"What do you think? Have we gotten away?"

"We'll give it a good run . . . the *Windraider* be the best. We got a chance . . ." his eyes flicked her direction, "for now." Blythe was frowning, thinking her own thoughts and so missed the disturbing end of his statement.

"She's a fine lady, isn't she." Blythe looked up into the intricate maze of rigging that tamed and reined the full, graceful sails above them.

"The best." Bastian took a deep breath that swelled his barrel chest. "Why, wi' a handful like 'er, Old Henry Morgan coulda taken the whole damned Mediterranean!"

"Bastian, just who was Henry Morgan? You and Raider and the lads . . . you all swear by sundry parts of the fellow . . ." Bastian's eyes widened on her, appalled by her ignorance of seafaring heroes.

"Why, he be the boldest, cleverest, finest piratin' captain who ever lived!" Bastian claimed, with a flash of ancestral pride. "He were a buccaneer in the old days . . . took enough plunder to fatten up all England . . . and he done it in style, Old Henry! Then he got rich and got pardoned and knighted an' were made Lieutenant Governor o' Jamaica. Not bad fer an old sea dog. Would that I coulda sailed with . . ." A certain wistfulness crept into Bastian's strong, blocky features.

"Piracy's fell on hard times of late . . . there be no denyin' it. Riffraff and bilge scum has sullied the ranks of what was once a fine perfession. Ye see, *proper* boardin' and pillagin' . . . it be turnin' a bit of trade, nothin' personal to it. Like with the gov'nor of St. Thomas. Nothin' personal . . . because Raider an' me, we always been perfessional. But bad practice has been creepin' in . . . and bad blood with it . . . stinkin' offal like Long Ben and his boys." He turned to look at Blythe's softened expression and felt an unholy urge to speak his fears.

"The seas be gettin' smaller, Wool-witch. There be navies now, and the old ways be dyin' out. Piracy . . . ain't what it used to be," the fire in his hazel eyes damped suddenly and his voice lowered as he spoke his conclusions and his fears, "nor ever will be again. We be the last . . ."

Blythe laid her hand on Bastian Cane's trunklike arm and gave it a gentle caress. There was a surprising streak of the romantic in Bastian Cane's overblown ideas of pirating, whether he liked it or not. "If you're the last, Bastian Cane . . . you're also the best. If I had to be kidnapped by pirates, I'm glad it was the best."

Bastian looked at the liquid prisms in her eyes and the fond smile on her face and felt a strange swelling in his chest. When she turned away, the image of her face lingered in his mind . . . her eyes becoming very blue, her hair becoming like cornsilk, her lips becoming fuller and pouty. In his mind, Bastian Cane was seeing Signe Thorvald and it seemed to him that the wind bore a taint of faraway jasmine just then.

His eyes closed to hold that sweet image a bit longer. A deep, splintering ache began in his chest, spreading into his loins, then pouring through his legs like the smoky ache of afterbattle. It was a new kind of misery, this wanting. For he sensed that not just any woman could slake it. It was curvy, responsive Signe Thorvald who he wanted to claim, to pleasure. What a bloody fool he was to have heeded her respectable, womanly tears and let her escape without enjoying her fully. Likely that was what caused his unholy ache for her, this haunting image of her he carried just at the backs of his eyes so that whenever he closed his lids for more than a second he saw her. It was a pure case of thwarted desire. He simply wanted her because he had never had her; that was all.

But he closed his eyes again and saw her as she had lain in his arms, quivering, arching, responding with a need of her own. Signe Thorvald was no sighing virgin, no timid brown mouse. She had known a man's hungers . . . the unleashing of a sailing man's fierce, bottled needs. And by her own admission, she reveled in them, come to crave them . . . storing her own needs during the separations to meet his when her man came home. Bastian shivered, stung sharply by the longing such thoughts produced in him. There had always been women for him in port, eager to satisfy his virile needs. But he never knew exactly which woman, which curves, what face would welcome him. Imagine . . . knowing voluptuous, full-blooded Signe Thorvald waited for him . . . heated and eager for his hands on her, aching for the feel of his body on hers. God. He swallowed hard, and forced his eyes open abruptly, cursing his own lusty responses and his fertile imaginings.

What was happening to him?! Damn and blast! He was acting like a mewling, moonstruck kid. Signe Thorvald was a respectable female . . . he was lucky to have escaped her. One look at Raider should remind him of the heinous fate awaiting a bloke who got himself stuck between a respectable female's thighs! He shuddered and tugged at his wide belt determinedly, turning . . . just in time to see Blythe step close to Raider and lay a caressing hand on his broad back. Raider turned to her, and Bastian watched the heated exchange of their looks, sensing that much was passing between them, though no words were spoken. He slammed his eyes shut and his lip curled in disgust. And there was Signe Thorvald

337

speaking to him . . . without a single word.

"Sweet Morgan's Blood," he cursed softly. Aboard ship, in the middle of the ocean, there was no place to run, no way to escape this wretched craving. He'd never see her again. What if he was doomed to suffer like the rest of his wayfaring days?!

Blythe looked up into Raider's taut, cloaked expression and poured all the warmth and trust she could manage into her gaze for him to see. It was a silent apology for her earlier lack of trust in his judgment. There was a long, breathless silence between them as they stood by the waist railing, the hand she'd called his attention with still on his shoulder. His features relaxed subtly and his polished jade eyes warmed in response. Blythe smiled at him and sighed relief when he put his arm about her and drew her tight against his side.

Wordlessly, he looked aloft and waited for the signal of a clear horizon from the watch in the crow's nest. When it came, he took a deep, shuddering breath, and in a strange way, Blythe felt the weight of his duty as though it sat on her shoulders as well. It puzzled her, until she examined it and realized that it had to do with the way they were joined, in feelings as well as in body. It was a small, reassuring revelation, this sense of sharing his life, his responsibilities.

She had no way of knowing that the sight of her glowing trust had just settled the weight of that responsibility all the more harshly on Raider's broad shoulders. He looked down into her bared heart as it was revealed in the tempting heart of her face, and knew a squeezing pain through his chest that he was hard-put to conceal. The time he had dreaded and the decisions he had tried to avoid were upon him at last. And this time they would not be denied. He brushed her forehead with his lips and sent her below to check with François about a bit of supper. And as she made her way around the mizzen toward the main hatch, he watched the casual enchantment of her sway and felt a physical pull on his heart, as though she were dragging it with her.

Raider was late coming down to their cabin for supper and

Blythe stood at the opened window, watching the rouged sky sliding into twilight as she waited for him. She was trying desperately to think, privately reliving that harrowing confrontation with pirates . . . *real* pirates. Beside them, Raider's and Bastian's crew looked positively respectable . . . something like a cross between fighting navy and small businessmen! The comparison seemed all the more apt, the more she thought about it. After seeing Long Ben and his repulsive and brutal jackals, she could never honestly call Raider and his men *pirates* again. They lived by a harsh code, they faced violence and death in their chosen trade, but they had moral limits . . . and they had hearts that moved and fierce loyalties that endured to the very boundaries of life itself.

"Turnin' a bit of trade." Bastian's words rang in her head, putting it all in a frame of reference she could comprehend and deal with in her own very sensible way. It was a business, sacking and plundering ships, *their* business. They were businessmen, if rather forceful ones, and Long Ben Harvey was their bigger, more ruthless competition . . . as Neville Carson had been hers. Raider and Bastian had been squeezed out of their Charleston markets by Long Ben's cagey maneuverings and vicious tactics. And it was Long Ben's foul depredations that had caused the Danes to form that pact with the British that had evicted the *Windraider* from her island base. Now their livelihood, perhaps their very existence, was threatened directly by Long Ben and his vile yellow armada. They were slowly being squeezed out of the profession . . .

Blythe swayed and caught herself on the windowledge as the powerful force of insight shuddered through her. Woolrich Mercantile and Freight had been squeezed in exactly the same way . . . albeit slower and with less noticeable violence. What a ninny she'd been not to have seen it before now! Neville Carson was Long Ben's "respectable" counterpart . . . greedy, unscrupulous, vengefully set on having whatever was denied him. How much of the misfortune she'd endured, how many of her mounting business catastrophes, had secretly borne Neville Carson's foul, unmistakable spoor? In her vulnerable, naive state, she'd raged against the inexorable fates and blamed her own mismanagement on lack of foresight . . . when it was probably Neville Carson behind the scenes, manipulating.

How could she not have suspected? Now, as she looked back, she realized that after every calamity, every small disaster, Neville Carson would appear in her offices, offering his oily condolences . . . his questionable assistance. And he would press his loathsome advances a bit further until she rejected his offers and made it clear she would stand on her own two feet. Missing wagons, fouled shipments, and waylaid correspondence . . . not to mention the frequent cooling and recanting of potential buyers and lenders, even after a deal was struck. She had taken the responsibility for all that on her own shoulders, convinced that others were reluctant to do business with a woman . . . a woman the fates seemed eager to consign to financial oblivion.

She groped her way to Raider's ivory tusk chair and sank into it weakly. If she'd known, she might have been able to fight Neville Carson somehow, rallied others with her. Certainly she wasn't the only one he had dealt with so treacherously. She chewed her bottom lip savagely and clasped her cold hands until they were white from the pressure. *Her* business problems were in the past. It was Raider and his men that mattered now. And with a sickening feeling in the pit of her stomach, Blythe realized that Raider's problems were not so easily solved as hers might have been. The challenge to their right to the business of taking ships was deadly vicious and the stakes upon losing would be their very lives. They were out-manned, out-gunned, and utterly without allies or support.

Blythe clamped her hands over her mouth and slammed her eyes shut, fighting the conclusion that convulsed her . . . hating its awful clarity . . . its perfect inevitability. Raider and Bastian and the lads were embroiled in a fight they could not win. *Could not win* . . . It beat in her brain and boiled in her blood. No matter how valiant, how strong, how fierce they were, they were still one ship, one crew, one captain. And there would be a score of those hideous yellow dogs, biting at their heels, tearing away pieces of them, sucking the very marrow from them, bit by bit. No matter how many battles they won, there would always be another on some distant horizon . . .

Identical thoughts were being aired topside at that very moment. Raider and Bastian and a large contingent of the lads were congregated on the quarterdeck and waist. What had begun as a conversation had slid into a major policy-making session. The dangers they faced were aired bluntly as each occurred in the lads' minds: lack of port, lack of alliances, lack of markets, and the frenzied pursuit of Long Ben's ruthless mob . . . which would escalate as the word spread. Every man amongst them knew he faced death at close range. But each had been their lot since birth, or at least since they strode their first deck—most when they were little more than children. Battle, or the sea herself, or illness; something would occur to take them down to old Davy Jones's locker. They faced it with subdued equanimity. A number of them had already exceeded their own expectations of life's span and said so openly. After a long silence, Old Willie rose and said just two words.

"Sail on."

Sail on. It became a mumble on their lips, a beat in their hearts, a pulse in their blood. It rose on the air around them, echoing a call to a bond by which other human relationships paled to insignificance. They were agreeing to fight for each other . . . and to someday die together. Raider paused, flicking a grave look at Bastian and called for a voice vote. The strength of the "Ayes!" was wrenching. Bastian had to turn away briefly, his eyes shining.

Raider lowered his gaze to collect himself, and when he looked up, he found Blythe standing at the edge of the group, near the hatch, stopped just where she'd exited. In the murky evening, her savaged lips were like bright cherries against her pale face, her eyes like dusky golden dubloons from some sunken galleon. The tumult in her face rattled him to the core. She'd heard everything.

"Is that what you're going to do? Business as usual . . . until Long Ben kills you all?" Her voice was hoarse as she came forward, weaving amongst the lads, turning those luminous, crystal-rimmed eyes on them, making them think other thoughts, making them recall all there was to live for. She made her way toward Raider and up the quarterdeck steps, everything in her twisting and churning. "There has to be another way—there just has to be!"

"Blythe—" Raider came toward her.

"There ain't no other way, Wool-witch." Old Willie lifted his weathered face to her. "We been over it, stem to stern. We be sailin' men . . . fightin' men. And we cain't throw in wi' the likes of Long Ben."

"But to just give up and die . . ." Her voice was thick with anguish, and several of the lads looked away with lumps in their throats. "We can't just sail away into oblivion! Good Lord— anything would be better!"

"Blythe, this is no good. We've been over it, like Willie said—" Raider tried to collect her against him forcibly, to take her below, but she shoved against his ribs and fought to remain on her own two feet.

"But there has to be something—" she groaned, refusing to give in to their gruesome fate. She cast a wild glance around her and her eyes fell on François, then on Stanley and on Harry and Clive and Richard. Dearest God, there had to be something they could do. Then it burst on her brain like a Chinese rocket. There *were* things they could do . . . every man-jack of them . . . *on land!*

"We—we could go on land . . . all of us!" She moaned, struggling against Raider's tightening grip. Raider's hands stilled. It was as though someone had bludgeoned the air itself, for it lay thick and stunned around them. Blythe swallowed her trepidations and hurried on before they could react. "Every one of you does something aboard ship that folk pay to have done on land. Stanley, you're a marvelous carpenter; François, you could cook in the finest hotel or the finest home in Philadelphia! And Harry and Alfonse—you could have your own wiggery or tailor shop. Black Jimmy, Washington's artillery needs experienced gunners, and Oars could do longshore work . . ." She was running out of breath. "You could take up your trades on land and settle down!"

"Go respec'able?!" Bastian found his tongue first and he reddened furiously as the impact off the words settled in. "Bloody Morgan's Spleen!" It set off a wave of incredulity that buffeted Blythe like waves.

"It'd be better than going to a watery grave or dying of torture in Long Ben's clutches!" she ground out, hoarse with despair.

"We've decided, Wool-witch." Raider ducked and swept her knees from beneath her, lifting her wriggling form easily into his arms. "And we'll not hear another word—*Respectable*—" he growled, striding for the steps.

A path opened for him as he made his way to the hatch and wrestled Blythe through it. He was down the steps quickly and banging through the cabin door, just managing to keep her squirming, protesting form against him. He dumped her on the bunk and stood over her, his face like red granite and his eyes glowing like jade fire.

"What's done is done, Wool-witch," he growled, every syllable costing him. "There's no going back now . . . I thought you'd have realized that by now. These are good fighting men . . . the best. They're like family to me. But I'd as soon run them through myself as take them on land and watch "respectable" society chew away at them. I know what they'd face. Respectable society is as cruel and corrupting as Long Ben in its own way. I can't do that to them . . ."

Blythe was in turmoil, her silent tears flooding, her shoulders trembling, her wits reeling. In recent days she'd forgotten Raider's contempt for the land-based respectables of the world. And how devastating it was to confront it fully again . . . to feel it biting into her heart like the cold steel of a splitting wedge.

Raider turned away, unable to bear the sight of her tears, feeling the weight of his responsibility for her like a stone slab across his lungs. He turned to look at her, her feet curled around her on the bunk, her lashes wet, her broad shoulders struggling to square and accept his decision. It was the most damning realization of all . . . that he'd pulled her into such a life . . . and that she'd trusted him enough to let him.

"Dear God, Blythe," the volume of misery in his deep voice vibrated the entire cabin, "I am . . . sorry." And Raider did that which he despised above all else in fighting men: he fled.

It was the middle of the night when Raider finally came to bed. He'd spent several hours in heated consultation with Bastian and a few of the lads. He undressed by moonlight and slid beneath the covers with her holding his breath as he leaned close to study her. As his eyes adjusted, he could make out the puffiness of her face and knew she'd cried a bit more. He sank onto his side, avoiding her inviting shoulders and thighs, praying he didn't disturb her. Her warmth seeped into his chilled frame and he turned his head to bury his nose in the tumble of her hair across the pillows. She didn't braid it anymore at night because she knew he liked to feel it around him. The thought clutched at him. Her fresh scent wafted through his lungs, into his blood, to flow into and curl agonizingly around his heart.

He lay a long time, listening to her, drinking in her warmth, storing these precious sensations in his heart for those awful days yet to come when he would lie alone, desperate for the feel of her beside him. He was glad she was asleep, for if she had seen his face, she would have known something was terribly wrong and he might not have been able to keep it from her. The reality of his agonizing decision was too new, the pain of it too fresh, to hide well. He needed the comfort of her nearness, the cloak of darkness to make peace with it.

He was taking his Wool-witch home. The wrangling and quarreling and waffling were done. He had tried every avenue, conjured every possibility, trying to find a way to keep her with them. But it was to no avail. They were outlaws and renegades wherever they went; to the colonial authorities, to the British who controlled many of the islands, and certainly to the pirate league who this very minute stalked them over the seas. They had one ship, no allies, no home port . . . no future.

Sooner or later, they'd confront a fleet of British ships or be caught by a pack of Long Ben's mangy henchmen. And the thought of Blythe caught in such violence sickened Raider all the way to his soul. If she weren't killed or maimed, she'd be taken as spoils and ravaged and abused or charged with piracy against the British and sent to some pest hole of a prison ship. Either way, she would soon wish she had died with the *Windraider*'s crew. He had no home to offer her, no protection, no future. His only recourse was to take her home to her family . . . to Philadelphia. If he lived, he would come to see her as he could. And when he died, there would probably be no one to carry her word of her widowhood and she might live the rest of her days not knowing . . . hoping to someday see him walk through the door . . .

His heart ground dully inside him. Lord, how he wished he

hadn't given in to his crew's demands and his own craven and selfish impulses to marry her! If she weren't Blythe Prescott, she might be able to forget him in time, to find a decent man and marry. By ensuring her "respectability," he'd also doomed her to a long, uncertain widowhood.

The Bahamas . . . that was where they were bound. The lads spoke of fine "swimming" beaches, with mischievous grins Blythe's way, and described snug natural harbors on as-yet-uncharted islands. And not even the fact that the islands were British possessions dimmed their enthusiasm for the project of finding a new base. They seemed to have regained most of their spirit since that fateful vote more than a week ago and went about their sail mending and deck scrubbing and gun tending with a firmness of purpose that clutched at Blythe's heart as she watched them. Their pride and resilience made thoughts of what awaited them easier to bear in some ways, harder in others.

The *Windraider*'s sails were full hung much of the time and they seemed to be making good time in the warm gulf currents. If only her relationship with Raider sailed as smoothly, Blythe thought. Since that night, a week before, the resurrected differences of their backgrounds and views of the future had lain between them like a huge, ugly lump. At night Raider came to bed later and later, and touched her less frequently and with greater then normal intensity. When he finally suggested she not wait up for him at night, Blythe was cut to the quick, and vengefully obliged him.

With characteristic Blythe Woolrich thinking, she assumed responsibility for the problems between them, deciding it was her lingering propensity for the respectable life that had offended him. As the days passed and she watched Raider's sensual stride across the deck, absorbed his manly, booted stance and the lithe movements of his arms and bared, oiled torso as it gleamed in the sun, her longing for him bloomed afresh and she determined to do something about the gulf between them.

Just at sunset, she ducked into the hatch, headed for their cabin with a determined, wifely glint in her eye. She was vaguely aware of someone standing in Bastian's doorway, her mind being set on

345

other things. But Bastian's voice sallied forth, plain as day, making her falter at the bottom of the steps.

". . . after we get done in Philadelphie."

She smacked into it as if were a stone wall. *Philadelphia?* "We" were going to do something in Philadelphia? How could that be, when "we" were headed for the Bahamas?! She reeled a moment and steadied herself against the wooden paneling of the passage as she sought some explanation from the figure silhouetted against Bastian's door. It was Clive, and he heard her small noise of confusion and whirled in the doorway. Bastian, seeing Clive's reaction, jerked the door open fully and caught sight of her paling face in the darkened passage. His own visage darkened and he sputtered, "W-well . . . W-wool-witch . . ."

"Philadelphia?" The soft vibrations of her whisper were swallowed up by the dimness. But Clive and Bastian heard it all the same. And both turned their eyes from hers, unable to face the inevitable question as it formed on her lips. "But why are we going to Philadelphia? I thought we were looking for . . . a new . . ."

Before her declaration was out, she knew. There was only one connection the *Windraider* had with Philadelphia . . . *her*. They were going to Philadelphia because of her! And that meant— Flame shot up her spine and lashed her brain to full, deductive power. It meant they were taking her home!

She turned and flew back up the steps with all the force of her exploding ire, nearly bowling Old Willie over at the top of the hatch. She caught a glimpse of Raider, forward on the fo'c'sle, and flew down the deck and up the fo'c'sle steps, ignoring the surprised stares of the Bosun Deane and Flap Danny, who were engaged in earnest discussion with him. She grabbed Raider's arm and turned him to her, planting herself before him with her hands on her hips and a preview of hellfire blazing in her eyes.

"Philadelphia!" she demanded furiously. "I want to know about Philadelphia!"

Raider froze briefly, and all movement and all talk on deck chilled with him. All eyes turned toward them expectantly. He had dreaded this moment in the very depths of his soul. And from the raw fury he could see building in her, he had been right to dread it. "I won't lie to you, Blythe . . ."

346

"Well, that would be a refreshing change," she hissed, sticking her chin up at him. "Let me hear it, Raider Prescott. I want to hear it from your own treacherous lips . . ."

"I'm taking you home, Wool-witch." It was as though he'd plunged into her fiery heart with a blade. Her eyes dimmed briefly as if her strength wavered, and she blinked and endured a visible shudder. But she stiffened and made herself face him.

"Morgan's Blessed Liver!" she spat, struggling for control of her waffling, womanly responses. "And you're going to leave me there, aren't you?! You won't go ashore yourself . . . or subject your men to the horrors of it . . . but you'll cast me up on it like a worthless piece of flotsam!"

"Wool-witch—" He grabbed her shoulders just as she reached the full boiling stage of anger, and his touch unleashed a stomp on his foot that sent him howling back.

*"Ow-w—*dammit!"

"How dare you even think of abandoning me, Raider Prescott?! I'm your *wife!*"

"I'm not abandoning you—" Raider's face caught fire, and an instant later he was ramming a shoulder into her middle, slinging her up over his shoulder, striding for their cabin.

"Lord!" she screeched as his hard shoulder pounded the breath from her and she pounded his rigid back, "this is just . . . like you! Tossing me around . . . like a wretched side of salt beef—" She smacked him on the buttocks with all the force she could muster and drew a satisfying flinch and a "Dammit!" from him. He jolted down the steps, oblivious to Bastian's horrified glower as they passed his door, and he banged her against the doorframe as he ducked into the cabin and slammed the door furiously behind them.

He off-loaded her onto the bunk, and while she was still flailing, he came down on top of her, clamping her wrists above her head and pinioning her thrashing legs with his steely thighs.

"I'm taking you home, Blythe—dammit! For your own good!" he thundered into her clamped, furious face. "Listen to me—"

"No!" She opened her burning eyes and gasped for air against his weight on her. "You promised me you'd never send me away if I didn't want to go. You promised!"

"And I'd never break that promise to you . . . except to ensure

347

your safety. And, God help me, I'd break a thousand promises before I'd see you hurt. I can't keep you at my side, knowing sooner or later Long Ben will catch up to us. I've already died a thousand deaths just thinking about what that maniac and his perverts would do to you. I have to take you home . . . I have to see you're safe!" He wanted to shake her and to hold her safe against him and to make mad love to her. He wanted to shelter her with his very body, to fight for her with primal male possessiveness. But he knew it was reason and the courage to follow it, not strength, that would keep her safe now. His only course was to set her on land, amongst her family, out of harm's way.

Blythe watched the turmoil in his face and read the rocklike determination that sat squarely like the ballast of his soul. Some of the fight drained from her. "You'd just abandon me," she charged hoarsely, scarcely able to believe it after all the loving he'd given her, the vows they'd exchanged.

"I'd never abandon you, Blythe, dammit!" he ground out. "I'm taking you home to your family—"

"I don't even know if I still have a family or a home there anymore. Neville Carson was going to foreclose on the mortgage to Woolrich House . . ." She felt him flinch.

"Then I'll find a way to set you up in a home of your own, Blythe. I swore to take care of you, to provide for you . . . and I will, with or without your help." Her eyes began to shimmer, alive with the pain of separation she was already beginning to feel. "Don't fight me on this, Blythe . . . it's hard enough . . ."

"You also swore to love me, Raider," she charged, finding his most vulnerable spot. She felt the tremor that went through his coiled body and felt his weight lifting from her. He slid from the bunk and stood looking at her, his chest heaving as he ran quaking hands back through his sun-streaked hair. His face tightened and he turned away.

"I have no right loving you, Blythe. I'm a damned pirate . . . it's my cursed *fate* in life . . . and there's no escaping it. I was born under a lawless star, I grew up a black sheep . . . was cast among thieves to live my life and find my death amongst them. You . . . weren't part of the plan, Wool-witch. Women like you . . . aren't intended for bloody pillaging pirates like me. Somewhere there was a mistake . . . a glorious, wonderful foul-up of fate. But it was a mistake, all the same. And now it's being reckoned . . . called back."

Blythe sat up, drenched with confusion and needing to clear her thoughts in order to refute his awful blend of fatalism and logic. The taut contours of his rigid body and the strained lines of his face were evidence of the genuineness of his beliefs. He actually meant it! He interpreted everything that happened in cosmic terms of predestination, taking it out of the scope of human action, out of the realm of possibilities, and thrusting it into the realm of dreaded inevitabilities!

"What utter bilge, Gideon Prescott!" She pushed off the bunk, her legs trembling, her head reeling as she swayed and drew herself up to face him. "This isn't *fate* . . . it's Long Ben Harvey! He's responsible for taking your markets, for getting you kicked out of the Danish Virgins, and for hunting you down like a fox gone to ground." She stalked toward him, her fists balled at her sides, the fire in her eyes stoked hotter as the truth took unmistakable shape in her mind.

"There's no such thing as *fate*, Gideon Andrew Prescott. What you call fate is just the effects of decisions you've relinquished to others or that they've taken from you. Don't you see . . . it was Bastian Cane's decision that you become a pirate, not your fate, that made you one. He needed you. And you weren't born under a lawless star; your father's wretched favoritism and your own youthful rebellion against it were what got you into trouble when you were young. There's nothing mysterious about it—it happens all the time between fathers and sons!" She took a step closer, daring the rest as well. "And it was a woman's betrayal that exposed you to the revenue agents and sent that cutter down on you . . . not some darkling *lord of fate!*"

"How do you . . . ?" His head snapped up.

"It wasn't so hard to guess." She seemed to soften before his eyes as though trying to absorb some of his pain. "You despise respectable women so; there had to be some reason for it. Experience is the most potent teacher . . . and someone had really driven a lesson home in you. Then, I asked . . ."

Raider turned away, struggling with the challenge of her logic and yet drawn to it as an extension of her bright, loving being. It was a radically different way of looking at things, a diametrical opposite to his view of his life . . . and their future. It was perfectly consistent with her sensible, responsible nature, with her willingness to take responsibility for everything that happened around her. His entire being was in turmoil, wishing it could be so simple; decisions, just make the right decisions . . .

But whether from fate or the decisions of others, the outcome was the same this time. The realization filled him with an even wider sense of despair. They were without allies, hunted. And no decision on his part could change that now.

"It makes no difference how it started or who was responsible, Blythe . . . some things can't be changed. We're still pirates—"

"No! You're not pirates . . . not like Long Ben. And you don't ever have to be," she wailed angrily, shaking impotent fists at her sides and wishing she could use them on every living soul who had ever betrayed Gideon Prescott's faith in free will and the goodness of respectable people. "You can choose. You can go on land in Philadelphia . . . take a different name . . ."

"No, dammit, I can't!" Raider growled. "I can't ever go back to that kind of life . . . never!"

"You mean you *won't!*" Blythe quaked with power of her assertion. "You've *decided* not to!"

"That's right," he thundered, "I won't! I won't go on land, skulking and hiding, and stifle under a hypocritical society . . . nor subject my men to the constant danger of discovery and hanging. I can't live that way, Blythe!"

"But you can live without me . . ." she charged, quivering and alive with hurt.

Those small, razor-edged words impaled Raider physically. Blood drained from his face, leaving him gray beneath his tanned skin. He couldn't speak, couldn't breathe, couldn't stand the choked anguish rising in him. He stumbled from the cabin and down onto the gun deck, where he leaned against the ladder, holding himself together with his hands.

He wasn't sending her away so he could live without her . . . he was sending her away so he could die without her.

Chapter Twenty-two

Raider didn't return to the cabin that night. Blythe knew because she spent the bulk of those horrible dark hours watching the door. In the cool gray light of morning she realized there would be no change of heart nor change of plan. Gideon "Raider" Prescott was an exceedingly stubborn man. Her fate was sealed by Raider's abhorrence of respectable life and his determination to live out his pirate fate. And no amount of logic or need or pain would change it.

What did change was the weather, presaging their speedy progress toward their northern destination. It grew sharply colder so that Raider and the lads had to wear coats and shoes full time, all except Sharkey—who was reputed to have the cold blood of his fierce namesake. Gray clouds dragged despondent heels across the sky as if in sympathy with Blythe's awful predicament. The looks she garnered from the lads matched them. They nodded soberly and smiled a bit forlornly, as though already consigning her to their collective memory.

She wandered about the deck feeling like a ghost, separated from the life she'd come to cherish, as she would soon be separated from the man she'd come to love with all her heart. She paused, clinging to the railing, realizing they were distancing themselves to blunt their pain. Stung, she whirled and caught sight of Raider braced against the stern railing, reading his dark future in the *Windraider*'s dissolving wake. He was doing the same thing, she realized, avoiding her and their bed . . . distancing himself. Her eyes closed and an ache rose up, deep inside her. She couldn't let him deny her this last bit of loving, these last memories, however painful they might be in the making.

Drawn by a desperate ache of desire, she went to him and took his hand, pulling him toward the hatch. He protested, but she turned to him with eyes so full of turmoil and longing that he followed when she began to tug on him again. When the cabin door closed on them she turned and slid straight into his arms, clasping his waist tightly, burying her face in his shirt.

"Blythe—" Panic welled inside him, stiffening his body as his defenses against her irresistible sensuality began to slide. "Don't."

"Please don't take your loving from me, Raider . . . not yet," she uttered in a choked whisper. "I can't bear it."

"Blythe, please." He tried to disengage her gently, knowing that every moment she held him weakened his ability to do what he knew to be right. She refused to be dislodged, and he tilted her face up to him, sucking a hard breath through his teeth at the teary splendor of her golden-eyed plea. "I can't. I could . . . make you pregnant."

Blythe gasped as though he'd punched her, and he felt her shiver in his arms. "Please, Raider, give me this much of you. Give me at least a chance for a child . . . for a part of your love to keep with me always." As her first tears slid, her hand rose to his cheek, feathering an eloquent entreaty across his beloved features.

He lowered his mouth to hers and tasted the salty sweetness of her mouth and the hunger in her response. And he knew he would give her the loving she craved, and perhaps even a babe, because she wanted it so. His body encompassed her, his heat invaded her, his desire claimed her.

Their clothes were soon shed and their bodies entwined in sinuous, changing rhythms that built in intricacy and intensity. And when their wild explosion of release came, charring and burning away the dross of pride and pain, they rediscovered in its steamy after-splendor the joy of pure loving. Here, in their bed, there was no future, no past, nothing but the mingling of self and other in marvelous unspoken ways that left each a little better for having risked and given.

It was enough to love so fully.

* * *

352

The closer they got to the Carolinas on their way north, the worse the weather became. Their *Windraider* was a strong lady, but in the huge Atlantic swells and fierce winds she was tried over and over. Everything from cannons to benches to tankards had to be lashed securely and the lads had to string lines along the deck for making their way about. Their was no risking fires for cooking, and the lads had to man the pumps in shifts to expel the water that crashed over the *Windraider*'s prow and sank like cold, relentless fingers down through her decks. Raider insisted Blythe stay below in the comparative dryness of their cabin and, for once, she felt no urge to defy him.

The black and treacherous seas seemed unending, giving Blythe a glimpse of a dark and deadly side of sailing that she hadn't realized existed. She braced, huddled in a comforter on the floor by the bunk, since trying to stand or sit in a chair were futile. She prayed earnestly that none of the lads would be washed overboard and felt the weight of their current peril descending squarely on her broad, responsible shoulders. If they weren't northbound, taking her home, none of this would be happening . . .

Nature's fury peaked finally in a full gale that raged up from the southeast and tossed the *Windraider* about like a leaf on the wind. In the dim afternoon light, Blythe could see sheer walls of black, forbidding water outside and her heart and lungs convulsed with terror. Raider . . . she could only think of Raider and the lads above, fighting to stay atop those heaving, smashing waves that sought to pound them to the very ocean bottom.

Darkness deepened as the sun fled from the sea's wanton violence and the wind's raw defiance. And just as the last rays of the sun crossed that heaving, dimensionless horizon, there was a shudder and a rumble deep in the *Windraider*'s hold as if something had struck her broadside. The valiant lady bucked and yawed for a heart-stopping minute, then lurched and righted herself like a tigress shaking water from her. At that instant, Raider's ornate, lacquered music box pitched from its shelf to smack into the middle of the cabin floor, landing near Blythe's feet on its side. She gasped and clutched her beleaguered heart, staring at the box's skewed lid and trying to subdue her brief panic. And above the roar of the storm came an odd, tinny tinkle of music, a strange lilting melody, half heard, half imagined, capturing her beleaguered senses.

Then as it had begun, unbidden, it suddenly stopped, mid-melody. Blythe shivered and collected it into her arms, staring at the smashed and sprung corners of the lid and the brass mechanism the breakage revealed. She managed to close it, and held it against her as the darkness deepened and the agonizing wait continued.

Topside, Raider felt the rumble, too, and watched the rogue wave take the *Windraider's* prow full under, only to relinquish it heart-stopping seconds later. And when they righted, he yelled for Bastian to go below and check the damage from whatever they'd struck. In the agonizing wait, Raider was surprised to feel the keel responding as though undamaged. And presently, Bastian returned to bellow through the driving rain and sea roar: "She be right as rain . . . no damage!"

No damage. The *Windraider* emerged into a tumultuous daybreak in surprisingly fine fettle. She was riding the lowering swells defiantly, refusing to even take on water. The lads shook their weary heads and shrugged and abandoned their pumps for a well-deserved bit of rest. On deck things quieted to a restless sea drone. Bastian went below for a bit of rest, and when the watch turned over, he came up to send Raider below for the same. Raider fell, exhausted, onto the bunk, not feeling Blythe peel his wet clothes from him, dry him, and wrap herself in the comforters with him to provide him warmth.

The seas continued to calm, and by the end of the second day, as twilight gloomed in upon them, Raider was back at his post, feeling very lucky to have escaped so bad a "blow" unscathed. Through his glass he searched the heavy gray horizon for signs of land or stars, anything to fix their position. And what he saw purely transfixed him. Stern lanterns. Three sets of them. A large ship nearby . . . a third-rate ship-of-the-line or better, gauging from the rows of lanterns he knew to accompany each level of upper decks. He handed the glass to Bastian with a motion warning him to silence.

Bastian looked at the ship and shared Raider's concern. They scoured the heaving, dark horizon for sign of other ships, finding none. They had no way of knowing whether she'd seen them or not, but passed the word to stand ready. And the storm watch became a ship watch through the long night ahead.

At daybreak, both the brilliant sun and a sense of expectation rose to light the *Windraider's* crew. The seas were calmer and the ship they had watched through the night was somewhat nearer, though they had made no effort to stay with her in the restless seas. Now she was clearly visible in the morning light; *not* a British third-rate warship, as they'd feared, but a British merchantman, retrofitted with guns . . . and riding deuced low in the water. More to the point, she'd suffered topmast damage in the storm and seemed to list as they watched her scull along. And nowhere on the horizon was there a sister sail that might come to her aid.

Raider and Bastian exchanged bewildered looks. How could they just come out of a near fatal storm with a fat, damaged prize literally in their laps?! Blythe emerged on deck just in time to hear them call the bosun and Black Jimmy and Clive together to announce their decision to take her. There was a burst of cheering from various corners of the *Windraider* as the word was spread, and soon a familiar contagion was racing through the crew like flames in dry grass. Blythe felt a squeezing in her chest as Raider came to her and took her shoulders, asking her to go below and to stay out of harm's way.

"I will not." She lifted her chin stubbornly. "I'm still a pirate wife . . . and I can swim now." She tossed her head, refusing to give in to her own craven impulses. "Besides, if Willie gets busy," she lowered her lashes and voice, "you might need me at your back, Raider Prescott."

Raider threw back his tawny head and laughed, for the first time in days. She was resilient, his Wool-witch, a fighter in her own way. With the odd lightening in his heart, he kissed her soundly and called for her pistols, assigning her a station on the quarterdeck. Then he turned his full concentration on the ship they were about to take and board.

The portly captain of the *Gastronome* looked into the dawn from the quarterdeck of his beleaguered ship and saw a hellish vision of destruction bearing down on him. Straight out of the blazing red sun on the horizon came a sleek black hull with bony-fingered masts that seemed to be reaching for him. Then that alarming apparition began to spread sail . . . unearthly canvas that gleamed blood-red, as though spawned by the fiery heat of the sun from which it seemed to materialize. He stared through grainy, sleep-starved eyes, dumbstruck. He was not by nature a superstitious man . . . no more than any other seafaring captain. But his judgment was riddled by strain and exhaustion and he read stark omens in the eerie sight the dawn brought him.

He'd barely weathered the hurricane-force storm. He'd been separated from his escort ships and sustained damage to his hull from a damned loose cannon that had ripped free of its lashings and rolled. Then he'd lost the topgallant sails on his fore and main masts because of fouled rigging and his wretched crew's incompetence. And he'd had to contend with squads of sick and panicking foot soldiers who'd been foisted upon him to "protect" his military cargoes . . . and watched half a dozen of them being swept overboard. And his first mate had been struck on the head by a broken spar and his below decks smelled like a vomit bucket and his helm was behaving like a bloody mule. He staggered on the quarterdeck and bellowed for his second mate and his bosun and his gunner. He had to put up some sort of resistance . . . to save face.

Sharpshooters were stationed in the *Windraider's* rigging, and the swivel guns were primed and aimed. They were close enough to see the Union Jack on the merchantman's forward flagstaff, and eager, wicked grins spread over the lads' faces. There was something almost heartwarming about taking a British bark. Raider called for hard to starboard and they began that infamous arching swing as they raced past the laboring *Gastronome* to cut back across her bow in impeccable raking position. There were red coats spilling onto her topdeck, and the sight sent blood pumping through the lad's veins and set them to fingering their well-honed blades.

Even under the best conditions, the *Gastronome* would have had difficulty keeping pace with the nimble *Windraider*, and damaged as she was, she might as well have struck all canvas and dropped anchor. Her battered crew and weakened guard watched the fluttering Stars and Stripes above the *Windraider*'s proud-breasted topgallants and stoked enough ire for loading muskets and unsheathing blades. But when the *Windraider* dropped open her rank of gunports and ran out her long, gleaming guns, they swallowed furiously, thinking of their explosive cargoes, and lost a good deal of their patriotic fervor for the Union Jack. The first rounds came frighteningly near the *Gastronome*'s prow and her heavily laden cargo holds. The second round took out her bowsprit and part of her head railing. Neither was an especially deadly injury, but to the *Gastronome*'s beleaguered captain, it was an ominous bit of finesse that warned of worse yet to come . . . especially when he considered the deadly barrels that jammed his holds. He grimly ordered sail struck and to prepare for boarding.

There were ominous pops of musketfire from the rigging of both ships as they breasted and drew alongside. Blythe was achingly aware of the cries and the bodies falling from the opposing rigging and soon realized only the *Windraider*'s rigging gunners remained, taking aim on the redcoats below who seemed to be giving orders. Grappling hooks whirled across the murky waters, and soon the *Windraider*'s lads were streaming over the railings and swinging down from the riggings to enjoin the battle on the deck of the *Gastronome*.

Blades flashed in hand-to-hand conflict and ever more of the *Gastronome*'s men went down until Raider reached the portly captain who had watched the tall, tawny lion of a buccaneer cutting a swath through the ill-seasoned soldiers toward his post. Discretion was the better part of valor. The captain did not even unsheath his sword, but unbuckled it and offered it over his arm to Raider with grimness etched in his soul. Then he called for his men to lay down arms and surrender. And within the space of an hour after the rise of the sun, *Windraider* had taken her richest prize ever.

The mopping up was now familiar to Blythe; the details of the stripping of arms, the taking of keys and examination of logs and cargoes. Raider stood on the quarterdeck overseeing the topside clean-up and dispatching the wounded back to the *Windraider*. Blythe watched Raider and felt light-headed relief at his apparent safety. She then searched the far deck, accounting for every *Windraider* lad she could find, while she helped Ali settle the wounded lads on the quarterdeck until the extent of their injuries could be determined.

Minutes later, she witnessed Bastian tearing up out of the *Gastronome*'s hatch, his face scarlet, his eyes wide and wild as they searched out Raider's familiar form. He went thundering up the quarterdeck steps gasping, "Guns . . . it be damned guns . . . and *powder* . . . tons of it!"

It was as though time skipped them briefly, for not a muscle moved nor an eye blinked on either deck to indicate its passage. Then Bastian threw back his head and let go a wild, joyful whoop of a laugh that unleashed a maelstrom of cheers and shouts and thumping and gyrating. A munitions ship—they were rich!

The storm had blown them farther north than expected. By Raider's position reckonings, they were somewhere north of the Chesapeake, closing in on the Delaware. It was decided to repair the *Gastronome* and to sail her into the safety of Delaware Bay, where they could scatter the Brits ashore to find their way to their own lines, then set about finding a colonial buyer for their lucrative military cargoes. Bastian took charge of the captured ship with a few of their lads and a few of the *Gastronome*'s worthier crewmen to assist. Stanley and the lads soon had the hole patched in her upper hull and replaced two of her broken spars so that she could spread enough sail to get by. They saw to her wounded and pumped her out and made the redcoats scrub her decks down with vinegar. In the space of a day, they were underway for the mouth of Delaware Bay.

Blythe watched Raider's fierce grin at his lads, and a shiver went through her heart. The elation of taking of a rich prize had temporarily overshadowed their original purpose for sailing into Delaware Bay. But that mission still rode beneath the flush of victory, gnawing at Blythe's joy in their good fortune. How could she find joy in anything, knowing she'd soon be separated from Raider, perhaps forever.

She stood on the quarterdeck that next evening, watching the sun setting and watching Raider's jovial mood with his men as they downed their grog. Not far off the port side, Bastian's ship labored along under partial sail and occasionally one of the *Windraider*'s lads could be seen waving at them. Blythe waved back, but she felt a heaviness in her chest that made it hard to smile while doing so. She pulled her short cloak tighter about her in the chilled breeze and started below . . . just as the call came from the look-out posted above.

"*Sail ho!* Hard to starboard! Triples!"

Sails? The lads raced for the starboard railing to have a look, and Raider sent Richard for his glass. Blythe and the lads watched Raider scan the specks on the eastern horizon and waited his word. He lowered the glass, his jaw set and his nostrils flaring, then he raised it again and uttered a "Morgan"-sounding expletive. He turned a hard look on the men around him and made that dreaded pronouncement.

"They're yellow."

Yellow. Every man aboard knew exactly what that meant . . . especially coming in three's. And Blythe's face drained as she realized it, too. Long Ben. She watched the torturous possibilities fliting through Raider's clean, sculptured features and felt his fury rising against all restraint. He shoved his glass at Richard with a snarl to stand by as he stalked back to the stern and stood with his legs planted apart and his tightened fists on his hips. Blythe could see his chest heaving and could feel his heart pounding inside her own ribs. She went to him, drawn by the desperation of two dreams dying inside him.

"Run for it." He voice came low and even, filled with a determination she little felt. "Run for the Delaware. He can't follow you full into Philadelphia Harbor."

Raider's jaws flexed, his shoulder muscles knotted, as he stared down into her irresistible face. Bastian was riding a bloody powder keg; there was no question of his joining the fight. And alone, the *Windraider* would never be able to stand off three of Long Ben's heavily armed barks. And there was Blythe's safety to consider . . .

She was there, offering him encouragement, alternatives . . . a choice. Searing-hot determination, drawn from her stubborn faith in his ability to choose, exploded up from the middle of him, showering through his shoulders and arms. He grabbed her shoulders and stared down into her golden eyes, drawing strength from her strength. It was his turn to trust her . . . and her very sensible creed. Her love, her certainty, poured into him and he decided to decide, to take his fate into his hands one more time. He touched her cheek with a brief wealth of meaning and lunged for the quarterdeck steps, bellowing news of their peril to the *Gastronome*, along with orders to hang every bit of canvas she had. They were going to run for it!

Two thinly spread crews leaped into action and soon they were cutting through the waves, catching every bit of breeze they could, while the *Gastronome* struggled to keep pace with the *Windraider*'s reined sails. They worked valiantly to bolster the *Gastronome*'s sluggish responses, all the while watching those vile yellow ships gaining slowly on them.

Then darkness fell, and with the bare sliver of silver moon above, it was excruciatingly hard to make a good estimate of that narrowing distance between hunters and hunted. Fortunately, the waning moon allowed clear view of the "steering" stars and Raider was able to fix their position as being blessedly close to the mouth of the bay . . . close enough for a glimpse of land just after daylight . . . if they made it that far.

Long Ben's ships made taunting gains on them through the night. By the light of dawn they were drawing within gunnery range of the *Windraider* . . . just as they rounded the first point of land that marked the bay. Raider stalked the deck, his polished jade eyes scouring deadly familiar names on those jackal-yellow hulls. He sent a message to Bastian to make straight for the harbor. And he trimmed his own sails to fall back and protect the *Gastronome*'s rear. His gallant maneuver worked, for as the *Gastronome* beat through the choppy bay waters, Long Ben's ships concentrated their fire on the *Windraider*.

Volley after volley boomed, falling short, but coming ever closer as the three ships jockeyed for position; one firing, then falling back while her treacherous mates skittered in to try from other vantage points. Soon the smoke of burned powder came thick on the southerly wind as the *Windraider* wheeled and zagged across their path to answer their fire. Just as she lowered her gunports, she took a hit. There was a shocking crash and explosive splintering of her stern railing.

The *Windraider* pitched and shuddered beneath the ball's impact, as though enraged by the assault. Her long guns fired in vengeful succession, rattling every timber, every body aboard. She took out a bit of rigging and a spar on Long Ben's lead ship, but they came on, their single, blood-red strakes like evil grins painted over their prows.

Another dreadful roar of volleys boomed and a ball ripped through the mizzenmast above Blythe's head, snapping its top twenty feet and sending tackle, splintering wood, and shredded canvas hurtling over the deck below. Raider dove for Blythe and bore her to the quarterdeck beneath him, sheltering her from the rain of debris with his body. And before the shock had registered fully in her, he had her by the arm, pulling her up and kicking debris aside, thrusting her around the carnage.

"Go below, dammit!" he bellowed with the force of a twenty-four-pounder.

"I won't—" she screamed above the agonizing intensity of battle noise and the thundering boom of cannon. She twisted wildly in his grip, her reason slipping as she fought to keep from being pulled down the steps. But suddenly he wasn't pulling any more . . . was staring past her, over her shoulder, over the water. His face grayed and the dark centers of his eyes narrowed to pinpoints in reaction to whatever he saw.

"What is it?" Blythe wrenched about to follow his gaze through the haze of smoke and made out ships—three large ships, bearing down on them out of the north.

"Dammit!" Raider flew past her, scattering debris as he headed for the railing to rake the advancing barks for some sign of identification. He turned and bellowed for his glass and Richard came running through the tangle of men and confusion, shoving it into his hands and waiting for the verdict.

"French!" Raider lowered the glass and wheeled, coming face-to-face with the Bosun Deane who had just come storming up from the gun deck, panting and grime-streaked. "They're part of the French fleet. *Dammit!*" he thundered.

"What will they do? Are they charging us?!" Blythe groaned, grabbing his arm.

"God knows!" He wheeled back to scour them, desperate for some sign of their intent.

They were caught between Long Ben's slavering pack and the charging French fleet. They hadn't a snowball's chance in hell of surviving a battle with either group . . . much less all six of them. What were the French doing . . . coming at them full bore?

A fresh cannonade from Long Ben's lead ship cut short his deliberation. Their zigzag course had allowed Long Ben's barks to gain on them, and a ball ripped through the stern, laying open the entire side of Raider's cabin and collapsing part of the topdeck and stern railing above it. The *Windraider* bucked wildly, and as she righted, Black Jimmy's lads drew vengeful beade on the waterline of the offending bark and sent two twenty-four-pound balls ripping into it.

Brief elation accompanied the yellow ship's violent rolling and slowing. It was enough time for Raider to turn back to the French ships bearing down on them. Two of them were peeling off toward his starboard, tacking hard into the wind, and his head snapped back and forth, measuring their tacking angle and projecting their point of engagement . . . at the rear of Long Ben's ships! Was that possible?!

He whirled back to Blythe and Bosun Deane and shot a look up his mainmast . . . where the colonial Stars and Stripes streamed proudly above his crimped topgallants. It flashed in his brain and rumbled out of him, "We didn't run the Stars and Stripes down after the *Gastronome* . . . they think we're colonials!" It was a gamble — a glorious, fate-defying gambit that just might work! He charged back to the wheel, shouting orders to make straight for the middle of the French pack and to fire only on yellow, nothing else. Then he sent Richard to the bow to get Bastian's attention aboard the *Gastronome*, signaling her to the same course.

The roar of long guns continued for a brief space, but it seemed all other noise aboard the *Windraider* had ceased, as if she held her breath to learn the outcome of her captain's gambit. The lads straining at the sheet cables paused, the gunners stared through their smoky ports, waiting. All felt prickles of expectation racing across their shoulders. And in those breathless minutes, they watched as one of the French ships reached the apex of her tack and swung back . . . headed straight for the side of Long

Ben's ships. And as if to announce her intentions, she fired off a warning round.

Stunned silence erupted into mad euphoria. Blythe went running to the railing beside Raider, jubilant, as a roar of relief went up amongst the lads. Raider swept her up into his arms and crushed her to him with near violent relief, spinning her around. Then he set her safely out of the way and made himself get back to the business of sea battle . . . with a new exuberance to his bellowing orders.

The French captains soon bit deep into Long Ben's yellow flanks, and when the jackals turned, the *Windraider* laid a full broadside into the lead ship, bringing the confusion on their decks to a visible boil. Matched numbers were not Long Ben's style of fighting, and his henchmen tried to reel off, running hard against the wind for the mouth of the bay and the freedom of the open Atlantic. The ship Black Jimmy's gunners had scored was left to fend for herself in the smoky confusion. She was listing badly, having sustained top damage from French guns, and the French were closing fast on her, signaling to demand her surrender.

The other Frenchmen, having accomplished their purpose, came about to cruise into parleying proximity, and Raider and Bastian found themselves being hailed in French, then in broken English. And when the ranking French captain beheld wind-tousled Blythe standing on the fo'c'sle, he decided to come aboard the *Windraider* to accept their gratitude personally as they escorted the "American" vessels into safe harbor.

Official gestures were exchanged as the dapper Frenchman, Captain André Ellemonde, came aboard, and it was plain that his eagerness to make Blythe's acquaintance accounted for his personal interest in the extent of the *Windraider*'s damage. He covered his disappointment at her being the handsome captain's bride smoothly, but when Blythe answered him in her best schoolroom French, his composure fled him and he expounded at length on the lovely sound of his native tongue on her rosy lips. Blythe sent a hapless, pleading smile to Raider above the Frenchman's head and was relieved to see his possessive scowl melt a bit. He shrugged, communicating his grudging acceptance of the captain's respectful enchantment . . . and his worry over the French presence on board. It seemed they were sailing straight into the Port

363

of Philadelphia, like it or not. And their first stop would be the harbormaster's offices.

Blythe watched Raider's dread of the coming confrontation with colonial officials, who were certain to charge them with kidnapping and piracy on the high seas. She was responsible for their present fix, no question about that. It was all because Raider and the lads were determined to take her home, to see her out of harm's way. Since she was responsible, she had to do something about it. And Raider probably wouldn't like it . . .

She tried to find a private moment to speak with him, but the dark-eyed Frenchman's devotion to her company was unshakable and she had to resort to a feminine bit of deviousness to escape him; she declared she just had to change clothes before going ashore.

As they cruised toward harbor, Willie and Richard salvaged what they could of her things and Raider's from their ruined cabin and trundled her into Bastian's quarters, which were relatively intact. And on the pretext of assuring her safety and convenience, Raider excused himself from the French contingent and went below as well. She actually was changing clothes, freshening up in a basin and getting ready to don her precious sea-green velvet gown which lay on the bunk. Clad in her chemise and silk petticoats, she went flying into his arms and opened to his possessive kiss with joyful hunger.

"We made it!" She slid her mouth away long enough to whisper huskily. Then she nibbled his bristled chin and grasped his face between her hands, showering it with breathless kisses. "Can you believe it?!"

"For now." He was being swept along in her current of relief, even though he knew their peril was far from over. She'd never felt so good in his arms. He kissed her deeply, and then drew a ragged breath as he loosened his hold on her. "At least we won't have watery graves. The Fates and the French seemed to have saved us for the rope."

It was said lightly, but Blythe sensed a great weight of meaning behind it. She pulled back in his arms to search his face.

"We're pirates, Wool-witch, have you forgotten?"

"Because you kidnapped me?" A fascinating, fiery glint inserted itself in her golden eyes. "I'll have you know I was never kid-

364

napped, sir. I was swept off my feet by a dashing privateer and went off to marry him . . . unexpectedly, but quite officially. Would you contest that story, sir? I'll have you know, I am a very respectable woman . . ."

Raider's jaw loosened as he watched her features take on the unmistakable hauteur of a society-bred female. "What . . . ?" He grunted a laugh, loosening his hold on her and stepping back.

"I said, I am a respectable woman, *Gideon* Prescott . . . in Philadelphia, anyway. They can't possibly charge you and Bastian and the lads with pirating away your lawful, respectable wife . . . and a Woolrich, at that. The Woolriches didn't have much left when I left Philadelphia, but at least we still had a very *respectable* name. I suggest we not mention the exact details of how I went from 'Woolrich' to 'Prescott.' "

Raider stared at her tousled beauty, at the fire in her eyes, at the new primness in her posture and the set of righteousness to her jaw. And he blinked. Lord, they hadn't even set foot in Philadelphia yet and already she was reverting to that most dreaded of social phenomena . . . the "respectable matron!" Changing, she was, right before his very eyes.

Then she beamed a satisfied little smile and carried the used water in the washbasin to the window and gave it a toss. She poured it full of fresh water and carried his razor and soap to him, giving him a wifely peck on the cheek.

"You'd better shave, dear."

Chapter Twenty-three

The two-mile-long Philadelphia Harbor was busy in the cold, wintry sun. But with a French military escort and bringing in a lucrative prize laden with military stores, the *Windraider* received priority treatment and soon was nudging a berth at the docks, beside the *Gastronome*.

Bastian met them on the quay near the customs house in Philadelphia, with the captured ship's manifests under his arm, looking justifiably nervous. He, too, had found time to shave and spruce up a bit; his formal eyepatch was in place. He nodded graciously to Blythe, complimenting her appearance, and shook Raider's hand, congratulating him on a "devilish fine" bit of sailing. Then, with a sidelong glance at their French escorts, he lowered his voice and spoke, barely moving his lips: "We be in fer it now, lad. They be ripe for a bit of hemp stretchin'. They got a passle of Long Ben's boys an' is itching to get on with the formalities. Shortly we could be dancin' a gibbet wi' 'em."

"You didn't kidnap me, so you're not pirates . . . I'll testify to that," Blythe assured him quietly, patting his arm beatifically as she spied her enamored French captain bearing down on them. But Bastian's tightly uttered retort speared her mind as she turned to raise her hand to her continental admirer. "That be as it may, we still ain't got letters o'marque."

They started off down the dock toward the imposing custom house, exchanging meaningful scowls and winces behind the Frenchman's back and over his head. Blythe felt a little sick. No letters of marque. Did he mean they'd never had them? Is that what Bastian meant when he'd so often declared they were true pirates? From the graying under Raider's tan and the grim set of Bastian's blocky jaw, that was exactly what they meant. And, unconsciously, Blythe's steps slowed as they approached the steps of the customs house. Her determined plan to save them from being hanged had developed a serious flaw. Apparently she wasn't the only thing they'd pirated over the years!

Blythe's shock was no less than that just sustained by a pair of slitted, bilious brown eyes as they fell upon her from some distance down the dock. Those fat-rimmed eyes widened, seeing Blythe Woolrich coming off a ship, moving along the dock . . . with a French military escort. Neville Carson blinked and stared at her and the tall, tawny-haired gent beside her.

"What the hell . . . ?" he cursed. "When the hell did *she* get home?!"

He was off, striding for the customs house, puffing furiously, batting away Dickey's insistent questions about what had roused his sudden ire. Dammit! Blythe Woolrich was back in Philadelphia . . . and not a word of it had reached his network of ears! How the hell could that be? Somebody was going to pay for this slipup! He hurried toward the customs house as fast as his hamlike legs would carry him.

"Thank you, sir." Blythe had removed her worn, short cloak quickly in the stove-warmed harbormaster's office, unveiling the enchantment of her lush velvet gown and the greater enchantment of her delectable shape. She graciously took the chair the balding, fiftyish harbormaster offered her.

"Well, sirs," the harbormaster turned to Raider and Bastian, "I am given to understand by the captain here," he gestured to Blythe's gallant Frenchman, "that you are quite the heroes, bringing in a full British munitions ship. May I be first to congratulate you on your daring and your sailing." He offered his hand to Raider, then to Bastian, who accepted it with a certain bewilderment, glancing at Blythe.

Bastian handed over the *Gastronome*'s manifests with a terse explanation that all could be verified by the ship's captain, who had been remanded into French naval custody. The little, bald harbormaster glanced through the sheaf of familiar-looking documents and nodded, impressed, then turned to empty-handed Raider for the *Windraider*'s manifests and documents. "And your ship, sir—"

"Blythe?!" A harsh volley intruded into the proceedings before Neville Carson's bulk could. "Blythe Woolrich—" He finally bounced and barreled past the young French officers who packed the broad doorway and came to rest on the far side of the harbormaster's desk, staring at her, panting rather indecorously. "You're home?"

Blythe blanched and pushed to her feet at once. Neville Carson was the last person she expected—or wished—to encounter just now!

"Blythe Woolrich *Prescott*, actually." Blythe hurried to make good her defense against the kidnapping charges she expected him to level at them. "Mrs. Prescott . . . and yes, I have come home." *If she still had a home!* For the moment, she forgot that Neville Carson had already met Raider and Bastian. "Neville Carson, may I introduce my husband, Captain Gideon Prescott, and his partner, Captain Bastian Cane." Thus, "Raider" was suddenly transformed into "Gideon". Blythe intuited that a Christian name like Raider might raise a few eyebrows, if not a few questions.

"Missus? You mean to say you've already married?" Carson reddened hotly as he stared at the full blossom of her womanly beauty . . . now irrevocably beyond his reach. "You married that Charleston fellow? But your father said . . ."

"My father?" Blythe's knees weakened at the mention of him. "I—I'm afraid there wasn't time to send for him to attend the ceremony, Mr. Carson. I know he'll be surprised . . . to find me home and already wed." Her joy at hearing her father was still around . . . and apparently still talking . . . was tempered by the thought of what he might have been saying. Good Lord! They thought Raider had taken her to Charleston? Carson sounded as though he had half expected her to be married . . . and called Raider a "fellow" from Charleston. An astonishingly ordinary way to refer to a pillaging pirate and a kidnapper!

"But Gideon was sailing so shortly," she flicked a meaningfully adoring look at Raider, "and I simply couldn't bear to be parted from him and left in . . . Charleston."

"Gideon?" Neville seized the intimate way she said the name and turned to glare at its owner, receiving a strong jolt. "Wait—I know you!" He stomped forward, propping his hamlike fists on the desk and looking remarkably like a bulldog as he stared Raider up and down. It suddenly came to him. "You're that . . . 'Gideon'!" He turned on Bastian, pointing, with "And you, you're that 'Captain.'" Then he turned to the harbormaster with fire in his eyes as he pointed at them. "They're privateers!"

"That we are, sir," Gideon Prescott stepped forward, his face a dangerous granite slate as his deep tones vibrated every fingertip in the place. "And deuced proud of it. We sail for these colonies, taking British ships to aid the effort for independence. We've just captured a British munitions ship . . . a tenth share of which will go for the defense of this fair city."

Carson scoured his mind frantically and could recall nothing incriminating in their brief encounter months before . . . except the very fact that they desired doing business with *him*. He glanced at Blythe and, seeing that she clutched a rolled, ribbon-tied document in her hands, determined to challenge them any way he could.

"Then let's see your papers, sir, your letters of marque . . . from the continental congress," Carson challenged.

"I owe you nothing, sir." Raider's deep tones calmed, and Blythe's alarm reached fever pitch.

"The *Windraider*'s documents were blown away and destroyed, sir." Blythe stepped closer to the harbomaster, drawing his fascinated, if somewhat bewildered, gaze upon her.

"A goodly part of my cabin was ripped off by the pirate cannon," Raider took it up, "the veracity of which is verified by the good Captain Ellemonde." He waved a deferring hand to the gallant Frenchman, who clicked his heels and nodded with exaggerated agreement. "I am afraid you must take my word, sir, or seek the verifying documents at the bottom of Delaware Bay."

"I don't believe a word of it." Carson's eyes narrowed on the peachy color in Blythe's heated cheeks. "Make them show the proper papers."

"Monsieur!" Captain Ellemond stepped forward with indignant fire in his black eyes. "Eez clear you know notheeng of these matters . . . and you know eeven less of ze zailing men and zeir code of honor. *Mais* . . . ve forget zees talk . . . *maintenent*. Yes?" He turned to the scowling harbormaster. "Ze cabin, zhe is blown off, zir." He dismissed the entire matter with a very French wave of his hand and Blythe rewarded him with a very liquid smile of gratitude.

"Produce the papers or forfeit the cargo . . . isn't that the rule?" Carson, now desperate, rounded on the beleaguered harbormaster. His jowls were aquiver, and in his heated state he gave off noxious fumes. Bastian's nose curled in revulsion.

"How dare you, Neville Carson?" Blythe saw an ugly impasse looming and forged ahead with a bit of a prayer and a lot of Wool-witch grit. She came to lean her skirts into the desk, her golden eyes scorching hot. "The Woolrich name has always stood for honorable dealings and integrity of such a caliber as to be rare indeed . . . the kind of reputation that most can only aspire to." She turned the full force of her indignation on the poor harbormaster. "You know the Woolrich name, sir, all Philadelphia does."

"W-well . . . y-yes Mis—M-ma'am," the harbormaster stammered, reddening. He knew it well from former days.

"Then you perhaps have also heard of myself, Blythe Woolrich. I ran my father's business before my recent marriage. I am a woman of a certain *reputation* in Philadelphia, I believe." And she thanked God hurriedly for the stern and priggish nature of it! She caught sight of Raider's and Bastian's jaws loosening.

"Y-yes, ma'am." The harbormaster blushed openly. Indeed everyone connected with commerce in the city had heard of the notoriously uncooperative Miss Woolrich and her trials with the British. Could this ravishing creature honestly be the same young woman?

"Then can you honestly imagine, sir, that I would wed other than a gentleman of the most impeccable family . . . and a staunch patriot?! Why, it is a pure affront to four generations of Woolrich honor, sir. And it is intolerable to let it continue. Though I have the proof here—" She lifted the rolled parchment in her hand and whirled, searching out the boxy metal brazier and hurrying the few steps to it. She used her skirt to grasp the hot metal handle and open the glowing box, then tossed the document inside with a vengeful flourish. She turned to the stunned room and waved to the spectacle of the parchment going up in flames. "There!" She raised a defiant chin.

"Now it is my word, sir . . . and the honor of *four* generations of Woolriches." In the shocked quiet, she strode purposefully to Raider's side and slipped her hand through his gentlemanly arm. "And, of course, nine generations of Prescotts . . . the earls of Suffington. Gideon is the current earl's son."

She lifted an adoring look at Raider's aristocratic face and he managed a composed, seemingly adoring smile down at her, before turning a very patrician look upon the wilting harborman. They were the very picture of nobly wedded privilege . . . perfectly paired and mated.

A bizarre beat was kept in the charged silence by the labored rush of Neville Carson's fulsome breathing. Prickles of dreadful anticipation crept up Blythe spine.

"W-well, of course . . . the cabin was b-blown away!" the harbormaster sputtered, seeming to come out of a trance state suddenly. "Good Lord, documents do get destroyed in such calamities! And the very fact of your being here, my lord, registering such invaluable cargo . . . paying the colonies' share willingly. Well, your word is sufficient for me." The harbormaster rattled along quite nicely, once he got started, and Neville Carson let a very foul curse, and with a vengeful glare at Blythe and Raider turned and shoved his way viciously from the room.

"Nothing to apologize for, sir, in the rightful performance of your duty." Raider was perfectly gallant in victory as he addressed their little, bald benefactor with a smile fully as charming as his wife's. "Philadelphia is indeed fortunate to have so watchful and . . . insightful a servant." The harborman beamed under the praise. "And I am not strictly a lord, sir . . . my esteemed father holds that title."

Afternoon shadows were lengthening in the cool winter sun when they reached the cobbled street that ran along the docks some time later. The good Captain Ellemonde and his young officers took leave of them finally, and Raider and Bastian watched Blythe wilt with relief. Raider caught her around the waist to steady her.

"Are you all right, Wool-witch?" Raider stared down at her with a certain wonder, and glanced over to find Bastian regarding her with the same bit of awe. They never knew what to expect next with their Wool-witch.

"I'll be . . . fine." She melted against his side and the back of her hand came up to press her brow in that mannerism peculiar to respectable females. "That was a near disaster. I thought we were completely undone when I saw Neville Carson. I've never been so frightened in all my life!"

Frightened? Bastian and Raider exchanged bemused glances. That incredible exhibition of aristocratic arrogance was actually fear in disguise? She had charmed and bullied and misrepresented and out-and-out lied them out of hanging, for Morgan's sake! They shook their heads. Their Wool-witch had the strangest damned way of looking danger straight in the eye until *it* blinked!

"Good Lord, Wool-witch . . . the Earl of *Suffington?*" Raider shook his head, as unnerved by her impulsive creativity as he was by imperious respectability. "There isn't any such beast."

"That just came tumbling out. I'm afraid I got a bit carried away." She inched away to stand solidly on her own two feet, feeling very much like addled Walter Woolrich's rattle-headed daughter just now. Her eyes were suddenly large and luminous; they belonged to that vulnerable young girl that had captured Raider's wayfaring heart so. And just now they unsettled him a great deal. She went from outraged doyen of society to vulnerable Blythe with bewildering ease. "I hope you're not angry with me."

"Carried away or no, ye kept us from gettin' carried off . . . permanent!" Bastian beamed a delightfully wicked grin.

"Ra—Gideon . . ." she sought his eyes, "you're not angry are you?"

"Angry? That you save the necks of me and my entire crew?" His arm tightened about her waist. "Not hardly, Wool-witch."

"I think perhaps I'd better be 'Blythe' to you now . . ." She looked around them to see if they were drawing notice, and Raider caught the glance and released her. She was going respectable on him in a damned hurry.

"Well, I was certainly shocked to learn you had a 'reputation,' Miss Woolrich." He affected gentlemanly indignation. "I had no idea you were so infamous. And what was all that about you with

372

some fellow in Charleston?"

"My father!" she jolted, eyes like golden saucers. "Oh, Raider—my family! I've got to see them—to find out what's happened to them—"

"Whoa!" He grabbed her arm and pulled her back, sliding his hands onto her shoulders. His smile was relief and devilment and anxiety mingled. The very thought of facing Blythe's family filled him with dread. "We'll go back to the ship first, to tell the lads what's happened. And then I'll get a coach to take you home." The devilment won out. "We can't have an earl's daughter-in-law walking home, now, can we?"

The coach looked rather strange, careening through the narrow dockside streets with rough and grizzled sea dogs either perched or hanging all over it. It was a small miracle, the surly driver grumbled under his breath, that the horses could move that much weight at all. By the time they reached Woolrich House, the lads were more than happy to peel themselves from the coach and plant their feet on paving bricks again. How landlubbers managed to stand those swaying, bobbling, rocking conveyances without heaving up their dinners regularly was a mystery to them!

Blythe stood in the street, regarding the familiar double doors to Woolrich House with a turmoil of mute emotion. Her eyes flitted over the tarnished brass knocker, over the aging but still respectable paint, and over the stately brick face of the still grand house. How strange that the same feeling could make her palms so damp and her mouth so dry. She had lived here all her life until the last four months. But was it still her home?

Raider and Bastian and the lads watched her struggle with old memories and private thoughts and read her reluctance with a wry bit of sympathy. Raider took her cold, gloveless hands in his and dipped into her gaze when she turned anxious eyes up to him. His smile was like a warm shaft of sunlight on her chilled heart.

Raider's head and gaze flicked meaningfully toward the door and Bastian was in motion, banging the brass knocker forcefully. They waited, watching the little clouds their breath made on the cold air and inspecting the faded shutters, the half-columns that supported the elegantly carved paraments above the doorway. Then there was a rumble and a sharp feminine tone that communicated ire through the heavy wooden door panels.

The door jerked open in the early-evening light and a rather frazzled Mrs. Dornly thrust herself into the opening with a forbidding scowl on her face. She froze at the sight that greeted her: Miz Blythe, standing there big as life, surrounded by a motley horde of males. The staunch housekeeper grabbed her breast, her throat, her mouth in exactly that order, her eyes growing ever bigger in her face. "Miz B-Blythe?!"

"It's me, Mrs. Dornly," Blythe managed, sounding a bit hoarse.

Mrs. Dornly's hand then made it to her forehead and she stumbled backward into the main hall, as though she might keep going indefinitely. Blythe hurried inside to help her, followed quickly by Raider, Bastian, and the rest of the lads who slipped inside to ogle both this very starched female and the homecoming proceedings with unabashed fascination.

Feeling Blythe's arm about her, Mrs. Dornly's customary Scotch-Irish sternness melted briefly and she touched Blythe's cold-blushed cheek with bewildered pleasure. "Lord be praised! You, lass, in the flesh!" She stammered a bit and finally embraced Blythe roughly, then pulled herself away self-consciously, and straightened her crumpled apron. "Lord, girl, where have you been? We been worried sick . . ." She shook her finger at Blythe, "an' not a blessed word you sent—"

"My father, Mrs. Dornly, and Nana . . . how are they? Are they all right?" Blythe took the woman's clasped hands in hers as she cast a frantic look about for signs of them.

"Well, yer poor father . . . he had a spell with his heart some weeks back. But he be on the mend now . . . back to the shop most days. He been worried sick about you, Miz Blythe—"

"His heart?" Blythe's own heart thudded dryly at that news. She glimpsed Raider's face going tight indeed. "Where is he?"

"He just come from the shop not long ago." The housekeeper sniffed, her gruff persona firmly back in place. "I'd best break the news to him. Wouldn't want to upset him too bad." She hurried off across the wide hallway, opening the double parlor doors, then closing them behind her.

"Blythe?!" They heard his voice just before the parlor doors slammed back. "My Blythe is home?!" He rushed into the hall, coattails flying, eyes wide and shocked. Then he saw her, standing in the middle of the hall, looking so pretty with her hair all done up in womanly curls. He stopped, feasting his eyes on her, trying with everything in him to absorb the reality that she was alive and that she was home.

Raider and the lads watched in hushed silence as Blythe stared at her white-haired father, seeing for the first time in years the light of reason in his blue eyes. They rushed to each others' arms, hugging joyfully, letting the tears flow freely as they twirled around, oblivious to all but their joy. In the rest of the hallway, eyes averted from the sight, some throats cleared, here and there shoes scuffed awkwardly against the black-and-white checked marble floor.

After a time, Blythe was able to draw back in her father's arms to look at him and, in so doing, caught sight of Raider, standing by grimly, witnessing her reunion with her father. "Father," she caught Walter by the arm and drew him toward Raider, "this is my husband, Gideon Prescott."

Walter studied the tall, tawny-haired stranger and Raider felt himself tightening inside, coiling defensively, expecting a furious denouncement. For the moment, he had forgotten Blythe's occasional comments on her father's eccentricities. By all respectable, even marginally decent standards, Raider knew himself to be everything a man should hate in a son-in-law . . . a wanderer, reckless, unconventional, lustful, and with a lawless past. Good Lord . . . he was the pirate who had kidnapped and bedded this man's innocent daughter and had kept her as a mistress until his own crew forced him to marry her!

"You're married?" Walter looked at Blythe with a puzzled frown and gestured to Raider. "To him?" Blythe nodded, swiping the last vestige of tears away. Then came the question Raider had been dreading. "But where did you meet him, Blythe?"

"In . . . our shop, Papa," Blythe answered softly and truthfully. "He came in one day to . . . sell us things."

"Well . . . is he a good man? Do you like him?" Walter's acceptance of her simplistic explanation and his guileless questions surprised Raider.

"Oh, yes, Papa, he's a very good man." Blythe's warm, liquid gaze flew to Raider's reddening face. "I like him very much."

Walter sighed, obviously confused. He looked at Raider, then at the lads, feeling like there were some pieces missing somewhere. But his lovely Blythe was smiling; she seemed happy to be married to the fellow. As Carrick said, she was a much better judge of who to like . . .

"Then I'll like him, too. Welcome . . . Mr. Prescott, was it?" He shook Raider's hand and shortly found himself introduced to Raider's "partner," Bastian Cane, and the rest of the lads, one by one. With great aplomb Walter made the acquaintance of Mr. Old Willie, Mr. Sharkey, Mr. Richard, Mr. François, Mr. One Tooth, Mr. Clive . . .

Then Walter led his daughter and her new husband into the parlor. The lads ignored the staunch housekeeper's forbidding stance in the doorway to push into the spacious chamber after them. No amount of throat-clearing from the blanched Mrs. Dornly would dissuade them from seeing how it all worked out between their Wool-witch and her pa . . . they were entitled! They wandered about the beautiful, albeit empty room, fingering the patterned walls and window drapes and Venetian marble fireplace, examining the premises openly.

There were only a few seats available and Walter requested that Mrs. Dornly round up the other chairs in the house for their guests. She sputtered, giving their "guests" a jaundiced eye and a sniff, and huffed off.

A cheery, warming fire had been laid and the lads congregated about it, some settling on the floor, some standing. Raider and Walter flanked Blythe on the settee and Bastian took the great wing chair nearby.

"You weren't by any chance married in Charleston, were you?" Walter regarded them dubiously as they settled.

"Charleston?" Blythe started. "No . . . not in Charleston. What is this about me being in Charleston? And with some fellow? Neville Carson said—"

"Then you've seen him? Mr. Carson?" Walter wagged his head. "I expect he'll be rather peeved that you've married someone else. Carrick assures me he had his heart set on you. Why ever did you go off like that, Blythe? We looked and looked . . . and after a while we had to think the worst. If you wanted to marry this chap

376

so badly, I would never have stood in your way."

"You . . . didn't get the note?" Raider asked, scowling at Bastian who shook his head and shrugged, disavowing responsibility with a wicked grin.

"What note?" Walter looked from Blythe to Raider to Bastian, then back to Blythe. "You wrote us a note? Then why didn't we get it? Good Lord, the worry your absence caused us—" He startled and suddenly began to pull vintage bits of yellowed paper from his pockets, perusing each and discarding it onto the floor distractedly. Above his head and around him, Blythe and Raider and Bastian were exchanging bewildered glances. The ransom note never reached them at all? They didn't know Blythe was being held for ransom by pirates? They'd sounded no alarm to the authorities?

Blythe began to giggle crazily behind the lips she was chewing and soon Raider was turning his head aside, fighting down laughter. Bastian's shoulders were quaking silently, and the lads finally caught on and coughed and rumbled chuckles. Walter's head came up and he flushed.

"Never mind, Papa." Blythe took his hands in hers to still them and he turned to look at her glowing face. "It wasn't important anyway. I'm home now, we're all together, that's all that matters." Walter smiled agreement and relaxed.

"What is it you do for living, Mr. Prescott? Blythe said you were selling us things. I'm a shopkeeper myself." Walter turned to Raider with a lucid, earnest regard.

"I'm . . . a sailing captain." Raider's defenses were on the rise again. "I have my own vessel. And these are my lads," Raider gestured to his men, "my crew . . . part of them anyway."

"Splendid." Walter clasped his hands between his knees like a young boy and his eyes shone. "You know, I've never been on a ship. I always wanted to take a voyage sometime. Would you mind if I came to see your vessel, sir?"

"I . . . would be honored." Raider gentled markedly at Walter's boyish entreaty and lifted eyes filled with remembrance and fresh understanding to Blythe's crystal-rimmed gaze.

"So I've a son-in-law." Walter smiled with new warmth, turning to Blythe and taking her hands. "You know . . . I always wanted more children." His voice thickened noticeably. "This pleases me,

Blythe, you bringing me a son. Do you know . . . I've missed you so."

Blythe hugged her father tightly, and Raider watched with a strange constriction in his throat. Walter Woolrich was the farthest thing possible of his conception of a "respectable" father-in-law . . . and he thanked God for it. He had to be the damned luckiest pirate alive.

The lads, while not catching quite all the finer points of things, recognized that Walter Woolrich was a bit soft in the "critical thinking" department. But then, so were Sharkey and Oars . . . and several more of their best mates. Just because a bloke was a bit peculiar didn't mean he wasn't all right. Walter sealed their acceptance of him by rising from his seat to insist that they all stay at Woolrich House with him and his daughter and his new son.

Mrs. Dornly, who was busily trundling in chairs that nobody was going to use, heard him and turned white as she beheld Sharkey's bizarre grin and Old Willie's toothless leer. "B-but . . . we ain't . . . prepared . . . for so many!" she protested. "We can't possibly feed all of 'em!"

"Moi!" Dark, glitter-eyed François stepped forward, giving his barrel chest a proud thump, *"Pour vous . . . je cuisine!"*

"There, you see," Blythe smiled sweetly, watching Mrs. Dornly eye Franco with overt suspicion, "you'll have all the help you need. François is a magnificent cook, Mrs. Dornly, a true French *chef de cuisine*. Just show him to the kitchen."

"By all means, Mrs. Dornly, do let us help." Raider rose with his most bone-melting smile turned full upon the staunch housekeeper. It was shamefully effective. "But if you wouldn't mind doing the marketing . . ." He strode over with a small pouch of gold coins that had been liberated from the captain of the *Gastronome* and placed it in her hands. "And a few of my lads can accompany you . . . to help carry things, won't you, lads?"

They nodded, crowding forward toward her. Her hand clutched at her throat as they bore down on her. But even more startling was the heavy bag of coins in her hand. Money . . . real coin . . . in hand! Being a devout pragmatist to her very core, Mrs. Dornly ripped her eyes from their grizzled countenances to peek inside the pouch. In those shining coins she saw a golden opportunity

. . . to settle an old score with Simmons the butcher. She stiffened and straightened and gestured for Sharkey, Oars, and Black Jimmy to follow her.

Lizzy came home shortly, having been to fetch Carrick from the shop for a bit of supper. She hugged Blythe joyfully and blushed furiously at Raider's gentlemanly greeting. Carrick endured Blythe's peck on the cheek with good grace and shook Raider's hand as though it were the most normal thing in the world for his erstwhile employer to have returned from a four-month disappearance with a husband and a pack of gritty sea dogs in tow. And if he thought her handsome sea-captain husband and his burly partner seemed a trifle familiar looking, he kept it to himself.

"Oh, Nana . . . I forgot Nana!" Blythe startled and quickly had Raider by the hand and was pulling him and the lads up the main stairs after her, headed for her invalid grandmother's room. She peeked her head into Nana's cosy room. "Nana, I'm home."

And shortly Nana Woolrich found her room filled and her bed surrounded by strange men . . . some of them exceedingly strange, to her discriminating eyes. In wordless shock, Nana accepted Blythe's hug, and when Raider bent over the bed to take her hand she stared at him, slack-jawed. Bastian was introduced next, then a few of the lads. When Old Willie leaned toward her with a grin on his wiley maw, she pulled the covers tightly up under her chin and found her tongue.

"H-have they no decency? Invading a lady's boudoir?" she shrieked.

Blythe flamed, remembering Nana's delicate state and asked the lads to wait outside for her. Under Raider's perceptive gaze, she answered Nana's probing questions about her absence and her marriage . . . claiming to have sent "a note." And she patiently endured Nana's sharp-edged rebuke and her grudging welcome home. And just as they turned to go, Blythe heard her mumbling and turned back to catch:

"A sailing man! Humph! Well, at least she had the sense to catch one with a respectable trade."

Supper was a fitting end to a tumultuous day . . . served late and under rather unusual conditions. Everyone pitched in to help extend and set the huge walnut table in the dining room, much to Mrs. Dornly's horror. The sight of grizzled, ham-handed sea dogs plowing through their table linen and examining and banging about what was left of their fine china and cutlery had her flurrying from china closet to linen chest to table like a hen on a hot griddle.

Then the entire house stopped dead as a blood-curdling scream issued from the kitchen, and Blythe and Raider came running from the parlor to find Mrs. Dornly pressed flat against the wall by the kitchen door, white as chalk, clutching her heart and babbling hysterically about that "madman" trying to kill her. No need to hear more; Blythe knew exactly who was meant and what must have occurred. She had Lizzy fetch smelling salts and explained patiently to Mrs. Dornly about François's unusually strong penchant for privacy while he was cooking . . . and about his southpaw curve. The poor, overwhelmed housekeeper sat in a chair in limp, glazed shock while a grinning Sharkey fanned her with a table napkin.

They did finally eat François's marvelous food; even Mrs. Dornly had recovered enough to appreciate it. And the lads had a chance to practice the manners they'd learned at The Raider's table aboard the *Windraider* in the last few months. Blythe looked down the table at them proudly and caught sight of Old Willie, looking strange indeed. His mouth . . . it was full of ivory . . . *teeth!* Unable to contain her surprise, she asked Bastian about it and learned that Old Willie had relieved the captain of the *Gastronome* of them . . . and they fit exceedingly fine. And when Willie smiled proudly in her direction, she felt her eyes misting and returned it with all the affection she could muster.

Few of the questions Raider dreaded materialized. Between Blythe's careful answers and Raider's gentlemanly maneuverings, Walter's simple curiosity about their "courtship and marriage" was easily satisfied. Then it was Carrick and Walter's turn to explain the remarkable survival of both Woolrich House and Woolrich Mercantile. Ironically, it was Neville Carson's treacherous network of "loans" that had kept them afloat until this very minute. It was his hope of satisfying his vengeful greed and his lechery toward Blythe that had prevented him from foreclosing and ruining them until now. But now that she was home and married to

380

someone else, it seemed his plans for revenge were at least partly thwarted.

Blythe expressed worry openly. She knew now the full extent of Neville Carson's cunning . . . and expected the worst to come from their irksome confrontation with them that afternoon. But Raider caught her hand beneath the table and squeezed it reassuringly as he spoke to Carrick and Walter.

"Loans may be repaid. I've always had a yen for a bit of the mercantile trade . . ." His glance at Blythe was so quick, only she caught it. She blushed in response. "Perhaps, if you'd like, I could become your new partner, Walter. Rather like . . . keeping it in the family."

"Oh, well . . . I think that would be splendid!" Walter looked at Carrick, whose birdlike head bobbed enthusiastically, and he beamed.

Blythe saw Bastian and the lads settled in guest chambers, where they bunked casually on beds, floors, and the few cots they were able to salvage from the old servant quarters. Walter retired for the night, Carrick went home, and Lizzy and Mrs. Dornly huddled in the housekeeper's room with a heavy bureau shoved against the door, keeping both sea dogs and sleep at bay.

Blythe took the last candle in one hand and Raider in the other and headed up the stairs to her old bedchamber and her very comfortable bed.

Chapter Twenty-four

Blythe stood in the middle of the worn carpet, looking at her old room, left exactly the way she had exited it on that chaotic morning more that four months ago. Well, not exactly the same . . . there was a blazing fire in the grate now, and in her hand was a candlestick with two candles spending themselves recklessly. She set the candles on the night table by the bed and turned to Raider, feeling strangely awkward, now that they were truly alone and uninterrupted for the first time in literally days.

"So much has happened. It seems strange to find my old room so much the same." Her voice was breathy as she gestured about her, and her eyes came to rest on him hesitantly. "The storm, the *Gastronome*, Long Ben's ships, then the French—"

"Strange turns of fate, every one," he mused uneasily. "By all rights we should be on the ocean bottom or stretched on a torture rack . . . or held in dock awaiting the gibbet."

"Yet . . . here we are," she swallowed, unsure how or whether to broach the subject of what lay ahead for them. Her questions must have showed in her face, for he spoke his mind plainly.

"I for one am content with that state. I have no desire to anticipate what more fate has in store for us." His tone had a declarative edge that Blythe understood and somehow welcomed.

He was right, she realized. This was no time, nor were they in any state to cope with the ramifications of what had transpired in the last four days. It was enough to be together and safe. The thought sent a tremor of relief through her and she smiled, appreciating his wisdom and his diplomacy with her.

"Thank you for . . . being so good with my father. He's so much better than he used to be. But he's still very much like a boy sometimes."

"I find him to be the most sensible of men." Raider's deep tones grew warm and sincere. His eyes fixed on the way she was silhouetted in the golden candlelight behind her. She was kissed with gold: her lustrous hair, her marble-smooth shoulders, her light eyes . . . a rare and wondrous golden prize. "He obviously cares for you a great deal and cares very little for the opinion of society. Remarkably good sense. Though he could probably have raised himself in my estimate if he'd tossed my pirate arse out in the street for my treatment of you."

His smile caught her lips and coaxed them up on the ends in response. "But you're not a pirate . . . anymore. We established that this afternoon, remember?"

His smile faded slowly. He remembered all too well. "For lack of a bit of paper, the lads and I might be bound for the tripletree this very minute. For lack of a few 'respectable' words on paper . . ."

"A few 'respectable' words were also what rescued you, Raider Prescott," she reminded him stubbornly, coming closer. "I think 'respectability' is a far more flexible state than you're willing to credit."

The irony of it was not lost on him. His ethical, responsible Blythe had boldly traded on her impeccable reputation and her family's respectability to cover his past sins . . . which consisted primarily of paperlessness. For want of a paper, a man like himself went to prison or to the noose; in possession of such paper, a man like himself became a solid citizen . . . even a hero! It was irksome and hypocritical. But somehow, with his Wool-witch at his side, he was beginning to see it through different eyes now. And it struck him that, loving Blythe, he might come to see quite a few things through different eyes . . . if she still wanted him . . . if he stayed . . .

The dark jade searching of his gaze on her sent a shiver through Blythe. His legs were spread, his gentlemanly coat was pushed back at his sides by hands that rested casually at his hard, narrow waist. She could feel the heat radiating from his powerful chest and lean belly. This . . . she welcomed a responsive rush of hot, Caribbean nightwind through her body . . . this had not changed. This would never change. And she sensed it was where they must start.

Raider watched her, wrapped in thought, swaying past him to stand near the fire, and he felt the caress of her presence like a warm wave lapping his body when she passed. All of him reacted at once, his senses, his blood, his loins. He swallowed against that grip of raw desire on his throat and reminded himself that she was "respectable" now. Several times today, she'd surprised him with a "respectable female" persona: correct, surprisingly controlled . . . sometimes downright imperial. Would there be a place in her "respectable" life for the lusty, reckless scapegrace of a noble house . . . who had never fit well into society's cramped molds and niches?

"Come." Blythe dragged the Queen Anne wing chair nearer the fire and patted its seat. He willed his balky legs to move, feeling the warmth of her in strengthening blasts against his skin as he approached. His uncertainty, the thought of this bold pillaging pirate in abject retreat, warmed her to him. She could almost read his worries about her in his face. When he sat down, she saw his long, muscular fingers grip the worn tapestry of the chair arms. He was bracing, she realized. And well he should. She had just vowed privately to make Raider Prescott's first night of respectability as memorable as possible.

With a sultry flicker in her golden eyes she stooped by his feet to tug at his boots. She felt surprise beneath his cooperation and soon she set his footgear and stockings aside and sank onto her knees by his feet. Her fingers began to loosen the front lacings of her gown; his fingers tightened on the arms of the chair.

She moved so that she nestled on her knees, between his bare feet, and pulled her lacings completely out . . . row, by determined row. The heat of the fires, both beside her and inside her, brought a molten glow to the skin she revealed. Her hands trembled slightly as she pushed her bodice apart, baring her full, coral-tipped breasts to him, watching his eyes drop to them hungrily. Then, like a temptress, she tucked both halves of her bodice into her sides, riveting his hot eyes to the hardening globes she brazenly revealed. His fingers dug into the chair.

"For you, Raider Prescott, my pirate lover," she said, though he could not have said whether it was her eyes or her lips that spoke. "This night is for you." She turned slightly and began to rub one taut, sensitive nipple against the inside of his calf and up to the inside of his knee. Her shoulders flexed and twisted, arched—catlike—then shuddered at the feel of his raspy hair against her sensitive nipple. She unbuttoned the knee bands of his breeches and pushed them up, to continue her soft, sensual massage up one leg, then the other. He saw her body moving against him, felt his blood crashing against his skin, surging to meet the erotic caress of her breasts. He couldn't breathe, couldn't swallow, couldn't move.

Then her body surged between his spreading legs and her fingers worked the buttons of his breeches to lay him bare. She rubbed her hard-tipped nipples up the length of his thick shaft, one at time, ripping a hoarse moan from his constricted throat. Then she touched him with her fingers, cool and silky, and suddenly he was surrounded by warm, satiny skin, cradled, trapped in the valley between her breasts. She moved like a caressing tide against a firm, beloved shore. Surging and liquid inside, she engulfed him over and over. He shuddered, his legs flexed with spasms of pleasure, and he slid to the edge of the chair, pulling her hard against him.

He sought her mouth with fierce, penetrating possession that left her air-starved and dizzy as he lifted them both to their feet and inserted his hands under the shoulders of her dress and chemise to pull them down. She removed her arms and helped him loosen the waist of her dress and petticoats and push them down over her hips. Stepping from the rings of her discarded clothing, she stood before him, clad only in garters and stockings.

"It's my maiden's bed." She glanced at the big, draped posters that had once sheltered her forlorn, girlish dreams of love. Her voice became a sensual rasp. "Come, help me make it into a marriage bed, Gideon Prescott." She turned and walked out of her slippers as she swayed toward those cool, expectant linens.

The provocative swing of her rounded buttocks sent flames climbing the walls of his body. Her broad, smooth shoulders, her narrow waist, her long, silky legs with their ladylike stockings and garters . . . He was quaking, thunderstruck. He'd never wanted a woman like this . . . never been so consumed by need that he couldn't even move!

She turned at the foot of the bed, glowing in the candlelight, a golden vision, a goddess. Not a cold, remote beauty that commanded a man's worship, but a warm, vital presence who breathed life and passion and joy into all she touched. And tonight, she had chosen to touch him.

He exploded with raw excitement, ripping his clothes from his body, flinging them into far corners as he went to her. He wrapped himself around her and felt the delicious shivers of her response as he kissed and nibbled her mouth, opening it, claiming it with flamelike strokes of his tongue. He clasped her to him, raising her, bending her back over his steel-thewed arms and moving her backward so that her bottom came to rest on the edge of the bed. Gradually, he came down over her, holding her arched over his arms as he kissed her throat, her breasts, her love-swollen lips.

His arms withdrew and he raised above her, poised at the edge of the bed. He nudged her dangling legs apart, fitting his hardened shaft against the silken entrance to her body as he adored her body's glorious shape with firm, possessive hands. He stroked and caressed her, taking her nipples between his fingers, rolling them with maddening sensual restraint. She was forced to move under him, to seek the delicious pressure of his hands on her that would quench the fires building inside her. Then his mouth followed his hands, and those fiery dartings of his tongue at her nipples sent her steamy, amorphous desire congealing into a driving, focused hunger.

She pulled at him, wriggled beneath him, undulating against his hot, pulsing shaft as it ground so tantalizingly across her burning womanflesh. She ached for the fullness and completion only he could give her. But he continued to stimulate her, touching, nibbling, caressing, mastering her, absorbing her throaty moans and entreaties into his fiery arousal, growing harder, hotter with need. Just when she feared she would die of wanting, he slid back, then slowly forward, seeking, penetrating the glistening entrance of her body. Slowly, he embedded his shaft in her creamy, quivering flesh, sinking his arms beneath

386

her, molding her to him.

Lifting her against his braced, driving body, he moved within her . . . long, searing strokes that took her breath and sent her soaring wildly toward a brittle barrier he refused to acknowledge as a limit. Climbing breathlessly, hot and pulsing, she breached it . . . feeling its explosive shattering all through her and around her. She contracted around him, pulling him with her, clinging to him, hurtling through vast reaches of pleasure while still held securely in the steamy cradle of his arms.

He moved them back onto the bed, spreading himself over her, sustaining that soaring flight with uncanny thrusts that raised her, over and over, like a golden leaf on hot wind. She had spent, released, only to feel that wanton, delicious pressure building inside her again. More, she needed more. Her fingers dug into the rippling muscles of his back and shoulders as he moved, ocean-like, above her and around her, invading, drowning her in liquid sensation. And he bore her up again toward yet another threshold, another realm of pleasure as yet unexplored.

Gasping, writhing in white-hot throes of passion, she gave herself up to him, letting him take her where he would. Soon that second threshold loomed. Time slowed and all things stood still for one blinding, breathless moment. Then all of reality exploded inside her body! Streams of searing light and violent eruptions of burning color and scorching heat rocked her body and shot along her limbs, freeing her from the weight of them.

He thrust deeply, unleashing his own life force within her, joining her—caught in the violent updraft of her wild, soaring pleasure. Then, through the storm of his release, he felt her presence, pulling, lifting him, surrounding him. And they were together, mingled in essence, floating free.

The blinding-hot lights slowly muted to cooler colors. The searing heat subsided, pouring out of them to produce a satiny sheen on their still-joined bodies and a wantonly squandered warmth. It was some time before their dallying spirits settled back into their spent bodies, bringing them back to consciousness of the soft sheets, the dull beat of the fire, and the delicious exhaustion they shared.

"Lord, Mrs. Prescott, you surprise me," he murmured hoarsely, lifting himself heroically on one arm to look at her damp, thoroughly sated body. She was flushed erotically, filled with wanton languor. The earth-deep look of feminine satisfaction in her eyes awed him. He couldn't recall ever seeing a woman look like this before.

"On the other side the door, I'm Mrs. Prescott." A mysterious, womanly curl appeared at the corners of her love-swollen lips. "Here, in our bed, I want to be your Wool-witch. I want to be your pleasure, to give you everything you want. And I want you to be my 'Raider,' to pirate and plunder me . . . in a thousand and one ways."

He stared at her, drinking in her meaning and stunned by it. His own speechlessness made him redden beneath his seafaring bronze. Smiling, she lifted a hand to his cheek to stroke it.

"But . . . you'll have to give up blushing like that, Gideon Prescott. Blushing is for maids."

"Lord." He gasped a half laugh, pulling her as tight against him as his tired arms would allow, dropping a wondering kiss on her irresistible mouth. "I'll work on it, Wool-witch."

Then he lowered his head to the bed beside her, nuzzling her neck, absorbing the piquant scents of her love-warmed skin and her fragrant hair. He took a deep, satisfied breath and was half asleep before it was expelled. That sigh was pure unabashed surrender, and Blythe's blood gave an exultant little trill in her veins. Then she succumbed to a dreamy sigh herself and went tumbling into sleep after him.

"We let the candles burn completely out," she murmured into his ear some hours later, rousing him to her loving presence when he turned onto his back.

"That's what candles are for, golden eyes . . ." He opened his gaze into those arresting features that had inspired the name he called her by in their tenderest moments. He was warm, replete. Somewhere in the night she'd pulled the sheets and comforters from beneath them to cover them. In the silvery-gray light, he was reminded of their island bed, of the sweet and steamy loving they'd discovered in their brief honeymoon.

His arms came from the covers to clasp her and urge her on top of him. His hands roamed her back, her bottom, her shoulders, enjoying the special feel of her. She was meant for his hands, destined to share his bed, his body . . . there was no denying it. Tonight was the ultimate proof. Now, what of the rest of his life . . . was she fated to share that, too?

Atop him, she snuggled into a comfortable arrangement, matching her curves and bumps with his mounds and hollows, reading in their meshing symmetries the perfectness of their match. Sometimes a body just had to take things into her own hands . . . had to decide to decide. Like when she offered Raider his "share" of her. If she hadn't, they might never have come to this splendidly intimate moment. From that conclusion, she drew a fresh bit of determination. She'd have a life with him if she had to wrestle Raider's damnable "fates" every step of the way.

"Baron Redbridge," Raider rumbled. She lifted her face to him and he could make out the puzzlement of her expression. "Lucian Prescott, Baron Redbridge. My father. You're a baron's daughter-in-law, not an earl's. Are you disappointed?"

She laughed and laid her cheek back on the hard mound of his chest. "Not in the least. I promise not to tell a soul."

He laughed, stroking her shoulder. "Wool-witch?"

"Um-hum-m-m . . ."

"What was that paper you burned in the harbormaster's offices today?"

"Our certificate of marriage," she murmured contentedly, rubbing her cheek against his hard, flat nipple. "Now I have absolutely no proof that you're my lawful husband. I'm utterly at your mercy."

He froze for a brief moment, taking in the impact of her revelation. With a low, fierce growl, he wrenched and dumped her onto the bed, pinning her beneath him and flashing a wicked pirate sort of a grin.

"You most certainly are!"

An unholy, blood-curdling shriek awakened Raider the next morning, and with reflexes honed by years of harsh survival he was bolt upright and springing from their bed before a single thought crossed his mind. He hit the floor with full faculties intact. His surroundings—Blythe's room; that sound—a human

389

screech . . . probably. He whipped a gaze about the bed and room as he jerked on his breeches. No Blythe. Lord, could that have been her?!

He ripped open the door, bounding into the hall, nearly colliding with Bastian, Old Willie, and half a dozen more of the lads, spilling out into the dimly lit upper hallway charged for battle. They'd heard it, too.

"Bly-y-ythe!" It came again, and Raider and the lads were down the hall like lightning, following it right to Nana Woolrich's door. *"Bly-y-ythe!"*

Raider grabbed the naked blade out of Bastian's hand and charged through the door with the lads at his back, coiled for resistance and stopping flat-footed in the middle of the room as the last vibrations of that unholy sound stilled. There was a frantic hush as they scoured the room, finding only Nana Woolrich, huddled under her covers, gasping indignantly.

"What the hell was that?" Raider stalked toward the bed, lowering the blade. "That caterwauling—" He raked a glance over the old woman whose chin was coming out from under the cover, jutting angrily as she recovered from her shock. "Morgan's Blood!" He fastened a look on her furrowing face. "That was you?!"

"How dare you invade my rooms . . . in such a disgraceful . . . *exposed* state!" Nana snapped.

"What was ye caterwaulin' fer?" Bastian stomped forward, his eyes blearing hotly and his open shirtfront and unbuttoned sleeves flapping.

"I was calling Blythe . . ." Nana stuck up her chin, "not that it's any of your concern. She's late with my hot water—"

"She's what?" Raider stalked a bit closer, narrowing his gaze on her, trying to imagine by what splendid catastrophe of inheritance Blythe had avoided being born in the old crone's mold.

"She's supposed to bring me my hot water of a morning."

Raider eased and handed Bastian back his blade. "Then that was my wife's name, that assault on the hearing of the eastern half of Pennsylvania. I see." He turned and asked the lads to wait outside a minute. When he closed the door and turned back, Nana was tugging her nightcap down and averting her eyes from his shirtless, bare-legged form. He looked down and found the flap of his breeches flap hanging precariously to one side, held by only two buttons. Vengefully, he left it that way, crossing his arms and coming to lean his muscular shoulder against the bedpost near her feet.

"Perhaps you and I should become better acquainted, Nana."

"Not until you've covered yourself decently. This is an outrage!"

"Your granddaughter doesn't think so, but then . . . she has that French 'hussy' hair, doesn't she. And those impudent eyes that never quite darkened enough to be acceptable to you. Not at all like your fine, upstanding, very 'respectable' self, is she? Come to think on it, there is one thing she took from you. She has your volume at times . . ."

"How dare you—" Nana sputtered. "I demand you leave at once!"

"I'm fair man, Nana. I'm predisposed to hate your very liver, but I'm willing to wait on that until I know you better." Anyone who knew Raider Prescott well would have been well warned by the wicked glint in his polished jade eyes. "In fact, being the downright generous sort I am, I'm going to see to it your every need is met from now on. My wife has other duties now, but I'll see you have the perfect attendant . . . a nursemaid, with special experience in 'invalid' cases." He turned to the door, with his lips a thin line of vengeful glee, and called Old Willie inside. After a minute's consultation by the door, they turned to the bed together. There was a wicked glint in Willie's wiley brown eyes as he went straight to the head of the bed and stuck his walnut-meat face down at Nana, giving her a steely-eyed appraisal that made her gasp.

"Surely you can't mean—" she gasped, clutching the covers tight under her chin, her eyes saucerlike.

"Oh, but I *do*," Raider nodded devilishly. "Willie here has special experience with the problems of invalidism. Don't you, Willie?"

Willie flopped his wooden leg up on the bed for Nana to see and gave it a resounding thump. "Aye. Persn'l ex-peri-ence."

"No! I won't stand for it . . . do you hear?!" Nana saw Raider turn and head for the door and her volume rose steadily. "I want to see Blythe. This is indecent! Get this wretch out of here! I won't be insulted in my own home . . . my sickbed! How dare

391

you?!".

Raider ignored her ravings and paused at the door for a gentlemanly nod before escaping into the hall. Raider looked so pleased that Bastian scratched his head and started to ask what happened. But Nana's voice rose hysterically through the closed door.

"Don't you dare touch me, you filthy beast! Help! Oh! Bly-y-y—" Nana was cut short, midbellow, and after a minute's uninterrupted silence, Raider rubbed his bare chest, satisfied, and strode off down the hall toward Blythe's room and the rest of his clothes. He and the lads met Blythe hurrying from the stairs.

"What's going on?" She hurried to Raider, casting a worried glance around her at the lads. "I could have sworn I heard Nana's call—" She realized they were coming from the direction of Nana's door.

"Oh, Willie's taking care of her this morning," Raider said casually. "He volunteered . . . knowing how difficult it is, being invalided."

"An' she took to him right off, didn' she, lads?" Bastian eyed them meaningfully and they nodded enthusiastically. Never seen anything like it, they vowed. Her an' Willie; two peas in a pod, they declared.

"Ye know," Bastian changed the subject quickly, pulling at his nose and frowning, "I ain't plugged up yet. I swear I can smell Old Franco's coffee clear up here."

"B-but Nana and Willie . . . ? Are you sure, Raider?"

"Oh, absolutely. And you'll have plenty to keep you busy as it is." Raider put his arm about her and turned her toward their room as the others rumbled downstairs toward breakfast. Once inside and alone, he kissed her hotly, burning worries about Nana from her mind completely and leaving her a little dazed.

Yes, she agreed helplessly, she certainly did have other things to do.

The next few days were busy for the Woolrich-Prescott household. Raider and Bastian found buyers for their prize cargo of munitions and finally unloaded some of the *Windraider*'s long-held cargoes for sale in the resurgent Woolrich Mercantile Shop. They also had repairs to oversee on their lady *Windraider* and the *Gastronome* and had to decide what to do with the second ship. Blythe was kept busy setting Woolrich House and the newly stocked shop to rights. François continued to cook for them, and Old Willie gave Nana all the "nursing" she could withstand. Richard divided his time between helping Blythe at the Woolrich shop and defending young Lizzy's virtue. Harry and Alfonse set up a sewing room on the little-used third floor and, after ogling ladies coming out of dressmakers' shops to ascertain the lastest fashion trends, proceeded to augment Blythe's rather limited wardrobe.

Walter insisted Blythe and Raider make Woolrich House their home, since it would be hers someday anyway, and horrified Mrs. Dornly by insisting that Bastian and the "lads" were welcome to call it home, too. The lads all came to the house, at one time or another, to pay respects and visit their Wool-witch. But, to the housekeeper's relief, most declined Walter's generous offer, feeling somewhat more comfortable bunked aboard ship or in a dockside tavern that provided comforts Woolrich House couldn't . . . like ale and wenches.

There were occasional disturbances, like the time Simmons the butcher came personally to deliver an order of meats and surprised François in the middle of making a mincemeat pie. And occasional limits had to be imposed, such as the one refusing admittance to any lad who showed up after ten o'clock or roaring drunk. Mrs. Dornly's matronly outrage was mollified a bit by Raider's assurance they'd be shipping out after a while and would be out from underfoot. And at his suggestion, Clive, Old Willie, and a few of the lads began to pitch in to help with the numerous chores of housekeeping. Scrubbing was scrubbing, he put it to them, whether it be decks or floors. On the whole, their adjustment to life in Philadelphia's Society Hill district went well for a group of sea dogs unused to stifling their impulses.

Walter's delight at having Blythe and his new "son" home with him was wonderful to behold. Just having their loving presence in his house and witnessing their tender gestures of affection seemed to draw him toward a renewed sense of purpose and pleasure in life. Nana, on the other hand, found the new conditions of her invalid state perfectly intolerable. Willie informed Raider that his suspicions were correct: the old woman's legs were far from withered and had full, normal feeling. He cited the way she nudged her feet away from her stoppered water bottle when it was too hot as proof. After a full week of Old Willie's single-minded nursing, she was desperate indeed. Willie appeared one afternoon in the parlor to announce to Raider and Blythe:

"That Nana woman be demandin' to see a preacher." His eyes twinkled and, as Blythe jumped up and went for her cloak to fetch Reverend Warren, he cast Raider a wicked, ivory-toothed grin. "I think we gots a miracle o' healin' comin' on."

Sure enough, after half an hour closeted with the good reverend, Nana came out of her room, toddling along under her own steam. Blythe was delirious with joy and embraced Nana and then Raider and Willie. Raider and Willie exchanged glances and declared it a "bleedin' miracle." Fortunately, Nana's physical healing seemed to have been accompanied by an improvement in her irascible temperament. And her surprise at the reemergence of Woolrich House's long-waning elegance and the reemergence of Walter's long dormant wits was enough to make her presence almost amiable.

News of Blythe Woolrich's marriage spread quickly through Philadelphia, owing to a fleet network of gossip and a conspicuous flow of "boughten" goods toward Woolrich House. It seemed Captain Gideon Prescott, formerly of Charleston, was bent on infusing much needed capital into both Woolrich House and Woolrich Mercantile. He arranged for the repayment of certain loans, which had fortuitously kept Woolrich Mercantile afloat in his wife's absence, and insisted on replacing most of the furnishings that had been sold to meet earlier debts. He was rumored to be an astute businessman who knew a choice opportunity when he saw it. At his insightful suggestion the basis of Woolrich Mercantile was changed to that of a shareholder company. No one took note that the names of the charter stockholders read like a ship's roster: Mr. Sharkey, Mr. One Tooth, Mr. Black Jimmy . . .

When Blythe and her captain were seen together in public,

heads turned to take in the striking, well-dressed couple. No one gave serious credit to snipets of gossip about the comings and goings of an unruly element of seagoing types to and from the household. And Mrs. Dornly herself was heard proudly confirming the rumor that they had imported an elegant French cook. Shortly after Eudora Frankel and Beulah Henderson visited the Woolrich shop and left wide-eyed, social invitations began to arrive at Woolrich House as well. Apparently nothing ensured social acceptance quite like a flourishing business concern . . .

. . . except for one Mr. Neville P. Carson. He stood by the window in his offices above Market Street, a week after his clash with Blythe in the harbormaster's offices, watching the new Mr. and Mrs. Prescott being greeted in the street below. Members of Philadelphia's elite who had expunged him from their very polite society, now rushed to embrace Blythe Woolrich's new husband as though he'd been born amongst them!

Blood gorged his puffy face and seeped into his eyes as pure rage welled up inside him. He lumbered to his desk and snatched up the bank draft bearing Gideon Prescott's gentlemanly signature. It was the settlement of Walter Woolrich's debts . . . delivered to him that very morning by the banker on whose establishment they were drawn. He hadn't even had the satisfaction of demanding payment, damn their hides, since the notes had yet another full month to run! Nor had Woolrich or this "Prescott" deigned to appear personally to settle the account. He'd had to surrender the documents to a go-between . . . a damned fancy errand boy!

He crumpled the parchment and threw it viciously across his disheveled office. They'd scorned and betrayed him . . . using his money to tide them over while the little slut cast about for richer "pickins" in Charleston! What a fool he'd been not to have seen it! Well, by damn, they'd regret making a dupe out of Neville Carson! So what if the little trollop was beyond his reach . . . or that he no longer held controlling interest in their wretched business?! There were ways of making them pay! He could *ruin* them if he chose. His obese body suddenly quivered with obscene rage at the thought.

"Dickey!" he bellowed, rushing for the door, panting. "You mangy whelp—where are you?!" Palorous Dickey met him in the door and Carson dragged his cringing minion into the office by the scruff of the neck.

"I want Woolrich watched . . . night and day," he spit savagely, giving Dickey a shake. "I want to know everything they sell, every time they bank . . . every move they make! And I want those damned ships watched . . . especially that munitions ship. I want to know when and where they move that cargo! Because, I'm going to be there—"

"B-but . . . Mr. C-carson," Dickey stammered, "I cain't do all that!"

"Of course not, fool!" he spat. "Talk to some of the boys at the docks . . . the ones we used before. Tell them I'll pay well for the information I want . . . and for a bit of muscle once I get it." His eyes were hot with fires of vengeance. "I'm going to destroy Woolrich Mercantile and Freight!"

Chapter Twenty-five

". . . I'm tinking on buyin' anot'er ship," Lars Olsen concluded, sipping from his wineglass and taking in his wife's reaction across the dinner table.

"Iss so?" she questioned him. "Vas iss her name, and vhere built?"

"British." He pursed his broad mouth and counted it a small victory that Hilde hadn't rejected the idea out of hand. "De *Gastronome*. You know, tat prize ship de privateer bro't in. She hass good strong timbers and tight holds. Ain't the fastest . . . not like that other ship . . . the *Windraider*, dey call 'er . . ."

The name brought his houseguest's head up in a flash. "What vas it you said? The *Windraider*? In port? Here?!" Roses budded, bloomed, then seemed to explode in Signe Thorvald's cheeks, turning her whole face and breast rosy.

"*Ja*," Lars, cousin to Jens Thorvald and a sailing captain himself, nodded. "You know, tat munitions ship, bro't in more'n a week ago. They're goin' to sell 'er."

Lars and Hilde watched Signe grip the edge of the linen-clad table tightly and watched her eyes unfocus, as though some mental image took precedence in her mind.

The *Windraider* in Philadelphia? Signe was suddenly dizzy. That meant Bastian Cane was here as well . . . strong, thick-bodied Bastian Cane with his firm hands and fiery hazel eyes. *Gud pa Himmel!*—the nights she had laid in her widow's bed, loathing herself for the stupidity of rejecting his loving. What a

397

silly, respectable fool she'd been!

She'd insisted on leaving her outraged brother's protection immediately and caught the very next British ship bound for New York. But she arrived home to a house occupied by British military, who offered to pay rent for the use of it but refused to be dislodged from its comforts. Tired and angry, she left immediately for Philadelphia and was received warmly by Jens Thorvald's cousin and his good wife. That had been a mere fortnight ago and only now was she settled enough to begin facing dismal thoughts of the future again. There were hints of marriage prospects from Lars and Hilde, but Signe could think of no man in that way . . . not with whispers of the pleasure Bastian Cane had made for her still coursing in her blood.

But now . . . the *Windraider* was here! Bastian Cane was here . . . somewhere nearby. She could feel her heart filling, her body responding at the mere thought.

"Signe?" Hilde was calling her back to them. "Signe, iss someting de matter?"

"Oh—" Signe flushed deeply and fidgeted with her table napkin. Her mind was flying. When she raised her face to them, her eyes were bright. "Lars, ve musst see your new ship . . . tomorrow, first thing . . . mussn't ve, Hilde?!"

So it was that the next morning, four days before Christmas, Signe Thorvald found herself being ushered up the gangway of the *Gastronome* beside Hilde Olsen. Once they were on the deck, Lars pointed overhead to the masts and spars that were being replaced, and he began to detail tonnage numbers and the volume of canvas she could bear. Signe heard little; her mind buzzed with expectation and not a little fear. What if Bastian Cane hated her, wanted nothing to do with her? What if he already had a woman somewhere . . . a wife? *Det Gud forbyde!*

Bastian sniffed and paused to give his broad black belt a final tug before he stepped out onto the *Gastronome*'s deck. Strangely, that peculiar head-stuffing ailment he always suffered when in smelly port cities was taking its time coming on. He was close to an agreement with the tough-bargaining Dane and he intended to clinch the deal this morning when the man brought his wife to see the ship. But as he cleared the hatch, he walked straight into a pair of sky-blue eyes, framed in a halo of cornsilk-yellow hair.

He stopped dead, staring, speechless. Signe Thorvald. His heart lurched and thumped wildly in his throat, then plummeted to pound frantically in his loins. His eyes burned dryly at the sight of her wide-eyed face, her lush, pouty lips, her enchanting womanly shape that his fingertips still remembered. His Signe . . . here . . . on this very deck! All he could do was stare.

Signe roused to the sound of her name, subduing the frantic thudding of her heart that made her voice noticeably breathless. She acknowledged her introduction to the man who had ravished her once on a moonlit beach and every night thereafter in her dreams with a proper nod and an extended hand. And when he touched her, gooseflesh rose all over her skin under her wrap. The sudden, familiar heat of his gaze, the lingering pressure of his hand as he continued to hold hers, the bronzing of his square, virile features . . . he *did* remember her! Her bones were near to melting by the time bewildered Lars and Hilde penetrated the charged exchange between them.

Bastian, fully occupied with thoughts of his curvy widow, urged Lars Olsen to take his woman all about the ship . . . and to take all the blessed time he needed. And when they were alone on deck, with only the hammering and the chaos of the carpenters above and around them, Bastian ushered her onto the quarterdeck with trembling hands.

"What be ye doin' here, Signe?" His voice was thick with the need to pull her into his arms then and there.

"I come to stay wit friends . . . British haf my house now." She swayed slightly at the impact of him on her starved senses. "And you? Vhat are you doing in Philadelphia?"

"We took a fat prize on the way to . . . bringin' the Wool-witch home. Blythe—her pa lives here, keeps a shop, and me an' Raider brung her home to stay." His feet were going weak and he had to clasp his hands behind his back to keep them from doing something shocking.

"Then . . . your voman musst be proud," Signe looked around her at the *Gastronome*, "tat you bro't in so fine a prize."

"I ain't got no woman, Signe." Bastian spoke the answer to her unasked question and Signe's melting blue eyes turned to him with what Bastian hoped was a bit of relief. He might have been a little shocked to know just what she was thinking just then: Oh, yes you have, Bastian Cane.

While the women drifted below to examine the spacious officers' quarters Bastian was joined by Raider for the final negotiations. Raider was a bit annoyed by Bastian's inattention to the proceedings and found himself doing most of the bargaining. A deal was struck and hands were shook. Then Signe Thorvald stepped out on the deck and Raider was stunned to be "introduced" to her and to have her greet him as though she'd never laid eyes on him before. He stood by, bewildered, as Signe Thorvald took Bastian Cane's blocky hand and invited him to dine with her and the Olsens that very evening . . . to celebrate the purchase.

Bastian stammered and agreed, flushing with fresh heat from his toes up. And Raider watched him staring hungrily at her swaying skirts until she was completely out of sight. It suddenly struck Raider that, to his knowledge, Bastian hadn't spent a single night away from Woolrich House since they docked, nor had he been seen rip-snorting drunk . . . not even once! No willing wenches? Raider glowered at the thought. That wasn't like Bastian. And not even a good all-night toot with the lads? And this randy, sea-beagle way he looked at curvy Signe Thorvald. Lord. He never thought he'd see this . . .

Bastian arrived at the stroke of seven for supper with the Olsens. He'd spent the afternoon braving a full tub bath and dandying up. He debated wearing his eyepatch, deciding to leave it at home on Blythe's womanly advice. And when he was admitted to the Olsens' fine parlor and saw sweet Signe sitting like an angel by the glowing grate, he knew it was worth it.

Supper was delicious, though Bastian savored little besides Signe's luscious presence across the table from him. His Blythe-tutored table manners came in handy and he acquitted himself in more-or-less gentlemanly fashion.

After supper, when it grew near ten o'clock and Hilde yawned, Signe seized the chance to send her host and hostess off to bed.

They stared at her, but acquiesced, trusting her to know the limits of decency and decorum. Signe closed the parlor door quietly and turned to Bastian with her throat tightening and her heart thudding. She went to the settee and patted the place beside her. Bastian filled it instantly, then clasped his hands together harshly to control their wanton yearnings.

Signe asked about Raider and Blythe . . . and about Franco and the lads. Bastian answered as fully as he could, explaining their bout with Long Ben and subsequent adventures, trying to control his urge to plunge into Signe's depthless eyes . . . and sweet, responsive body. Lord, this was hard . . . this gentlemanly restraint. How did Raider ever manage so long without laying the Wool-witch flat on her back?!

Bastian ventured the opinion that it was good of Signe to hold no grudge against them for holding her for ransom. And things got very still and very thick between them, as if the smallest movement would spark a massive explosion.

"I . . . have tho't of you, Bastian Cane," Signe's voice came low and full. "Often."

"You have?" Bastian could hardly reply for the grip of desire on his throat. He was being engulfed by heated, womanly scents he'd never smelled before: faint attar of roses, the warm musk between breasts and legs, the winey sweetness of warm breath. His nose had rarely been functional around his "shore" ladies. Smelling a woman was a new experience for him . . . and an excruciatingly erotic one!

"And . . . I haf regretted . . . leaving you that night." His eyes lifted to hers and she trilled physically at the light she recognized in their hazel depths. "Life iss short, Bastian Cane, and hard. Loving iss too precious to waste."

"I . . ." he swallowed hard, "thought of you, Signe. Morgan's Blood, how I thought of ye." His hands parted and hovered near her shoulders as waves of heat fanned through his body. Even as he hesitated, Signe gave in to the impulse and touched his broad, muscular chest.

He crushed her softness to him, sinking into her kiss, welcomed into the velvety sweetness of her mouth. Lord, it was like paradise . . . burying himself in her scents, feeling her, cool and soft, against his flaming body. Even better than he remembered! She was curved to fit his hands, she was firm and soft and silky and strong—

Her arms clasped Bastian's brawny back, her burning breasts sought the heat of him as she wriggled closer . . . closer. Then his hands found the tingling, hardening tips of her breasts and she felt jagged streaks of fire radiating all through her at the way his knowledgeable fingers did exactly what she wanted. She wriggled closer, frustrated in her quest for him, by the cramped quarters of the settee. She wanted him in her bed . . . she wanted to feel his big, muscular body driving hers beneath it into those heavenly soft mattresses. And she wanted a little more . . .

"Bastian, my Bastian," she slid her bruised lips from his long enough to moan, "I want you."

"God, Signe . . . I want you, wench!" he growled against her throat, on the way to her heated breasts. Her cool hands trapped his face and lifted it to meet hers. He could see desire dancing in the darkened centers of her eyes, could feel the yearning in her quivering body against him.

"I am twenty-seven years, Bastian Cane. Not so young, but not so old. I vas married five years . . . and Jens Thorvald gave me no children. I do not know if I can bear. But . . . marry me, Bastian Cane. And sail your lady *Vindraider* as you musst . . . and come home to my bed vhen you can . . ."

The raw hope, the desire in her husky words drove straight into Bastian Cane's heated core. *Marry* her?! It ripped through him like a carronade round. Marry her?! He was suddenly choking, strangling on his own desires. He saw Signe's shock as he pulled away and held her from him for one heaving, tortured moment. Didn't she understand? He was a pirate . . . a rover . . . and she was a respec'able female . . .

He looked into her wide, sky-blue eyes, seeing hurt washing in . . . seeing the turmoil of the risk she had taken in speaking her heart. God, he couldn't stand to see it! He staggered to his feet, churning, confused and furious all at once. She lay against the back of the settee as he left her, crumpled now, crushed by his withdrawal. He was in turmoil . . . drawn to her and her strength and her delectable loving, yet horrified by the thought of being trapped, snared, imprisoned in a respectable world.

"Signe," he panted, having run from her and ready to run yet again, "Signe . . ." But he couldn't make himself say it . . . say anything. He backed to the door as Signe sat up, her eyes luminous with tears, her chin quivering with humiliation. Bastian Cane, bold, pillaging pirate, lover of women and leader of men . . . turned and fled into the frigid night.

Signe Thorvald felt the draft of the open street door all the way into the parlor. Its chilled fingers crept over her heated skin and invaded her aching heart. And her tears began to fall.

Bastian Cane blew through the dockside streets like a raging hurricane, intent on getting drunk as a sea slug. He found the tavern several of the lads had endorsed for its potent rum, healthy ale, and willing wenches. And he downed a good bit of rum, chasing it with the stout, dark ale.

He didn't honestly see the tavern wench's winks or feel the suggestive press of her breasts against his blocky shoulder. His mind, his blood were full of Signe Thorvald. Lord, what a bilge-brain he was, not to have seen it coming. She was a respec'able female . . . and he knew exactly what that meant. Gawd. Just look at what happened to Raider!

Yes—some unsoaked part of his brain took control—just look at what happened to Raider! Raider was lying snug and content in the Wool-witch's arms this very minute, maybe lovin' her up a bit, while swaggerin', independent Bastian Cane sat drinking himself into a stupor in a cheap dockside tavern. Raider had a wife now . . . a permanent bedmate . . . and more. Bastian had watched the covert tenderness of their exchanges and been brushed occasionally by the hot current of sexual need that often surged between them. It made him feel that strange weakness in his feet, and then Signe Thorvald would appear out of nowhere in his mind. Raider had the Wool-witch to talk to, to laugh with . . . at secret little things that got on Bastian's nerves at times. And Raider was always thinkin' up little things to do for her, like a bolt out of the blue, as if she were always on his mind. Like Signe was always on *his* mind, he realized.

Lord. He took a desperate swallow of his ale before his throat closed altogether. He and Signe Thorvald already shared secrets . . . and secret looks. And how many times had he wished he had a woman to talk to . . . to share things with. Signe knew about ships and sailing, and the things that mattered to a sailing man's mind.

Go "sail the *Vindraider* as you must," she'd said to him. Lord, she even understood a man's longing for the sea! And she was willing to be there to welcome him home . . . to give him everything a man's heart could long for. What a sorry bastard he was . . . a slime-slogged bilge rat . . . a lily-livered, short-sighted squid brain! He could go on all night with such erudite self-abuse . . . and Signe's bed would still be cold and he'd still be sitting in a cheap dockside tavern hating himself for hurting her and for denying that he wanted her more than . . . more than his damned precious freedom, whatever the hell that was anyway.

He got to his feet and found his legs still functioned nicely. He wasn't as drunk as he feared. He was just drunk enough not to realize that his determination to see Signe, and see her right now, was perfectly scandalous. The frigid December air slapped enough sense into his pounding brain for him to recall the way to Lars Olsen's house.

There was a frightful pounding on the street door of the Olsen house and a bellowing that might have raised a few dead in the nearby churchyard. Lars and Hilde came pouring out of their door into the upstairs hallway, candle in hand and Signe, in her loose nightgown, with her golden hair atumble, was close behind. A roused servant woman stepped back to let the master answer so dreadful an assault, and as soon as the door was open, Bastian pushed inside, roaring Signe's name, demanding to see her.

There was a moment's confusion as Lars tried to wrestle Bastian back into the street, then Signe's scream stopped them all in their tracks. It hung a moment on the air, vibrating, dying. He looked up from Lars to find her standing on the staircase in her bare nightdress with her hair in disarray.

"What do you want, Bastian Cane?" Her voice was choked, her eyes were reddened, though still luminous. She'd been crying, he could hear it in her voice.

"I be two years short of forty, Signe," he declared boldly, praying it wouldn't make any difference to her. "An' I got my share o' scars."

"And?" There was a tremor of hope in her voice.

"And I want you, Signe Thorvald," Bastian shook Lars's stunned hands off and came to stand below her, spreading his legs to keep from toppling, "if'n you'll have me."

There was stunned quiet in the hallway. The serving woman thought to close the front door and slipped out. Signe came down the stairs slowly, her big eyes fixed on Bastian. "Iss all right, Lars, Hilde. Go back to bed. Mr. Cane and I musst talk."

But the Olsens couldn't move as they watched her walk straight to Bastian and stop before him, looking small and vulnerable. Bastian was thinking the same things about her himself . . . hoping against all hope that she *would* still have him.

"Vhad did you say?" she asked, her heart rising into her throat as his tortured heat engulfed her.

"Marry me, Signe Thorvald. Be my woman, my . . ." he swallowed and made himself say that, too, "*wife.*"

"You mean it?" she whispered, both a question and a prayer.

He nodded, feeling hot and molten inside, feeling very ordinary suddenly and afraid of losing her. "Marry me, Signe!" It was ground out in a groan that came from the bottom of his very soul.

"Yes, Bastian Cane," she whispered, "I vill marry you. Oh, yes, I vill!"

Bastian crushed her to him and she hugged him tightly and squealed with girlish joy as he lifted her off her feet and swung her around and around. The fullness of her eager response seeped through her thin nightgown under his hands and he planted her on the ground again, covering her back and bottom hastily with his hands, pouring a lusty, thorough kiss over her pliant mouth while the Olsens, dumbstruck. She molded herself to his body and with hoyden heat and returned his searing kiss with all the promise and passion in her.

"Sig—" Hilde's outrage was stopped by her husband's fingers against her lips as he nudged her back up the stairs.

"Iss not decent to vatch, Hilde. Come to bed."

Shortly, Signe and her Bastian were alone in the hall, trembling in the grip of fires that threatened to rage out of control. Bastian finally pulled his mouth from hers and asked hoarsely what she wanted to do . . . now.

"I know ye be a respec'able woman Signe." It was agony to add this next. "I'd not shame ye before yer kin, takin' ye afore we're wed."

"I'll not deny you, Bastian Cane, ever again." She swallowed hard, torn between his gallantry and her need.

It was Bastian Cane, bold, pillaging pirate, leader of men, and lover of Signe, who pulled away and took a deep breath, then another. "I'll wait for ye, Signe, till tomorrow. Wed me tomorrow."

Tears came to Signe's eyes. "Tomorrow is fine, my sweet Bastian. But you musst not leave me tonight. Vait—" She turned and ran up the darkened stairs, returning shortly with a lighted candle and a big, downy comforter.

She pulled him into the parlor and then into her arms on the settee. They snuggled and bundled, exploring and discovering each other as they spun plans for a married life. And that's how Hilde and Lars found them early the next morning, sleeping in each other's arms.

Actually, it was to be two days before they were married. Preparations, Hilde said. There *had* to be preparations. Celebration, Blythe insisted. There had to be a proper celebration . . . and time to plan it. Bastian and Signe forebore and waited until the afternoon of the second day to say their vows in the jammed parlor of Lars and Hilde's comfortable home. Then they adjourned to the larger Woolrich House where Franco had laid on a proper wedding feast, sugarcakes and all.

Raider and Blythe watched the newlyweds, a little stunned by their happiness and wondering how they could have missed something so obvious. As they watched Bastian and Signe depart for the Olsen's house and their nuptial night, Raider drew Blythe's back against his chest and wrapped his arms around her, nuzzling her ear. "This . . . this is how we missed it," he rumbled, drawing her shivering laugh of agreement. "We were just too busy to notice."

"Um-m-m." Blythe rubbed his strong arms, then turned in his embrace to mold herself against him. "Let's get 'busy' now."

Raider laughed and lifted her boldly in his arms to carry her up to their room.

The Olsens had gratefully accepted the Prescotts' invitation to remain at Woolrich House that night, leaving the newly wedded couple alone in their house. Bastian was quiet and Signe was nervous during the coach ride to their temporary home. But when they shed their coats and mounted the stairs to Signe's room, Bastian enveloped her hand in his and that shared bit of warmth thawed the air around them.

He poked at the glowing coals in the grate and built up the fire while she sat at the vanity and began to take her hair down. He watched covertly, fascinated by the pots and vials and combs arrayed before her. He'd seen a few women brush their hair in his time, but he'd never observed a respectable woman's toilette . . . much less a wife's. And it struck him that there were probably other things, maybe a lot of other things, he didn't know about respectable women. Including how to make love to one.

But Signe had responded to him once, he reminded himself; she still responded in his arms. Would being wedded change all that? Would she be horrified by the things he wanted to do with her?

He poured the wine Lars had left on the bedside table and brought a glass to her as she finished with her shining hair. He knelt on one knee beside her, taking a lock of her hair in his hand and burying his nose in it, luxuriating in its mingled scents and softness. Then Signe turned to him, her laces loosened, framed in a silky halo, her lips rosy and scented with wine. Her eyes were like pools of evening sky. He suddenly had to know, had to try . . .

Bastian drew her into his arms and kissed her, gently at first, tasting the warmth of wine on her lips, sensing her hesitation. As she warmed and opened, he plunged deeply into her kiss and her arms slid around him. Her body strained toward his, hungry now for the feel of him against her, for the joining of her body with Bastian's.

He paused and loosed her dress with hands that trembled like a stripling's. Then he lifted it over her head and tossed its pale silk perfection aside to enjoy the silky perfection it had covered and caressed all afternoon. Signe's petticoats and corset came next, and soon she stood under his questing hands, reveling in the pressure of his firm grip, weakened to the marrow by his tantalizing light strokes and quicksilver caresses.

She was beautiful, womanly, his Signe, Bastian thought. He lifted her and carried her like a precious jewel to the bed, laying her down, covering her with the cool, crisp sheets while he disrobed. He felt her eyes on his emerging, battle-scared frame and wondered fleetingly if she could find him desirable. When he sat on the edge of the bed to remove his boots, her nimble fingers answered his fears. She rose onto her knees behind him, tracing the scars of old wounds on his back and feathering her hands possessively over the healthy muscles beneath. She slid her arms around his waist and ground her full breasts into his back, igniting the fire in his loins that would be quenched only in Signe Cane's voluptuous body.

Then, like a Viking woman of old, she bit his shoulder, lightly, but leaving her intimate mark in his skin. He whipped about to find her chemise now shed, and the smoke of desire in her Viking blue eyes. Signe was no sighing virgin, she was a full-blooded wife . . . who had found her pleasure in his hands before. He wasted no more time on clothes. Bare-chested and bootless, he bore her to the bed beneath him with a growl and her squeal was pure delight.

He invaded her mouth, possessed her breasts, and claimed her curvy waist and hips with relentless strokes. Soon she arched and writhed and wriggled beneath him, demanding more, pulling his mouth to her breasts, pushing his hands to her thighs and melting into puddles of pleasure when he found the lush, creamy heat between them.

He was wonderful, Signe soared. Big and hot and so hard. Her hands caressed and kneaded his back, his shoulders, and cupped his firm buttocks through his breeches. She laughed a throaty, exultant laugh at his impatience for her and pushed him back to reach for his buttons. Freeing them quickly, she caught her breath at the great thickness of his rod. She stared at him, her eyes dancing, her body wriggling with eagerness.

Bastian Cane read the invitation, the challenge in her flickering body and parted her legs and lowered himself to her. He watched the exquisite arching, the rippling of her body as he entered her and then had to wait, to calm himself before he could continue. Signe held him tightly, luxuriating in the feel of him, in the weight of him, in his salty, sealike smell that meant pure loving to her.

Then they moved and joined with thrusts and tight embraces. He plunged into her core and she absorbed the very essence of him through his virile thrusts. Over and over they came together, soaring higher, burning hotter. And suddenly everything exploded between them, within them, expanding into a broad, luxuriant sphere of pleasure and light. Buoyed up on currents of joy, they joined again and again as they floated slowly back to earth.

Signe would not let him leave her body and he had to settle for canting across her onto a pillow. They were damp, exhausted, glowing. Bastian was not a particularly smooth man with words, but he had a great urge to tell Signe how he felt.

"I knowed it would be like that, Signe. It were . . . purely wonderful."

Signe looked at her husband with all the love in her eyes. "I tink I knew it, too, Sebastian. I love you. I tink I decided it the day of the ransom. I couldn't leave witout your kiss."

"What ye mean, decided?"

"I tink vhen I saw you . . ." she shrugged, "I decided to love again. To love you. You were zo strong, zo much man . . ."

"But what if ye never saw me again?" he frowned, stroking her lovely breasts, thanking God things hadn't worked out that way.

"Den . . . I love you always, wherever you are. Vhen you love, Sebastian Cane, it does not matter how far away you are. You

409

still love. When you sail, I vill still love you . . . and vait for you." She smiled a very adoring smile at him and he kissed her love-bruised lips lightly and hugged her fiercely before dropping his head to the pillow.

They lay together for some time in drowsy contentment before Bastian's voice rumbled close to her ear. "Are ye goin' to call me *Sebastian* now, Signe?"

"Iss your name," she murmured, lifting lazy lids to smile at him.

"Ye don' think it sounds . . . sissy?" he winced.

Signe's sultry blue eyes fluttered down Bastian's thick chest and firm belly to the heavy rod he wielded like a warrior king. "No man who loves a woman as you do, Sebastian Cane, need ever vorry about that." And she threaded her fingers into his wiry hair and sealed her pronouncement with a fierce Viking kiss.

Chapter Twenty-six

"We been thinkin', Raider . . ." Old Willie spoke for a small contingent of the lads as they approached Raider and Blythe in the parlor of Woolrich House on Christmas Day. They'd had a modest but satisfying Christmas celebration, owing to their continuing recovery from the great revelry that accompanied Bastian Cane's marriage only two days previously. And now, as they sat in the newly refurbished parlor in a state of pleasant fatigue, the lads came for a bit of a talk.

They weren't the first to report such extraordinary behavior . . . "thinkin'." There had apparently been quite a little bit of it going on since the shock of Bastian's unexpected nuptials. It was as though his vows had unleashed a tidal wave of accumulated changes. The very day after the wedding, Stanley had approached Raider, asking to strike his name from the *Articles* and to withdraw his "share" in order to take up carpentry and cabinetmaking as a profession on land. Then, only this morning, Harry and Alfonse came to him with the idea of setting up a tailor shop and haberdashery in the city . . . which meant they'd be leaving the *Windraider*'s crew. Now it was Old Willie, Richard, Oars, and François.

"I could do the butlin' fer Miz Blythe, here. That old feller she got cain't remember his own name most days. Richard, he been helping out at old Walter's shop and has got to hankerin' fer the 'mercantile,' " Old Willie explained and Richard nodded agreement. "And Franco here be happy as a clam stuck in muck in 'at big galley." François snorted at the comparison, but nodded affirmation. "Oars, here," Willie turned to the brawniest member of the *Windraider's* crew, "he's a mind to try drivin' a wagon fer Old Walter, on account of he gets on so good with th' mules. Like comin' to like, I guess. It'd be like we was . . . takin' care o' the Wool-witch for ye, when ye be at sea. I reckon we be askin' fer release, Raider."

Raider studied their averted eyes and shifting feet and knew what it cost them to bring their petition to him. They'd weathered much together, good times and bad. The lads aboard the *Windraider* couldn't have been closer if they'd had the same birthmother. His throat seemed clogged and he had to clear it.

"You've thought it out, then . . . decided?" Raider felt a strange heat rising up in his stomach as they glanced at one another, then nodded. "Then I'll wish you well in your new life. I'm pleased you've chosen to stay . . . nearby." He shook their hands and turned away toward the window with a grave expression as they filed out.

She went to stand behind him, close but not touching. Beneath his calm exterior, she could feel the molten swirl of his troubled mood. Bastian's marriage to Signe had come as a great shock to him. It presaged a drastic change in a partnership that had endured nearly a decade in a profession where death and treachery and rivalry were the rule. Now it was all changing, shifting beneath his feet like a deck in a furious squall. The time had come for him to do a bit of thinkin' himself.

Since that first night at Woolrich House, neither had directly raised the topic of their future nor made reference to more than their most immediate needs and plans. Though both had felt the question of their future lying unresolved between them, Blythe had come to hope, to believe it would all work itself out, given time. She had watched him observe and judge and test the parameters of this strange new life. His suspicions, his contempt, and his prejudices about respectable society were slowly surrendering under the onslaught of his success as a respectable sea captain and his understanding of the surprising flexibility in colonial society. No small part of the change in his thinking was caused by the openness and comparative freedom of Blythe's unusual family and their hybrid sea/land household. And there was Blythe herself, that intriguing, rousing blend of the sensual and the sensible, the responsive, and the responsible.

"It's all changing, Blythe." He felt her presence and spoke to her, though he could not see her.

"Yes, it is." The ache inside him was flooding into her as well.

"I can't make it all out," he admitted softly. "I can't see where it's headed. Every morning I wake up holding my breath . . . sure I'll find you gone . . . that I'll be back in that pesthole prison in Algiers, dreaming all this."

"I'm here and I'll always be here." She touched his back and he turned to look into the loving turmoil of her face.

"No," his jaw clamped against an aching rush in his chest, "it'll turn again . . . it won't last."

"It's real, Raider. I'm real!" Hot frustration swelled inside her and she took his hand and pressed it over her breast, holding it there. "My love for you is real . . . the loving we make is real."

"Blythe—" He tugged his hand, but she held it trapped against her. "You don't understand. There've been good things before . . . but they never last. It's my—"

"Fate?!" she finished hotly. "Morgan's Wretched Liver!" She dropped his hand, furious with him and his wretched "fates" for threatening her love and her life with him. "I'm sick to death of your precious 'fate.' There isn't any such thing! What there is . . . is choices . . . those we make and those others make for us!"

"So everything has a damned reasonable explanation, does it?! It's all just a matter of choices . . ." He stalked forward, pushing her back with his heated body and growling. "Tell me—just whose choice was it that we didn't sink under that rogue wave during the storm? And just whose choice was it that we come out of a storm with a fat, damaged prize in our bloody laps?! Did the *Gastronome*'s captain decide that . . . or did I?!"

"A storm is just wind and water, Raider. The *Windraider* is a wonderful ship and you're a master at the helm—you fought it and won!" she shot back, trying to hold her ground. "And the *Gastronome* was just caught in the storm with us . . . separated from her escort—"

"And what about Long Ben's ships appearing . . ."

"You said yourself he was probably already looking for you before Port-au-Prince!"

413

". . . catching us so close to harbor," he completed it. "And the bloody French being there . . . just at the right time . . ."

"You forgot to strike the Stars and Stripes, remember? Captain Ellemonde said they were tired of sitting . . . doing guard duty. They needed a bit of action and thought we were colonials. They had orders to protect American shipping and *decided* to come to our rescue." She was shouting now, furious with him. "Things happen for reasons, Gideon Prescott!"

"And you have a neat tidy little explanation for everything, don't you?!" he thundered at her, feeling bullied by her logic and trapped in the web of his stubborn beliefs. He saw her chin pull back, saw her cheeks burning and the angry tears forming in her molten eyes.

"I don't claim to know everything," she rasped, fighting through suffocating waves of despair. "Things happen that I can't explain . . . like your loving me. I still don't know why you love me, Raider. And there are miracles sometimes . . . like Nana's walking . . . things that I can't explain. But I have to explain the things I can . . . to make sense of what I can make sense of . . ."

"Nana's . . . ?" He snorted angry disbelief. "That was . . ." . . . hardly anything miraculous, he bit off and finished silently. The old harridan was faking, pure and simple, and he and Willie had called her on it . . . and on her taking advantage of Blythe's loving, sometimes vulnerable nature. He straightened, resisting the quiver that threatened to curve the ends of his mouth up into a smirk. How ironic that her example of a "miracle" was something he himself had engineered!

The thought sank in his brain, then through the entire rest of his heated body, chilling every single nerve. In the heaving silence, the logic of it transferred inescapably. He'd been behind the scenes of Nana's "miracle." Then . . . was it just possible that someone . . . others . . . were behind the things that happened to him . . . his inescapable "fate"?

He reeled, feeling the deck beneath his feet heaving yet again. Lord—it crashed over him—it was possible! Then that meant—

In a haze he wheeled and stumbled for the doors, slamming them back and snatching up his cloak from the bench in the hall. In seconds he was stalking blindly through the cold, cobbled streets, wishing he could escape the relentless onslaught of his own thought processes. But every step pounded that wedge of reason deeper into the core of his long-held beliefs.

His father's favoritism, Noraleen's betrayal of him, and Bastian's need for a navigator — Lord! how could he not have seen it? He'd been condemned as bad seed by his father . . . and was betrayed by the woman he loved. One thing led to another . . . then to another — a chain of decisions others had made about him or concerning him. With such killing strokes against him, it was easier to conjure and blame "fate" than to admit he'd been wronged by the father he'd wanted to please and that he'd been a callow youth in love with a hard-eyed woman of the world. And that Bastian had taken him . . .

Perhaps it was true, he realized. What if his sensible, responsible Blythe was right? Then was it all just a matter of how you looked at it . . . and how you reacted? Could it really be so simple as just deciding to decide?! Not that the decisions would always be easy . . . or unopposed. But it would mean he was no longer doomed to a life at the hands of capricious and incomprehensible forces like "luck" and "fate."

With every step he took in the cold afternoon sun, he felt old bonds and shackles falling away. He was being freed, buoyed, given back his life. And he knew exactly who to credit . . .

Blythe had watched the anger and shock trading places in Raider's face and felt the eruption of his fury in the rumble of the front doors. All of life, even breath, was suspended in the crushing desolation she felt. He was gone. And if he never returned it would be her own blessed fault.

She tottered weakly to the settee and sank down on it, her spirits sinking even lower. She'd railed and argued like a regular shrew. No, like a nagging wife. The thought skewered her. Was she turning into that very thing Raider loathed and dreaded most . . . a clinging, demanding, selfish female?

But was it so selfish to want to spend her life with the man she loved? To want him safe, to need his strength, to want to share the joys and woes of life with him? If it was, then she was irretrievably lost, for it was a desire within her that would never change . . .

She heard a rustle and looked up to find Nana standing nearby, watching her with those piercing gray eyes. "That 'Willie' beast your husband just made into our new butler—he said Gideon Prescott is a pirate."

"He was," Blythe sighed, not expecting Nana to understand. "I don't think he knows what he is now." And that insight astonished her. That was exactly the problem! All this prattle about the past and fate and choice—when what really mattered was what Gideon "Raider" Prescott was now . . . and what he wanted to be.

Nana came forward and settled on the brocade settee beside her, taking her hand and studying it with a frown. Blythe felt herself tightening inside, but Nana's soft tones surprised her.

"I've made some mistakes, Blythe. If I had it to do over I wouldn't try to remake the people around me as if they were outmoded dresses. Especially the people I love." She raised tired gray eyes to Blythe and her cool, blue-veined hand came up to trace Blythe's flushed cheeks. Love, hurt, weariness, and apology mingled in Nana's wizened features. Blythe was stunned.

"A man has to be whatever he is inside, Blythe. Men . . . and women, too, I guess . . . aren't made of clay or metal that can be shoved into a mold and reshaped into something 'acceptable.' Lord knows I tried that with Walter. And it nearly killed him." Her eyes filled with tears for the first time in Blythe's memory.

Blythe responded, drawing Nana impulsively into her arms. And as the tears slid down her cheeks, Blythe absorbed Nana's dearly bought wisdom into her aching heart:

"Your man has to be whatever he is. All you can do is love him."

Raider blew through the front doors just at sunset with his coattails flying, roaring her name through the hall and the parlor. He found her in the dining room with Willie, Richard, Nana, and Mrs. Dornly, preparing for a light supper.

"Out!" he bellowed at full steam, and when they just stared at him, he added a furious lunge and a wave of his arms. "Out, I said—and close the damned doors after you!" But he grabbed Blythe's arm and held her back, growling, "Not you!"

"R-raider—" She shrank from him, feeling both the icy cold of his coat and the seafire of his eyes. She saw the alarm on the others' face as the door closed and it gave her own fears a swift boot. "Raider, please—" His hands clamped on her arms and he pulled her toward him.

"You're right, dammit. You win!" he ground out, deciding to corral her protesting form against the table. He pushed her backward with his body until she was wedged between two chairs and against the linen-draped edge of the table.

"There is no damned *fate*. I'll give you that much." He towered over her, bending her backward over the table as she struggled to avoid him. "I was betrayed and forced and flattered and fleeced into making my living taking ships on the high seas. But I'm damned good at it! I'd be a rich man twelve times over if I hadn't spent most of it feeding my blessed crew . . . and keeping Bastian out of trouble!"

Blythe's golden eyes were huge with the shock of his furious mood and the unleashed heat of his big body against hers. She'd seen him like this once before. This was Raider Prescott under full *pirate* sail! His hands clamped about her waist and he hoisted and plunked her bottom down on the table between plates. Then his broad-oak shoulders came down on her, pushing her beneath him onto the tabletop.

"Now what do we do about the fact that I'm a damned pirate, Blythe Woolrich," he growled, setting her skin atingle with his low, savage vibrations and the hungry heat of his breath on her bare skin. "I like striking and boarding and fighting hand to hand. I like the way my blood pounds in my body before a battle. I like matching wits against another captain . . . bringing it down to a fight . . . and winning. I get a randy itch for it sometimes. What'll you do with that, Wool-witch?!"

Raw excitement sparked through her skin at the flash of danger in his glittering eyes, the fierce sea-hawk hunger in his bronzed features, the carnal set of his full mouth. His body had pressed between her legs and now pinned her to the table with its potent force. Heat uncoiled like a whip inside her, lashing up from her loins, setting every sensitive inch of her skin aflame. Desire galvanized her body, her throat, allowing her only a small moan of confusion.

"No answer for that, Wool-witch?" He rasped an animallike

growl as he lifted her head toward him. His voracious lips sent his challenge searing through her warming flesh, igniting the full force of her passions in a way she'd never experienced.

Her arms lashed about him, demanding the feel of him above her, and he suddenly levered himself to oblige—heedless of the moan of the table beneath them. He plunged deeply into her kiss, plundering her, raking the hot, honey sweetness from the yielding surfaces of her mouth. He nibbled her lips and dueled with her tongue, possessing her, inciting in her a primal instinct for sensual combat.

"Henry Morgan used to pillage his women captives after dinner . . ." he panted as he devoured her cheek, her throat, her jutting breasts. "Right in the middle of his damned table, dishes and all . . . with his men shouting encouragement." His ragged whisper said he was considering a version of the same. "Bastian thinks Morgan was a prince. He had guts, Old Henry . . . but in many ways he was a pig."

He lifted from her aching form and when his feet hit the floor, he pulled her upright and scooped her up against his passion-hardened body, striding for the hallway doors. He kicked them open, unpleasantly surprising several heads that were pressed to the other side.

The cool air of the hallway fanned Blythe's steamy responses enough for her to make sense of the outraged looks they were receiving. "Raider—what do you think you're doing?"

"I prefer to do my pillaging in private, Wool-witch." A sensual smirk stole over his lust-bronzed face and he began to take the stairs by two's, as though her weight were nothing to him. Shortly he kicked the door shut behind them and dumped her on the bed in their chamber.

"Take your clothes off, Wool-witch." His guttural order sent a tremor through her, and she skittered off the end of the bed. When she hit the floor, she drew herself up with a glint in her eyes that matched his. Both of his coats came off at once, and his waistcoat and boots were doomed to go next.

"I will not." Her voice was husky and her stance defiant. "If you're pillaging me, Scourge of the Seven Seas, then you'll have to do it yourself." He laughed, a wicked pirate kind of a laugh at her challenge, and his lust-polished eyes narrowed determinedly on her. A sensual shiver of expectation vibrated her erotically sensitive places and she felt herself going liquid with desire. She watched him rip his shirt off and come for her, his body coiled, explosive with need.

Her laces didn't stand a chance; he had them pulled completely out in a few dexterous moves. Her garments were pulled from her with practiced, relentless precision, and when she broke and started to flee, he clamped her to him with a steely arm and finished his work one-handed. He carried her to the bed clad only in her stockings and frilly garters, and held her beneath him, her wrists pinned at the sides of her head.

"Strike colors or prepare to die, Wool-witch." He panted an ageless pirate ultimatum, breaking into a lecherous grin that riveted her gaze.

"And if I fight on?" She tossed her head with provocative sensual defiance.

"The end will be the same, wench."

Her body was fluid and molten inside, her breasts were flushed with arousal, and her nipples were pebble hard. She was aching for the feel of his weight on her belly. He parted her thighs and slid his thick, pulsing shaft against her, rubbing slowly over her burning pleasure center. Her body jolted and she sought to intensify his languorous movements by wriggling her pelvis against him.

"Then you'll just have to pillage me, Captain . . . *please!*"

Raider's laugh was carnal triumph as he sank his arms beneath her and his shaft inside her. She moaned and arched and writhed in splintering ecstasy at the raw power of his loving and at the depth of her need. His kisses were fierce, breathtaking, and her caresses were like possessive cats' claws on his broad back. They arched and strained in white-hot splendor until the fires they stoked exploded out of control, propelling them up through searing, jagged peaks of successive pleasures.

"What do I do about this hungry pirate in me, Wool-witch?" Raider murmured his question again as they lay nestled together some time later.

"Again? Already?" Blythe raised on her elbow and sent widened eyes to his very resilient manhood. He laughed and pulled her elbow from under her, bringing her down, nose-to-nose, with him on the pillows.

"Not that hunger . . . exactly. I've been a sea raider a long time, Blythe . . ." His beautiful jade eyes were perfectly serious and he was surprised to see her grinning.

Yes, he certainly was a pirate . . . one who pillaged and devoured her, but was too much of a gentleman to actually do it on the dining-room table. Heaven help her, she wanted them both — refined, gentlemanly Gideon and fierce, sensual Raider. She had to find a way to reconcile them . . . so she could have them both. But for now . . .

"Well, you get to be a pirate sometimes." She sent a mischievous hand down his lean hip to encourage his hardening manhood. "And you get to be *hungry* whenever you want."

Chapter Twenty-seven

"They moved it yesterd'y, Mr. Carson. The day afore Christmas." Dickey flinched, fully expecting the raw oath that followed his news. Neville Carson heaved himself out of his chair, lunging straight at his scrawny hireling. Christmas Day was no different from any other for Neville Carson, having no family and no particular faith. He had worked at his office all day, stewing at the inconvenience others caused him by closing their banks and shops and offices to celebrate. He was in a mood for better news.

"Then why didn't I know about it yesterday . . . or last night? What the hell am I paying you for, you miserable maggot?!" He grabbed Dickey's shirtneck and wrenched it tight.

"Nobody thought they'd move it Christmas Eve. And it were done quick. They off-loaded themselves . . . no longshoremen." Dickey felt his eyes bulging and added, "The warehouse be located just down the dock and half the stuff's still in wagons they hauled it in. Makes our job easier . . ."

"Yes!" Carson released him forcefully, his eyes narrowing in calculation. "Call the boys together . . . now!"

"But it's Christm—" Dickey stopped at the evil flame in Carson's eye.

"What better time to move? All we need now is a diversionary bit of vengeance . . ."

"Raider?!" Clive came bursting through the front door of Woolrich House. The day after Christmas, they were gathered in the dining room for breakfast. "Raider, where are you?!" By the

421

time he stumbled into the dining room, Raider and Willie were halfway to the door.

"Fire—" Clive collapsed against the doorframe panting. He'd run all the way from the docks and was heaving so furiously he could scarcely get it out. "The *Gastronome* . . . burning! I already got Bastian . . . hurry!" Raider was instantly in motion, making straight for the door with Willie, Richard, and Oars cutting along through his wake.

Smoke boiled black and evil out of the foc's'le of the *Gastronome*, obscuring the flames. The air all around was thick and acrid, and visibility was nil. Raider ran all the way, arriving first and having to bend over, coughing and heaving for air. It was that sound that allowed the Bosun Deane to find him in the gray smoke.

"Bastian's here—*Le Tigre* and the *Antoinette* sent over spare pumps and a few lads," he explained, leading Raider aboard. Raider wetted his handkerchief in the stern water barrel and tied it over his nose and mouth. The heat and smoke stung his eyes savagely as they fought their way toward Bastian's familiar bellowing.

"Cain't do much from here," Bastian shouted to him above the roar of fire and the men's shouts. "She's spreadin' forward—outta reach!"

"Then let's rip her open!" Raider shouted back, wheeling to shout orders to break out axes for smashing through the topdeck to the fire below.

Blythe arrived to find the smoke thick and nearby streets clogged with gawking onlookers speculating obscenely on how many men the burning ship would take down with her. She fought her way through them and then through the cordon of French sailors from Captain Ellemonde's *Le Tigre* that had been assigned to keep the growing crowd back.

It was a horrifyingly long time before anyone emerged from the billowing wall of gray that shrouded the ship. Bastian and some of the lads materialized and collapsed onto the dock, coughing and gasping for air. She carried them water and tried to piece together what was happening on the smoldering ship from what they were able to tell her. Raider was all right, working like a fiend to rescue the ship, Bastian managed. Then

Signe was there, cradling Bastian in her arms, and Blythe went on to help others.

The fight continued in shifts for most of the morning and twice Raider came out of the smoke to collapse at her feet. She gave him water and washed his heat-singed face, then had to relinquish him back to the grip of duty, for he would not hear of abandoning their prize to the flames.

By noon the fire was mostly extinguished; only a few smoldering timbers remained. Captain Ellemonde led his Frenchmen aboard to do the final mopping up, and the dock was soon littered with exhausted crewmen and those few longshoremen who had joined the firefight.

When they were able to get to their feet, Blythe found a wagon and ferried them straight to the Woolrich Warehouse, which was near the docks. There they could recover in some warmth while she made arrangements for food and drink.

The story came out slowly, pieced together from a bit here, a word there, as the sooty, exhausted men sprawled over the crates and platforms inside the main room of the warehouse. Darkness had hidden the first traces of trouble. Then the watch posted on the *Windraider* smelled the smoke and made an immediate check of that ship, finding nothing. Other lads were roused, and shortly the smoke from the *Gastronome* was spotted and the alarm was sounded.

"Where was the watch on the *Gastronome?*" Raider demanded. "Who was assigned?" He located the Bosun Deane and learned that Collin, a lad from the *Windraider* had that watch . . . and he was unaccounted for.

Raider and Bastian were grim as they withdrew into the warehouse office with several of the lads and Blythe and Signe. According to Stanley, their ship's carpenter, the damage was extensive enough to require major shipyard work . . . and to squash the planned sale to Lars Olsen. It was a blow; they'd counted on the sale to disburse proper shares amongst the lads.

Blythe watched Raider's exhaustion and read unsettling thoughts in the hard lines of his jaw and the cold flint of his eyes as their losses were tallied. Too well she remembered their argument and his certainty that their "good luck" was transitory. And now, when he looked at her, she could see echoes of his fatalistic prediction in his face.

"Damned bad luck," Bastian scowled as he sat in the warehouse office, savoring the ale Signe brought him and reaching up to hold her hand as it rested on his shoulder.

"It's not bad luck," Blythe corrected with a determined eye on Raider. "It's a fire . . . with a cause. What was there on board that could have started it?"

"Naught I can think of." Bastian shook his head. "Not in that part of th' ship. One o' the lads smokin' mebbee. Cain't figure why the watch didn' sound out. Collin be a capable man . . ."

Walter and the Bosun Deane joined them, and together they raised and examined every possibility: an overturned lantern, rum brought aboard illegally, lamp oil, crewmen smoking aft of the galley in forbidden areas. Nothing seemed to explain the swift spread of the blaze except "damn bad luck."

. . . until Carrick ushered Captain André Ellemonde into the office. The gallant Frenchman greeted them soberly, and from his dapper belt, pulled a long, horn-handled knife.

"Ve find a body . . . wit thees." He handed it to Raider, and every eye in the room fastened on that crude blade.

"Small man?" Bastian's voice was thick as he rose. "Young?"

"*Oui.*"

"Collin." Raider blanched behind the heat-scorched red of his face. When his gaze lifted from the knife, it locked on Blythe. "Somebody set the fire . . . and had to kill Collin to do it."

"B-but who?" Bastian drew Signe into the protective circle of his arms. "An' why? Why'd anybody burn an empty ship?"

In the charged silence they studied each other. And it hit Blythe in a sickening wave. How stupid she was not to have realized he'd do something to strike at them!

"Revenge." She took Raider's arm as she lifted pained eyes to him. "There's only one person who'd go to such lengths to hurt us. Neville Carson. He was responsible for the disappearance of Woolrich's wagons . . . and for who knows how many more of our prior 'misfortunes.' He cloaked it so it would appear to be Indians or British . . . or just 'damned bad luck.' But he always came around after each catastrophe, wheedling and bullying to get us to give in. When he couldn't force or bribe his way into Woolrich Mercantile or make me marry him, he swore I'd pay.

424

Oh, Raider, it's him . . . I know it!"

Raider stared into her tortured expression and saw again the slitted fury of Neville Carson's reaction in the harbormaster's offices that first afternoon. He had watched the murder borning in Carson's eyes and seen the way he detached from it, as though setting it aside for another time and place. Raider recognized that process . . . he'd seen it often enough in the faces of ship-taking captains, including the scurrilous Long Ben. A sea raider had to learn early to set his urges aside, to decide when to fight and when to withdraw . . . to fight another day.

"As soon as the men are rested, we'll sweep the harbor area." Raider turned to Bastian. "If it was Carson, he wouldn't have risked setting the fire himself . . . he'd have had help. There's probably a 'torch' or two in the area. We have to find them, before . . ." He stopped suddenly, staring at Blythe.

"Before he tries something else?" Blythe shuddered. "Raider, the warehouse . . . he'd love to get his hands on the guns and munitions!"

Bastian was already in motion, rousting a detail of men to accompany him to the warehouse to strengthen its guard. Raider relented to Blythe's insistence that he go home, to eat and rest before setting out to find what had happened. But as he saw to his men and thanked the French captain for his assistance, Bastian blew back through the door, panting, having run the several blocks from the warehouse.

"The guns and powder . . . gone . . . stole out from under our noses. The warehouse be empty!"

"When? How?!" Raider started, sweeping Blythe's burning face with a look.

"Pro'bly whilst we was fightin' the fire this mornin'." Bastian staggered forward into Signe's arms. "The lads on guard was pulled away. There was so many people . . . everthin' was confused. Raider . . ." he looked meaningfully at Raider as he recovered, "it were Carson, all right. I smelt him. Onions . . . I swear I smelt onions."

"Morgan's Bloody Bile!" Raider spat, turning away with impotent anger evident in every line of his hardened frame. "It was a bloody diversion—" The full range of Carson's cunning and ruthlessness was only now becoming clear to him.

425

"He set the fire aboard the *Gastronome* . . . to get his hands on our cargo! Dammit. Burning and pillaging and murdering . . . the kind of stuff I'd expect from Long Ben and his jackals. What the hell is he, a businessman or a damned pirate?!"

He whirled and stared at Blythe. For the first time he realized the kind of forces she'd been up against . . . alone and vulnerable in a harsh male world of trade. It was a small miracle she'd held the business together as long as she had. He straightened, feeling a familiar heat trill through his blood and a powerful coiling in his gut. His visage changed before their very eyes. There was that dangerous pirate gleam in his eye and that predatory fierceness to his aristocratic features.

"You run with a tough pack, Wool-witch." He strode to her and took her shoulders in his hands, appreciating fully now just how broad they were. "But we've run with tougher, haven't we, lads?"

Bastian laughed as the gleam in Raider's eyes ricocheted from Blythe's surprised face into his own eyes and the bosun's. "That we have!"

"It occurs to me that there may not be as much difference between pirating and 'respectable' business as I thought," His statement brought a sputter from Blythe and spread an enchantingly wicked grin over his face. "Each has its sharks. I think what Woolrich Mercantile and Freight needs now is a bit of muscle in the marketplace . . ."

That night, one-eyed Bastian and a few of the lads stalked into the Contrary Mary Tavern, spreading out slowly in the smoky, sour haze, searching for information. Bastian's coin bought a bit of cooperation from the bloke behind the ale-soaked bar, who nodded toward two men in the corner. "Them two's for hire . . . for anythin'," the barman whispered. Bastian smiled his most beguiling smile and strode over to where Runyon and Spars were absorbing the last of the liquid reward purchased by their latest venture . . . a bit of heistin' from a warehouse.

Bastian came to stands over them and Runyon lifted bleary eyes to register a face that was alarmingly familiar. And as recognition filled Runyon's face, the same light entered Bastian's

426

heated visage.

"You!" Bastian confronted his paid henchmen of several months ago. "Damn, ye be a sight fer sore eyes!" he bellowed, his determination belying the geniality of his words. "Lookat who we got here, lads!" He turned toward his men and rasped, "Bring 'em!" under his breath as he strode for the door.

Once outside and down a nearby dark alley, Bastian renewed his acquaintance with the two and introduced the *Windraider*'s lads. The introductions had quite an impact on Runyon and Spars and shortly they were babbling like brooks about the guns and powder kegs and formed lead that they helped load into wagons. And they were even moved to share what they knew of the goods' destination.

"You're staying here, Blythe!" Raider commanded, stuffing a long knife into his belt and checking his pistols one last time before he left their candlelit bedchamber.

"Don't you dare come righteous and respectable on me, Raider Prescott." She blocked the doorway. "I can ride a horse, which is better than most of your lads can do . . . you'll be lucky to get them there in one piece. And I'm a fair shot with a pistol—"

"No, dammit! You're going to stay here like a proper wife and—" He grabbed her waist and she struggled briefly, thinking he was setting her aside. But he pulled her hard against him and poured a lavish, bone-draining kiss over her. His tongue stroked hers, seducing it into full, greedy compliance. Heat was flaring dangerously between them when he pulled away. His voice was gratifyingly hoarse. "And wait for me."

Weak with carnal need, Blythe watched him grab his coat and felt his husbandly peck on her forehead. It was a long moment before she could react to what he'd just done.

"That was low, Raider Prescott," she growled. "And if you think you'll get by with it, you're dead wrong!" She ran straight for the wardrobe and dug past her pretty new dresses to seize her leather skirt, waistcoat, and Wool-witch boots.

The *Windraider*'s lads gathered by torchlight in the Woolrich warehouse. Expectation pulsed in their blood, joining them in purpose and determination. In true pirate tradition, each man had been responsible for his choice of weapons and a mount of some sort. They came armed to the teeth, though most were riding Walter Woolrich's wagon mules. Raider walked amongst them, clasping arms, speaking low, spreading the fire in his eyes through their midst. Then he sprang up onto a crate, his booted legs braced, his hands on his hips, and he told them what they had to do.

"The guns and munitions are in wagons, headed north for the Howe's British encampments around New York. Carson's thugs have several hours start on us, but they're dragging quite a load." There was a surly expression of pleasure at that and Raider held up his hand for quiet. "There's a driver and a guard on each wagon and, as best we know, there are outriding guards, front, sides, and rear. They're keeping off the roads, under natural cover as much as possible. We'll have to move quietly . . . using with a minimum of shot and powder. We can't risk losing our cargoes to a stray ball." There was another murmur of understanding and approval. The lads were itchin' for a good hand-to-hand fight.

It sounded impossible to Blythe . . . whose heart hammered wildly against her ribs as she pulled Walter's old coat closer around her at the back of the crowd. But as she listened to Raider's proud, pirate-fierce tone, she could feel the heat, the certainty rising inside her even as it rose in the lads. They had cunning and sea-honed strength and agility on their side. They had The Raider to lead them and a wrong to avenge. And they had futures at stake—every man-jack of them.

It began with a word, became a chant, then a pulsing drone—a wordless sea call to battle, a fierce thundering tide of determination. Raider jumped down into their midst and led them out through the wagon doors to their mounts waiting outside in the frigid night. Blythe waited until most were gone, then hurried outside to find the horse she'd borrowed, praying that she hadn't forgotten how to ride. She made to mount, and the animal shied and banged sideways straight into another bloke trying to get aboard a hard-headed mule.

"Hey!" Richard growled angrily, "it's bad enough—" He found

himself looking straight into a pair of doubloon gold eyes. "M—miz Bly—you cain't come!"

"Oh, yes I can," she glowered regally. "Now give me a leg up and keep your voice down." When he hesitated, she added the potent threat, "Or I'll personally lock Lizzy's door every night of her life from now on!"

Soon they were both mounted and trailing the expeditionary force, heading north.

Tracking and trailing on land was vastly different from ocean-going hunting. It was virtually impossible to cut a straight line between two points with trees, houses, hills, and fences in the way. On the other hand, there were folk to ask and heavy wagon-ruts to mark the way. Impatience was the major difficulty they encountered at first . . . that and balky, infuriating four-leggers who seemed perfectly bewildered by their new role as saddle mounts and by their riders' total ineptitude. After the first two hours, there were audible snarls and vitriolic curses heard, disparaging their land-based transport. And when they stopped at daybreak to water their mounts and stretch, some of the lads found themselves scarcely capable of walking.

Blythe pulled her borrowed cap low over her face and hung back behind Richard, rubbing her numbed posterior and wondering if any of them would be fit to fight when they finally caught up with Neville Carson. Raider must have wondered the same thing, for he strode amongst the men and animals, assessing the damage with a dangerous glare.

"Ye got to do somethin', Raider." Bastian stomped stiffly after him.

"Me?" Raider was near an explosion. "Just what the hell am I supposed to do about it?" Bastian sputtered and jerked his blocky chin back.

"Well, them mules . . . they be females, ain't they?"

Raider jolted back, a bit unnerved. He turned to look at his men's expectant faces, then went to stare the closest "jennie" in the eye. A crafty light entered his jade gaze and he pulled the mule's head down to whisper in her ear. The lads murmured superstitiously as the flesh on her neck flickered and shivered under his touch. And as Raider went from one mule to another, touching, whispering, the lads broke into lascivious grins. Apparently The Raider's touch worked on all forms of females!

Soon he turned and addressed the lads in his deepest bass tones. "My arse hurts, too. But it's Neville Carson who'll get the blisters! Let's ride!" He swung up into his saddle with a furious set to his jaw and the lads rumbled approval and remounted, their confidence renewed.

They set off at a punishing pace, stopping only to confirm directions for most of the morning. The mules honestly did seem more cooperative as the lads' animosity toward them abated, making the going easier. As Raider intended, every bit of discomfort they suffered was being stored as coiled rage, awaiting release on Carson's ill-paid thugs.

Midafternoon they found themselves in wooded hills and Raider sent scouts out to locate the wagons and report back. They split into two columns and trailed as slowly and quietly as they could through the stark, wintry trees. There were few sounds: the creak of harness, the cold thud of hooves on ground, and the rustle of leaves underfoot. The mood grew expectant, and the lads fingered their blades and checked the priming in their pistols and muskets.

Ahead of them, Sharkey slipped through the trees on foot as though gliding through an underwater bed of kelp. And like his namesake, his senses were tuned to detect the slightest disturbance and interpret it as prey. When the rustling came, he froze, locating the source. A lone rider, musket carelessly draped over his arm, plodding forward. A twig underfoot snapped loudly and the fellow jolted in the saddle, lifting his gun. There was a humming quiver on the air and the sharp, surprising sting of the shark's steel. The man toppled with a dull thud from his nervous mount. Sharkey caught the reins and steadied the beast, crouching, watching. Movement up a far rise caught his eye and a small flash of red . . . a cap . . . drew him forward. He stole along after them to locate their counterparts on the far side of the valley and to catch a glimpse of the last wagon disappearing around a bend below. He'd found the wagons and their flanking outriders. His strange grin spread and he turned and slipped back through the sea of trees to warn The Raider.

Sharkey, Clive, the Bosun Deane, and four other lads were assigned to take out the outriders and slipped off through the trees, relieved to see action at last. An instinctive military tactician, Raider sent Bastian's contingent onto the high ground across the way as it broadened into that little valley. They were to move quickly, without signals, and to draw bead carefully and fire one round, taking out as many of the drivers and guards as possible. Then there would be the rush . . . and it was every man for himself.

They unsheathed their weapons as they hurried through the trees. But when the wagons came into view, there was the additional, unexpected obstacle of a dozen mounted guards roaming the sides of the file of wagons. Raider let a low curse. Carson was a very careful shark. He ordered his sharpshooters to take aim on them first, trusting Bastian to stick with their former strategy and concentrate his fire on the drivers.

"Make every damned ball count; you won't have time to reload." He moved back through his men, scarcely noticing the old cap drawn down over the face of the lad on the far side of Richard. Muskets came up and Raider went back to the head of the file, moving quickly now toward the place ahead where the treed slopes gentled to provide the perfect entry for attack.

The ache of battle-angst gripped every throat, tightened every gut. Blythe felt it, less like fear than she'd experienced before. She knew the sound of musketfire, knew the smell of blood and the fierce sounds of battle. That familiarity both chilled and reassured her. She swallowed hard, harnessed the pounding in her blood, and met Richard's look with Wool-witch determination. She was going to be at Raider's back—

Ahead, Raider turned and waved them down, cutting out of the trees with a bellowing cry that had sometimes turned hot pirate blood to ice in his enemies' veins. Shouts of alarm broke out amongst the wagons and the drivers whipped their teams into violent motion, some careening recklessly off the path to get around the slower ones in front. The mounted defenders startled around to face Raider's guns. Those few seconds of confusion gave the *Windraider*'s lads the advantage of the first volley. Fully half the mounted henchmen were taken down by that first round as the lads rushed in. The surprise impact of a fierce, armed force swooping down out of the hills from two directions prevented most of those remaining from using their guns until it was almost too late.

The rush soon engaged hand-to-hand as Bastian and Clive and Black Jimmy stormed the wagons with their men, braving the point-blank fire of the wagon guards Bastian's men hadn't taken down. Blythe heard screams, pops of musketfire, and saw Stanley take a ball and career off a wagon bed. Clive soon pounced on the wagon guard who'd shot him, and his needlelike blade flashed, ripping into the man's coat twice . . . striking home the third time. Richard tried to stick by her, shouting for her to ride for cover, but he was dragged from his horse into a grappling life-and-death struggle against a wiry older bloke. Blythe saw it and knew a minute's agonized indecision as she caught sight of Raider, riding hard after the two lead wagons that were making off.

She wheeled her horse back and crashed through the heaving turmoil of bodies and screaming mounts toward Richard. It was pure, primal rage that raised the pistol in her hand as Richard sank to his knees, with a blade heading straight for his throat. She squeezed the trigger and the recoil and the sight of the bloke falling struck her in the same instant. There was a second's stunned immobility as Richard shook the fellow off and staggered to his feet, seeing Blythe with the smoking pistol, staring down at him.

"God, Wool-witch, get outta here!" he stormed waving his arms in her horse's face. Her mount reared, bringing her back to reality and she threw down the empty pistol and managed to rein around. Raider . . . she had to find Raider!

She dug her heels in and hugged the horse's neck as it lurched and clambered through the chaos of thrashing bodies on all sides. Suddenly they broke into the clear, and the nervous animal jolted into a thundering gallop with Blythe hanging on for dear life, scarcely able to realize they were moving in the direction she'd originally intended. She was jostled and pounded as she tried to right herself and take command of the reins, and finally the horse responded to her commands, reining off to the right, following nothing recognizable except blurred motion on the trail ahead.

She raced for it, the icy wind stinging her face and burning her eyes. She could hardly breathe. Her numbed fingers scarcely registered their frantic grip on the butt of the other pistol.

One of the wagons racing pell-mell left the irregular path to pull around its mate and struck a rock, overturning into the path. The first wagon driver was hard-pressed to keep from slamming into it and very nearly overturned his wagon before bringing it to a rocking stop.

Raider was on them in a flash, dodging and returning the fire of one wagon guard, wounding him. He pounced to the ground beside his mount, reaching for his sword, a sharp dirk already brandished in his other hand. He found himself face-to-face with a wagon driver, a guard, and a heaving-furious Neville Carson.

"Don't just stand there," Carson spat at his henchmen, his spittle foaming, "kill him—damn you!" He wallowed back behind them, panting, watching with a sickening light in his eyes as Raider faced two knives, from two directions. Raider lunged at one, sending him back, while the other thrust in, slashing wildly, coming perilously close with a deadly arc.

"How did you find me, Prescott?!" Carson taunted, hoping to sway Raider's fierce concentration. "No matter, you won't hold me . . . you'll never get me. They're going to kill you, Prescott . . . so I can have your guns and your little slut both!" His laugh roiled, raking over Raider's shoulders, producing a hitch in Raider's movement as he parried a blade. "See—?" Carson jeered, "they're going to wear you down, Prescott, going to stick you—make you bleed. But not before you hear what I intend for your little whore—"

"You'll never touch her, Carson." Raider feinted left and struck, catching one of the henchmen on the arm, but not putting him out of commission. He had to take one of them out! "When I dispose of these two, I'm coming after you. I'm going to carve you up like you did Collin—"

"You'll be dead, Prescott, you and your wretched crew. Already they're breaking ranks, running away like the yellow bellies they are!" Carson snarled. A horse was bearing down on them from the distance and he seized on it, hoping to break Raider's concentration. "There's one of my men now—three against one! You haven't got a prayer!"

Raider parried and lunged murderously, catching one opponent off guard with the bold move, sending a blade through his shoulder. The wretch cried out and sank to the ground as Raider whirled for better position, to get a glimpse of the approaching rider. What he saw set a chill through his blood . . . a banner of tumbled dark hair flying. Blythe.

"It's her, Prescott, how convenient. I won't even have to go back to Philadelphia to claim my pleasures," Carson tormented. The driver of the second wagon had been thrown free of the wagon and winded. Carson saw him rising, shaking his head to clear it, and began to move, as if to meet Blythe. Raider moved, wildly parrying thrusts and slashes to keep Carson in his sights, distracted momentarily by Blythe's intrusion into the volatile situation. As Carson hoped, Raider didn't see the driver fumbling in the wrecked wagon for a musket . . . raising it . . .

But Blythe saw it. Like a bizarre theatrical tableau, it was all taken in at a glance, movement discounted, irrelevant. Carson, prowling at the edges of the conflict, Raider blade-fighting—one man at his feet, another approaching from the rear with a gun, taking aim— She didn't call his name, hardly thought to rein up as she approached. Her eyes were riveted on that steely cylinder pointing at broad shoulders that belonged to her! With raw feline instinct, she pounced to the ground, wobbling as her shocked legs took her weight. Then she raised the pistol in her hand and fired at the startled driver before he could decide where to spend his shot.

The fire and the shock allowed Raider's opponent a slight edge; he had seen it coming and his blade nipped into Raider's arm. The pain shot through Raider, exploding red and hot in his brain, unleashing an eruption of molten fury. Three frenzied slashes and Raider sent his sword through the man's midsection.

It was a shocked moment before Carson lunged at Blythe and pulled her back against him, clamping his arm against her throat, holding her viciously. Raider wheeled, heaving, red-eyed with fury.

"I've got her, Prescott!" Carson began dragging her toward the upright wagon, using her to shield him as he searched the ground desperately for a weapon. "You'll have to kill her to get to me—" She groaned and made a strangled sound as he tightened

434

his arm viciously against her throat. And as he eyed the waiting wagon, calculating his chances of reaching it, his arm slid on her throat. Frantically she turned her head to relieve the pressure and found his hand near her mouth. She opened her mouth and bit down with everything in her!

Carson strangled a screech and shoved her to the ground, lurching for the wagon. But Raider lunged with perfect timing, stopping him on the point of a bloodied sword.

Blythe scrambled up, staring at Raider, scarcely able to believe they were both still alive. She wobbled over to the driver she'd shot and lifted his musket, leveling it straight at Carson's porcine heart.

"I should kill you here and now," she growled, stalking forward, her gold eyes blazing. It was gratifying indeed to see his jowls quivering with fear, to see sweat popping out on his forehead even in the cold air. Her finger twitched near the trigger. Some small movement drew her eyes toward Raider. He was easing, watching her, his eyes glowing. The spreading red stain on his sleeve jolted her back toward reason. "Maybe you'd better find something to tie him up with," she managed hoarsely.

He took a deep breath and lowered his blade, slicing into the ropes that held the cargo on the overturned wagon. And soon Carson was trussed and his virulent curses were stopped inside his own head with a piece of canvas. When Carson was stowed in back of the upright wagon with the rest of the cargo, Raider took the gun from her trembling hands and scooped her up to set her on the wagon seat. He tied the horses at the back, then climbed aboard to take up the reins.

He didn't want to look at her, didn't want to open his mouth until he had himself well in control. But when he felt her sag against him and looked down, he found her eyes closed and her pale face half buried in his bloody sleeve. She didn't respond to her name and he knew exactly what had happened. He needed to be furious with her, but a helpless grimace of a smile tugged at the corners of his mouth as he wrapped a possessive arm about her shoulders and lowered her unconscious form to his lap.

Chapter Twenty-eight

Blythe awakened on a cot in what appeared to be a darkened canvas tent. She tried to sit up and her entire body erupted in revolt. Burning cinders exploded in her shoulders and showered along the nerves of her lower back and legs. She lay back down with a groan and waited for the flashes of pain to subside before trying again. Biting her lip, she managed to get her feet over the side, shove the blanket back, and push upright. She rubbed her face and stared at the flickering dance of reddish light on the canvas walls and the slice of darkness visible through the tent opening. It was night . . . but where was she?

It came back to her in a rush . . . riding that godawful beast for hours. The fight—Raider was hurt! She stumbled to her feet and made it to the tent opening before the wave of nausea hit. She held her head and stomach and waited for it to subside. When she emerged into the cold night, she nearly collapsed with relief at the sight that greeted her.

Just outside the tent, Raider, Bastian, the Bosun, and Richard were seated around a blazing campfire with a few men clad in blue military uniforms. There were other tents around, other smoky fires visible beyond. Stalking toward them on brittle legs, she caught Bastian's eye and he pushed up.

"Wool-witch?! Be ye all right?"

Raider was up and around in a flash, heading for her. The rest of the lads and the military-clad strangers found their feet quickly, meeting her bewildered look with grins. Raider put his arm about her shivering shoulders and drew her toward the warmth of the fire.

"Where are we?" She sagged against his side, looking up at his red-bronze face and thinking she'd never seen him looking so blessedly healthy. Her eyes and fingers flew to his arm and found it bandaged neatly beneath his ripped coat sleeve. "Are you all right?"

"General Greene's camp . . ." He witnessed the charming confusion of her newly wakened state and tried not to be seduced by it . . . or by the tenderness of her touch. He had every right to be furious with her. "Let me present my wife, gentlemen, Blythe Woolrich Prescott. Blythe, these gentlemen are General Greene's staff. We came across a patrol on the way back to Philadelphia and they offered to escort us to their camp. The arms and munitions were destined for the general's men anyway. It seems Carson's little foray only speeded up delivery of the goods a bit."

Raider called each of the officers by name and they stepped forward to take her hand and speak their admiration for her in effusive terms. Their gentlemanly gazes caught on her unusual eyes, her fair, cold-blushed skin, and the thick jumble of soft hair over her shoulders. It was hard to believe she was the hard-riding, straight-shooting woman who'd saved her husband's life only a few hours before.

"Carson? What happened to Carson?" Her eyes were adorably wide as they poured over Raider's handsome features, still seeking reassurance of his health.

"The general is seeing to charges of theft of military stores, possible spying, and a few other things," Raider informed her. "When the army is through with him, he'll be sent back to Philadelphia, to stand trial for arson and murder. I don't think we need worry about him as competition for Woolrich-Prescott Trading Company anymore."

"Woolrich-Prescott Trading—?" She frowned and swayed noticeably, feeling the heat of his eyes melting the last strength of her legs.

"Excuse us, gentlemen, it seems my wife is still rather weak." He turned her forcefully back toward the modest tent, snagging

437

an oil lantern to carry along. Once inside, he set the lantern down on a paper-littered camp table and bent over her in the cramped space, taking her shoulders in his hands. He was trying desperately to decide whether to rave at her for defying him or to congratulate her daring and thank her for saving his life . . . again. "Blythe—"

"Are you all right?" She feathered her hands eagerly over his face, his throat, his chest, relieved to find him whole. "Thank God." She slid her arms about his waist and gave him a thorough hugging despite his stiffness. "Did we . . . lose any lads?"

"Not a one—though Stanley is in a bad way. I've already sent for Ali to come and tend him . . . he'll pull through. Blythe—" He honestly tried not to hug her yet, but she was so soft and so warm and—Lord!—it felt good to be alive, to be holding her! He completely forgot his outrage for a moment and crushed her to him, squeezing a small groan from her before he gentled.

"What was that about a 'Woolrich-Prescott Trading Company'?" She pulled back in his arms to look up into his face. Her heart was hammering.

"I'm your new partner, Wool-witch, like it or not. This mercantile business can get rough. I never realized it could be . . . so . . . stimulating. I think I could probably make a good businessman. I could see to it that Woolrich-Prescott is a force to be reckoned with . . . in more ways than one." He couldn't quite read the look in her face and decided he'd better lay it all out. "I talked it over with Walter on Christmas Day. He said he'd be delighted to have a 'son' in the business with him. And I talked with Bastian this evening . . . told him I've decided to stay on land . . . to run the trade and find the buyers. He's decided to try sailing as a straight merchantman for a while, now that he's wedded."

She was stunned. "You mean it? You want to stay with me on land? Really stay; share my bed every night . . . take up a life together . . . have babies . . . become a 'respectable' merchant?!" She would have her Raider and her Gideon both?! When he nodded, she hugged him ferociously, then pulled his head down to kiss him with the same exploding joy.

438

"A merchant . . . Raider, a week ago, you'd have been furious at the mere mention of it," she gasped, trying to take it all in.

"Yes . . ?" he bronzed a bit, "well . . . this little clash with Carson put it all into a new perspective. And I'm willing to give it a try."

Blythe broke into a wry smile. "Poor Neville—it seems his scheming always turns to my benefit in some way. He was responsible for our meeting in the first place, sending you to my shop. Then he kept Woolrich afloat with his treacherous loans. And now . . . he's helped you decide to stay on land with me."

"It's probably just his fate," Raider mused tauntingly. And he laughed at the spark that struck in her eyes. "Or maybe not. It could be just his lousy choices . . ." His laughter rumbled through her where their bodies were pressed together. Soaring joy lifted her heart again . . . only to have it crash into a very broad wall of raw male prerogative.

"Wait, you mean to say you've . . . already talked about all this with Papa . . . and Bastian?"

"It's all settled. Bastian will have shares in the company and carry cargoes for us. And as soon as the *Gastronome* is rebuilt and refitted, we'll launch her as well, maybe under Bosun Deane—"

He stopped abruptly, realizing that he'd allowed his husbandly ire to be waylaid totally.

"Dammit, Blythe, you might have been killed!" he growled, making her draw back with a scowl. "It's lucky I had my hands full when I first saw you riding like a maniac, straight into the jaws of death. You deliberately disobeyed me!"

"*Disobeyed?* Don't you dare rave and bellow at me, Raider Prescott! I saved your wretched hide . . . again!" she growled back, her golden eyes blazing. "And how dare *you* go around deciding our lives behind my back . . ."

"Behi—" He straightened, lifting the top of the tent with his head. "I thought you wanted me to stay with you . . . to find some 'respectable' trade."

"I did . . . *do,* dammit!"

"Then what the hell's the matter with you? And just when did you start using words like 'dammit'?"

439

"You never thought to discuss it with me, did you? My life . . . our life together . . . You talked with Bastian, with my father, probably with your whole blessed crew!" She pushed back furiously in his arms. "And never once did you think to mention it to me, your wife . . . who's supposed to be sharing it with you!"

"Dammit, Blythe, it's my duty to decide and to provide and care for—"

"Partners, you said." She jabbed her finger into his coatfront. "Well, I won't have a partner who doesn't consult me on things!"

"Well, I won't have a partn—a *wife* who gallivants about the countryside in defiance of her husband's orders—dressed half in men's clothes and packing pistols! I'm going to be a respectable businessman now, Blythe Prescott, and you'd better learn to heed your husband and behave as a decent, respectable wife should!"

"Well, maybe you just better learn what it takes to control a *pirate wife*, Raider Prescott," she growled furiously, shoving back hard enough to break his hold, "because that's what you've got on your hands. I sailed with real pirates!" She was at full gale now. "I was ravished by the Scourge of the Seven Seas and became his mistress before I was your very respectable wife! I've helped take ships on the high seas and I've shot two men protecting my husband's back. And if you think I'm going to dandy up and decorate your settee all day, twiddling my thumbs, you've got another thing coming!"

The silence crackled with ultimatum as they faced each other, both a little shocked by her declarations. The burning golden disks of her eyes and the defiant tilt of her dented chin battered Raider's righteous new respectability.

Lord, he felt the same himself . . . It had been his biggest fear these last weeks on land. After the excitement, the heady, blood-pounding thrill of the stalk and the hunt, after the exhilaration of victory in sea battle, would he be able to settle down to a quiet "respectable" life on land? He stared at her heaving breasts, at the curvy, womanly form beneath those fitted leather clothes he'd had made for her life on the seas. He'd exposed her to such a life . . . and she'd come to relish parts of it, just as he

440

had. She had brains and courage and determination, and just because she was a woman didn't mean she couldn't crave adventure as he did.

"I have to be your full partner, Prescott, or—" Her voice clogged with turmoil. Her vehement responses to his proper male attitude shocked her a little. What if she really meant it? What if she couldn't settle back into a respectable, wifely role now that he was finally coming to reconcile the disparate halves of him?

Raider watched that vulnerable young girl emerging from beneath the bold pirate wench and every bit of resistance in him melted. He thought of the many intriguing creatures she was inside and knew a crashing wave of relief. With Blythe at his side, respectable life would never be too dull or predictable. Suddenly he had to feel her against him, had to hold her and share this new confidence with her. Pulling her reluctant form into his arms, he tilted her heart-shaped face up to him.

"Be my partner, then, Blythe . . . in bed, in the mercantile, in our home. We were pirates together. We can find a way to be respectable together, too." His eyes locked in hers and his head lowered. He captured her parted lips and coaxed them wider with a stunning sensual entreaty of a kiss. A pleasurable chill raced through his limbs when her arms came up to slide beneath his open coat and clasp his muscular ribs. His mouth massaged and nibbled and caressed, reclaiming all the pleasures of kissing her. It was a long time before he could drag his mouth away.

"If you ever do something crazy like this again, I'll lock you up—I swear on Morgan's Spleen, I will," he uttered in tones so hoarse and deep they vibrated her entire, aching body. But when she managed to open her eyes, he was grinning his lusty, wicked pirate sort of a grin. "And I'll make love to you until you come to your senses."

He turned down the lamp to a smoky glow and pushed her down on the cot.

"Oh-h-h—" she groaned, her poker-stiff body throbbing with misery as he came to lift her feet up onto the cot. She moaned, then bit her lip as he lowered himself onto the cot beside her and covered them both with the blanket. "Oh-h . . . I swear on Morgan's Liver, I'll never get on another horse as long as I live . . ."

He chuckled. "I'll take you home tomorrow, Wool-witch." He moved his hands over her tense, aching limbs, soothing and caressing carefully. "And I'll personally bathe you in a big, hot tub of water and rub your entire body with coconut oil. And I won't let you out of bed until we've worked all the soreness out."

"Oh . . . ooh . . . ow!" She tried to wriggle as his warm hand found the peak of her breast, but it hurt too much.

He grinned and dipped his head to taste her waiting mouth. When he raised his head, he was surprised to see her face drawn into a troubled frown. "Did I hurt you?" He checked the press of his body against hers, then relaxed it when she shook her head. After a moment her voice came . . . small and worried.

"Raider . . . what do we do about the Wool-witch in me?" Her golden eyes widened, forming a clear window on her fears, her desires . . . her unconditional love for him.

He laughed, his wickedest pirate laugh. "Let's let the pirate in me deal with her. They're two of a kind."

The corners of her warm cherry-red lips quivered and soon she was laughing—and complaining that it hurt.

Epilogue

The fates do love their dice. And while some call them "fickle," it is simply a fact of their nature that they love to be wherever there is excitement . . . rather like people. And unlike lightning, they have no compunctions about rolling the same number over again, or landing in the same place twice . . .

"Oh-h-h —" Blythe groaned, straining and shuddering with the exertion of the final throes of childbirth. The firstborn American Prescott was thrust into the world just as the first rays of the sun crossed the unseen horizon. Outside, thunder boomed and lightning split the swirling sky in a ferocious late-summer storm. The bedchamber itself seemed to tremble as one last massive stroke of lightning blasted through the sky and its echoes roared and rumbled all around Woolrich House.

In the mingled light of dawn and candles, turbaned Ali handed a squalling red male child to the very pregnant Signe Cane, asking her to clean and wrap the child while he attended to Blythe. There was a commotion at the door and Nana put her tear-soaked handkerchief in her pocket and flew to block the entrance bodily.

"I told you heathen pack, you're not coming in!" she stormed — right into Raider's dripping face. "Oh, it's you." She melted back to admit Raider, tossing a glare into the crowd of sea dogs who waited anxiously in the upstairs hallway. "It's

443

about time you got here."

"The bloody bridge was washed out—I've ridden all night!" He grabbed Nana's shoulders frantically, his eyes fixed on Blythe's slender figure swathed in tangled bed linen. "Is it over? Is she all right?!"

"She's fine." Nana patted his hand on her shoulder and fresh tears came to her eyes. "That Turk of yours knows what he's doing, I guess."

Raider approached hesitantly and melted with relief when Ali lifted his head and smiled, waving him on toward Blythe's head. He stumbled forward and knelt beside the bed, taking her slender hands in his. Her eyes fluttered open, glowing with pride and love.

"Did you see him?" she murmured, stroking Raider's wet hair.

"Him?" Raider showered kisses on her hands, her temples, and brushed her lips lightly, as if afraid of bruising her.

"Your son, Scourge of the Seven Seas, you can't have forgotten . . ." she teased, raising her head to look past him. Disentangling her hands, she reached for the bundle Signe brought her. She nestled their son near her breast and poured all her love for Raider and more into her first glimpse of the new being their loving had created. "He's beautiful," she sighed, her eyes misting. "He looks just like you."

"Well, of course he's beautiful." Raider's voice was clogged and wavery. "He has the most beautiful mother in the world. You're all right, aren't you? I mean—"

"I'm fine, Raider, really," she assured him, reaching for his hand and pressing it to her cheek. "I love you."

"And I love you, Blythe." He grinned through the rims of moisture in his eyes. "I have to be the luckiest damned pirate who ever lived."

Walter squeezed past Nana at the door and, after a quick teary-eyed visit with his daughter, went to throw open the door and announce to Raider's former crew: "It's a boy!"

There was a huge, delirious uproar in the hallway, not unlike the last rumbles of thunder that had preceded it in rattling the bedchamber. Mrs. Dornly and Lizzy, Nana and Walter succeeded in restoring enough order to close the door to give the new family some privacy.

"I wonder what you'll be when you grow up," Blythe murmured to her son, sniffing quietly, her eyes shining.

"A wealthy merchant? Like his father?" Gideon whispered, thoroughly awed.

Blythe's laugh was husky as she looked at him. "Or a pirate? Like his mother?"

Raider laughed, too, stroking her glowing face and his son's downy cheek. And he murmured a prayer of thanks that the tide of his fortunes had changed forever when he claimed the prize his pirate's heart craved . . . the love in Blythe's golden eyes.

Author's Note

I hope you enjoyed the story of Blythe Woolrich and her gentleman pirate. Raider's dilemma, not knowing whether he was a pirate, a privateer, or a small, seagoing businessman, was actually a rather common one in times of war. There was an exceedingly fine line between privateering and piracy, between patriotism and self-interest. The emergent United States of America had no navy during the war for independence and commissioned private warring vessels, privateers, to combat the British on the seas and keep lines of trade open. These privateers were so successful, they took more than six hundred British ships during the conflict and greatly benefited the war on land.

The various seafaring traditions portrayed on the *Windraider* are based in fact; from grog lines and "double-tubbing," to signing the *Articles* and the rarity of decent food, to punishments for stealing and the strategy and details of sea battle. The life portrayed aboard Raider's ship embraces the developing American seagoing practice of the day and the traditional practices of true piracy. "Real pirates" like Long Ben did certainly exist in 1778, but, as Bastian noted, they were the dregs of the sailing world and their fortunes and numbers were in decline. In another thirty-five years, piracy would be all but eradicated from most of the world's seas.

As to the "dice of fate" . . . I am personally inclined to favor

Blythe's views, that it is man's free will—the choices of ourselves and others—which shapes our lives. But, being a rational sort, I must also admit that there are things which cannot easily be explained in these terms. Extraordinary good fortune and calamity have always, will always, puzzle humankind's greatest thinkers. The "dice of fate" might be as good an explanation as any . . .